What has been said about the

L. Ron Hubbard
PRESENTS
WRITERS OF THE FUTURE

ANTHOLOGIES

"This has become a major tributary to the new blood in fantastic fiction."

GREGORY BENFORD

"From cutting-edge high tech to evocative fantasy, this book's got it all—it's lots of fun and I love the chance to see what tomorrow's stars are doing today."

TIM POWERS

"I recommend the *Writers of the Future* Contest at every writers' workshop I participate in."

FREDERIK POHL

". . . an exceedingly solid collection, including SF, fantasy and horror . . ."

CHICAGO SUN TIMES

"A first-rate collection of stories and illustrations."

BOOKLIST

"It is rare to find this consistency of excellence in any series of science fiction and fantasy stories. The well-deserved reputation of L. Ron Hubbard's *Writers of the Future* has proven itself once again."

STEPHEN V. WHALEY
PROFESSOR ENGLISH & FOREIGN LANGUAGES
CALIFORNIA POLYTECHNICAL UNIVERSITY, POMONA

"The untapped talents of new writers continue to astonish me and every WOTF volume provides a well-spring of the greatest energy put forth by the ambitious writers of tomorrow."

KEVIN J. ANDERSON

"This contest has changed the face of Science Fiction."

DEAN WESLEY SMITH
EDITOR OF *STRANGE NEW WORLDS*

"Some of the best SF of the future comes from *Writers of the Future* and you can find it in this book."

DAVID HARTWELL

"Not only is the writing excellent . . . it is also extremely varied. There's a lot of hot new talent in it."

***LOCUS* MAGAZINE**

"As always, this is the premier volume in the field to showcase new writers and artists. You can't go wrong here."

BARYON

"*Writers of the Future* is the leading SF pathway to success."

ALGIS BUDRYS

"This contest has found some of the best new writers of the last decade."

KRISTINE KATHRYN RUSCH
AUTHOR & EDITOR

"I have been fortunate enough, myself, to make use of L. Ron Hubbard's *Writers of the Future* anthologies for a number of years in my own classroom, and my students have learned much about what constitutes good writing."

DR. JOHN L. FLYNN
ENGLISH PROFESSOR
TOWSON UNIVERSITY, MARYLAND

L. Ron Hubbard

PRESENTS

WRITERS

OF THE

FUTURE

VOLUME XV

L. Ron Hubbard
PRESENTS
WRITERS
OF THE
FUTURE
VOLUME XV

The Year's 12 Best Tales from the
Writers of the Future
International Writers' Program
Illustrated by the Winners in the
Illustrators of the Future®
International Illustrators' Program

With Essays on Writing and Illustration by
L. Ron Hubbard • K. D. Wentworth •
Leo & Diane Dillon • Tim Powers

Edited by Algis Budrys

Bridge Publications, Inc.

Blade of the Bunny: © 1999 Jim Hines
A Man More Ordinary: © 1999 Manfred Gabriel
Bearing the Pattern: © 1999 G. Scott Huggins
The One-Eyed Man: © 1999 Gregory Janks
Dream the Dream: © 1999 Leo & Diane Dillon
The Unbound: © 1999 Nicole Montgomery
Out of the Blue: © 1999 Ron Collins
By Other Windings: © 1999 Franklin Thatcher
How I've Been Passing the Time until Waiting Is Filled: © 1999 K. D. Wentworth
My Son, My Self: © 1999 Amy Sterling Casil
The Price of Tea in China: © 1999 David W. Hill
The Great Wizard Joey: © 1999 W. G. Rowland
Holding Bogart's Fort: © 1999 Tim Powers
Great White Hunter: © 1999 Don Solosan
The Vampire Shortstop: © 1999 Scott Nicholson

Illustration on page 8 © 1999 Julia Armstrong Murphy
Illustration on page 45 © 1999 Yuri Chari
Illustration on page 56 © 1999 Victory
Illustration on page 100 © 1999 Paul Butler
Illustration on page 151 © 1999 James Matt Frantz
Illustration on page 212 © 1999 Lukasz Laskowski
Illustration on page 238 © 1999 Tomislav Tomic
Illustration on page 289 © 1999 Lee Seed
Illustration on page 314 © 1999 Robert G. Kmiec
Illustration on page 338 © 1999 Ludmila Ryabets
Illustration on page 403 © 1999 Scott Schomburg
Illustration on page 426 © 1999 Igor Pogodin

Cover Artwork: © 1999 Bridge Publications, Inc.

ISBN 1-57318-163-3

Library of Congress Catalog Card Number: 84-73270
First Edition Paperback 10 9 8 7 6 5 4 3 2 1
Printed in the United States of America

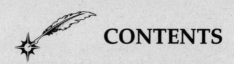

CONTENTS

INTRODUCTION

Written by
Algis Budrys

This is Volume XV of L. Ron Hubbard Presents *Writers of the Future;* fifteen years of an anthology that is unique in many ways. It has brought an unprecedented number of solid talents into the science fiction and fantasy fields, both in writing and in illustration. It has also published a great many essays of advice and nuts-and-bolts articles on how to write and draw. And that is precisely what L. Ron Hubbard intended. He wanted to help deserving young writers and illustrators at a crucial early point in their careers, giving them the opportunity to earn significant payment and, more important, to take the first steps up the ladder of recognition. There is nothing else in the world like it.

As you run your eye over the fiction contents, you will hardly see a name that is recognizable. That is because the stories were written by people who had only published a maximum of three stories when they entered the Contest from which these annual volumes derive. If you will look in previous volumes, going back to Volume I, you will find scores of famous names listed in the Contents: Leonard Carpenter, Karen Joy Fowler, Nina Kiriki Hoffman, Dean Wesley Smith, Mary Frances Zambreno and David Zindell in the first volume alone. . . .

Over the years there have been many, many more . . . including Dave Wolverton, who went from contestant to First Place winner to Grand Prize winner to First Reader of the contestants' stories to Coordinating Judge of the Contest. And I expect that as we proceed onward into the future, the names from Volume XV will become equally well known.

It is a process in a way analogous to what happened with *Astounding Science Fiction* magazine in the late 1930s and the 1940s. In those days, the new, unknown names were Isaac Asimov, Hal Clement, L. Sprague de Camp, Lester del Rey, Robert Heinlein and A. E. van Vogt, among others, besides a completely reconstructed Clifford Simak, and a man who was already a legend in all other fields, L. Ron Hubbard. It was on those shoulders that editor John W. Campbell built the golden age of science fiction, and it is on the shoulders of L. Ron Hubbard's *Writers of the Future* that a new golden age is being built, illustrated by the heirs to such Campbell illustrators as Hubert Rogers, Charles Shneeman and Edd Cartier. It is a legacy of immense proportions . . . and a legacy that is still growing with each year that goes by. L. Ron Hubbard passed on in 1986, but who is to say that he is not still vigorously alive in the artistic sense?

Enjoy this book. Not only for what it is, but for what it promises.

BLADE OF THE BUNNY

Written by
Jim Hines

Illustrated by
Julia Armstrong Murphy

About the Author

Jim Hines was born in 1947 and grew up in Holt, Michigan, where he's been reading science fiction and fantasy most of his life. He currently teaches composition at Eastern Michigan University and is working toward his master's in English. While finishing his undergraduate degree in psychology at Michigan State, he realized he was devoting more time to a novel he was writing in his spare time than he was to his term papers. Essentially, he has not looked back since then.

He would like to dedicate this, his first professional publication, to Margaret, for her encouragement, and to his parents, for supporting him through his multiple early career shifts.

About the Illustrator

Julia Armstrong Murphy has been interested in art, science fiction and fantasy for as long as she can remember, and she was especially fascinated by the intriguing artwork that graced book covers.

With a degree in mathematics and a minor in art, she is currently employed as a physical scientist. Julia paints and draws in her spare time, and specializes in studio art and fantasy illustrations.

Someday my luck will run out. I'll end up twisting at the end of a rope, feeding the flies for crimes I committed years ago. Then I'll be hauled up before Josenn Ko, the god of judgment, who will decide my eternal fate. But while I wait for him to decide where the name James Lapan is to be written on the scroll of life, I'll have a few questions of my own to ask. Does a man ever really know what a woman is thinking? for example. And why does trouble always seem to start when I'm out watering the trees?

I had only been gone a few minutes. Three mugs of ale had cried out for freedom, and I had been helpless to resist. So, after liberating my libations, I made my way back into the Blind Griffon, where two things immediately caught my attention.

The first was a woman. My wife, to be precise. We had been married for two weeks now, and it was still an odd feeling to look at her and think, *this woman is my wife*. It felt so natural, being with her. But there were also times that it felt a bit unreal. I stood in the doorway and took a moment to look at her.

I must be honest—I have, in my life, met women who were more beautiful than Alycia. Her red blond hair was cut short, above the ears, and her round cheeks were slightly flushed with drink. An old knife scar ran in a diagonal line across her chin. Lively blue eyes met mine as I walked back into the bar. I saw the silent message there and took a seat, allowing her the space to resolve the situation herself. As I said, there are women more beautiful than Alycia. But I've never met one who was more fun. I ordered another ale as Alycia returned her attention to the wall of muscle and hair that towered over her.

"Wall," as I dubbed him, was the other thing to catch my eye. Mostly because of the way he was staring at my wife and licking his upper lip. Between the background noise of the Blind Griffon and the fact that Wall was slightly intoxicated, I had to strain to make out what was being said.

"You dress like a man," Wall said. It was true. Leather bracers covered Alycia's sleeves, and black pants were tucked into her low-cut boots. It was a dramatically different look from the cleavage-thrusting shirts worn by the barmaids. Wall leaned closer, grinning. "You like getting into a man's clothes, huh?"

I mentally gave him a few points for cleverness. But I knew my wife. I couldn't begin to count the times that, as I congratulated myself for some witty remark, she had pierced my pride with a few well-aimed words. She didn't disappoint me. She looked up at Wall and blinked her eyes seductively.

"Why, yes, I do. Do you happen to know where I could find one?"

I raised my drink in salute. Attack, riposte, and Wall was down. And angry. Even from across the room, I could see the muscles tense. He was armed, I noticed. A large sword was strapped across his back, and a hunting knife hung at his left hip.

"You insult me?"

Alycia shrugged, returning her attention to her drink.

"Apologize, and maybe I'll forgive you." He leered. "You'll find I can be *very* forgiving."

Alycia shook her head. "I'm not."

Wall seemed to be losing his patience. He reached out and grabbed the mug from Alycia's hand. "I will give you one more chance, because I'm in a pleasant mood. I suggest you apologize."

At that point, the mug cracked in his hands. Alycia had seen my knife coming and jumped back to avoid being splashed. Wall was not so lucky. He shouted angrily and threw the mug onto the floor. The handle of my knife still protruded from its side.

I already had another knife by the blade, ready to throw. Alycia glared at me, as if to say, *I was doing fine without your help.*

I shrugged. *I couldn't help myself.* It's true. I can never resist jumping into the thick of things. And I tend to have a bit of a protective streak about Alycia. Even though, truth be told, she ends up bailing me out of trouble more often than not.

Wall was glaring at me now. His hand slowly reached toward his sword. "That was a mistake, little man." No more games. His voice was low and dangerous. I could feel the tension in the bar. Conversations stopped, and people turned nervously to watch.

Wall studied the distance between us, trying to decide if he could get to me before I could throw. He couldn't, but I wasn't sure if he knew that. I've known how to use a knife since I was six. But I hated to spill blood in my favorite tavern in Larindale. So I was grateful when Alycia whistled to catch Wall's attention.

He wasn't stupid. Well, not mortally stupid. He might have tried to get to me before I could throw. But with Alycia and me both watching him, daggers poised, he backed down. "She's yours?" he asked.

Illustrated by Julia Armstrong Murphy

Alycia raised an eyebrow at me, daring me to answer. "We're married," I said diplomatically. Wall looked back and forth between us, then nodded. "Good luck," he said to me. Then he turned and left.

I walked over to my wife's table, giving her a quick kiss before I sat. A serving boy, a short kid by the name of Devin, handed me the knife I had thrown. I quickly returned it to its sheath. Alycia, however, kept her blade out.

"That was *my* drink," she said, nodding toward the spilled mess that Devin was quickly mopping up.

I held up my hands. "Please, milady, if you would allow me to buy you another?" I gestured at Devin, who ran off to fetch a new mug.

She narrowed her eyes, trying to decide if that was sufficient. Finally, she set her knife down on the table. "Very well." Then she grinned. "What were you thinking, James? Throwing a knife in a crowded room. What if you had missed?"

"Missed?" I raised a hand to my heart. "You wound me, milady."

At that point, Devin returned with the drink. As he set the mug on the table, his gaze fell on Alycia's dagger, and he stared. I couldn't blame him. The six-inch blade gleamed like polished glass. But it was the hilt that attracted the most attention. It had been carefully carved to resemble a leaping rabbit. The blade met the hilt in the rabbit's mouth, while outstretched ears formed the crossguard. Perfectly smooth inlaid dots of amethyst gave it dark, gleaming eyes.

"Careful, boy," I warned him. "You gaze upon a magical blade of power." I could practically hear Alycia's eyes rolling skyward.

Devin looked skeptically at the blade. "Is it really magic?" He reached out to touch it. As his fingers drew close, the eyes on the hilt blinked suddenly, and the nose wiggled. Devin jerked his hand back as if he had been bitten. Which, had he been a hair slower, he would have been.

"Where did it come from?" Devin asked.

I leaned back in my chair. "It started a little over a month ago." I reveled in the attention as others in the bar turned to listen to my story. Alycia just sipped her drink and shook her head. Her expression was one of affection mixed with amusement.

"Alycia and I were both third circle initiates in the guild."

"The guild?" Devin asked.

"The Guild of Thieves."

●●●

It was before Alycia and I were married. The life of a thief doesn't tend to promote family stability. But we had been a couple for several years, off and on. More off than on, lately.

I was breaking into a small warehouse on the riverside. It was an odd job for me. Generally, I confined my exploration to the business district. High risk, high payoff. But this assignment had come from the guildmaster herself. She said that a shipment of cloud-silk was being aged in the warehouse, and she had a buyer who would pay several hundred in gold for the feather-light material. So I tucked a large sack into my shirt and headed for the river.

Cloud-silk was imported from Parvous, a tiny island far to the east. It grew stronger with age, and took several years before it was strong enough to be used for anything beyond the flimsiest veil. But after a few decades, it was nearly indestructible. I wondered how much I would be able to pinch for myself. Maybe just enough for a nice sash. Something to add a touch of class, not to mention giving me another place to conceal a knife.

It was late, but there were still people moving about, loading and unloading ships at the dock. I staggered toward the warehouse, pretending to be drunk. It was my favorite act, though there were some who said I did too much research into the routine.

A sailor moved toward me, but I clutched my stomach and made retching noises, and he quickly vanished. At the warehouse, I knelt down and pretended to vomit. Loudly. Just in case anyone was paying attention. Then I used the door as support while I tried to rise. Eventually I would get to my feet, but in the meantime, it gave me the chance to explore the lock with my tools.

At least, that was the plan. Instead, the door swung open, and I fell forward into a dark room. The door had been unlocked. It hadn't even been latched.

"Grab the door," a voice shouted.

Even as I turned, the door slammed shut. I immediately grabbed for the handle, but there was none. I couldn't even find the outline of the door. I was trapped in complete darkness with no way out.

I pulled my knife and waited in silence. I didn't know who else was in here, but there was no way they were going to sneak up on me. A moment later, I realized that the voice was familiar, and I groaned.

"Alycia?"

Another moment of silence. Then, "James?"

Together, "What are you doing here?"

Suddenly the room lit up with a quiet *whoosh* as four torches, spaced evenly around the room, burst into flame. I squinted painfully as my eyes adjusted. When I could see, I looked around a room that was nearly empty. No chests of cloud-silk, as I had been led to expect. A few empty crates were smashed open, and the chains that had once kept them secure lay uselessly on the floor. A door in the back probably led to an office. Aside from that, there was just myself and Alycia, standing with knives drawn, and a third man waiting patiently at the other end of the warehouse. He was tall. I had an instinctive dislike of tall people, having never exceeded five foot three myself. But I shoved my feelings aside and studied him cautiously.

Pure white hair was pulled back into a short braid. Black, bushy eyebrows shadowed dark eyes. He had strong cheekbones and an outthrust, cleanshaven chin. He wore an expensive blue shirt and black trousers, with a black cloak thrown over his shoulders. But it was the red triangular pendant around his neck that caught my eye. A wizard, then. The red triangle indicated a wizard of some power, if I remembered the ranks correctly.

I was now thoroughly confused. So I waited. Patience is one of the three cardinal virtues for a thief, after all. I waited a grand total of about four seconds before demanding, "Who are you? What do you want?"

"I am Hadar." His voice was relaxed, confident. It made me nervous. "I am here to hire you."

"I was told there was a shipment of cloud-silk here," Alycia said accusingly.

I turned to stare at her. "Who told you about the cloud-silk?"

"The guildmaster."

"But she gave me this job," I protested.

"Then you're late," Alycia said. "I was here an hour ago."

Hadar interrupted our discussion. "Your guildmaster deceived you because I paid her to do so. I wanted you both here."

"So why not just be honest with us?" I said. I still had my dagger out. I didn't like being manipulated.

"Honesty with thieves." Hadar chuckled. "I was told that you were two of her best, but that it might be difficult to persuade you to meet together."

It was true, I conceded. Alycia's and my last breakup had been far from civil. She had picked the pocket of the woman I had been planning to rob. Personally, I think she was jealous, though she never admitted it. And while I thought that we had kept the whole thing relatively subtle, I had long since given up being surprised by the extent of the guildmaster's knowledge.

"What do you want?" Alycia asked. Her eyes were beautiful when she was angry.

Hadar moved his hands, and several chairs appeared. He sat down, offering us each a chair. We both refused, and he shrugged. "I need you to retrieve two things for me."

"Not interested," Alycia said.

"I've already cleared it with the guildmaster, and I'll pay you a thousand in gold. Each."

I sat down. Alycia remained standing, but she was listening.

"A few weeks ago, a young colleague of mine stole two things of immense value," Hadar began.

"What did he take?" Alycia asked.

Hadar frowned. This was not a man who was used to being interrupted. I watched him bite back his annoyance. "A knife. An enchanted knife. The blade is magically sharp. The handle is carved in the shape of a springing rabbit."

"A rabbit?" I repeated.

"A jack rabbit, actually. It was made several hundred years ago, by a tribe of desert nomads. It has been in my family for over a century."

"Excuse me," Alycia said, interrupting again. "Why does such a powerful wizard as yourself need to hire a pair of thieves?" The sarcasm was dripping freely. I knew that tone, and how much it could get under a man's skin. Hadar was no exception. His jaw clenched as she continued. "Why not just pop in with your magic and take what you want?"

Hadar looked pained. "The young man who stole these things from me is also rather gifted in the magical arts. I know, because I was his teacher. A magical battle between us would attract far more attention than I would like. I could defeat him, of course, but I prefer to keep this matter as quiet as possible."

"You want us to steal from a wizard?" I started to rise. "Sorry, I never steal from anyone who can turn me into a frog."

I heard a choked laugh from Alycia. "Who'd know?" she asked. I glared at her.

"I asked for the two of you because of your skill with the knife," Hadar said loudly, trying to regain our attention. "All the magic in the world can do nothing against a blade in the back. If necessary, kill him."

I cut him off. "We're not murderers." A glance at Alycia told me that, this time, we were in agreement.

Hadar continued as if I hadn't spoken. "If you can catch him by surprise, you can bind his hands to prevent him from using his power. But this is irrelevant, as you'll be going at night, and he will be in bed, asleep. So long as you don't disturb him, there will be no need for confrontation."

"What is this second thing we're supposed to retrieve?" I asked.

Hadar smiled, an odd half-smile. "An item of greater value than the first. You will know it when you see it. And now I must know, will you accept this job?"

Steal a magic dagger and an unknown item from a wizard. There's a term for that sort of job. It's called a noose-walk, because it's the same as walking to the gallows and putting your head in the noose. Still, a thousand in gold was a lot of money. I wouldn't have to work for a year. But gold was of no use to a corpse.

I started to shake my head. Hadar saw, and nodded sympathetically. "I understand your fear."

"Two thousand," I snapped. There was no way I'd let it be known that I passed up a job due to fear. In the guild, reputation is everything. Let him be the one to back down.

"Done," he said with a smile. He clapped his hands sharply, and two large, heavy sacks appeared on the ground before us. "The deal is made. I will provide your guildmaster with the information you need."

Hadar waved absently at the wall of the warehouse, and the door appeared. "You are now wealthy thieves," he said, and left.

I cautiously nudged one of the sacks with my foot. It was heavy, and clinked. Two thousand in gold, I thought, suddenly stunned by the wealth before me. I turned to Alycia.

"You're an idiot," she said calmly.

●●●

True to his word, Hadar gave the guildmaster all the information we needed. The young wizard's name was Tomin. He lived in a small cabin in the forest, about an hour's walk out of town. It was magically guarded, but we were given a paste to rub on our eyelids that would enable us to see through the enchantments. He trusted us to deal with any mundane traps we might encounter. As we left, the guildmaster reminded us that we had given oath . . . and that failure would be looked upon with "disappointment."

Alycia swore at me for a good five minutes as we left, but there was nothing she could do. She was trapped by our membership in the guild. My oath was binding for both of us. If she didn't complete the assignment, her life would be forfeit, as would mine. After her initial bout of cursing, we walked in silence until we reached the cabin.

In the light of the full moon, it was beautiful. That's coming from a man who rarely appreciates beauty beyond the glint of gold or the shine of stolen jewels. But this was a work of art. Live oaks formed the four corners of the cabin. Branches snaked along the walls, helping to hold the wooden planks in place. The doorway was tall and arched, with flowering vines that covered the door. The cabin blended perfectly into the forest. It seemed to belong there, a part of its surroundings.

Something grabbed my arm, hard. My knife was out before I realized that it was Alycia who was cutting off the blood to my left hand. "James . . ." she hissed, pointing at the door.

"I need that arm," I whispered. She ignored me. I stuck the blade between my teeth for a moment to try and pry her fingers off. I had never realized how strong she was. Finally, after freeing myself, I looked to where she was pointing.

On the face of the door, dozens of tiny dots moved amongst themselves. Spiders, I realized. They were crawling back and forth among the vines. "Do you think they're poisonous?" I asked, after taking the knife out of my mouth.

"I hate spiders."

I looked at her. Her face was pale, and she was biting her lip so hard I expected to see blood at any second. "Take it easy," I said. "Let me go look."

She stayed there, frozen, as I approached the door. I had gotten within about ten feet, when something landed on my hand. One of the spiders had jumped onto me, from the door. I almost panicked, shaking my hand violently to try to dislodge it. It was still there. Thoughts of poison raced through my head. I dropped the knife and smashed the damn thing with my palm, twisting viciously to make sure it was dead. Then I retrieved my knife and backed away quickly, wiping the smeared remains on my pants.

"They can jump," I commented to Alycia, trying to calm my breathing. From the muffled whimper, I didn't think I had reassured her. I glanced back at the cabin. "Wait here," I whispered. She nodded, never taking her eyes off the door. I had never known she had such a fear of spiders.

Moving slowly and silently, I began to circle the cabin, looking for another way in. As I did so, I began checking what I carried, looking for anything that could be used against the spiders. My dagger was worse than useless. I considered taking my boots and using them to smash the spiders, but that wouldn't work. I could smash perhaps a dozen at a time, and while I did so, the rest would leap onto my body. Not to mention that the noise would alert anyone in the cabin to our presence.

Then my hand brushed against the magic paste Hadar had given us. I stopped and closed my eyes. There were times I thought my father was right, and I really did have the brains of a rutabaga. I quickly uncorked the small jar and dabbed a bit of the green gook onto my eyelids. It was messy, and I could feel my eyelashes clumping together, but I finally finished the job. With an evil grin, I put the jar away and returned to Alycia.

It was dark enough that she shouldn't see the stains over my eyes. "There's no other way in," I said quietly, keeping my attention on the door. It was all I could do to keep from laughing. There were no spiders. No vines, either. Just a black, painted spider web that covered the entire door.

I took a deep breath. "I'll go first. Maybe if we move slowly and don't startle them, they won't bite us."

●●●

At this point my story was interrupted as Alycia rose from the table. She smiled at my audience, then came over to stand behind me, her arms snaking around my chest.

"I'm going to go get something to eat," she whispered. And then, in what must have seemed to be a loving gesture to anyone watching, she proceeded to bite my ear. Hard.

I stifled a yelp. A moment later she released my throbbing lobe, whispering, "You finish your story."

●●●

Taking a deep breath, I walked toward the door. I allowed myself a quick glance back, to see Alycia staring at me. At about ten feet, I jumped suddenly, as if spiders had begun boarding my body. I was rewarded by an audible gasp from behind.

"It's okay," I hissed. Very slowly, I moved closer. It would be a while before she called me an idiot again, I thought in satisfaction. A minute later, I reached the door. Here, professionalism overcame my desire for revenge and I sobered. There was a faint light from within. The hinges were on the inside, which caused me to swear silently. I always liked to give the hinges a quick drop of oil to prevent squeaking. But that was impossible this time.

There was no knob or handle. I gave the door a soft, slow push, and it cracked open. Unlocked. My wariness increased. I pushed a bit more, and was rewarded by a quiet squeal. Damn it, I hated that sound. My heart jumped as I waited for any sign that I had been discovered. There was a rustling from inside, but when a minute passed without my being transformed into a frog, I decided that the noise had gone unnoticed.

The door was open wide enough to slip inside. I turned back to Alycia and waved for her to follow. She didn't move. I waved again. She bit her lip and took a tentative step forward. Then she stopped.

I closed my eyes and shook my head, as if I was suddenly remembering something obvious. Donning a deliberately sheepish look, I took out the jar and tossed it to her. Even in this light, I could see the expression of rage on her face as she realized what it was. I shrugged, as if to apologize, then slipped inside.

The room was rather large, covered in a soft, patterned carpet. The light came from beyond a slightly open door in the far wall. More rustling came from behind the door. A light sleeper, I thought, cursing our luck. Then something caught my eye.

A robe hung from a hook in the far wall, next to the door. From the same hook dangled a leather belt, a sheathed knife still on it. It couldn't be this easy. Still, I crept closer, always watching for any sign of traps.

I reached out and took the dagger. It was just as Hadar had described, a beautiful blade, with a handle carved like a rabbit. The carving was so fine and detailed that I could almost feel the animal's fur. An instant later, I stifled a curse. The damn thing was looking at me. It was the most disconcerting feeling, to have this magical weapon watching me like that. I grabbed one of my own knives and switched them. If I was lucky, it would take a while before anyone noticed the switch.

I turned around and came face to face with Alycia, who smiled at me. That smile made me even more nervous than the dagger. Anger, embarrassment, rage, all these I could have dealt with. But that smile was too much. Alycia is very patient. And she never forgets an offense.

She walked to the door and peeked through. I followed. As I looked into the bedroom beyond, I recalled Hadar's words of assurance. It would be simple, he had said. Tomin would be in bed, asleep.

Well, he was in bed all right. But he wasn't asleep. Neither was the young woman he was with. Suddenly I had an entirely different interpretation of those rustling noises.

Alycia was already backing away. I continued to watch, purely out of professional caution, until Alycia grabbed my hair and tugged me back.

Neither of us spoke until we were outside. There, I said dryly, "They're awake."

Alycia ignored my comment. "I'm not poking around a wizard's cabin unless I know he's asleep."

"He *did* seem rather distracted," I offered.

Alycia glanced around anxiously. "I didn't see the knife or Hadar's other item."

The other thing we had promised to steal. I thought about my quick glances around the cabin, searching for anything that could have been our intended prize. But I had seen nothing.

At that point, my thoughts were interrupted by a loud squeal that seemed to come from my belt. No, not from my belt. From the magical dagger at my belt.

"What's that?" Alycia hissed.

"The knife." For an instant, I thought she would kill me herself. The squealing continued. I placed my hands over the hilt, trying to muffle the sound. A moment later, I was rewarded by a sharp pain in my palm. "It bit me!"

Alycia rolled her eyes. "Stay there," she ordered, and vanished into the dark.

•••

At this point, my wife returned. I winced in anticipation as she gave me another quick peck on the cheek, but this time there were no teeth involved.

"It would have served you right if I had left you there," she commented, offering me a torn hunk of bread. "Hungry?"

I nodded. Around a mouthful of bread, I continued speaking.

•••

I was left standing outside the cabin with a screaming knife. I thought about running, but it would have been pointless. If I kept the knife, I would be too easy to find. If not, I failed my assignment. Either way, I was in trouble.

I glared at the dagger in frustration. Then my eyes widened. There was now a total of six knives on my belt. One was my own, still in its sheath. The stolen blade was on my other hip. And four other blades gleamed nakedly in the moonlight, all tucked neatly through my belt. As I watched, another blade popped into existence.

"What in the hell?" This made me very uncomfortable. There was a thief I had known by the name of Derek. He stole a jeweled dagger from a weaponsmith one night. With the unsheathed blade in his belt, he began to sneak away. Unfortunately, the weaponsmith's cat, an ancient, half-blind tom, woke up and started yowling. Derek began to run, tripped over the cat, and fell to the ground. *Slice*, instant celibacy. So the sudden appearance of sharp blades at my waist was less than reassuring.

"One of the properties of the dagger you've stolen," a voice answered. "The weapon is always kept isolated, never with another knife. Otherwise, it tends to . . . reproduce."

Tomin had a calm voice, which seemed out of place as he stood there in his hastily donned robe. The woman was right behind him, watching.

"I must ask that you return the dagger," Tomin said.

I nodded, trying to look defeated. In truth, I was nervous. I wanted to know where Alycia was. She wouldn't have just left me here. Even after my little joke. She wouldn't break oath just to get back at me. I was having a hard time convincing myself.

Finally, the dagger had stopped squealing. I now had a total of nine daggers on my belt, where before there had been two. I unfastened the belt, jumping back as one landed, point first, by my foot.

I tossed the blade to him, still sheathed, and he stepped forward to retrieve it. As he bent down, the woman behind him frowned, then cried out, "Tomin, wait!"

There was a blur as Alycia jumped down from the roof, landing on the wizard's back. They tumbled to the ground, rolling around briefly. When they stopped, Alycia's knife was pressed against Tomin's back. Gods, I loved that woman.

I wondered briefly where that last thought had come from as I raced forward and used my belt to tie Tomin's hands. Together, we pulled him to his feet. Then Alycia cried out and dropped her knife. Her hands went to her head. Ignoring Tomin, I caught Alycia as she fell. Her breath was coming in quick, tight gasps. I looked at the other woman to find her gesturing with her hands. Two wizards. A minor detail Hadar had neglected to mention.

I kicked the back of Tomin's knees, and he landed beside me. Scooping up one of the fallen knives, I brought it to Tomin's throat and yelled, "Stop, now!"

Instantly, the woman's movements ceased. Alycia took a deep breath and slowly pushed herself up off the ground. She seemed uninjured, but weak.

"All we want is that knife, and one other item," I said. I kept one eye on the woman, the other on Alycia, and wished for a third to keep on Tomin.

The wizards looked at one another. I pressed the knife closer and tried to appear menacing. Finally, the woman nodded. She offered her hands to Alycia. "You may bind me if you wish."

"Lana, don't," Tomin protested.

"It will be all right," Lana answered. She was a tall woman, with dark eyes and prominent cheekbones. Unbrushed brown hair formed a bushy halo around her head. She waited with quiet dignity as her wrists were tied. "What is this second thing you want?"

Alycia and I glanced at each other. "We . . . don't know," I finally admitted.

"Not only are they thieves," Tomin muttered, "but they're incompetent thieves."

"Enough," Lana snapped. "Let them search the cabin. They can take what they want, and be gone." Then she frowned, studying Alycia closely. Her fingers reached toward Alycia's eyelids. Alycia raised her knife threateningly, and the fingers stopped, inches away. "Where did you get this?" Lana asked.

Alycia was silent. To give away the name of one's employer was punishable by death. Not that it turned out to be much of a secret.

"Hadar," Lana said quietly. She gave Tomin a look of concern. I could feel his shoulders tense.

"Of course," he said bitterly.

I cocked my head at Alycia, silently asking, *Do you know what's going on?*

A shrug. *Not a clue.*

"I believe I know what this second item is," Lana said with a half-smile.

The expression on her face was familiar, and suddenly I knew. She had the same dark eyes, the same proud chin. "It's you," I realized. "His daughter?"

"Say nothing," Tomin said angrily.

Lana shrugged. "They already know."

"I told you we should have gone south. Hadar knew about my cabin. Of course he'd find us here."

Lana's eyes narrowed. "And perhaps if you hadn't been so spiteful as to steal his dagger, he would have been less angry."

Tomin laughed harshly. "He'll kill me either way."

"Shut up, both of you," Alycia shouted, cutting off the argument. She turned to Tomin. "Nobody's going to kill you. You're free to go." Then, to Lana. "You have to come with us. We have no choice. But I don't see why you can't just leave after we deliver you."

"You don't understand," Tomin said bitterly. "It's forbidden for a member of the Order to take a lover. And Hadar would never allow Lana to leave the Order. The last man who tried to woo his precious daughter ended up a turtle, swimming the Marona River."

Lana nodded. "He would already have destroyed Tomin, except that I can sense his presence. Had he approached, I would know. But once I'm gone, Tomin is as good as dead."

"Take the knife," Tomin said. "Lana's right, it was stupid of me to steal it in the first place." His voice dropped, became a plea. "But please, allow us to leave. I love her."

"We can find a way to pay you whatever you want," Lana added.

Alycia shook her head. "We gave our oath."

Lana nodded slowly. "I understand." She looked at Tomin. "If you flee now, you might be able to escape."

Tomin snorted. "I'm not leaving."

"You'll die."

The young wizard shrugged. "So be it. I'm not leaving."

Suddenly I felt low. They obviously loved each other very much. And here we were, breaking up their romance and practically sentencing one of them to death. I had been a thief for my entire adult life, starting at age eleven. But I was no murderer. I locked eyes with Alycia, and saw the same conflict there.

"We gave oath," I repeated.

Alycia nodded. "We swore to bring back both Lana and the knife."

My heart felt heavy, like a stone in my chest. I reached down to retrieve the magical dagger. This time, I made sure it was the only knife on my belt.

"Come on," I muttered. "We have no choice."

• • •

I waited in the small back office. The door had been locked shut when I arrived, but the lock was poorly made. It took only seconds to break in. There were no windows. Wooden rafters cast odd striped shadows on the ceiling. An old oak desk sat by the far wall. The only light came from a small oil lamp that burned hotly in my hand. Lana sat, still bound, in one corner. I could hear footsteps in the storage area, gradually growing louder. Shadows danced oddly as they neared. A minute later, Hadar stepped into the room, carrying a softly glowing stone in his hand for light. He set the stone on the desk, where it illuminated the entire room in a pale blue glow.

He smiled when he saw me. "Daughter," he said, turning to Lana. She said nothing. With a shrug, he looked at me. "Where is your friend?" he asked.

I closed my eyes in an expression of pain, then shook my head, shoving the feelings aside. "She left. She wanted nothing to do with this."

"A pity," Hadar said. Dark eyes scanned my body. "You have my knife?"

I pulled it from my belt. "What's going to happen to her?"

"Nothing at all," he answered, still smiling. "Lana is quite gifted. She will return to her studies, and all will be forgotten."

"And Tomin?" Lana asked, speaking for the first time.

Hadar's gaze hardened. "He disobeyed me. He was my student. Discipline must be maintained." His eyes burned into mine. "I'm sure you understand. I'm told your guild has similar standards."

"If this is about discipline," Lana snapped, "then punish me. Not Tomin."

Hadar smiled, and for an instant I saw true affection in his eyes. "I love you, Lana. I could never hurt you."

"It would be better to take that blade and kill me now. That way you would only kill my body. Instead you murder my soul."

I was impressed. Lana had a bit of a flair for poetic language. But her words only seemed to enrage Hadar.

"Enough," he roared. When I first met the wizard, I had seen a glimpse of his anger. Now his temper was fully revealed in that way that only family can evoke. His hands wove patterns in the air, and Lana jerked back in fear. Then, regaining control, Hadar clasped his hands tightly together.

"Tomin will be punished. You will come home with me."

"No." Lana sounded calm, but a rage equal to her father's flashed in her eyes.

"You would challenge me?" Hadar asked. His voice was dangerously low. "That is, of course, your right." He waved a hand, and Lana's ropes fell to the floor. He waited, a vision of confidence, as Lana massaged her sore wrists.

Their eyes locked, and for a moment I thought I was going to end up in the middle of a full-scale war between angry wizards. Not the healthiest of positions. But with the way my luck had been lately, I wouldn't have been surprised.

Then Lana looked down. "No, Father."

Hadar nodded, full of forgiveness and control. Control both of his own magical powers and of his daughter. He held out a hand to me, and I slapped the hilt of the knife into it. "You may go."

Hadar turned his attention to Lana. I watched her for a moment, head bowed in defeat. Then, shaking my head, I opened the door and stepped back.

I love drama. I would love to say that it was a fierce battle, full of flashing blades, powerful magic and incredible courage. If I was lucky, someone would take a serious wound, but still rally the strength to carry on to the bitter end, a glorious, triumphant end.

Instead, Alycia moved noiselessly through the door, braced herself behind Hadar, and slammed him in the back of the neck with the butt of her dagger. He fell like a rock.

It was beautiful. She moved with a grace that even I, with all my skill, could never match. She turned to me and bowed. I applauded softly. She had a length of chain from the storage area of the warehouse that she used to bind the wizard at the wrists and elbows. I had forgotten how well we worked together. For the first time, I realized that I had missed her.

Once Hadar was secure, we both turned to Lana. "Thank you," she said quietly. But she looked sad.

"Thank James," Alycia said. "It was his idea." I grinned and tried to look modest. I failed, but I did try.

Lana knelt down in front of her father and kissed him softly on the forehead. When she rose, her tears left a shiny trail down her cheeks.

"Tomin is waiting," Alycia reminded her.

She nodded without looking. Very quietly, she said, "Goodbye." Then she turned and left.

"We make a good team," Alycia commented, coming to stand beside me.

I said nothing. Instead, I kissed her. I'm pretty sure I hadn't planned to do that, but somehow our lips ended up pressed together. I thought that perhaps I should pull away, in case I had offended her, but that would have been difficult with her hands locked so firmly behind my head. Alycia was a very strong woman.

Hadar woke up a little later. He tested his bonds for a few minutes, but Alycia knew her craft. Hadar was bound tight. He couldn't even stand. And he was furious.

For an instant, I felt fear. If he should manage to escape, the remainder of our lives would be spent in agony. But he merely spat, "You broke oath."

Alycia shook her head. "We brought Lana, as we promised. It wasn't our job to keep her here."

"As for your knife . . ." I slammed the dagger into the desk, where it quivered briefly.

Together, we turned to go. From behind, Hadar's voice followed us. "Hope that your guild kills you. I promise you that my punishment will be far more painful."

The man had bothered me ever since I met him. Apparently he had the same effect on Alycia, for she drew her dagger and stepped forward.

"Punishment. Discipline. You would keep your own daughter from happiness, just to satisfy your pride."

Her words were wasted. Hadar brushed them aside as if they were dust. "You should kill me," Hadar said. He seemed to have no fear of the knife Alycia was pointing at his chest.

"You're right," Alycia snapped. She set her dagger on the desk and grabbed the wizard's shirt in both hands. "We should. Or Lana should. Or Tomin."

"You lack the courage," Hadar accused.

Alycia shook her head in disgust. Without a word, she stood up and left, dropping Hadar to the floor with a thud. I followed, locking the door behind us.

"You know he'll come after us," I said.

She frowned. "I'm not sure." She bit her lip, as if she were struggling to remember something. "I think I left my dagger on the desk." She looked at me and shrugged innocently.

I heard two sounds as we left the warehouse. The first was Hadar, shouting after us in rage. The second was an animal-like squeal which quickly rose in pitch.

•••

"What happened to Lana and Tomin?" Devin asked. The young waiter hadn't moved from his spot. I allowed myself a twinge of pride in my storytelling abilities.

I shrugged and took a deep swallow of ale. "Don't know. Never saw them again."

Alycia tapped my arm. "We should be going soon."

"What about all that money?" Devin said.

I grinned. "Dirt. Hadar tricked us. We did the job for a few sacks of soil." I tossed a few coins onto the table and stood to leave.

Devin's hand darted out, and the money vanished. "That's a good story," he called out to us. "But I caught you."

I turned and raised an eyebrow.

"If you were real thieves, you wouldn't go around bragging about it. The city watch, they'd string you up in a second." He folded his arms, looking smug.

"Clever kid," I said, throwing Devin a mock salute as we left. The night was dark, and I breathed in deeply, loving the cool air.

"Quite," Alycia agreed. She slipped a hand into mine as we walked. "We should do something about the watch."

"That reminds me, we should double-check tomorrow's shipment."

She nodded in agreement. Hand in hand, we walked in the direction of our warehouse, where four thousand, five hundred and thirty-eight daggers waited for delivery. Our price was amazingly low. The Larindale city watch had been thrilled at the offer.

ART vs. EATS

Written by
L. Ron Hubbard

About the Author

L. Ron Hubbard's remarkably productive writing career spanned more than half a century of literary achievement, and had a lasting creative influence. Its scope and diversity eventually embraced more than 560 works—over 60 million words—of published fiction and nonfiction. And though he was always, foremost, a writer's writer, his zest for adventure, his inexhaustible curiosity and his galvanizing personal belief that one should live life as a professional led him to outstanding accomplishments in other fields—as an explorer and prospector, mariner and aviator, filmmaker and photographer, educator and artist, composer and musician.

Growing up in the austerely rugged frontier country of Montana, he was riding horses by the time he was three, and by the age of six had been initiated as a blood brother of a Blackfoot medicine man. While still a teenager, before the advent of modern commercial air transportation, he journeyed more than a quarter of a million miles by sea and land into remote areas of the Far East rarely penetrated by Westerners, intensively broadening his knowledge of other peoples and cultures.

A master mariner and helmsman, he subsequently led three separate voyages of discovery and exploration under the flag of the prestigious Explorers Club.

Returning to the United States from the Far East in 1929, Mr. Hubbard studied at The George Washington University where he became president of both the Engineering Society and Flying Club, and wrote articles, stories and a prize-winning play for the school's newspaper and literary magazine.

A daredevil pilot, he barnstormed across the United States in gliders and early powered aircraft, becoming a correspondent and photographer for the Sportsman Pilot, *one of the important national aviation magazines of its day. At the age of only 25, his reputation already prominently established as a writer of popular fiction, he was elected president of the New York Chapter of the American Fiction Guild, whose membership at the time included Dashiell Hammett, Raymond Chandler and Edgar Rice Burroughs. Shortly afterward, he worked successfully in Hollywood as a screenwriter and script consultant for Columbia and other studios.*

All of this—and much more—over the breadth and range of his professional career found its way into his writing and gave his stories a compelling authenticity and an exciting sense of the texture of life, or of the way things credibly might be in some possible future or alternative dimension, that continue to attract and engross readers everywhere.

Beginning with the publication in 1934 of The Green God, *his first adventure, in one of the hugely popular all-fiction "pulp" magazines of the day, L. Ron Hubbard's outpouring of fiction was prodigious—often exceeding a million words a year. Ultimately, he produced more than 260 published novels, novelettes, short stories and screenplays in virtually every major genre, from action and adventure, western and romance, to mystery and suspense, and, of course, science fiction and fantasy.*

Mr. Hubbard had, indeed, already achieved broad popularity and acclaim in other genres when he burst onto the landscape of speculative literature with his first published science fiction story, The Dangerous Dimension, *in 1938. It was his trendsetting work in this field, particularly, that not only helped expand the imaginative boundaries of the genre, but established him as one of the founders and principal architects of what remains its most celebrated—and legendary— period of productivity and literary invention, the "golden age of science fiction" of the late 1930s and 1940s.*

Such timeless L. Ron Hubbard classics of speculative fiction as Final Blackout, Fear, Ole Doc Methuselah *and* Typewriter in the Sky, *as well as his powerful capstone novels, the epic alien-invasion story* Battlefield Earth *and the sweeping ten-volume* MISSION EARTH® *series, continue to appear on bestseller lists and to garner critical accolades in countries around the world.*

The single biggest science fiction novel in the history of the genre, Battlefield Earth *was, in fact, given singular recognition when it was voted third in the Random House Modern Library readers' poll of the one hundred best English-language novels of the twentieth century. Production of a major motion-picture version of* Battlefield Earth *began in July 1999, for release in the year 2000. Meanwhile, an original L. Ron Hubbard screenplay about look-alike spies,* Ai! Pedrito!— When Intelligence Goes Wrong, *novelized by Kevin J. Anderson, was published in 1998 and immediately became a* New York Times *bestseller, the seventeenth Hubbard title to do so. This was followed in 1999 with the publication of* A Very Strange Trip, *an original new L. Ron Hubbard story of time-traveling adventure, novelized by Dave Wolverton, also becoming a* New York Times *bestseller directly following its release.*

L. Ron Hubbard's extraordinary 56-year career as a professional writer was distinguished, equally, by his deeply felt lifelong commitment to helping amateur and aspiring authors of demonstrated merit. This culminated in 1983 in his establishment of both the Writers of the Future Contest—*now marking its fifteenth year as the largest and most successful merit competition of its kind—and the annual anthology of the winning best new, original stories of science fiction and fantasy.*

The companion Illustrators of the Future Contest, *for whose winners this anthology also provides an important international showcase, was inaugurated five years later.*

Mr. Hubbard's initial work with fledgling writers, however—undertaken while still in his 20s—found salient expression in lectures given on how to get started at such schools as Harvard and The George Washington University.

He also began, as early as 1935, to publish sharply practical "how to" articles about writing as a craft and profession, which appeared in major writers' magazines and continue to be used today in writing courses and seminars, and as the basis for the Writers' Workshops held each year for the winners and published finalists of the Writers of the Future Contest.

In the essay that follows, L. Ron Hubbard addresses the ages-old question of "Arts vs. Eats"—whether it is better to have been read (and possibly forgotten) than never to have been read at all—and brings fresh insight and informing wit to the answer.

It was midnight in the Village—or maybe three or four. The longhaired exponent of the moderns stabbed a slab of ham and somehow navigated the tortuous course through uncombed shoals and to his mouth. He pointed his fork at me.

"But it's tripe! You know it's tripe. You aren't creating anything. You are taking a predetermined plot and garnishing it to suit the puerile taste of fatuous editors. You are shoveling out words as though they were so many beans. Ugh!" And he speared some scrambled eggs.

"My wares are read, anyway," said I with wicked malice.

"Read! By whom pray tell? Taxi drivers and white wings and vapid stenogs! By garbage collectors and housemaids . . ."

"And doctors and lawyers and merchants and thieves," I snapped.

"Why not? But what of it?" He emptied his fork into his bottomless cavern and again waved it before my nose. "What of it? I say. You'll end up your days by never writing anything truly great. All you'll have to show for it is a stack of dogeared magazines, each one forgotten the instant it is replaced on the stands by the next number."

"Is there anything wrong with that?" I said. "Is it so different to lay away magazines than to stow unpublished manuscripts? When it comes to that, my pro-nothing friend, I think it far better to have been read and forgotten than never to have been read at all."

"You dissemble. At least I am earnest. At least I am striving to write something truly great. At least my wares are not beneath my dignity, and if those few I have published went unpaid they at least added their small bit to the true literature of the day. You fictioneers make my hair crawl. You prostitute a God-given gift for the sake of your stomachs. Mark my words," he said, ominously striving to put out my eyes with his useful fork, "you will live to regret it."

At the time I was quite amused, for it was I who paid for that ration of ham and eggs he had so manfully mauled. For a long time afterwards I related the story to my brethren amid much applause. It was so funny, you see, for this shaggy half-bake to berate the source of the money which had paid for his much needed meal. But through the din of laughter there still hovered a small doubt. What he had said was perfectly true. In fact it was so true that I was made very uneasy. To write millions and millions of words for the magazines was wonderful from the financial standpoint. But money isn't everything—or is it?

Now it so happens that this argument started long before two of the Pharaoh's chief poets fanned it into the raging flame which has carried it so far down the ages. On one hand there is the fellow who consoles himself with the thought that his work, unread, is too great; and on the other, the man who says that though his work is not great, it is widely read.

In such a way do we all maunder. If we write "trash" we apologize for it. If we write "art" we bellicosely defend our right to starve. In such a way do all writers put themselves on the tilt field with their resulting wounds. Few indeed are the fellows who feel neither one way or the other about it.

This argument of art vs. eats is without foundation. It is a chimera. According to Voltaire, if one must argue, one must define his terms and, certainly, it is impossible to draw a line between art and trash, for where one ends and the other begins is wholly dependent upon the taste of the man who makes the distinction.

Unless, then, it is possible to discover some generality whereby these matters can be reconciled, we will continue to stumble and stagger and apologize.

Quite accidentally I discovered what appears to be such a generality. Occasionally in this business of writing, a fellow is called upon to stand up before aspirants to the profession and utter magic words. Rarely are the words very magic; usually the writer states that it is a fine business, that editors read manuscripts and that one has to produce to sell. Beyond that the wise speaker never ventures—for he would find himself as lonely as an eagle in the blue so far as understanding is concerned. Unless one has experienced editorial reactions, he cannot understand them. Unless one has been confronted with the woes of technique in their most inquisitorial form, he cannot discourse upon relative merits. Unless one has a rather mysterious gift in the first place, he cannot write at all. And so it goes.

But on this one particular occasion I was confronted with the epitome of impossibility. In so many words it was requested that I "talk for forty-five minutes and tell all about the writing and marketing of short stories." And as one could talk for forty-five years without getting deeper than the surface of the subject, the cue was for laughter. Anytime men find themselves confronted with impossibles, they laugh.

Still, the thing was a challenge. To tell *all* about the writing and selling of short stories in forty-five minutes would be an alp to climb. And that I refused to climb it irked me. I dislike the acknowledgment of impossibilities. It couldn't be done and it never had been done and it never would be done . . . unless I could figure out some generality which would cover the whole subject in one grand sweep.

A MAN MORE ORDINARY

Written by
Manfred Gabriel

Illustrated by
Yuri Chari

About the Author

Manfred Gabriel was born and raised in the Chicago area, where he graduated from Loyola University with a BA in communication. He now lives in western Wisconsin, with his wife and two dogs. He manages a bookstore, which over the years has given him access to all sorts of reading, and has shown him that though writing can be a tough business to get into, success stories happen all the time.

About the Illustrator

Yuri Chari was born in Lvov, Ukraine, and graduated from the Lvov Polygraphic Institute. He now lives and works in New York City. He has participated in numerous exhibitions worldwide, including the National Museum of Warsaw, Pompidou Center in France, the National Museum of Stockholm in Sweden, the State Museum of Heidelberg in Germany and quite a few others. He is an acclaimed painter, illustrator, printmaker and lecturer.

As soon as I saw my brother Phillip at the kitchen door, I went upstairs to get my gun. I crept into the bedroom, finding my way in the dark to my side of the bed. Slipping my hand beneath my pillow, I felt the warm metal of the loaded .38. As I pulled it out, Kelly stirred.

"Can't sleep again?" she asked, half rising.

"Yeah," I whispered. "Just need a glass of water. Go back to sleep." I leaned over to her, placed my hand on her shoulder, settled her back against her pillow. I doubted she could see the gun in the dark, but I kept it behind my back all the same. As I kissed her forehead, it weighed heavily in my hand.

Out in the hall, I peeked into Suzanne's room. She slept soundly, her breath steady. Gently, I closed her door. Then I headed downstairs to the kitchen, hoping Phillip had changed his mind and gone.

He was still waiting though, his bulk filling the door's frame, his eyes peering through its lace-curtained window. He hadn't knocked, or rung the bell, he was just standing there, as if sure I would notice him eventually.

Not wanting him to see the gun, I slipped it into the junk drawer where we kept scissors, pens, paper clips and other odds and ends. I had bought it a month before, as soon as I learned of Phillip's escape. I took a course in how to handle it, fired several rounds. Still, the gun was a foreign object to me. I hoped I wouldn't have to use it. I went to the door and opened it halfway, leaving only the flimsy, locked screen door between us. The night air was hot and still. Crickets chirped. Phillip smelled like he hadn't bathed in days.

"Aren't you going to let me in?" he asked.

I shouldn't have, I know. I should have gone to the phone, called the police and kept him locked out until they arrived. But he was still my brother, and I missed him. Besides, I had turned him in once before, and I didn't want to go through that again.

Hesitantly, I clicked open the door. He entered and followed me into the kitchen. He headed to the fridge, foraged until he found a can of beer, popped it open, guzzled half of it down. I stood near the drawer where I had tucked the gun, watching him. His hair was long, wild, uncombed. He had grown a beard, scraggly and somewhat gray. He wore a pair of dirty pajamas, striped like a concentration camp uniform, and his feet were bare. He looked so different from the last time I saw him, buttoned down and cleanshaven, wearing his best suit. That was in court, when he was found guilty but insane and sentenced to the institution. I still remembered how he glared at me as they led him away, and how I looked down to avoid his gaze.

"What do you want?" I asked, trying to sound calm.

He sat down at the kitchen table, his back to the window. Fireflies danced beyond his head. "Want? I don't want anything. I'm just here to say hello, and maybe repay a favor."

The last word dripped off his lips. I stiffened. I calculated how long it would take to pull the gun out of the drawer, if I could do it before he sprang at me. I

wondered if he still had the speed and reflexes from his
college running-back days.

"You look so nervous," he said. "Don't worry. Have
a seat." He patted the chair next to him. I remained
standing.

"Tell me, how are Kelly and Suzanne?"

"Fine," I answered. "They're out of town for the
weekend."

A grin shone from beneath Phillip's beard. "You
never could lie, Little Brother. It was just a polite question. Don't worry, I've always liked Kelly. I remember
when I was your best man, standing up there, thinking
how pretty she was, how you were lucky to have her."

The air conditioning clicked on, humming softly. The
artificial breeze blew up at me from the vent at my feet.
A bead of sweat rolled down my forehead. The gun was
just inches away. I wondered, if it came down to it, if I
would have the guts to pull the trigger.

"And Suzanne, how old is she now, sixteen?"

"Fifteen," I replied coldly.

"Practically a woman," he said. He sipped his beer,
leaned back, confident, sure of himself as always. I
thought of my daughter, so innocent, unaware of any of
this. I was sure she had questions about what had
happened to Uncle Phil, but she was too young to
understand at the time, and it wasn't something we
talked about anymore, even since his escape. She was
still my little girl. I wanted to shield her, at least for a
little longer.

"You have the life, you know that?" Phillip continued.
"Nice family, nice house, nice neighborhood, good job.
Still working at Tellinghouse Labs, I take it?"

I didn't say anything. He could have had the good
life, too. He was smart—valedictorian, *summa cum laude*,

Illustrated by Yuri Chari

masters in information systems. He was pulling down six figures just freelancing before he snapped. That sunny spring afternoon when he walked into that bank and started shooting, killed a teller, the bank manager and wounded three customers before taking off, coming here, asking me to hide him, just for a few days, until he could figure out what to do next.

When I didn't reply, he went on. "Good place to work. I turned them down once, you know. Too corporate. Still, you can work there until you retire. Live the fat life. Yes, you've got it good. Shame if someone, something, took that all away."

I almost pulled out the .38 then, threatened to make him leave at gunpoint, go and never come back. But he hadn't done anything yet, and something in the way he was talking made me curious about what he was up to.

"They're looking for you," I said. I thought of the police, who had given up their stakeout only a week before.

"Haven't found me yet."

"Still, they will," I replied.

He leaned forward in his chair. "Only if you turn me in again."

The words stung me. "I had no choice. You were all over the TV. Cops were everywhere. They were watching my every move. I could have gotten in a lot of trouble if they found you here. You needed help."

He sat back. "I just needed a little time, that's all. It would have been nice if you understood."

But I didn't understand. He had always been so normal. We had good parents. He had plenty of friends, an education, he was intelligent, funny, athletic, lots of women, lots of money. He had everything. I always looked up to him, longed to be like him. It crushed me to see him crash and burn so fast. My fallen idol, a wasted life.

"Why did you do it?" I asked. It was the first time I had the opportunity to ask the question since his arrest.

He looked down at his hands, fingers splayed as if examining a manicure. "I don't know. No reason. I just couldn't take it anymore. It could have happened to anyone. We have a lot less control over our lives than we think. It just happened to me, that's all. Besides, none of that matters now."

He finished his beer, crinkled the aluminum can in his hand. "You know where I've been these past few weeks? You know how I managed to escape?"

I shook my head. I didn't know, and neither did anyone else. The institution was maximum security, he was strapped down at night. Yet in the morning, his bed was empty, the straps still buckled, his door still locked, the bars on his windows untouched. There had been no sign of him leaving the grounds. Dogs couldn't pick up a scent. It was as if he had never been.

He closed his eyes and he frowned, as if trying to remember. "I lay in bed, immobile, eyes wide. A new drug I had been given made it difficult for me to sleep. The shades were drawn and everything was dark. Then I heard a crackling noise, and in the corner of the room a large hole appeared in the wall, a rift in the fabric of space, darker than even the room, black as death. A tingling sensation swept over my body, starting with my toes and working its way up. Then I passed out."

He didn't say anything for a time. The air conditioning clicked off. The sudden silence scared me. "Go on," I urged. I figured as long as he was talking, I was safe. Kelly and Suzanne were safe. And maybe I was wrong, maybe he came here just to talk after all—no revenge, no hatred, just a conversation. Brothers again.

Then I remembered what he said about repaying a favor. My hand slid over the handle of the drawer that held the gun as he continued his story.

"When I awoke, I was sitting in a cold metal chair in a dimly lit room. My vision was blurred so that I couldn't make out any details. At first I thought that I was still at the institution, that the blurring was due to the new drug, but then there they were, staring at me. Three of them. They have these eyes, like pinpricks of light, all gold, no pupils. Spooky." He opened his eyes slightly, squinting, as if to try to imitate what he described.

"In the blurring, all I could see clearly were those eyes. I'll tell you this, though, these things weren't at all like people say—too many limbs, too much of what I thought was hair. They were black, except for those eyes, and then they had these voices."

Phillip cleared his throat. He spoke suddenly in a high-pitched tone. "*What doyousee in yoursleep? Whereareyourhands when they arenotinuse? Canyour bloodbe reformed?*" A shiver ran up my spine.

"They asked all sorts of questions." His voice was back to normal again. "Nonsensical, confusing questions, like those of small children. They patiently waited for answers, which I tried to give them even though I didn't understand what was happening. The questions kept coming, and I kept answering, but they never seemed satisfied."

He looked at me then, seemed to read what was on my mind. "What, do you think I'm making this up? This isn't the *X-Files*. I'm not Whitley Strieber. These things were real, and they never even heard of Roswell.

Otherwise, how do you explain my escape? I'm smart, maybe even as smart as you think, but I'm no Houdini."

He had a point. Still, he was capable of anything. "But why you?" I asked. I didn't see why he of all the people would be taken. I wanted him to see it too, and hoped by answering the question he would see his delusion for what it was.

He let out a small laugh. "I asked them that, and you know what they said? Accident. They don't travel in spaceships. They fold time. Unfortunately, their calculations aren't perfect. They don't know exactly where they will come out. That's how they ended up in my cell. It seems they've never been here before. God knows how they learned English."

His voice changed tone again. "'Howwouldyou characterize yourpeople?'

"'We are selfish, stupid barbarians.'

"'What wouldyourpeopledo if we revealedourselves to them?'

"'We'd kill you the first chance we got and take your technology for ourselves.'

"They seemed shocked at that. They didn't believe me. I don't think they know what war is, or physical violence, for that matter. Funny thing is, being kept by them was worse than anything I suffered at the institution."

"How do you mean?" I asked. These aliens were an obvious extension of him, and by learning about them, maybe I could learn what had made him this way.

He turned his head, looked out the window. The fireflies were gone. The night was black. He looked back at me. "At least at the institution I got to go outside, got regular meals, was left in peace sometimes. But these things, they kept me in that chair all the time. I wasn't strapped in, but I couldn't move. They hardly ever let me sleep. I didn't get anything to eat or drink for what seemed like days. Even then, I had to beg, screaming at the top of my lungs until they brought me some water and some stuff that tasted like moldy bread. Their questioning gave me splitting headaches which lasted hours. Once, I asked them when they would let me go. They responded with another question.

"'*Areyousoprimitive you cannotfunctionoutside of When?*' they asked. I couldn't answer them, because I had no idea what they meant. The headaches became worse. Then I told them what I had done at that bank. They seemed to get sick, and had to leave the room. For a time, the headaches even went away. Like I said, they didn't seem to understand physical violence."

He stood up, walked over to me, looked me right in the eye. "That felt good, you know, seeing them retch. It felt as good as what I had done at the bank, letting off steam like that. I wasn't crazy, you know. I knew exactly what I was doing. Banks. Money. Capitalism. Gets in the way. I was better than all that, all of them. I proved it. I would have gotten away, too, if it wasn't for you."

He took a step closer. This was it. The payback. I had no choice. I reached into the drawer, pulled out the gun. I fumbled with it before I got a good grip and had my finger on the trigger. I pointed it at him. My hand trembled.

Phillip slapped down on my wrist and the gun went off as it fell from my hand, the bullet digging into the kitchen table as the .38 clattered to the floor. He shoved me up against the fridge. He leaned on me, his whole weight pinning me, his face inches from mine. I could smell his breath, stale with beer.

"Don't worry," he said. "I'm not going to hurt you. You're my brother. I would never hurt you."

He eased up on me, walked over to the sink, looked out the window above it. The fireflies were back. Kelly and Suzanne appeared in the hallway. Kelly started to say something, but I held out my hand to silence her.

"You know why they let me go?" he asked.

"N-No," I said.

"They said they didn't want me anymore, said they didn't think I was a typical human being. They wanted someone more normal, a man more ordinary, they called him."

He turned around, faced me. He didn't seem to notice Kelly and Suzanne. My back was still up against the fridge. "That's when I told them about you, Little Brother. You with your nice family, your nice house, your nice life. I said you were exactly what they were looking for. They had me lead them to you. That's why I'm here. To tell you they're coming to take you away."

"This is insane," I said.

Phillip reached into the breast pocket of his pajama top, pulled out a pipe. He tossed it on the counter between us. "Go ahead," he said. "Pick it up."

Cautiously, I reached out, picked up the pipe. It was only about two inches long, with a short stem and a large bowl. It was black, like the ebony of piano keys, but it wasn't ebony. It wasn't wood, or plastic, or metal. I couldn't tell what it was made of. I would have to bring it back to the lab and do some tests. All I knew for sure was that it wasn't made of anything I knew.

"They smoke this blue powder with it," Phillip explained. "Smells bitter, like roasted almonds. Gets them high as a kite. One of my interrogators couldn't get enough of the stuff. I lifted that one to show you that they weren't from here. I knew you wouldn't believe me without proof."

He nodded towards the door. "Not that it matters anymore. They're waiting outside. You'll be gone before the sun's up. They'll get quite a bit from you. And maybe, someday, they'll let you come back. And I'll have repaid you for what you've done to me."

"And what about you?" I asked.

"Me? They could care less. I'll disappear. Go to another city, take on a new identity, a new life. Alaska, maybe, or the Caribbean. It won't be hard."

"I don't believe any of this. You're just trying to scare me." I was trying to convince myself more than him. I ran my thumb along the pipe.

"Goodbye, Little Brother."

Phillip walked out, letting the door shut behind him. I leaned against the counter, shaking. Kelly told Suzanne to call the police, and went to me, put her arm around me. She was asking me questions, but I didn't hear them. I was looking out the window. My face was reflected in the glass. The fireflies were still there, but I realized suddenly that they weren't blinking, weren't moving, weren't fireflies at all. I stared at them. Eyes, like gold-plated stars, stared back.

BEARING THE PATTERN

Written by
G. Scott Huggins

Illustrated by
Victory

About the Author

Scott Huggins entered the realm of science fiction through the Clarion Writers' Workshop 1997. His two goals in life are to make SF a more respected literary genre and to become Emperor of The World. It's difficult to say which he is making the more progress toward. This is his first professional sale.

About the Illustrator

Victory currently works as the manager of the Fantasy Gallery in Houston, Texas. She has been drawing since she was two, gets most of her inspiration from music, lives in the boonies, has various and sundry pets, and tends to do things at the last possible moment. As a native Californian, she is never afraid to try new and different approaches, techniques and styles.

he gun was heavy, and little drops of water—perspiration—trickled from above the trigger down to my hands, tickling all the way down to my elbows. I came to the balls of my feet. Footsteps. Soft footsteps, just around the corridor.

It had taken all my patience to let him come to me. And he had. Slowly, I gathered air in my lungs.

I jumped.

Everything happened together; the hallway leapt into focus and with it, Heath, eyes going wide at my yell, then another high yell, a yellowish white blur in front of my face, and then stinging pain and numbness all up my wrists as the gun was ripped from my hands to clatter against the far wall. The momentum of my leap carried me across the corridor, where I landed squarely on my ass.

"What the hell . . ." I spluttered, looking up, and I froze.

About ten centimeters from my nose hung three thin, silvered blades. They bobbed a little from side to side, warping my crazily elongated reflection when they moved. Beyond them, a curiously small, pale face stared down.

Out of my peripheral vision, I could just see Heath staring, mouth open, his own watergun hanging limply in his fingers. I didn't dare take my eyes off the owner of the blades.

Illustrated by Victory

She was almost kneeling, but was still about one and a half meters tall. She was holding the blades in her right hand—no, the blades were fixed to her wrist *above* her right hand, and she was holding her forearm with her left.

Both arms were encased in bone.

In fact, *she* was encased in bone. From her neck down to her false ribs, she was a single plate of dun armor, thick enough to give only a vague impression of the breasts that lay beneath. A joint revealed a series of smaller plates, reaching from her sternum at the apex to down between her legs. Between her legs there was nothing but a small knob of bone. Her legs were also armored; a ridge of bone the thickness of a femur ran the length of each, broken only at the knee joint. Her feet were a series of thin, interlocking surfaces. Now I could see that her arms were more lightly armored, wrapped in spider-web frameworks of supporting bone, like a grid. Between the grid supports, the armor was about the thickness of a fingernail. Her elbows and shoulders were heavily knobbed. Three large sections, like huge vertebrae, climbed up her neck, the last of which arced high over her head, splitting her black hair down the middle. Thin runners of bone branched to the sides, leaving shoulder length hair to grow from the sides of her head.

Of course, I had heard about military bioarmor. This was the first time I'd ever seen it.

Now she rose, and I could see she was well over two meters tall. "Excuse me," she said. Her voice was soft, but cool. "You startled me. I did not mean to hurt you."

I let out a long, shuddering breath and flexed my fingers. The feeling was returning in a rush of needles. Nothing hurt, but they wouldn't stop shaking. I closed them into fists behind me and got up. "Uh, I'm all right."

Heath made a noise like a strangled gurgle.

She seemed to scratch the plate on the top of her head. "I must be more careful," she said absently, almost like she was talking to herself. She said, "I'm slightly nervous today. It won't happen again."

"I see," I lied. My mouth switched to autopilot. "Well, as long as we've met, I'm Carl Shire. This is my friend, Heath." I extended my hand automatically.

She hesitated, then took it. Her hand was small, warm, dry and completely normal to the touch. Over it there was a cuff of bone and three slits that just might be housings for blades. I fought not to stare.

"Marta Krovikian." She turned and offered her hand to Heath, who gingerly took it.

"Are you visiting a friend?" I asked.

No one else was in the room. She must have been standing right in the doorway when I'd jumped around the corner.

"I am a student like yourself." Her voice was flat.

"I thought that all soldiers had their armor removed before mustering out."

The words were out before I knew it, and I wished I hadn't said them. Her eyes arched.

"I chose not to," she said, slightly louder, now, looking around. I followed her gaze.

The hallway had about ten people in it, all in various stages of moving in. Every eye was on her, a tower of reinforced ivory filling the door to her room.

"Well, it was, uh, nice to meet you. I've lived here for a year. My door's open if you have any questions." She said nothing. "See you around." I turned and picked up the watergun where it had fallen.

It was completely unbroken. I turned back to Marta, but her door was closed. Heath and I looked at each other, and I followed him back to his room.

I stepped over the boxes and sat in the room's empty chair, accepting the beer Heath handed me.

"Well," I said brightly, "that was interesting." I took a long pull of the beer to quell the shaking I felt beginning to crawl up my spine.

"You okay?" Heath asked. "I've never seen anyone move so fast."

"I'm all right. Or will be." At least I thought so. Now I had time to be scared. To distract myself I asked, "What do you know about things like that?"

"I know I wouldn't use `things like that' as a description where she could hear you."

My head jerked up. "Hey, I meant the armor, not her."

Heath shook his head. "With that stuff, it's a little difficult to make the distinction. Don't you know?"

"I'm a poli sci major, Heath. I know how much it costs, not what it does."

Heath shook his head in mock sadness, then went on seriously. "They have to grow that directly onto her own bones. Her muscles are underneath. Highly augmented. It's artificial cell division. So she can't take it off."

"I knew that, but not why."

"Well, it's hard to explain, but she's designed to destroy tanks. Don't get in another fight with her."

"I didn't . . ." I began, but saw Heath laughing over his beer. I gave him a disgusted look and finished mine. Then I walked back to my room to finish my own moving in. It was hot, and I'd suggested the waterfight to cool us both off. It had worked. I could still feel chills, even if not the way I'd planned. I passed Marta's room several times. The door remained closed. Eventually, I stopped thinking about her.

2

The floor orientation meeting was a week later. Heath and I were among the last to enter the large triangular common room.

Marta protruded in the room like an upthrust rock spire in a busy harbor. The dun tones of her armor reflected a red, ghostly reflection of the clear red sunset shining through the glass. She sat on a chair that was comically small for her, next to an empty sofa. I circled around in front of her, taking one of these seats while a large number of people sat on the floor, a good three meters away. Heath gave me a look, but followed, sitting on the other side of me. I smiled at her, and in return got a cold lift of the eyebrows. Her nostrils flared, as if smelling something unpleasant. Well, now what had I done?

"I thought I'd approach slowly, from the front, this time," I said, with a small laugh.

That seemed to do it. A corner of her mouth quirked upward, and a little of the ice in the royal blue eyes thawed. I looked around, and became conscious of more eyes. Measuring eyes. Questing eyes. No one was, of course, rude or brave enough to stare outright.

Under the broken gazes, I began to understand that my gesture of sitting next to her might have been taken as the act of a particularly gauche spectator.

I fidgeted uncomfortably with this thought. Marta's eyes wandered, but mostly stayed fixed on the door in the center of the hall—the private apartment of our

Resident Assistant, who was late. I opened my mouth, but then thought better of it. There was no time to explain about Peacey, anyway, and she was coming in the door as soon as I abandoned the notion.

Paige Crenner was a tall blonde with the tendency to remind one of a crane, in both senses of the word. She was striking, and aware of the fact. She wore her hair in short spikes, except for thin, trailing wisps that ran to waist length. Her clothing almost always conformed to the lines of her body, which was in very good shape, thanks both to nature and the fact that she was a karate instructor. Hoops hung and protruded: ears, nose, eyebrow.

Except for her current girlfriend, Nenya, everyone called her Peace, after her initials and politics.

She sat down languidly, next to Nenya, and began her speech about how she welcomed everyone to Kassebaum Hall and Kansas State University, how honored she was to be the RA this year, et multiple cetera. Soon, she turned to the obligatory beginning-of-the-year state-your-name-and-major ritual. "First of all, I'm Peace Crenner, and this is my partner, Nenya. I'm the president of Free Women for Choice on campus, majoring in sociology. I'm on the Debating Team, I'm the treasurer for the Separate Society here, and I like to do work for the Green Party. Okay, next, please?" She turned with a smile to a morose-looking freshman on her right.

I was still trying to think of worthy things to say about myself when Marta stood. There was a swish of indrawn breath. Sitting beside her in an open room, I felt even smaller than I had a week ago.

"My name is Marta Krovikian," she said, just loud enough to be heard. "I am a former combat specialist in the United States Army. For those of you not familiar with it, I am currently bearing the Standard Combat Growth Pattern of Osteoplastic Armor. It functions as a bodily organ, much as your skin does. It permits full range of motion." Just slowly enough for the eye to follow, she spun on one foot, collapsing to a crouch and then reaching up to touch the ceiling. "Like so. In addition, the Pattern provides for unarmed combat."

She twitched her fingers, and all six of the blades I had seen a week ago unfolded over her shielded knuckles. Then she turned so that the back of her head was to most of the room, and pointed to three tiny gleaming black spheroids mounted on the back of the skull crest. "These simple eyes give me the ability to detect motion beyond my normal range of vision.

"I realize that I look unusual in this setting, and wish to allay anyone's anxieties now. Having done so, the subject need not be raised again. Unless there are any questions?" She surveyed the room, almost daring.

Peace raised a hand. Her expression was unreadable; perfectly neutral.

"Could you tell us why you still wear your armor?"

Marta regarded her calmly. "I bear the Pattern," her stress on the verb was slight, "because I choose to." There was an instant of tension between the two women. Then Peace inclined her head, seemingly in acknowledgment, though what she was acknowledging, I could not then have said.

3

Two weeks later, I saw Marta in the hall while taking out the trash. It was the first time I'd seen her since the floor meeting. She was either out or in most of the time.

Nobody knew which. Nobody ever knocked on her door, as far as I could tell.

The empty bucket in her hand said that she had just done the same thing. As I dumped my can, a small piece of paper with hasty writing on it caught my eye. I picked up the crumpled thing and straightened it out without thinking.

It said: "Armored Bitch Go Home."

I was actually surprised. I shouldn't have been. Despite its success, the South China War had made the military unpopular. I heard it in my classes: War was unnecessary, soldiers were unnecessary. After NATO put down the czar in 2025, the problem was worse. But I had tuned it out. Few people cared, at Kansas State. Fort Riley museum was occasionally vandalized, but the ROTC program was very small and ignored.

But now I was surprised. It had gotten *personal*. I put my trash can back in my room and went to Marta's door. I knocked loudly, and realized, to my horror, that I had no idea what I was going to say.

I didn't even know why I was doing it. I didn't know Marta. Maybe she deserved it. Maybe I just didn't like her getting picked on.

Maybe I liked sticking my nose into other people's problems. I *was* a poli sci major.

A muffled "Open" reached my ears, and the door slid aside.

She looked at me across one of the small standard-issue tables that come in every dorm room, crouched over it on the chair, knees high, looking much like a praying mantis. On the table was a chessboard with half the pieces remaining, interlocked in patterns of block and attack. Unfinished work glowed above the computer.

"Yes?" she asked in her perpetually neutral voice.

Like a drowning man, I grasped at the board presented to me. "Chess problem, or unfinished game?" I asked in return.

"Problem, actually. I pulled it off the Fifth Net," she said, looking at me measuringly. "You play?"

"In high school, I did." I looked at the pieces, and the problem appeared. "Queen to king's—" I broke off. I had just set white up for checkmate. I was rewarded by one of Marta's tight smiles.

"That's the obvious. Next guess?"

"It's got to be a pawn move; it's always a pawn move," I muttered, social problem forgotten in favor of chess problem.

"Be my guest," she said.

I went through all the possibilities, none of which were useful, most of which were fatal. We stared at the board together for long moments. Then I bowed my head, laughing quietly. "Oh, tricky," I said. Marta looked at me quizzically. "Queen takes bishop."

Marta looked at me like I'd gone insane. "Rook takes queen."

"Exactly, and now pawn takes pawn . . ."

"Oh!" Marta's eyes flashed. "Very good," she said, after a minute. "Would you care for an entire game?"

"Sure." She yielded the chair to me and moved the table so that she could sit on the bed. The game opened fast, and I found myself taxed merely to stay on the defensive. I sighed in mock irritation as I sent a knight to cover my threatened bishop. "Don't you have work to do?" I asked facetiously.

"Yes," she said, seriously, "but chess has always helped me to relax when things get tense."

"Relax?" I asked. She nodded. I fished out the crumpled sheet of paper from my pocket. "Would this be one of the reasons things are getting tense?"

She took the sheet of paper and scowled darkly. "Where did you get this?"

"You dropped it by the trash."

"What right have you to intrude in my affairs?"

"Look, I just wanted to help . . ."

"I don't need your help."

This wasn't going the way I had thought it would. "No one says you do, but I didn't think . . ."

"Correct, you didn't. I think you should leave."

"Marta," I began. She rose and looked down on me. Hard.

"Out."

I stood, moving very slowly. What exactly triggered those combat reflexes? I hoped it wasn't anger. "Very well," I managed. "I apologize deeply for troubling you with my assistance." I turned my back to her and left. The door shut behind me. Nenya was walking by, and she gave me a supercilious glance.

I wanted to hit something. Dammit, I'd done the right thing. Or I'd tried to. And she'd made me look like an ass. But she'd been hurt, too. I didn't know whether to be angry at her or pity her.

The next day, I saw another note on her door, and checking quickly to make sure she wasn't around, I peered at it closely. This one said: "IRON MAIDEN BABY KILLER."

Disgusted, I ripped the note down and tore it up. Because she still didn't deserve it, I was sure of that.

Two hours later, while poring over a download from the library, there was a buzz at the door.

"Open!" I sang out. The door slid open, and Marta ducked under the doorframe. For a minute, I was afraid that she had somehow seen me take the note from her door, and had come to talk about more "interference," but she didn't look angry.

"Yes?" I inquired, politely.

"I've come to apologize," she said, in that same flat tone that never altered. "You were concerned. I appreciate that. I . . . sort of acted on instinct. I won't say that it won't happen again. But I should not have been angry."

Against all logic, I was smiling. "Won't you sit down?"

"Actually," she said, giving me that smile that looked like she was afraid of breaking her mouth, "I was hoping you'd come back over. I'd hate you to think that you could get out of losing to me at chess by getting yourself thrown out of my room."

"I was hoping you wouldn't see that," I mock-groaned.

"I almost didn't," she said, softly.

I continued the game of chess and won it. We played again, and she put me soundly back in my place. Then it was time for class, and I left.

She never knocked on my door again. But I watched hers. And every two or three days, there'd be something new on it. Obscene cartoons, sometimes, but mostly invitations for the homicidal, armor-plated, baby-killing bitch to go fuck herself. I pulled them down.

The next week, I got two myself, one calling me a warmonger and the other depicting me with a drill between my legs trying desperately to penetrate the shell of some mutant crab thing. I spat, and trashed them, thinking black thoughts about Nenya, and whomever she'd told.

Conversations tended to stop when Marta Krovikian entered a room. No one dared stare at her, but they didn't want to talk around her, either. Even Peace, who at least always greeted people, seemed to find other things to occupy her attention when Marta was there. But at least she left Marta alone. So I thought.

One day, after a chess game, on our way to the dining hall, Peace passed us. She mumbled greetings. Marta waited until she was gone. "She is annoying," she said.

I agreed, but was surprised to hear that statement come from Marta, who I didn't think had been around long enough to learn that.

"What makes you say that?" I asked automatically.

"She's like a friend I had, once." Her eyes focused on a point somewhere long ago. "She . . . surrounds herself with mirrors, and builds up images before her, of how things should be. She doesn't care about the way things are. Or the way they might want to be."

I was amazed. "Marta," I said, "you're a poet."

I got a quirky smile and a shake of the head.

"Has she been bothering you?"

"She wants me to visit some of the groups she belongs to."

"Well, in fairness to the groups, their members can't all be as, ah, emphatic as Peacey."

"Their mirrors won't reflect me."

"What, are you a vampire?" I laughed.

Coldly, "I may have tasted enough blood to qualify."

"I was kidding," I sighed.

"I know." Now the smile was sad. "I didn't drink any of it except my own. I guess I don't qualify."

"I guess not." I hesitated. "Marta, if I may, I think you could stand to take the world less seriously. You could even laugh once in a while."

She stopped. "The world is serious, Carl. The world is deadly serious about everything it does. Even when it laughs, the world never forgets how important it is. You're intelligent enough; but you haven't learned that."

Annoyed, I let it drop.

The place was full, and there were no free tables. We got our meals and sat with the rest of the sixth floor in its traditional corner table. For once, conversations didn't stop. Peace was giving some poor freshman her views.

". . . oh, but you're male. You obviously have great understanding of women who want to be sistermothers. What gives you the right to an opinion?"

"The Constitution," Marta interrupted, not looking up. I winced. Well, Marta had to learn, sooner or later.

"The Constitution?" Peace repeated blandly, rolling her eyes. "A piece of paper created by white males to legitimize their own power? It doesn't even guarantee civil rights for women. I thought about being a sister-mother once," she said, turning back to her original opponent. "I guess you think I'm not capable of raising a child?"

"That's not what I meant."

"Well, it's what you said!" Peace bridled. "Maybe if people would pay more attention to what they say, we wouldn't have a need for people to wear things like Marta does."

Marta slowly turned her head to face Peace squarely. "I swore an oath to defend the ideals on that `piece of paper.' And the Pattern is descended from an art form older than language. Its kind will not be removed from the earth through controlling language. What we say does not start wars; what we do, does."

Peace smiled and put a hand gently on Marta's ribbed shoulder. "Well, of course they made you swear an oath, but people are more important than ideals. They wouldn't let you into their army without—"

"Take your hand off me."

Peace froze. The massive forearm swung up and knocked her fingers aside.

"Off!" There was a moment of charged silence. Marta spoke again.

"What do you mean, 'their army'?"

Peace drew her hand back and looked hurt. "Well, I was only trying to be helpful!" she huffed. "Their army, of course; the army of this country that uses people to oppress people, all over the world!"

Marta raised a massive fist. She spread her fingers. "Very well. I see that you believe me to be"—she ticked the points off on her fingers—"a tool, a traitor and possibly an idiot. Which is it, please?"

"I never said—"

"You most certainly did. Only a tool would swear a coerced oath. Only a traitor would permit her use against her own. Only an idiot would swear an oath without knowing its implications. I ask again, which do you take me for?"

Peace's look changed to one of purest sympathy. "I'm so sorry. I didn't realize what they must have put you through. It's not surprising that you feel a kind of loyalty, it's a common technique—"

"Stop it!" But Marta's voice was softer, and she spoke as if to a child. "*Their* army didn't do anything to me. I neither need nor want your excuses. I am what I am. Would you want me," she glanced at Nenya, "making excuses to people here for what you are?"

Peace's face became deadly expressionless. "Oh. I see. Simple heterosexual bigotry. Well, I was born lesbian; I have a right to be who I am, and I'm proud of it!"

"There we have the difference and the likeness between us, then," said Marta, calmly. "I was not born the way I am. It's not natural. But I, too, have the right to be what I am. I, too, am proud of it."

Peace stood. "Proud? You've subjugated your body to those who buy only death!" She strode out of the dining hall. Nenya half rose, looking at Marta in fear, anger, and something else. Then ran to follow her partner.

"Better the body than the mind," Marta said quietly, and went on eating. Conversation did not resume.

4

From then on, the number of notes on Marta's door, and mine, doubled. A letter to the editor denounced the "hate language" used by "a militarist" to insult a "dedicated, open-minded woman" like Peacey. About four days later, though, as I reached to take yet another piece of paper off her door, I paused. The script was neat and even, not jagged and hurried:

> Individualism is a fatal poison. But individuality is the salt of common life. You may have to live life in a crowd, but you do not have to live like it, nor subsist on its food. You may have your own orchard. You may drink at a hidden spring. Be yourself if you would serve others.
>
> —Henry van Dyke

An ally? But who? I didn't care. I hoped it would do some good.

Two days later I saw the results. Marta Krovikian stepped into the lobby—in blue.

She was everywhere blue. The ribs of her arms; the plates of her legs and torso. The ridges were highlighted with white and lighter blue, while joints and gutters were velvet navy—almost black. A dark, double-beaked, abstract bird of prey launched skyward on her chest plates. Only on her face, hands, and exposed neck was there no trace of color.

She gazed defiantly into the lobby, a third full with morning studiers and breakfast-goers.

Slowly, a low clap rang out, and then another. Then the whole lobby was applauding. She gave the lobby an amused half-smile with a gracious bow of the head. She took the step that put her beside me.

"Shall we eat?" she asked quietly. I bowed deeply to hide my blush. When I looked up, I saw Peace standing in her doorway. There was a look on her face I couldn't interpret. Rage mixed with knowledge of a defeat, mixed with . . . what? I gave her a wide smile as the elevator door opened, and about ten people, including Marta, stepped inside.

The questions around Marta changed. It wasn't, "What kind of person goes around in armor anymore?" It was, "Where did you learn to do that?" To this, Marta only answered that she had had little formal training. And I began to notice that while I was still removing hate mail from her door, there was much less of it. Sometimes, there were things like this:

Genius is the power of lighting one's own fire.
                                                                —John Foster

It was the same person who had written the first note. Whoever it was, I wanted to meet that person. Being Marta's friend was hard work. Just below it was one saying: "30,000 DEAD IN TWO WARS. HOW MANY MORE WILL YOU KILL?"

I mentioned it in the caf one day when I was eating with Heath.

"I'm glad someone's been able to break through to her," he said, chewing on an alleged dinner roll. "No one should be alone that much. But she sort of does bring it on herself."

I nodded, even though his remark grated on me. Did she really? Was it her attitude or just her armor that kept people away? I said, "I wish she were a little more alone, in a way. Those notes get pretty vicious."

I looked up and saw Nenya sitting down about three chairs away from me. I felt anger flare up in me. I'd pulled a swastika off my door just two days back, and I was pretty sure she was one of the chief rumormongers about everything that allegedly happened between me and Marta.

5

A couple of days later, I was playing chess with Marta in her room. She was quiet, even for her, looking blankly at the board. Her blue eyes contrasted with the flowing blue-purple-black color scheme of her armor.

She advanced a knight. I began considering the implications, when I heard her say softly, "I have been unwise."

I looked at the board more intently. "If that move was a mistake, I don't see it . . ."

"Not about the game, Carl." I forgot the board.

"Is there something wrong?"

"Possibly." She looked away for a moment, and then said, "You know the old man who preaches at the union?"

I felt my eyes roll. "Oh, yeah." Fred Morrun was the progeny of an old-time preacher family who had made it their personal crusade to deliver the student body of Kansas State from their sinful ways, real or imaginary, for literally generations.

My imagination caught up with me. "What did you do?" I asked, trying to fight a smile that was forming somewhere around my stomach. Marta actually looked guilty.

"Well, I wouldn't have done anything," she said, "but there I was just walking by when he pointed me out, standing there with those thick glasses, yelling about how I'd disfigured the temple of God by bearing the Pattern, and . . . so . . ." The words came out in a rush. "So I walked up to him, told him his glasses didn't suit his temple very well either, and before I knew what I was doing I'd grabbed them off his face and thrown them over Anderson Hall. It wasn't my fault that he tried to hit me and just about broke his hand. *Stop laughing!*"

I did, instantly, at that tone of voice. Her blue eyes blazed fiercely. "I could have killed him," she whispered. "He could have died right there in my hand. Because I was angry."

I began to see. I'd dreamed of hitting Fred Morrun; I didn't know anyone who hadn't, but this . . . "I'm sorry," I said.

"It's all right. I decided to tell you." She paused. "And I suppose, from your point of view, it *was* funny."

The door chimed.

Marta blinked, then said, "Open."

It was Peace. I felt my stomach sink.

Peace looked at us both, and raised an eyebrow. Then she decided to ignore me.

"Yes?" said Marta.

"I . . . wanted to tell you how sorry I am about what I said earlier. I mean . . . I heard about what you did to that asshole by the union. I didn't mean to hurt you. Well, I did, but I didn't understand you then. I was hoping that we could be friends."

Marta looked up, then away. "Neither understanding nor being friends is an easy thing, with me. But your apology is accepted."

"May I . . . sit down?"

Marta gestured. Peace sat.

"Marta, I don't want to impose on you, but I would like you to help us. You showed today that we can use men's weapons against them. You're really very inspiring."

Marta tilted her head. "Whom do you mean by 'us'? Inspiring to do what? Act against men? I don't act against men. I acted against *a* man, and only because he was being a hypocrite in public, and using me for an example. If you want action against men, you're far more effective."

Peace sat a little straighter. "Ah, but not as effective as you could be. That armor of yours . . . you've made it a wholly feminine power. I was wrong about that, before."

Marta frowned. She carefully picked up her queen from the board and held it up to the light.

"It's all a game to you, isn't it? You don't want a friend. You want a playing piece. And here I am. So well positioned; your lady in painted armor. But every queen starts out as a pawn. Thank you, but I do not want to be yours." She wrapped her fingers around the piece. "Why do you hate them so much?"

Peace's face flushed dark and when she spoke it was low and ugly. "You know, or should. Men are rapists. Nenya knows. Because they cause the wars that plague half the world. Because they use all of their strength, even *our* strength, to subjugate us, to keep us as chattels. Isn't that reason enough?"

I rose to leave. Marta looked up. "Sit down, Carl."

It was less than a command; more than a request. Her face was even harder now. She turned to Peace, almost gently. "Do you really believe that women would do it better? Not differently, but better?"

Peace leaned closer, and clasped Marta by the forearm. "Of course we would, we could . . ."

"Take your hands OFF ME!"

Peace recoiled, but found herself caught by a twist of Marta's wrist, gripping hers like a vise. A broken, jagged look was on Peace's face as she stared into Marta's eyes, and I knew: *Peace was in love with Marta Krovikian!* But there was not, could not, be reciprocation. . . .

Marta leaned into Peace's face, holding her painfully. "Don't you see," she hissed, "that if a man did to you what you are doing to me, you would call it assault? Don't you hear yourself becoming what you hate?"

Peace lost all semblance of composure. "But we're women! We don't destroy everything we touch! We're not like them!" she cried furiously.

Marta's face went terrifyingly blank. She took the point of Peace's jaw gently in her hand and turned it up to face her. "Never tell me that again. And never return."

"No, wait . . ." But there was no waiting. Marta altered her grip, forcing Peace to her feet with a gasp of pain. Marta marched her through the door.

"Out! Lock!" The door closed and locked, shutting out the sight of Peace slumping against the opposite wall. Marta took two steps back, unseeing, and folded herself on the bed. She put her head in her hands, and began massaging her face, and then her hands together, and then her face, and lower neck. Her hands seemed to recoil from the armor, and at the same time seemed to try to cover every exposed area of her body.

"Marta?"

She jumped and stared at me. For the smallest second, I knew what it was to be the target of a deadly weapon. "Carl." She took a deep breath. "I don't think I can finish our game right now."

"We can't anyway," I said, trying to force a lighter tone. "You've broken the queen."

Marta opened her fist and looked at the splintered plastic as if she'd never before seen such a thing. "I'm sorry," she said quietly. But she didn't seem to be speaking to me. I felt cold. She looked scared.

She put the pieces on the board, and took a bottle from under her bed and filled a low tray with the liquid. She dipped a dirty washcloth into the solution, and began cleaning her right leg. Where the solvent touched her armor, the intricate, rounded, purple-blue-black enamel dissolved and ran, leaving clean, yellow white organic.

"What are you doing? Marta, this isn't because of that idiot in the union, is it? You couldn't have taken that seriously?"

"No, but I take that seriously," she said sadly, not stopping, and gesturing toward the door. "I take those seriously." She pointed to her desk, and I noted a pile of papers on it, all sizes. I looked through them.

I'd never seen such a differing array of messages. There were notes; all the kinds I'd torn from her door and many others that I'd never seen, proposing everything from a date to crude sex to undying love. What in the world?

Marta was looking at me with one of her small smiles. "Well, don't look so surprised, Carl. Even your efforts can't stop people sliding them under the door." I winced. For all my self-congratulation, I had simply never thought of that. Somewhere among the hundreds of notes, it dawned on me that Marta was many things to many people, and all in their minds. They built castles around her, put swords in her hands, killed her, and removed her armor with their minds, thousands of them. Because whatever else you could do with Marta Krovikian, you couldn't ignore her. Not and still be alive.

"I understand," I said again. My eyes burned. Her legs were yellow gray again, and the color was being stripped from her arms.

"No, you don't, and neither does she, and neither do they. This," she indicated the tessellations on her armor, "was a mistake. All I want, all I have wanted, is to be left alone, and none of them will ever understand. I really want to be alone, Carl. It's what I've wanted for so long that I don't remember the last time I was lonely. I can barely comprehend the concept. And it seems that they either hate me for it . . . or don't believe it's possible."

"I don't hate you for it."

"No, you don't."

"Then if you want to be alone so much, why do you tolerate me?"

"You let me be alone with you, Carl." She looked at a far point on the ceiling. "You don't demand. I suppose that's why, here, you're the closest thing to a friend I have."

I didn't feel offended. I just nodded, and rose. "Call me when you're ready to play." I think it was at that moment that I finally began to understand Marta Krovikian.

6

But she was right; nobody else did. They were curious as to her sudden reversion to type, but their questions, polite or probing, were rebuffed, with increasing intensity. It didn't work in her favor. I could see the fame she had won facing the dear reverend deteriorating into something worse than ambivalence. Her reputation as something cold and inhuman was back. And there was something worse. A directed enmity marshaled against her, and it lived on the floor, in the big room off the common area. I was reminded of the proverb "Hell hath no fury . . ." when I saw Peace looking at Marta Krovikian. That was certainly something which wasn't restricted to one orientation. And why was I surprised about that?

The notes started to reappear. It was about that time that I caught one of the perpetrators. I had just turned off the light when I heard a soft step in the hall. Ever so faintly, there was a scratching. I walked to the door and looked through the peephole. Someone was holding a piece of paper on Marta's door, working on a message. I was just sleepy enough to be pissed and heedless. I opened the door, stepped out, and spun my victim around by the arm in one smooth motion. "What the fuck do you think . . . ?" The words died in my throat as my grip was expertly broken. I backed off quickly and came up with my fists raised, one tingling badly.

Nenya stood facing me, her face a mask of rage, her own stance promising a much more refined way of fighting. I was much stronger than she was. But I remembered Peace's black belt. "So Peacey can't even write her own shit these days, is that it?" I asked, breathing heavily.

Then I noticed the large blue splotch below Nenya's left eye, how thin and drawn she looked. I saw the note where it had fallen by the door:

"No one respects a talent that is concealed."
                              —Desiderius Erasmus

"Holy shit," I breathed. "It's you. Why?"

She stared defiantly up at me. "As if you could ever understand." She shook her head. "Step back."

Without thinking, I did so, and she picked up the note, fixed it to the door. Looking me straight in the eye, she said, haltingly, "I . . . *ask* you . . . not to tell Peace about this."

I felt my eyes widen. "You mean she *doesn't know?* And she still . . ." Nenya blushed, the bruise dark against her cheek. I shut up.

"The day I tell Paige Crenner anything I think she wants to know we'll see a windchill factor in Hell," I said evenly.

She nodded, straightened, and left. I went back to bed. I was a long time getting to sleep.

Nenya's secret efforts did not hinder Peace. It took time, but there were complaints. A couple of residents

expressed misgivings about living in the same building
with a person who was so effectively armed. Armed
deliberately, if stories told by the army were true, to kill
armed opponents. Not long thereafter, an open letter,
put forward by the Separate Society, appeared on the
editorial page of the school paper expressing its "real
regret that the relevant authorities have not seen fit to
ensure the security of the majority of students in regard
to keeping the campus free of weapons."

Once started, the thing proceeded with alarming
speed. Rumors mentioning Marta Krovikian by name
began to circulate, always in vague terms, alleging
"threats." Other groups on campus began also to show
their "concern," as well. And when the opportunity
presented itself, Peace acted. One day, the paper
mentioned a minor drunken brawl. One of the residents
had pulled a folding knife, and had been arrested. I was
in the room, sitting, as usual, over the chessboard when
the door chime sounded.

"Open."

Peace stepped into the room, and there was nothing
of peace in her face. It was a mask, hard as ivory. Marta
stood, eyes blazing. "I told you not to return."

"I'm afraid you don't have that right, Ms. Krovikian.
I am a Resident Assistant and have the authority to enter
the residents' rooms for the welfare of the students."

"Really? And what might justify concern over
student welfare here? Is playing chess dangerous?"

"I have reason to believe that there are weapons in
this room."

Marta spat. "Yes, you would believe that, wouldn't
you? Be my guest." She swept a hand around the room.

"I don't think a search will be necessary. There are six
knives, right in plain sight."

Marta's eyes narrowed. I didn't get it either. "What do you mean?"

"On your wrists, there. Three on each hand. It is against the rules of this hall to keep weapons in the rooms of residents."

Marta slowly made a fist and the three mirrored blades slid into view. "You aren't talking about these?" Her voice was frozen lead sliding on velvet.

"I'm afraid I am. You will have to give them to me."

"Be careful what you wish for, Ms. Crenner."

"Are you threatening me, Ms. Krovikian?"

"The threat is in the ear of the hearer."

"Then I repeat, you must surrender your weapons."

"My 'weapons,' as you call them, are a part of my body. I believe, in certain circles, your hands and feet are considered deadly. Do you remove them?"

"Hands and feet are not legally recognized as weapons by the university," Peace said, primly. "I'm afraid double-edged blades are."

"If you have been listening to me at any point in the year, which I doubt," said Marta, implacably, "you know that no part of the Pattern can be removed short of major surgery."

"Then I'm afraid I'll have to file a report of noncompliance with Residence Hall regulations."

"You go ahead and do that."

Peace was not stupid. Theoretically, she could have called the police and had Marta Krovikian removed from her room immediately, but a police officer might not have seen Peace's brand of reason. Therefore, a report was filed through campus authorities. Protests were raised. In less time than I believed possible, the bureaucracy, motivated by hundreds of correct shoves at the right time, reacted. Marta stood in my room holding a sheet of paper one week later. She ran her hand over her exposed face, probing the flesh. She sighed, and the eyes looking out of that shielded head were tired. "It appears that our Resident Assistant has won. I am to present myself to the student tribunal. I must prove that I am no danger to the student body. Failing to appear will result in discharge from the hall."

"You can prove you're no danger, can't you?" I asked hopefully.

"Carl, don't be stupid. Of course not. I am a danger to the student body. A controlled danger, but I am dangerous." She sat.

"I underestimated her. She had more resources than I let myself think. The tribunal will consist of at least a majority of her allies. They will merely seek to prove that I can kill a student on this campus, if pressed. And I can. I can kill anyone on this campus, and no one within reach could stop me." It was not a boast. "And even if they could find me safe enough to live with, she knows that this is exactly what I most wish to avoid. She has dragged me into the spotlight."

"Could you move off campus?"

She laughed bitterly. "Oh, really, Carl! Would I be on campus if I had another choice? Why would I subject myself to the stares, the whispers, the thousand invasions, if I could live alone? But do you think any landlord in town had a room for me? Strangely enough, they were all filled the second I walked in the door."

"Why are you here, Marta?"

"I just *told* you . . ."

"I don't mean the dorms. Why are you here? In school. Why don't you just become a hermit someplace quiet? If you hate being around people so much, then why are you even here?"

Her face had turned the color of concrete at noon. "I thought you were my friend, Carl."

"The only one you have, and I'd really hate it if you had to leave, so stop trying to distract me and answer the question." I began to have that detached two-seconds-after-the-car-wreck feeling.

"I'm not independently wealthy," she started.

"Oh, stop. You called me intelligent once, don't pretend you were lying now. You could make a decent living holding cars up one-handed for a mechanic who can't afford a hydraulic lift if you wanted to; why are you here? What's more important to you than your solitude?"

"I don't want to be just a tower of armor for the rest of my life, Carl!" she snapped. "Maybe I'm trying to deal with this the best way I know how. I thought college would be . . . different, somehow. Maybe I'm naive." Her voice had softened.

"Good, at least now I know you won't just give up." I picked up the letter. "This is bullshit, you know. If anyone but you faced this kind of prejudice, Peace and her friends would fall over themselves helping you. Let's use their own arguments against them. They want fair, we'll give them fair."

"How?"

Feeling giddy with the surreal feeling of absolute hopelessness, I stood. "My lady, I am a . . ."

"Poli sci major," she said with me, rolling her eyes.

"*And*," I continued, "this sort of bullshit is my business. I do not intend to have my chess partner kicked out from under her roof without a fight. Come with me."

An eyebrow raised. "Where are we going?"

"We're going to the library. Then we're going to the Student Senate and look for precedents. Then we're going to find manifestoes from every group that's crucifying you and hoist them on their own petards."

"We're going to lose, Carl. We have a week."

"And what are you going to do with it, lie down and die?" I snapped.

The quirky smile I knew so well finally reappeared. "Lead on. I suppose I might as well learn some research before I get kicked out of school."

That night, I plowed through the library looking for anything that would help us. I looked up legal precedents, anatomical definitions, statements of purpose, anything. At three in the morning I read the same sentence five times and sleepily suggested we call it a night.

"Oh, by the way, Marta . . ."

"Yes?"

"Whatever you use on that Pattern of yours, to decorate it? Use it. From now until the hearing."

"Carl, we've been through that. It's over."

"No. Public opinion is important on this. You had a lot more allies than you can believe simply because of how you looked. One of the rumors going around is that you're still on active duty and were ordered by your superiors to stop defacing the uniform. That's bad. Admittedly, it won't be much, but it's got to help."

We took it up at noon the next day. Marta appeared in brilliant pigments, an explosion of red and black in a fiery pinwheel that licked up her limbs, moving with her. We worked through that night and started another day.

By eight on the third night I had enough material to choke several committees and was starting to formulate my plan of attack. But I had to have a break before I went on. I couldn't take any more chess, so Marta suggested that we go down to the weight room.

My weight training is strictly low key. I picked up one of the short arm-curl bars as we entered the empty room and found a corner. Suddenly, Marta called out, "Catch!"

I jumped and yelled, staggering under the weight of the ten-kaygee bench-press bar she threw into my hands. She picked up its mate, one-handed, and blurred it through the air, twirling it like a baton. It *cracked* audibly onto her right wrist, and she held it like a quarter-staff. She essayed a shy smile. "I wanted to be a cheerleader, once."

"You what?" Truly ridiculous mental pictures formed in my mind.

"So long ago. So foolish." She looked into the mirror as if trying to find the past. "We trained with these in unpowered combat." She began to slide weights onto the two ends of the metal staff. Twenty kaygees first.

"You don't mean you hit each other with those?"

"It's the greatest confidence builder in the world to be hit by a drill instructor armed with one of these things and get up with no more than a sore back, Carl."

"What if someone took one in the face?"

"We had visors." She was done. The assembled weight was at least seventy-five kaygees. Slowly, under her wrist muscles alone, the massive barbell began to rotate in the air. She twirled with it, now on one foot, now on the other. A quiet croon came from between her lips; a long, wandering descant. Now the weight was twirling very fast, and she was using her arms, one over the other, to keep it going.

"These are speed kata exercises in our school of martial arts. I'm forbidden to teach it, but you certainly can't apply it." I nodded mutely. Now the dance became more intricate, and the weight became a spinning blur, described by a flashing gray border of moving iron. She moved to the large punching bag in the center of the room. Then she started striking. The huge barbell lashed out, once, twice, three times, and each time it grazed the surface of the bag, ever so slightly, and a metal on plastic *zing* rebounded through the room. Then legs and arms flashed out of the dance, each barely missing contact with the surface. It went on and on, faster and faster, Marta dodging the blows of an unseen foe, and then a foot leapt out of the red black maelstrom, striking the bag dead center with a BOOM! The bag jerked, reaching an angle of forty-five degrees before it swung back down, meeting the unyielding rod in the hands of Marta Krovikian. She stopped it, and then set the barbell down, breathing hard. "Pity I had to pull the punches, but a full bar strike would have split the bag."

"I believe it."

She ran her hand along her opposite arm, along the main bone crest superior to the ulna. "It's so incredible, and yet it cannot keep me safe. It can only keep me whole." She put her hands to her face, then looked at me. "Carl, in a few days, the questions about the Pattern, and why I bear it, will begin, and I will not be answering them. Do you know why?"

"You choose not to."

A rueful laugh. "You *have* been listening. It was wrong of me to tease you. But you if anyone deserve to know. And because you do not seek it," she paused as if before some inner barrier, "I will tell you," she said.

"If you don't want to . . ."

"Let me." She flicked her blades in and out, convulsively. "I might not be able to again."

I nodded. She sat on a bench-press machine, dwarfing it.

"My unit was sent in against the new czar. There weren't many of us. There didn't need to be.

"You'll never know the confidence we felt that day. We were killing machines, armed to our artificial teeth. I went in with a slow microreactor on my back powering a Gauss antitank cannon and a fléchette thrower that could shred anything unarmored. Lasers, grenades . . . oh, we had it all. Eight-man platoons, traveling in pairs. We ran at fifty miles an hour, and were sent scouting into the heart of enemy territory. And Hank and I ran into the center of the Pit."

"The Pit?"

"Part of the war you didn't hear about. The czar, now, he wasn't quite as stupid as you'd have him made out to be. The Custer of Crimea, they called him. Hell, I did, going in. The war only lasted three days; this was the first of them. And contrary to the rout you heard about, the czar's soldiers held. They died, but they didn't rout.

"The czar was tricky. He had his forces all over the peninsula, positioned to meet our beachhead. So Hank and I went in from the coast, around the curve of the Black Sea. What no one knew was that the czar had militia reserves all through the desert. The biggest of these, the best armed, lay hidden, ready to take our lead elements as they pursued the retreating *zashchitniki*. This was the Pit. We ran right into the middle of it. We were monitored for about a hundred miles, never knew it, and then . . . then the forest came to life.

"There were bunkers, all through the ground, and they just sprouted, like cottonwood, all at once. Hank and I, we stood back to back, yelling for backup. They'd jammed the net. They ran at us waving anything they had: new guns, old guns, swords, fists. At that range, a fléchette gun doesn't kill; it . . . strips." She shuddered only slightly, and went on. "Skeletons fell at my feet, just like parts made by robots, and I couldn't pause to do more than reload. And reload. Women, children." Her voice was a whisper. "Reload. Then there were no more reloads. We were in a hailstorm of fire, but it was too small to really hurt us; their few heavy weapons couldn't fire without hitting their own people in the back. I fought. Hank fought. And then I couldn't lift my leg anymore because there were twenty people holding it down. And then it was like falling in a screaming ocean. There were a hundred people on each of us. We weren't even hurt. But we couldn't move. They kept us pinned, and the ones nearest kept . . . kept *touching* me, trying to find the joints in the armor, trying to find some way in. The Pattern was the only thing that kept them out.

"The local commander arrived, too late to salvage Hank. They'd pretty well torn his helmet off, along with most of his face. But I was still alive. How could I be kept that way?" She seemed to shrink.

"They drove their one tank across my feet, Carl. That's how they kept me there. And even this bone has a breaking point. My feet were crushed, and the only reason I didn't bleed to death in the desert was because our blood is loaded with coagulants. So I lived. I lived while they drove trucks over my hands, keeping me spreadeagled on the sand. I lived and was conscious while they discussed how to rape me. And the women stood back and provided . . . ideas. They ordered me to surrender and take off my armor."

"You didn't surrender."

"I never surrendered." Her teeth showed spasmodically. "But I lay there helpless while they tried with knives, swords, rifles. It all just bounced off, even at point blank range, as they tried desperately to penetrate, right here." She tapped her featureless pelvis. "It only lasted three hours. That's all. They felt me, probed me, for three hours, trying to find the secret. They didn't. They got angry. Took off my helmet, broke my jaw, urinated on me. But at the end, they heard the radio telling them that they were needed at the front, because the rest of the force had landed and there weren't going to be any troops left to lead anyone into their trap. So the commander ordered their tank to back off my feet; I nearly passed out from the pain. I awoke just in time to see them lower the turret gun at the same point they'd been hammering at all night, and fire." Her hands went to her face. "I won't try to describe it. If it had been a modern round, I'd have been blown in half. But it was an old, light tank. The shell blew the armor in and left me slowly bleeding to death. Then, they finally left. By the time the helicopter found me, I was nearly dead. I survived. They put me back together again. I did not surrender. I can never surrender. And because the Pattern kept out those hands, I can't bear the thought of losing it. I don't think I could stand to be touched without it. The thought of sex . . . you have to surrender, you see? But sometimes, sometimes I miss feeling." She held her palms up. "Now you know."

"Now we know." Peace stepped into the room with Nenya behind her. The door had been closed, so how . . . ?

Then I remembered the tiny vents, set low in the doors. I looked to Marta, betrayed by her own words to a simple eavesdropper. She rose, and her face was immobile as the rest of her body.

"Coward," she whispered.

Peace's jaw dropped, theatrically. "Coward? Coward? You have the gall to stand there in that abortion of armor and call *me* a coward? You slaughter people for pay and call me a coward?" Her eyes went cool and mocking. "You didn't get half what you deserved."

"*Dammit, no!*" Nenya's shout wiped the triumph from Peace's face, and she looked down on her smaller partner in disbelief. "What's happened to you, Paige?" Tears of anger were running down her cheeks.

"I thought we didn't do this to each other. You told me we didn't. You told me it was never our fault! She was *raped*, Peace, and you say she deserved it—"

She was cut off by Peace's hand around her throat. "You little bitch. You think I don't know you've been looking at her, this whole time?"

Nenya's hand came around and cracked into the side of Peace's head, and she howled. She thrust Nenya from her and kicked viciously into her stomach. Nenya crumpled. Peace stood over her, punctuating words with blows: "*She* . . . wasn't *raped!* She was *shot* . . . butchering *people* . . . in that damned *invasion!* She's a *traitor*. . . ."

Then Marta was standing over her, bending Peace's right hand back, back away from Nenya. Peace's scream rose as her wrist cracked. Somehow, even then, she broke away, and stood facing Marta, one hand dangling limply, snarling hate.

I leapt up, crying out, "*No!*"

Marta *blurred.* The women flowed together, Peace's karate reflexes trying to block a bioarmor fist. Tin shield against the cannon. Peace folded over, and horror stared out of her eyes.

She coughed once, and blood poured down her chin, onto Marta's forearm. Three silver blades were buried in her lower gut. I was stone.

Marta's wild eyes stared into Peace's and she whispered, "This is how it was, and it is not rape?" Peace's mouth worked; she coughed. Blood spattered. Marta lifted her, on the blades, off her feet. The world spun, and my stomach emptied on the floor; still I heard Marta, screaming:

"This is how it was, and it is not rape? Answer me!" A wet, retching sound: someone trying to inhale.

Marta set her down and pulled the blades out, dripping. As her opponent fell, she whispered, tears streaming from her eyes, the words fueled by hate and the last of the air in her lungs, "That is . . . how it was."

Blood pooled underneath the crumpled form. Nenya gasped from her place on the floor, staggered to her feet, and stumbled out the door. Marta looked at her blades, now red black with blood. She seemed to wake up from some other place, and turned to me, almost as if she wanted to ask a question. Then she collapsed, falling beside Peace.

I did not pass out. I spent the longest minutes of my life in a gym waiting for the sirens to arrive, and watching Marta Krovikian, her rage spent, massaging her face with her hands.

7

The police took her away, and she went without resisting. I was taken too, for questioning. I answered.

"Where is she?" I asked the detective in the brown suit, when he was done.

"Via Christi, in Wichita. They're doing all they can."

"I mean Marta."

"Don't worry about her," said Brown Suit, grimly. "We'll take care of her."

"She's my friend," I said, softly.

"Oh." He was startled. Then his eyes narrowed, but softened at the same time. He spoke into a phone, then faced me again. "Her attorney's with her now, but . . . she isn't expected to be competent to stand trial. She won't talk; hasn't said a word. Follows simple instructions. We're calling a doctor to confirm."

"What happens after that?"

"She'll be consigned to a hospital, indefinitely, after they cut her out of that armor."

My mouth went dry. "You can't do that."

"We don't have much of a choice, Mr. Shire. We can't afford to have mental patients around that stand a good chance of winning an argument with a tank."

"She'll die. You've got to listen to me! You'll be condemning her to death without trial."

"Son, they do this sort of thing all the time," said Brown Suit, placatingly.

"Not to her! You don't . . ." I couldn't go on. "Can I see her?"

"When they're done."

Two hours later, I was led to her cell. I was surprised to see a mountain of metal and bone standing outside of it. But it wasn't Marta. It was unmistakably masculine, and even taller than she was. A large, open-barreled magnetic cannon hung by his side, and there were corporal's chevrons on his shoulders. He stared straight ahead, into the cell, at a point on the wall. Marta was sitting with her feet up on the bunk, face in her hands.

Her red-and-black coloring was partially removed in ugly, dun strips where something had been applied to take the blood off. Faded red mixed with muddy gray in runners.

"Let me in."

"Oh, no," said Brown Suit. "Not on your life. I'm not going to be faced with a hostage situation. She could kill you by patting you hard."

Anger flooded me. The detective looked at me as if to say, "Take it or leave it." Then he went out. There was nothing I could do but look through the bars.

She looked at me with the same old neutral mask on that she wore every day in public. But now there was a deadness in the blue eyes. She did not speak.

I knelt down, leaning against the cold bars, and whispered, "Marta, please, you've got to talk to them. They'll take away the Pattern without even a trial if you don't. They think you're insane." She looked up, and I half expected to see the old quirky smile, and hear her say, "Are they wrong?"

I didn't.

"Marta, maybe you can plead temporary insanity, and I'll testify all the way to back you up. Please, Marta. You can't surrender now. Fight this."

Slowly, she stood up. I felt the mountain of the corporal turn and move behind me, watching her intently.

Slowly, very slowly, she approached the bars and knelt opposite me. She looked me in the eyes, her hand emerging from the cuff of the synthetic bone. Under the three hidden knives, five soft fingers reached between the steel and touched my face, sliding along my nose, cheek, and neck, softly caressing my throat, then my shoulder, then my ribs.

Everything blurred, and her hand traveled back up to the shoulder, down the arm to the hand. She held my wrist as if she were afraid of breaking it, and gently pulled my hand to her face.

I sat unmoving, as she held my hand to her forehead, closed her eyes, and felt my fingers with her cheek. Then she dropped my hand, and bent her head, looking down. I blindly groped my way out of the jail, and before I knew it, found myself on a street, walking. I didn't stop until dawn, in the middle of a field, far away from everything.

A week later, they performed the operation that removed the Pattern from Marta Krovikian. I tried to see her. I was told that she was "severely disturbed" and was not allowed to have visitors. Three days later, I read the obituary.

The funeral was small. Nenya was there, too. All she said was, "I'm sorry," and then we cried. We keep in touch. We remember Marta. There were a few soldiers, ex-soldiers. They were very cold; distant. I suppose it was only fair. Who could tell them differently? We had never borne the Pattern. Marta bore the Pattern. It destroyed her, and saved her. It kept her alive and killed her. It was beautiful, and it was horrible. Marta always talked about "bearing the Pattern." And Nenya said maybe we all have one; something that kills even as it strengthens, heals as it wounds. "Peace was my Pattern," she said. "And Marta was the way out of it. For better or for worse." I don't know what my Pattern might be, but I'm keeping an eye out for it.

Because if it's anything like Marta Krovikian, it will be worth seeing. Whatever happens.

THE ONE-EYED MAN

Written by
Gregory Janks

Illustrated by
Paul Butler

About the Author

Gregory Janks grew up in Johannesburg, South Africa, graduating from the University of Witwatersrand with majors in mathematics and economics. But his first love has always been creative writing; his mother read The Lord of the Rings while pregnant with him.

He currently lives on Long Island, where he spends most of his time being cynical while masquerading as a State University of New York graduate student in math.

About the Illustrator

Paul Butler is a graphic artist from New Jersey. Mostly self-taught, he took occasional art courses in high school and college. He graduated summa cum laude from Rutgers with a degree in medieval literature; he also won the Donald Saunders Award for combined excellence in art and technology for his computer art/animation. He has since then exhibited this art form prominently at numerous science fiction conventions, been very active in the gaming community and is also a member of the Society for Creative Anachronism.

The truth of history flickers before my eyes. It is grainy and black and white.

Dirty hands fill the screen. They ferret about in a confusion of shapes: this close up, the details are lost to static. Joyce's voice is muttering in the background. "Where is it? Where did she put it?" His accent is clipped and educated, but his voice meanders, as if his words are orphans. "I know she had it. Where did she put it?" His hands are thick and fleshy, the knuckles lost in envelopes of fat. The nails have been gnawed upon. A viscous syrup coats his searching fingers; covers the broken terrain through which they dart. The lack of color is unsettling.

"Where is it? She has it; I know she has it."

Suddenly, sharply, the picture pulls back. Distance provides clarity. Joyce's arms and the top of his legs become visible. He is wearing pajamas; they are old and spotted with elephants. His sleeves are rolled up, but in a vain gesture. The pajamas are saturated with the same fluid that stains his hands.

With woman's blood.

From this new angle, I can see the central portion of her body. She is a black-and-white etching, an opened wound. It is deep inside her body that Joyce's hands are hunting. "Where has she put it?"

She is his wife.

The picture lurches down, down inside her. The terrain of her anatomy becomes blurred, her organs reduce to obstacles. The hands pluck. "Oh, my god, my god. She has it; I know she does. Told me so, she did, told me how she'd found it. Said she'd hid it somewhere safe." The picture is terribly close; he has his head inside her, searching.

I watch with the fascination of the involved. Watch the screen and the contours of brutality. Watch the court watching the screen. Honorable Yang is focused, her attention solely on the evidence. Somehow, there is no horror in her eyes, as if obligation has blinded her to atrocity. The technician, Harreson, avoids the details of death. He hides his eyes in his machinery. I imagine the colors of his console, the reds and greens, the yellows of his gauges. The wardens stand by the walls, their eyes on us and their hands on their prods. The trialists around me sit with private thoughts. To my left, Linus and two others whose names I do not know joke quietly amongst themselves; to my right, the expressions are uniformly sober but for Balbo, who is sleeping, and Vox, who watches with a sickness in his stare. There are eleven of us in line. I am sixth.

And I watch Joyce watching himself. He sits quietly, his head slightly tilted, and does not blink. His face is tinged with melancholy. I watch the silver snake plugged into his skull, watch it writhe with information, a thousand metal rings forming a tunnel for truth. With a twitch, Joyce rubs his ear on his shoulder. His fat fingers are curled around the arms of the chair; he is still wearing his wedding band, too tight for his flesh.

On screen, those same fingers alternate between frenzy and fatigue. Fatigue is winning: the episode is drawing to a close. Joyce's muttering loses its vehemence and winds down. Bit by bit, he dispenses with words,

until only a shrill, high keening remains. The picture
jostles about, in and out of the wreck. I see every
conceivable angle of the woman's gouged stomach and
opened chest. I see flashes of her legs (they are untouched) and her bloody arms. She has a mole beneath
her right knee, stretch marks line her hips. I see the bristle
of her armpits and the paleness that once ran beneath
her breasts. Now it is black on white. I see the beginnings of her thick neck, and even a hint of many chins,
but never her face. I see the Joyces' living-room carpet—
dark, but not so black as blood. And I catch a hurried
glimpse of their furniture, an old-fashioned collection:
cracked-leather recliner, reupholstered sofa, wooden
corner table. And no electrics. In his madness, Joyce
shows none of the modern essentials I would have
expected to crowd their home.

And I see the knife, haunted by darkness, discarded
on the floor.

The more Joyce tires, the more the picture steadies.
Slowly, he subsides to silence and heavy breathing.
Then, gently, the view descends for the final time. With
my mind's eye, I see Joyce lie beside his wife and place
his head in her ruined lap; see him take her hand in his.
Sure enough, as he settles, the image on the screen
swivels, until only the ceiling can be seen, far away and
clean. And that is all the evidence. As the groan of
Joyce's breath gentles and his eyes close, the screen fills
with an inevitable darkness.

Honorable Yang waits a few moments longer. Who
knows why: she is no more likely to see exonerating
evidence than Joyce is to rewrite history. They are long
moments, silent moments, a time of shuffling. Eventually,
when she is satisfied, Yang nods at Harreson. The technician plays his hands across his terminal, tugging at the

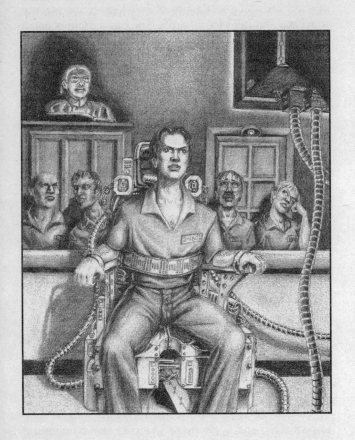

Illustrated by Paul Butler

appropriate switches. The screen flashes, then fades to a reflective sheen. Joyce's rasp is cut off. Harreson stands and straightens his clothing. He is balding and clean and middle aged and white and small. A residue of mustache clings to his upper lip; his remaining hair is starched to his scalp. With a sullen gesture, he unplugs the metal tubing from Joyce's neck and lays it on the floor. Even though he is wearing plastic gloves, Harreson avoids touching Joyce.

When the technician has completed his duties and returned to his seat, Honorable Yang crinkles her face to sternness and faces Joyce. "Walter Joyce," she says, "you are charged under penal code 274 in the high scale, in that you did knowingly and with malice aforethought commit upon your wife, Sherry Hoptree Joyce, murder in the first degree. After a careful review of the evidence, as properly elicited by an authorized court technician, I find you guilty as charged. I therefore have no choice but to pass upon you the sentence of death. Do you have anything you wish to say?"

Joyce's gaze is down in his shoes, his hands are folded in his lap, his shoulders are bowed. "I was looking, just looking," he mutters, "I meant no harm. Sherry was . . . losing things. Important things. She wouldn't have minded, Your Honor. Not my looking."

"Very well then," Yang says, "may God have mercy upon your soul." She taps the keyboard concealed within her podium. Now that the sentence has been pronounced, the black door warden leaves his post and removes Joyce from the truth machine. Joyce slides easily from the entanglement of tubing and stands downcast with his hands in front of him. The warden binds those hands, takes Joyce by the biceps and hustles him from the court. Joyce goes meekly and without a sound.

Honorable Yang glances at the court's large display. The blackness crackles. In red letters, the screen says: "Walter Joyce: guilty. Sentenced to death." Beneath the verdict, large numerals give the time—5:02 post meridiem. Yang is an old woman with narrow eyes and sallow features. Black is not her color; her robes seem more like curtains than clothes.

With a frown, she says, "Given the hour, I have decided to end the current session of this court. We resume tomorrow morning at 8:30 with the case of"—she peers down at her private terminal—"Bradley Mo, charged with rape in the first degree on the high scale. Mr. Mo, I strongly suggest that you and your conscience meet for a discussion tonight. You will find no refuge from the truth in this courtroom." She pauses, more for emphasis than anything else. "That goes for the rest of you as well." Her eyes are as calm and all-seeing as a raven's. Yang takes the time to examine each of us, a look of promises, then she stands and makes her way from the room. Her stride is short and tight. I watch Yang's back as she leaves, watch the shadows and creases of her cloak, until the door slides shut behind her.

•••

Nemma Jean was expecting me. The sensor above her door blinked a mute red. I could not understand its technology. How did the devices tell friend from foe? Max, for example, never set the thing to screaming, even when the system was armed. Me, it hated. I leered up into its crimson silence and pressed the doorbell.

Perhaps I should have brought flowers.

• • •

The wardens march us from the courtroom in single
file. The chamber has four exits, one on each wall.
Behind the podium is the door that leads to Honorable
Yang's office, to the inner sanctums of justice. It is
this door that Harreson uses every morning, creeping
in before the judge, his breakfast clinging to his
mustache, his hands already scuttling in anticipation
of his equipment.

The doors of guilt and innocence lie on opposite
walls, staring at one another. The door of guilt, Joyce's
door, always has a warden alongside it. It is painted
black. The door of innocence is wooden and unpainted.

Mine is the final door. A metal door, built for function. A camera is embedded in its frame and the
wardens halt each of us by it, recording our continued
participation in the process of justice. I've heard that it
never stops, this camera. That it plays its panoptic eye
across our backs as we sit in court, watching other
men's trials.

Once we leave the courtroom, we are escorted down
a windowless antiseptic passage. The walls are painted
passive green. A red line runs down the length of the
floor, enjoining our feet. Small cleaning remotes decorate the ceiling. They make a slight whistle as they pass
above our heads, though their scrubbing pads are silent.
There are no chance encounters in this passage. No
extra guards cruise the hall. I have seen no other trialists, no functionaries, no technicians. It is a passage
made solely for us and our daily tryst with Honorable
Yang.

At the end of the passage is an elevator. The elevator
is large, large enough to hold twenty men without their

touching. It has a wire mesh screen instead of doors. I've heard that this wasn't always the case, that once the elevator had proper, heavy doors. But there was an accident, a prison accident. Somehow, someone accessed the elevator's control system and disabled the safety feature that prevented the door's closing while a passenger stood between them. A trialist was ambushed: as the doors closed, an invisible push sent him into their path; broke all his ribs, narrowed his face.

The elevator's control panel is on the wall. Inside the lift, there are no buttons. The lettering on the panel is cryptic. I cannot understand it. But the guards can: one of them punches a button and the screen rises. We are ushered inside like cattle. "All right, boys," the head of the detail says, "you know the drill. Keep them grubby hands in plain sight. Try and control yerselves. No one's got away with nothing in one of these cars, so you all try 'n behave yerselves." He stops to swallow, then continues in a more serious, more bored, tone, "I'm required by law to remind you all that touching another trialist while on this elevator is a criminal offense."

He signals to the guard at the control panel. The wire mesh descends; there is a click as it locks in place. Around me, the others shift their weight from foot to foot. Claustrophobia dirties the air, as tangible as sweat. As the lift begins to rise, I feel the motion in my stomach. Our bodies sway to stop from falling. We are almost away when I hear the warden's voice again. "Of course, if you all want to go ahead and kill yerselves, that'd be fine by me."

The elevator creeps silently up into the justice center. Each man looks straight ahead; the air is starched with silence. It is too much for Vox. I hear his soprano voice from somewhere behind me. "Bru, you heard the one about the dyke frogs?" No one answers, no one turns around. Linus is standing in front of me and I keep my eyes glued to the fuzz that grows at the base of his neck. But Vox knows we're all listening. "Yes, sir, the one turns to the other and says, 'We do taste like chicken.'" No one reacts, not for several seconds. Then a man to my right releases a snort of laughter. I see the cords in Linus's neck tense as he too chokes on his mirth. Then it breaks out in earnest, and everyone is laughing: the workers and the daydreamers, the habitual criminals, the guilty and the innocent. Even me.

As we near our destination, fresh light spills through the wire mesh. Laughter is forgotten. The detention guards are ready, waiting for us. The chief warden on my level is a big, bald man, black as grime. His name is Coates. "Good evening," he says. "Let's see those hands. Come on, boys, you know the rules." He pushes a button on his control panel—his panel is identical to the one on the court level—and, with a click, the mesh screen rises.

"All right, boys, one at a time." We file out of the elevator onto another red line. As we wait, wardens run hand-held scanners over our bodies. The machines are gray and small, concealed in the palms of their shifting hands. They possess neither lights nor readouts, but rather emit a steady muted beep. Coates whistles tunelessly along. When the searches have been completed, we are marched into the holding area.

On this level, the cells are wrought from old-fashioned iron. There is no forgiveness in their solidity. Apparently on the women's level, the bars have been replaced by invisible force shields. Here, each room is a barren gray block. The cells are identical to those in the long-term facilities which the guilty are shipped to, although there—it is said—three men must share a cell. At least here I have a private internment.

I have placed nothing in my cell. No art, no pictures. I have left the walls as they are: a diary of previous inhabitants; a litany of names and dates. I have not yet had the strength to read them. My bed folds out from the wall. It is made from some clever plastic, hard yet serviceable, and is dressed in a regulation brown blanket. I lie on the bed and stare up at the vent that haunts the ceiling. The room is centrally heated, but I have no control of the temperature. The vent makes a subtle sucking sound, a between noise: the sound of justice.

I curl up beneath the blanket, my knees on my chest, and wonder what Sherry Joyce might have looked like in a softer time. As sleep engulfs me, I paint a picture of her face upon my eyelids.

Maybe it's not her face at all.

• • •

"Mr. Hallutio? Mr. Tom Hallutio?"

"Yes," I replied.

"Mr. Hallutio, I'm Investigator Rawlings and this is Investigator Chu. If you wouldn't mind, sir, we'd like to come up and ask you a couple of questions." The one officer, Rawlings, held a badge up to the camera, but I couldn't read it. They were well dressed; suits and ties and starched white collars that showed up well on the monitor.

"What about?" I asked.

"About the accident, sir."

The other detective, Chu, elbowed his partner aside and leaned into the camera. "Mr. Hallutio, sir, it's raining out here. We'd like to come up now."

The interruption was badly timed. I was in the middle of a sketch, my fourth attempt to capture the nuances that drifted across a silver statue that I'd found in a flea market on Lucent Street. The statue possessed a magic in its umbra. So far I had been unable to replicate it; my studio was littered with the debris of my efforts. It was a woman's body, the statue. Her eyes were closed and her head was askance.

When they knocked on the door, I still had my paintbrush in my hand.

"Sorry to disturb you, sir," said Rawlings.

"No, it's all right," I replied, "come in." Water dripped off the men onto my carpet. They were both heavyset. Up close, their clothes looked worn. Rawlings had a creased transit timetable in his coat pocket. *Four-seventeen* was written across the top of it in red ink. As he passed me, I smelt his aftershave, heady and invasive, the scent of burning sugar.

Chu came behind him, eager to look me in the eye. His eyes were brown, but not so dark as mine. We peered at each other for a long moment. They were not faint, his eyes. Then I looked away. The detectives took up a position opposite one another in the middle of the room. "Something to drink?" I offered.

"No, thank you," Rawlings replied. Chu moved off and began to wander about the studio. He kept his hands in his pockets as he moved from sketch to sketch, pausing a moment at each. I couldn't tell what he thought of them, his expression didn't change. Rawlings was still talking.

"I'm sorry," I said, "you were saying?"

"Yes, sir, I was. I wanted to confirm that you were at Ms. Nemma Jean Backs's apartment on the evening of the twenty-sixth." Rawlings spoke in an even tone, a voice of information. He had a little hand-held out and was looking at it as he spoke.

"Yes, I was. I made the call to Emergency Services."

Rawlings nodded, tapped a key on his computer. "That was at about 8:20 in the evening?"

"I have no idea what time it was."

"It says 8:20 here."

I gave him a smile. "Then I'm sure that's what it was. Would you like to sit down?"

"No, thanks," he said, "we won't be long. Where were you when Ms. Backs fell?"

Chu was at the statue, staring at it. It held his attention longer than my paintings. I watched from the corner of my eye, watched as its magic tempted his hand from his pocket. "Please don't touch that!" He turned and glared at me, turned back to the statue, leaned in close to it, and spoke in a rasping voice.

"You were in the bathroom."

"I'm sorry?"

Rawlings picked up from his partner. "You were in the bathroom when Ms. Backs fell."

"Yes, I was."

"And when did you know something was wrong?" Rawlings continued.

I crossed to the easel and put my brush down. "When I came out of the bathroom, I found Nemma Jean on the floor of her living room. She'd hit her head on the side of the table. Hit it badly. And there was blood, a lot of blood. She wasn't conscious; she didn't respond when I touched her. There was a gash, a bad gash." I held my hands up about five inches apart. "And blood, lots of blood. In her hair, on the table, on the carpet. Her hair. It was . . ."

"When did you call the ES people?"

"Right away. I could see that she was hurt badly. Well, not right away. I knelt beside her and tried to stop the blood, tried to wake her up. But she was gone."

"You knew she was dead?" Chu asked from the other side of the room.

"No, no, I didn't. My god, I couldn't tell; all I could see was her blood."

Rawlings consulted his hand-held. "That's when you made the call?"

"Yes. About then."

The two detectives exchanged a glance. Rawlings gave a little cough, took out a handkerchief, blew his nose into it. "Damn weather," he muttered. A little puddle was forming about his feet. He asked, "Why do you think she fell, sir?"

"Why did she fall?"

"Yes, sir, why did she fall?"

"That I don't know. I thought you'd know. Didn't they test her? Didn't they . . . do tests?"

Rawlings looked up at me. He had bleary features, red cheeks. I could smell his aftershave from here. He replied, "I'm sure they did, sir. We were just wondering if you knew of any medical conditions that the deceased might have suffered from."

"No, no. Nemma Jean didn't have any medical problems."

"You knew her well?"

"Yes, I did."

Chu had moved on from the statue. He'd made a complete circuit of the room, casting his eyes over all my art. Now he was looking out the window, watching the rain strike the plastic. Neither man spoke for a moment. Still, even as the silence developed, I knew what their next question would be. And who would ask it.

Chu said, "You were intimate with her?"

"We were seeing each other, yes."

"Was she seeing other men?"

"No."

"Were you seeing other women?" His voice was like oatmeal.

"No, Detective, I definitely wasn't."

Chu turned from the window and gazed down at me. His eyes were virile, reflective. "You were in love."

"I thought so."

He nodded, as if this confirmed a suspicion. "You must be devastated, then."

"Detective," I said, "I'm trying to answer all of your questions as best I can. How would you feel if you found your wife dying, her head shrouded in blood? If she died while you were watching? While you clutched her skull together with your hands?"

"I'm not married."

I took a step toward him. Chu didn't move, didn't frown. We stared at each other again, a duel of glances. My peripheral vision sharpened: I saw the rain whipping about behind him, saw Rawlings fidgeting with his handkerchief, saw the statue as it battled with the light, saw Nemma Jean on the floor, her face white and red and white. Maybe Chu saw it too. He nodded at me, ever so slightly, and I looked away. At that, Rawlings replaced his hand-held in his pocket and said, "Well, thank you for your time, Mr. Hallutio. We appreciate your cooperation; sorry to have disturbed you."

The detectives walked to the door. I shook their hands: Rawlings's tight and wet, Chu's as rough as sandpaper. As he followed his partner from my studio,

Chu turned to me and asked, "Is that statue your work? It's very good."

I tried to smile. "No, I bought it."

"I see," he said, and was gone.

•••

Dinner is served every night at 6:30 in a large barn of a room. It is a room bereft of windows, but still the walls are covered with scenery: prerecorded landscapes have been installed. It is as if we eat in the middle of a large prairie. Tall corn billows on either side; mountains of white clouds fill the sky.

The food is all one color, cooked into an acquiescence somewhere between gray and brown. I eat slowly, with a plastic spoon. The tables and chairs are one-piece units, also made from plastic—a firmer plastic. They are uncomfortable, like a long journey. I sit with the men of my line. Coates and his crew stand nearby.

Vox is talking in his ridiculously high voice. "So I heard about this one guy, see, name of Alecto. A real crazy guy, mean son of a bitch. They say he grew up in the gutters, never knew his parents. Killed his first man when he was fourteen; leveled him with a poker.

"Now, you won't believe me, but the thing of it was, Alecto was blind. Was born that way, blind as a bat. It was real freaky to be with him: he'd turn around and look you straight in the eye, like he could see right through you. I heard this one time, some other guys, you know, guys who were pissed at him, tried to sneak up on him, get him while he was sleeping. But a guy like that never sleeps. Alecto was waiting for them. Took 'em all on: punching and kicking and stabbing, never missing. Killed 'em all, just like that."

Vox stops to stuff his mouth with gruel. He shovels his food with a mechanical action, not even looking down. Most of the men are watching him intently, their own food forgotten. I am more interested in Bradley Mo, first man in line. Mo looks like he has been eating candles; his nostrils are wide, his cheeks imploded, the look of a man whose memory is on trial.

"Yeah, Alecto was a savage beast," Vox continues, "and he had this thing for girls. You know, little girls. I can't even tell you half the things he did to 'em; sick, bad things. I saw one of the little things after he was done with her, down on the docks, all broken and bleeding, like a chewed-up toy." He gives a sly wink; shows a lot of teeth. "Don't know how he used to catch 'em, though. Man must a had radar or something. Used to sit there, perched over the street, sniffing away every time some little skirt walked by beneath him."

"This story got a point?" Balbo interrupts.

"Yeah, bru, I got a point. Got a point concerns us all. One day they came down and picked Alecto up. Six of 'em, in their fancy armor and guns and cars, all shitting in their pants, I can tell you. But Alecto didn't even put up a fight. Just went with them and smiled. They mouthed off at him, telling him he was gonna pay for all the sin he'd poured down those little girls. But he didn't care, just smiled his blind-man's smile and went off with 'em, like he was an angel or something.

"Sure enough, they arraigned him, booked him into one of these funhouses, and hooked him up to the machine. The tech did his job, you know, fiddled with his switches, tuned the damn thing in. Here was Alecto, rapist and murderer and all-around evil son of a bitch, and when they bring him to trial and try and play back the evidence they don't get nothing. He was blind, bru! Hadn't seen nothing, wasn't no witness to nothing."

Some of the men at the table smile into their bowls and nod sagely, but Balbo will have none of it. He slams his fist into the table and juts his chin out. "Aw, come on, that's a load of crock. It's goddamn Goldilocks, man; pure poison."

Balbo lowers his tone, and looks around the table as if to give advice. "Don't listen to this stuff, boys. I been around; not my first time in this place." The socket at the base of his skull bears witness to that. "There's ways to beat it, sure, sure there are, but I heard this Alecto story before, or one just like it, and it's no help. Friend of mine, named Charlie West, heard this story, same as you boys. Charlie believed it, more's the shame—went and put his own eyes out with a burning stick. Man cried for a week; sockets never stopped smoking. Yeah, he thought it would give him immunity. But it didn't. He was blind, boys, blind: impotent."

"Is that true?" Linus asks.

"I swear it. I knew him. Charlie West was a real person, not like this Alecto crap."

Vox almost spits. He shrieks back at Balbo, "It ain't crap. I knew the guy. Was a mean son of a bitch."

"Give it a rest," Balbo retorts. Soon, the whole table is involved, debating crimes real and imagined. Only Mo and I take no part. He is fading fast, his color shading to green even as I watch. I can see his mind racing. Suddenly, I realize that he will not appear in court tomorrow. No, at some time during the night, he will take the low scale and save himself. The thought pleases me not at all. Indeed, I envy him greatly.

He has no need for truth machines.

● ● ●

Oh, God, she fell. Her eyes glimmered with vertigo and her feet betrayed her. Fast and gravity-gripped, like a puppet whose strings had been cut, she fell and fell and fell.

And I watched her falling.

•••

Long before I see him, I hear Coates as he makes his way down the cellblock. He walks sternly, but with a slight limp. The sound of his boots on the concrete, the moaning of the air vent, these are the sounds of the night. I am on my bed with my eyes closed, listening.

Someone is playing music, harsh and atonal and modern. There are lyrics mixed in with the drumbeat, but I cannot make them out. A toilet flushes. Coates is walking again, from cell to cell, peddling bargains. Somewhere, two men are talking to one another, but very softly. Whispered words seep through the bars, words of home and women and futures. I hear a faucet: on and off and on again.

They would make an interesting painting, these noises: a murky green for the sounds of ablution, a series of isolated browns for the whispered words, a sprinkling of metallic colors for the vent and its practicings at language. The hoarse music would be yellow; the fading light, gray. And to warn of Coates's ever approaching feet, jagged red spikes.

"Evening," he says.

I squeeze my eyes tightly shut and roll over so that my back is towards him, the blanket between us. He taps his prod against the cell's iron bars: *rat-a-tat-tat*. Then again, louder.

"No use in playing dead, son. It's regulations, neither of us have any choice in the matter."

"No, thanks," I mutter.

"It's up to you, but we both know you're making a mistake. The arraignment went three-zip the wrong way. Know what that means? The truth's against you. Listen to me: you don't want to go up against that machine. You won't win."

"I'll take my chances," I say. My eyes are still closed; the words sneak between my teeth.

"I still have to make the formal offer," Coates continues, "and I can't go home until I do, so you may as well sit up and listen. If I were you, I'd take the low scale. It's a guarantee."

We wait for a moment. He stands quietly, passively. Overhead, the vent goes through its cycle. Soon it will be lights out. I feel like I am battling the tide. Eventually, I roll over and sit up. Coates is looking at me; his face is bored, his walnut eyes droop like a basset hound's. He has returned his prod to his belt and now holds a small display screen and a light pen.

When he is sure that I will listen he reads, "You are charged under penal code 276 with murder in the third degree on the high scale. At this time, however, you may admit to the crime with which you are charged. Should you choose to do this, the court will show mercy: your sentence will be shifted to the low scale. Do you understand this right as I have related it to you?"

"No," I whisper.

Coates asks again in the same tone, his voice laden with inertia. "Mr. Hallutio, do you understand this right?"

I look up at him, try to look through him. When I answer, I sound like I'm lying. "Damn you, yes, I understand the right."

"Do you wish to take the low scale?" he asks.

"I can't," I reply and turn from him back to my bed.

•••

Nemma Jean opened the door and smiled her crooked smile. She was wearing a red top, tight at the neck. "Tom," she said, "come in."

I followed her to the living room. Max the cat was lying on the couch, licking his fur and trying his best to ignore me. The TV was on, more for background noise than anything else. I pushed the cat to one side and sat. There were no lights, only the flickering glow of the television. Fresh roses lurked in a vase on the table.

Nemma Jean followed me. "I just have to finish up in the kitchen, honey. Won't be a moment. Can I get you something to drink?"

"No, thanks," I said and aimed the remote at the television. Without much interest. I dialed across the net: a live feed of a windswept coast seen through someone else's eyes, an advert, an obscure sports ritual, a discussion group on falling literacy rates, an advert for the army, a silent movie, another advert, the local weather, boxing, European news, a music concert, an infosite on ordinance seventy-three, naked women in a cosmetic advert. Nothing on. Halfheartedly, I signed into a chatroom discussion on pastel shading. Six people were debating the effectiveness of contrast in chalk drawings.

"Won't be a minute," Nemma Jean called out from the kitchen.

"No rush," I replied. Her lounge was minimally furnished: the sofa, the glass table and its roses, the television, and a large wrought-iron candlestick sulking in the corner. There wasn't much art in the room, only an old man's portrait that hung above the TV, wisdom haunting its face. I'd never liked the picture. With one hand, I started stroking Max. Paint residue sullied my fingers, but the cat didn't seem to mind. On the television, a woman was crushing chalk. The screen had a small readout that displayed the time: 7:39.

Nemma Jean came in from the kitchen, sipping see-through wine. "So how was your day?"

"The same. I'm nearly finished the big piece, though I don't think they'll be happy with it."

She sat down beside me and pulled Max onto her lap. "Screw them, then."

"Yes, that's what I'd decided."

The wine glass looked fragile in her hand. She took another sip, then put the glass down on the table. "What are we watching?"

"Nothing," I replied, "some art site." On screen, they were showing one of those large black-and-white emotion pieces that some fool with too much time had ejaculated across a canvas.

"Supper will be about fifteen minutes," she said. Casually, she leaned in toward me. Without touching me, she began blowing in my ear. Up close, she smelled like soap. When I spoke, I could hear the bitterness in my voice. "I thought we'd agreed not to do this."

She pulled back, petulance written across her face. "God, I don't know what you want." With an angry hand, she threw Max onto the floor. He gave her a reproachful glare, then prowled off toward the corner and the candlestick. "What do you want, Tom?"

"I don't know," I said.

The people on the television were starting to sign off. The thought of looking for a new channel was too much for me. I stood and said, "I'm going to the bathroom."

Nemma Jean reacted quickly, with a panicked anger: "The hell you are!"

I turned away from her, towards the portrait on the wall. "Haven't we had this conversation?"

"We've never finished this conversation." She rose from the couch and took me in her arms. "Tom, the past is the past. You've got to leave it alone. We're here now, together. We could be happy. Shouldn't that be enough?"

Her body was hard against me, her arms tight on my shoulders. In the light of the television, her hair looked like water. Almost everything about her hinted of cleanliness. Oh, but she was close. I looked away, up over her head, at the wall and the face behind the glass. Dimly, I heard myself speak. "It happened, Nemes, and you can't pretend it didn't."

"Jesus, Tom, it was over a year ago. Tom! Goddamn it, look at me when you're talking to me!"

I didn't need to look at her, didn't need to see the mystery of her eyes. Her face was too familiar; I'd tried at least a hundred times to paint it, but those eyes refused me. I felt her body, stiff beside me. Desperately, I tried to find a meaningful way to speak, but her betrayal reduced my mind to aphasia.

Impelled by my silence, she released me and walked away. When she spoke, her voice no longer hinted at reconciliation. "You wanted me to do it, you sick bastard, and you're lying to yourself if you say otherwise. If you can't start acting like a grown-up, then maybe you should get the hell out of my life."

I wanted to protest, to scream "Me, the child?" but cowardice controlled my larynx.

"Say something, please!" she continued. "Tell me you hate me, tell me you love me, tell me anything.

Listen to me, Tom: I'm sorry; God, I'm sorry. Please believe me, I'm so very sorry. Can't you see?"

I should have spoken, should have dredged my memory for speech, should have mortgaged forgiveness from my mind, but my imagination wouldn't allow it. Even as I tried to form the words, picture after picture flashed before my eyes: Nemma Jean doing this and that and that—and smiling!—a cartoon of stolen intimacy.

"Speak, goddamn you!"

My tongue rasped against my palate; my lungs held no air. What could I say? I was no more blind to the past than I was to her pain. The pain bled tears from her eyes. Her mouth contorted with restraint. I felt the heaviness of the air upon my shoulders. Desperately, the sounds of the TV dimmed and color fled from the wall. My view narrowed, until all I could see was Nemma Jean Backs. In slow motion, she came at me. Her mouth was moving, but I couldn't understand her speech. She was saying something important; I couldn't hear it.

As she neared, her hand curled back behind her head. In the instant before she reached me, my vision collapsed to nothingness, as if sanity demanded blinkers. For a moment, I embraced the clarity of blindness.

Nemma Jean's fist impacted against my face. The clarity imploded and my senses roared. The television was screaming, flashing lights. The walls were a vast expanse of paint. My ears filled with a distant crack, like a sonic boom. Her nails sliced against my cheek and I felt their heat. I felt her power and sin, tasted the flavors of her need. In an unholy apotheosis, my senses united in the salty amber burning trace of Nemma Jean's love upon my face.

● ● ●

I am right: Bradley Mo no longer heads the line. In total, six men have used the cover of night to opt for the low scale. Their places have been quickly filled. Nine new trialists have joined the queue in Honorable Yang's courtroom. A heterogeneous collection, sixteen men awaiting the embrace of the truth machine. I am fifth in line.

Harreson is late this morning. He hurries into the courtroom with his top button undone and a bagel clenched in his right hand. His eyes reflect the entanglements of a morning commute. He slides into his console and punches several buttons. The machinery trembles. I hear it wheeze into life. Harreson is still straightening his tie as Honorable Yang shuffles into the room. The new men sit with stone faces and watch the judge as if she were a disguised vulture.

Yang takes her place upon the podium and the order of justice begins. The judge's voice is as old as her face, the sound of a brush upon the canvas. "Is Mr. Alberto Balbo present?"

Two wardens escort Balbo from the line toward the truth machine. The big ex-convict is freshly shaved. He has cut himself: a red scratch mars the bulge of his Adam's apple. Still, Balbo wears a certain cockiness in his mien. He stands before the judge with a straight back and when he speaks, I am surprised to hear the sound of hope in his voice. "Yes, ma'am. Alberto Balbo, present and accounted for."

Yang looks up from her console and fixes her stare upon Balbo. "Mr. Balbo, in accordance with the law, I am obliged to offer you a final chance to alter your plea. Do you wish to do so?"

"No, ma'am."

"Very well then. Mr. Harreson?"

The technician has finished his bagel and is busy wiping his hands on his trousers. He sniffs, then pulls on a pair of plastic gloves. Seemingly at random, he flicks switches on his console and checks several readouts. When he is satisfied, he nods at the two wardens, who strap Balbo into the truth machine. He does not resist, and is soon sitting comfortably, a bemused expression on his face. Harreson stands and gathers several cords from the floor which he plugs into cylindrical outlets on his console. When he is quite sure that everything is set, he goes over to Balbo and takes a thin metal probe from his pocket. Harreson speaks to Balbo, but I cannot hear their words. Balbo leans forward and reveals the socket at the base of his skull. With a practiced motion, Harreson inserts his probe. Balbo does not react. After several seconds, the technician removes his device and checks its display. Obviously satisfied, he mutters a few words, then picks up the large ringed tube that lies waiting at the base of the chair. He polishes the tube's mating collar and clicks it into place in Balbo's spine.

Harreson returns to his seat and begins adjusting the largest dial on his console. The court's large screen flickers into life and fills with static. Slowly, the distortion resolves. I see the interior of a convenience store: row upon row of cans and bottles and food and accessories. The merchandise's labels are impossible to read, and without color I cannot differentiate between the various products. Apparently satisfied, Harreson cues the audio. I hear several voices, none of them familiar, and none of them directed at Balbo.

As if on cue, the screen fills with the looming image of Balbo's hand. The hand momentarily blocks the light.

When the picture returns, it has deteriorated sharply, as if the convenience store's lights have been turned off. Given the prevalent natural static, it is almost impossible to make out what is happening. Then I understand: Balbo has donned a pair of high-filter sunglasses. I glance across at him, plugged into the chair. He is watching the screen intently, swallowing absent-mindedly.

Over the audio system, I hear a loud cough. It is a signal for action. Inside the store there is a commotion. I can't make out the cause. As Harreson desperately fiddles with his instruments, I struggle to interpret the picture. Most of the screen is filled with a bank of whiskey bottles. Only the very top corner shows anything of interest. In it, I can discern the shape of several people. Oh, but he is so very sly. I imagine the interior of that convenience store, see Balbo and his gang. They must have planned it this way, so that none of them is looking at what they are doing. In effect, they are trying to do the robbery blind.

As if to answer me, an anonymous male voice floats from the screen. "We can see you just fine. We're all trained shots; we've done this before. No one panics, no one gets hurt."

The sunglasses are effective. I couldn't possibly identify any of the people involved. I can't even tell those who are committing the crime from those who are being robbed. There is a haze of motion; I think someone has dropped a sack onto the floor. The voice returns: "Right, I want everybody to place their money cards, their watches and their jewelry in the bag. Get a move on, people. Remember, violence is an option."

There is a great deal of movement in the store, but Balbo is studiously ignoring it. All I can see are the whiskey bottles. And that's all there is to see. Several minutes go by. I am forced to study the bottles. Eventually, I make out the brand name. *Dark Horse*. In reality, the labels are blue.

"Thank you, everybody; have a nice day."

The picture jostles. I see Balbo's feet. He is wearing leather boots, I think. It is hard to tell. The convenience store floor is a tile mosaic. I see a flash of pants, another man's legs. Maybe he is wearing jeans. The view jerks up: I see a glass door, and then sunlight, remote and hazy.

All in all, it is quite a performance.

Honorable Yang motions to Harreson and he approaches her podium. The two of them confer in hushed tones. Harreson is shaking his head; Yang is scowling. She stands and exits the room. While she is gone, Harreson tries several tricks to tidy the images that we have seen. They rush across the screen again and again, but without any additional detail. Several of the men around me are growing restless, some are even tittering. They earn harsh glares from the wardens.

Balbo is still sitting in the truth machine. I see him wink at Linus, but he does not smile, nor gloat openly. His fingers are drumming on the side of his chair.

Eventually, Yang returns. When she is seated, she looks at Harreson, but he can only shake his head. The judge sighs. "Mr. Balbo, it is obvious to me, and to everyone in this court, that you are guilty of the crimes with which you are charged. Furthermore, you have participated in an incredibly foolish scheme to delay the passage of justice. I can assure you that it will not work.

"I have been in communication with several other justices, some of whom are scheduled to preside over the cases of your accomplices in this matter and we are sure that enough evidence will arise to convict the lot of you. Do you have anything to say for yourself?"

Balbo doesn't even try to look sheepish, there is too much triumph in his eyes. "Your Honor, I was only in that store to buy myself some whiskey. That's all. Just looking for whiskey."

"I thought you might say that," says Yang. "Are you sure that's all you were doing?"

"Yes, ma'am. Just wanted some whiskey."

Now it is Yang's turn to smile. "Then perhaps you can explain to me why you didn't oblige when the robbers ordered you to surrender your wallet and valuables. Why didn't you put your money card in the bag like you were told?"

All at once, the color drains from Balbo's face. He stammers, "Your Honor, Your Honor."

Yang is already typing. "I'm listening, Mr. Balbo," she says.

Balbo can say nothing.

Yang almost smirks as she sentences him.

•••

As Chu slipped the plastic ties around my wrists, he whispered in my ear, "I knew you did it. Knew right from the start. I could see it in your eyes. Always can."

•••

The day passes slowly in Yang's courtroom.

Inexorably, the men before me are removed and placed in the truth machine. Their stories flash across the screen and are gone, the details of their crimes allowed to blur in a medley of discontent. One by one, they are sentenced as Honorable Yang's busy fingers write their names into the log of justice.

It is a parade of the poor, of the guilty. None of these men have the resources to fund a private hearing. None of them can afford the gentler services of their own technician. They are statistics, not news; men who lack the ambition to be innocent.

So I watch their recklessness until it dulls my eyes. Watch them exact their small measure of brutality upon the world through petty thieving and pernicious rapine. All in all, it is a sullen evil, devoid of glamor: the evil of ignorance, the evil of circumstance.

I watch and watch and watch.

And when the day ends, it is simple arithmetic that plays most heavily on my mind. Sixteen men started the day. Twelve remain.

Now I am first in line.

• • •

She opened the door and smiled her crooked smile.

• • •

Coates does not allow me the privacy of my cell.

He comes while I am still in the dining hall, after I have finished my supper. The evening news is being piped through to one of the hall's long scenery displays. A small war is consuming a country I've never heard of. The images of the war occupy the screen. Frozen images of frozen bodies alternate with personal moments of terror and action: a group of guerrillas have given the reporter access to their memories, presumably in the hope of winning international sympathy. The segment lasts for thirty-eight seconds, then the network breaks for commercial.

It is during this break that Coates comes. I am sitting by myself, though many eyes are upon me. He moves away from his men and limps toward me. I watch his approach out of the corner of my eye. The huge screen is making a salacious offer to sell me a piece of the sunset.

"No one else left now," he says.

I ignore him and try to keep up with the TV.

"You want to quit?" he asks.

"Go away," I answer. He does not respond. Surreptitiously, I watch his black face. I am beginning to think he owns only a single expression. We remain like this for a while. For at least three adverts. I try to forget he is there. Then he speaks.

"I've been thinking about you," he says, "when I go home to my wife and kids. Got four sons, four good sons. I've been thinking about you when I'm with them, because at first I didn't understand you and that bothered me. I've seen a lot in this place, seen a lot of men and a lot of crime. I've seen the guilty, even seen a few who're innocent. None of them bothered me: I do the job, I go home.

"But I didn't think I'd seen one like you.

"I even went and read your file. You're an artist, or something. An educated man, been to a couple of schools. Must of had a pretty normal life, 'til you killed your girlfriend. That I've seen before. Plenty of normal guys come through here because of one insane moment. Most of those guys listened to me when I told them not to fight the chair. But not you. You dismiss me as if I were a figment of your imagination. Still, I've seen that too. Plenty of racists in this world.

"What I haven't seen a lot of is this . . . this waiting. What are you waiting for?"

The volume of his words pulls me away from the television. I stare at him with unblinking eyes; he is a slack-jawed man. A tributary of sweat runs down his forehead. When he realizes that I will not reply, he continues. "Of course, I've seen my share of fatalists, but most of them have a kind of serenity about them.

"Then last night, for the first time, I understood. Took me a while, but I figured it out. You're not special at all: you're just another fool." He gives a short, sharp chuckle. "Hell," he says, "you could be me, that's how ordinary you are. Sure had me going for a while."

At last, I say, "What do you want?"

He leans in close. "You aren't going to take the low scale, are you?"

"No."

"No, you're not," he continues, "so I thought I'd save myself a couple of hours and get home early tonight. Reclaim that time for my family. I figure you owe me that much. I want to take you to get fitted out now. Shouldn't make any difference to you."

"No difference," I say.

"Good," Coates says, "come on, then." He slips a plastic tie from his belt and gestures at me. I bring my hands together behind my back and he binds them. With a nod to the other wardens, he takes me by the arm and leads me from the hall. I have to slow my natural pace to match his. Neither of us speak as we move through the sterile passages of the vast court complex. Coates's breathing is heavy. I have never been this close to him. He smells vaguely of mothballs.

We take an elevator I've not seen before. This one has a normal set of controls, but requires a fingerprint

ID to activate it. Coates presses a button marked with a
large *S*. The doors slide shut and the elevator descends.

When we reach our floor, we walk in silence down a
short white-walled corridor that ends in a glass door.
Coates knocks on the door and a muffled voice answers.
He opens the door and pushes me through.

It is a small surgical office. Plastic cabinets line the
wall. They are filled with the paraphernalia of medicine.
The doctor is a dwarf. He is on his knees, rummaging
through a cupboard. He does not look up, but waves a
hand in the general direction of an uncomfortable
looking chair that takes up the middle of the office. It
looks like a dentist's chair. Coates leads me to it,
removes the tie from my hands and sits me down. The
chair's armrests have metal cuffs and Coates fastens
them around my wrists. There is also an angular neck
brace, but this he does not fiddle with. When he is sure
that I am secure, he limps over to the doctor's desk and
leans against it.

The doctor finds what he is looking for and emerges
from the cupboard. He is a hairy little man of obscure
origins, not four foot tall. Unusually, he wears spectacles. They make his eyes bulge. When he speaks, his
voice is heavily accented. I cannot place it. "Ben," he
says to Coates and goes over to the sink. There is a small
metal stool placed there, onto which he climbs. As he
washes his hands, he speaks to me. "So, my name is
Fermer. The doctor here, for this section. You are going
to the machine tomorrow?"

I say nothing. Coates sneers, "Oh, he's going all right."

"Very well," Fermer says. "Then you must be able to
talk to the machine. I am going to make it so you can do
this. If you have questions you must ask them to me. The
law says I must be answering them. You understand
this?"

"Yes," I reply.

"Good! To be answering your first question then, you will have no pain. I am giving you a little injection." He has scrubbed his hands three times while he's been talking. Now, he clambers down from the stool and drags it across the floor, until it rests behind me. It makes a brittle noise, like nails on a chalkboard. Fermer climbs back up. He has tiny, perfect hands like those of a child. They are cold on my neck. He fastens the brace so that I cannot move my head. "You will not be feeling this," he says. There is an intense, sharp prick in my neck. Instinctively, I try to jerk away, but I can't.

"No, no. Not moving. Very delicate," Fermer says. I hear the sound of a drill. "I am placing a hole in your neck. This is for the shunt."

Despite myself, I ask, "Can it be removed?"

"Oh yes, yes. Very easy. Plug 'n play. It is clever stuff, this wetware. Might be giving a bit of a scar though. Also sometimes, the court is saying not to take it out. This is if you're often coming back." I can hear the sound of the drill biting into meat, but I can't feel anything.

Fermer jumps down from his stool. He crosses to one of the cupboards and removes a shiny vacuum-sealed packet. There is a bright yellow label on it. The doctor touches the side of his stool, then opens the packet and, with his fingertips, removes the shunt. I can't see it very well from this angle, and I can't move my head, but I catch the impression of a small, limp squid. Then Fermer is back on his stool, chattering away. "You will be feeling not much when you are on the machine tomorrow. Sometimes, they say it is like water is trapped in your ear. Like you are swimming, or having the shower. This is natural. You are not to be worried. Just a little bit of lost electricity, nothing in your ear. You are hearing me?"

I hear the scrape of metal on bone. A loose cord flaps down my back. Fermer speaks to Coates, "You bring me that looker there. That one."

He wants a probe; Coates fetches it for him. "Just a minute," Fermer says. He lifts the loose cord. I hear him grunt, and something clicks. "Right." He takes the probe. "Tell me if you are feeling anything."

I don't.

Fermer leaves the probe in my neck for several seconds, then slides it out. "Yes, it is fine. You are going now. Goodbye and good luck."

Coates releases me from the chair and reties my hands. Fermer has already forgotten us. He is back inside his cupboards. I see his tiny legs sticking out as Coates takes me from the surgery.

The journey is silent. Coates's eyes are heavy on the back of my neck. The cells are empty; the other trialists are not yet back from dinner. It is a small mercy. Coates escorts me to my cell and, when I am inside, reaches through the bars and removes the tie. Immediately, I slide my hand up my neck. The socket is cool beneath my fingers, round. It feels like the inside of a bottle.

"You might be wondering," Coates says, "if I'd normally walk a prisoner on my lonesome like that." His voice sounds far away. "Of course not. But like I said, I figured you out. I know why you're here." He shakes his head. As he turns to leave, he offers me a final promise: "Tomorrow, then."

I am still busy fingering the plug. But I force myself to speak: "I'm not a racist."

This time, it is his turn to enjoy the silence.

• • •

When Nemma Jean opened her door, she gave me a short, sharp smile. She hadn't dressed up, her pink blouse was casual, buttoned to the neck and tucked into faded blue jeans. Her hair was up in a ponytail. The smell of supper floated over her shoulder.

While she finished up in the kitchen, I waited in the television room. An awkward time of day: the armistice between day and night, too early for artificial lights. As the darkness deepened, the television's glow grew more prominent, until its effulgence was the only thing separating me from blindness.

I was half asleep when she came in. She'd let her hair down; it lingered over her shoulders like a thin coating of ice. "You should turn a light on, Tom. You'll ruin your eyes."

I grunted noncommittally. She was drinking white wine from a half-empty glass. "How was your day?"

"The same. I'm nearly finished the big piece, but they won't like it."

She sat down beside me. The cat, Max, prowled in. He was a heavy cat, rich with fur. With a natural grace, he leapt up into her lap. "They're paying for it," she said.

"It's my painting."

She laughed. "You have to eat, Tom." The cat began kneading her stomach with his paws; he snuggled in close to her and began to purr. Nemma Jean drained her glass and put it down on the floor. "Supper will be another quarter of an hour."

The television glimmered dully with an art show on chalk painting. It wasn't a technique that I much liked. We watched in silence. Without any warning, Nemma

Jean put her hand on my thigh, leaned in close, and began blowing softly into my ear. Her scent assailed me, soft and soapy. "Damn it," I whispered. "You promised."

"Don't you like it?"

I pulled away from her, stood up. The spot where her fingers had rested bristled with false emotions. Her voice sounded so small. "What the hell do you want from me, Tom?"

"I have to go." I was already walking toward the door.

"The hell you do!"

She didn't have much art in the room, just a dreadful portrait of an old man she'd found in a pretentious uptown gallery. The picture lacked humility and warmth. To make matters worse, the old man's eyes glittered with an unearned wisdom. Like a martyr's, or a prophet's. "Haven't we had this conversation?"

"We've never finished this conversation," she half howled. "Tom, please. Leave the past alone. Isn't the present enough? We could be happy." I heard her creep up behind me; felt her arms as they coiled about me. Her hair fell about my neck. She pulled me around, stared up at me. Her body pressed into me, hard and soft. In the television's light, her hair looked like water, so very clean. I couldn't look at her, couldn't speak.

We stood locked together in silence while the television importuned us. She waited, but I could not speak. In disgust, she released me. When she spoke, her voice was sickening. "You wanted me to do it, you bastard, and you're lying to yourself if you say otherwise.

"Goddamn it, talk to me! Tell me you love me, tell me you hate me; just speak. I'm sorry. Please believe me, I'm so very sorry."

Her tone was so threatening, I forced myself to study her. Tears mocked her eyes. She had beautiful eyes, better than blue; eyes that evaded artistry.

"Speak, goddamn you!"

Her pain was so apparent, it began to seize my sight. The distraction of the television dimmed, the walls receded. The outside noises of the world, the inside voices on the screen, all faded. I saw her lips as they shaped at words. Knew I needed to hear what she was saying; couldn't hear what she was saying.

All my senses could show me was the outside of Nemma Jean Backs and the future.

•••

Eventually, I sit up. My bed is hard beneath me, unyielding. I throw my blanket to the floor and curl my knees to my chest. The air is close to silence. My eyes are salted with weariness, my forehead tight with the hour. Prospects taunt me. I cannot combat the coyness of sleep.

•••

As if caught in the gravity of history, she fell away. Assailed by grief and the television, I could only watch. She fell and her eyes denied the light. With a low snapping sound, her head hit the side of the glass table. The vase and the roses trembled with the impact. I stood, my mouth wide, and waited. She did not move, did not speak. Her hair was splayed across the floor like a failed parachute. I blinked hard. Blinked again. Finally, the fetor of the burning supper forced me to motion.

•••

"Mr. Hallutio, in accordance with the law, I am obliged to offer you a final chance to alter your plea. Do you wish to do so?"

"No, Your Honor, I do not."

"So be it," Yang says. She gestures to the two wardens who stand beside me. They are blocky men, identical. Before they can touch me, I am already moving toward the truth machine. Up close, it is a clickety-clack chair, a moulding of cogs and levers and coils of flimsy wire, more a socket than a seat. Its surface is potent with edges and angles. The view from the gallery has lulled me into a nervous complacency.

I lower myself into its embrace. The wardens lose no time in strapping me in; a large belt slides over my torso and locks into place. My wrists are fastened to the machine's thin arms by plastic restraints. I feel something sharp press into the small of my back. The seat feels almost archaic, as if I am secured to a spindly throne. It is anti-modern. The chair does not encourage movement. I am impelled to look forward, toward the court's screen.

Harreson is fiddling with his console. I can see more of his controls from here, a feast of knobs and needles. The instrumentation is carefully color coded. Harreson throws the start-up switch and a gentle vibration runs along his machinery. Several readouts tremble, a circular gauge volts to attention. The chair itself feels no different. Harreson checks over his displays, then stands.

When he is ready, he comes over to me. He is older than I thought and has more wrinkles. Loneliness stains the bags beneath his eyes; several nose hairs creep from his nostrils. He has small eyes; they are green and lurk beneath overly large lids.

"Good morning," he says. "My name is Dr. Harreson. I am the operator of the evidence retrieval unit in this courtroom. You are entitled to see my qualifications." He does not look at me while he speaks. Rather, his eyes dart about the straps and wires of the chair. A thick gel glimmers in the wisps of his hair. When I don't reply, he asks me to lean forward. I do, with some difficulty. The pressure at the base of my spine increases. Harreson removes a probe from his belt and holds it up to the light. It looks like a cross between a dagger and an old-fashioned thermometer. "Look down," he says. I feel nothing as he runs the probe into my neck. I wait for several seconds in this unnatural position, until Harreson jerks the device from my shunt.

"Your adrenalin is very high this morning," he comments. He is wearing plastic gloves. Through them, I can see that he bites his fingernails. He says, "We are ready to go. Sit tight; there's nothing you can do to influence what's going to happen, no matter what you've been told. You can't project images, you can't conceal memories, you can't resist. I suggest you try to relax." He bends from the knees and picks up the serpentine tube that lies on the floor.

The waiting is almost over.

I hear a click as he plugs the truth machine into my spinal column. With that done, he trots back to his console and twists a dial. I swallow. My eyes are locked on the screen. I swallow again; it is not nervousness, something doesn't feel right. My sinuses complain, as if I've undergone an abrupt change in pressure. The sensation starts to fade, until only my ears are affected. It feels as if water is trapped inside them, deep down, where my fingers could not hope to reach.

The screen awakes. It is enough to divert my attention. In black-and-white beads of static, I see the door to Nemma Jean's apartment. The picture quality is not good; I am forced to concentrate. The door opens. I see Nemma Jean. She is frowning. Her shirt is white; it constricts her throat. "Come in, Tom," she says. As if on cue, the images lurch into her lounge. The cat is sleeping in the corner of the room, curled around the candlestick. A crackle runs across the picture. When it passes, the screen is occupied by her television set and a dance of channels. Nemma Jean's voice floats into the courtroom. "I have a few more things to do in the kitchen. It won't take long. Can I get you something to drink?"

I hear myself reply. "No, thank you." It is awkward hearing my voice twice filtered through my ears. The court's screen relays her television signal. The display flickers and changes rapidly, until I sign on to an art site. Several minutes pass. The replay wanders about her room, now focusing on the chalk discussion, now studying the long-stemmed roses on the table, now glaring at an old man's portrait hanging on the wall.

Nemma Jean's voice returns. "Put on a light, Tom. You'll ruin your eyes." The picture swivels and she comes into view, drinking from a wineglass. "Did you have a good day?"

"I finished the big piece, but I don't think they'll be happy with it."

She sits down beside me and tosses her hair over her shoulder, then runs her fingers over a seam in the sofa. Her nails have been painted. On screen they appear black. "They are paying for it, Tom. You can't ignore them."

"Screw them," I hear myself say, "it's my painting."

Nemma Jean chuckles conspiratorially. "Yes, and it's your stomach." She takes a dainty sip from her glass. "What's on?"

"Nothing," I reply, "something on chalk paintings. You can turn it off." She doesn't reply, finishes her wine and places the empty glass on the floor.

I take a moment to look around the courtroom. Most of the trialists are watching, although they seem bored. Harreson is having an easy time with my mind. He is leaning back, his hands cupped over his stomach, concentrating on the show. Because he is a caricature of smugness, I cannot help but hate him. Although technology has gifted him with the ability to locate an instant in my mind, he's never considered the absurdity inherent in such an action. Real stories have no beginning. As for Honorable Yang, her face is impossible to read; her eyes are consuming the evidence.

It doesn't matter how closely she is watching; it's impossible to tell what happens next. One minute, the display is occupied with Nemma Jean's television and the next, it is filled with her petulant face. Her mouth is curled up at the corners. My voice sounds hollow as it comes over the speakers. "Damn it. I thought we'd agreed not to do this."

"God, I don't know what you want," Nemma Jean replies, "I thought you'd like it. What do you want from me, Tom?"

The view changes as I stand. "Maybe I should go."

Nemma Jean's voice is laced with anger. "The hell you should!" The portrait on the wall looms into focus, fills the screen. Despite the static, I can see the divine myopia that haunts its eyes. "Just once, we have to finish this conversation. Tom, the past is the past. You've got to leave it alone. We're here now, together. We could be happy. Isn't that enough?"

For a while, the screen shows only the picture on the wall and its gilt-edged frame. I say, "It happened,

Nemes." Then, as if forced, the view swivels. Nemma Jean's face consumes the screen. Sitting in the chair, I am forced to study it. To my surprise, it's not quite right: her features are blunter than I remember; there is a smudge of dirt beneath her ear. In black and white, her eyes are reduced to organs.

A moment of silence endures, then her face retreats. "Goddamn it, talk to me, Tom. Act like a grown-up. Tell me you love me, tell me you hate me. I'm sorry. You know I'm sorry." Tears form in the corners of her eyes and begin to melt down her cheeks. Her mouth twists in upon itself.

I glance around the court. Now, everyone is watching.

On screen, Nemma Jean's body tightens. As she leaps forward, at last, I hear her.

She screams, "Can't you see? Can't you see?"

The image dissolves into a kaleidoscope of hair and nails. I see flashes of Nemma Jean, see her fist, see the static and the lurid light. I see the cat, startled, raise its head. In glimpses, I see the walls of her apartment and the shadows of her furniture. I see how little space there is between us. I see my own hands, stained with dry paint, as they try to restrain her. I see her strike me, kick me; I see her frenzy.

But finally, I hear her words. "Can't you see? Can't you see?"

Almost I whisper, "Show me."

Through the crackle and the static, I watch Nemma Jean's last moments. She comes at me, raging. The picture is unsteady, falling backward. My hands flash across the screen, trying to intercept her blows. Despite the chair's restraints, I lean forward, ever so slightly. I feel the air leak from my lungs; my eyes are on fire.

I see my hands push. I see my hands pull.

I see her fall back, very quickly; see her head hit the table. But it's all wrong: the sound as her head bites into the glass is almost imperceptible; there isn't enough blood. And it's all too quick. When she fell, she fell in slow motion. I remember her eyes; I can't see her eyes.

Nemma Jean lies beside the coffee table and does not move.

But I've heard her. "Can't you see? Can't you see?"

The screen fades to darkness. I am frozen in the chair, the eyes of the court upon me.

And maybe, at last, I can. It has been an obscuring irony, that justice is locked in cahoots with the two-eyed. In my story, Nemma Jean Backs opened her door and smiled—to that, this court remains blind. Quietly, I close my eyes and surrender.

Like the Cyclops in the aftermath of Odysseus, I see what I cannot see.

DREAM THE DREAM

Written by
Leo & Diane Dillon

About the Authors

Leo and Diane Dillon are legends in the world of graphic arts. Their beautiful work has adorned hundreds (perhaps thousands) of venues for decoration. They are known far and wide for their line, draftsmanship and their unique color sense.

Both attended the Parsons School of Design in New York City, graduating in 1956. They were married in 1957, and have always collaborated; they have felt no need to ever do otherwise. Soft-spoken but positive in their opinions, diffident but unyielding, they are an ornament to our staff of judges.

Times are changing. The electronic revolution is having and will have an effect on the field of illustration. We have no idea how it will ultimately change what we do but there are constants that should not change: the knowledge of good design and composition, an understanding of anatomy, color theory and the ability to draw.

Observation, the ability to see, is learned through experience. Drawing until it "feels right" is part of talent. That feeling comes with practice. We see an idea in our heads, can work out problems, even change things in our vision and think it's all worked out, but when that idea begins to take form on paper we realize how amorphous it actually is. That's when skill and discipline take over.

Is art fun? With every new job there is always a period of doubt, fear, anxiety, during the development of the art. When almost everything is worked out, when we're comfortable with the technique we're using, when all we have to be concerned about is perfecting what is already there and touching in highlights, only then does it approach fun.

We use varied techniques and media to express what we want to say. They are our graphic vocabulary much as words are to a writer. Just as the writer must study vocabulary and grammar, so must the artist learn new techniques and experiment with different materials. To work with unfamiliar materials is difficult but with use they become comfortable. Experimenting can be frightening. We have to keep telling ourselves that we are in control, not the medium. We will correct, change things and decide when we have what we want. Ultimately, we will be satisfied or we will destroy and rebuild. There is a power in knowing that and when we have worked through a problem there is triumph. These are the artists' battles.

One major weakness we see in student work is observation of the human figure and objects in general. It is a mistake to believe we can draw only from memory. The mind is tricky. Try this experiment: Imagine an object and draw it from memory. Then find a photo or the actual object and study it. You will see curves, seams, details, how the light highlights the form—many details you may not have noticed before that make that object real and believable. Then redraw that object from life and see the improvement.

Let's say we want to create "plant people." First we will look at plants and details. How would limbs grow from the main stalk? Might the skin show veins like a leaf, have ridges or fuzz? Even if we intend to distort or exaggerate, we're starting with reality which makes the end result more convincing. Studying plants will give us ideas we could never have come to and will enrich our imagination.

We're not saying to copy. Especially if you are using someone else's photograph. Using a photograph for details and inspiration to create your own image is one thing, copying it exactly is another. That is illegal and artists have been taken to court for copying a photograph without the photographer's permission. It is useful for artists to be able to use a camera and photograph their own models and for other visual research.

Of course photographs can be scanned into a computer, manipulated and distorted beyond recognition. We're concerned about that. The calisthenics of drawing and knowing what to do to make a form correct will enhance what is done mechanically.

The computer is a tool, the artist is the creator. Our skills will get flabby relying too much on a keyboard. A major danger an artist can fall prey to when using the computer is using too much color and too much imagery because it is easily available with a click of a mouse.

The second weakness we find in students' work is composition. Often the complete surface of the picture area is filled with art, every plane as important as the others. The negative space, or the space where nothing is happening, is extremely important. It can direct the eye to the main action. It can balance the picture and create interesting shapes.

For centuries the written word has been the basis for what is called civilization. Now we are entering a visual age, yet it seems there is less interest or appreciation for art. Art departments are the first to be cut in the corporate world and public schools. Students today are not exposed to art history or music appreciation. Art is a part of our lives in what we read, what we wear, what we use and what we live in. There is an attitude that art is a luxury. Some think art is something to hang on a wall or place on a pedestal. It is that, but it is also what makes a page easy to read or what makes a label successful in conveying the contents of a package. Art is the design that makes a chair comfortable to sit in or what makes a room comfortable to be in. It is not separate from our lives. Art is functional and art is decorative. What we are saying is that to us art is a sacred thing. It feeds our soul. All kinds of art through all the centuries have been our inspiration, from sculpture to painting, from architecture to crafts. Looking at great art spurs us to work.

In terms of making a living as a freelance artist, it is a long, hard road. At the beginning we took almost everything that we could get. We did type design, record album liners, corporate reports and textbook illustration before we finally got our first book jacket illustration. With every new job we learned something and considered those jobs as a way of being our own patrons.

Freelancing is an isolated profession. There is a danger in being out of touch with what is happening in the industry; what to charge, what an agreement should cover, whether the art is being used for reproduction only and is returnable to the artist or whether the art is being purchased as a work for hire where the buyer owns the art and all rights including the authorship. Freelancing is a business. It is important to know these things. Talking to other artists is helpful. A book titled *The Pricing and Ethical Guidelines*, published by the Graphic Artists Guild, has extremely helpful information on contracts, pricing and ethical issues for all the disciplines.

It is important to have a knowledge of bookkeeping, a system for billing and record keeping. A system for tracking art, knowing what is out and what is due back, is a necessity if you don't want to lose your art. When we started out, we "just wanted to do the work." In those days it was sacrilegious to mention money in the same breath with art. Sometimes we forgot to bill for a job sent in and once we billed twice for the same job. Months later we received a letter from the publisher who found they had paid us twice and we had to send back the overpayment, which had already been spent. That was painful since we were always counting pennies.

We had no idea we were selling reproduction rights and not the original art and lost a lot of original art that we never even asked to be returned. In those days we did not know our work would have value.

Something else students should be aware of is using good materials. Materials are expensive but so is the potential of the art years later after you have made a name and the work has value. Using cheap paper and fugitive colors can render the work worthless. Early on in our career we weren't concerned about those things and we paid the piper.

We have learned from our mistakes and perhaps they are the strongest lessons, but we hope by sharing our experiences, other illustrators starting on the journey will be better armed to protect themselves from some of the pitfalls.

It is a privilege to be doing what we love to do. Each new job is a different challenge. We are seldom bored. To see a project through from start to finish is fulfilling. Our career has spanned over forty years and we are still working. From this end we can say it was worth the sacrifices, the doubts and the struggle. Often we thank our good spirits, perhaps the spirits of artists past, for such a great gift.

Dream the dream, aim for the best you can do, and make the next job better than your last.

Bon Voyage!

THE UNBOUND

Written by
Nicole Montgomery

Illustrated by
James Matt Frantz

About the Author

When Nicole Montgomery was nine, her mother took away all her books in an effort to make her play with other children. This did not work— Nicole started writing, instead.

Now, while she is studying at Gonzaga University, Nicole only has three loves: reading, where she can take herself to worlds more interesting than ours; teaching, where she is paid to talk about her favorite subjects; and writing, where she will get those people out of her head and onto paper where they belong.

About the Illustrator

Born in 1973 in Cincinnati, James Matt Frantz studied art in various local schools of art and design. Currently, he is a senior studying fine art at Miami University in Oxford, Ohio, and has also taken classes at Xavier University and the Art Academy of Cincinnati. In addition to art, he is interested in creative writing and music, though he believes his true talent is in art. After he receives his bachelor's degree, he plans to attend graduate school. He hopes to eventually be involved in the visual end of the entertainment or publishing business.

They came out of the sky like gods. Three monstrous birds, the sun gleaming off lethal tapered hulls, wings outstretched. They blocked the sun—at once terrifying and familiar. No one yet living remembered the first time they had come, when, indeed, they had been thought gods. No one remembered the terror and wonder of watching the enormous birds disgorge their strange passengers for the first time. No one remembered a time when Iridel had not been ruled by outworlders.

What the Iridelli remembered was that their imperial masters bled and died. They remembered the last Imperial Governor's head adorning a pike over the central square, while Iridelli chanted and danced around it. And they remembered the exultation of being free.

The Iridelli killed their gods, consigning their bodies to earth and their spirits to hell. Then they found they no longer knew how to live without them. Hunger allowed little time for feats of daring. Cold sapped the will to chant slogans and give fine speeches. Pride filled few bellies, and righteousness did not rebuild shattered cities.

Far below the circling ships, one who scavenged through the rubble stopped and stared. Clutching a precious piece of discarded plastic, he laughed a soft, bitter laugh to himself, his tail lashing. They had said the Empire would never come again. They'd said Iridel had shown the Empire they would take back their destiny. He'd known, though, that it was merely a matter of time.

He saw the faces of his people, now, as they peered at the beautiful, deadly birds, arrowing for the plain outside the city. Gone was triumph, gone was fear. What he saw on the faces peering from broken windows and ragged tents was deliverance. He scurried on his way, for above and behind the ships loomed the first dark rumbling clouds of spring.

The gods had returned. They would demand their due.

•••

Rogan Kor, Commander of the Fourth Draconian Fleet and newly appointed Imperial Viceroy of Iridel, picked his way among the rubble, both living and dead, that had been the shining city. He felt his stomach turn over. Iridelli bodies, in varying states of decomposition, lay strewn like so many discarded toys over and between the piles of stone and mortar and wood that had once been buildings. Fires still raged throughout the city, but this area, the first to fall, was nothing more than charred smoking refuse. He felt, through his insulated boots, something soft beneath his foot, and risked a glance down. An arm without a body lay across his path as if to bar his way. With distaste, he stepped over it.

He stopped in the center of the broken, littered square and surveyed the ruins. His heavily armed and armored men surrounded him—he would never have entered an unsecured area—and they paused to await his orders.

"Find me the palace, and get Toran on the line. As soon as our position is secure, deploy the troops and start cleaning up this disaster. Draft work crews if you must, but I want this city fully restored before the month expires." Hand at his waist, resting easily on his lasgun, he narrowed his eyes on the broken and battered city.

A line of cowed and frightened Iridelli, wide fearful eyes in dirty furred faces, stood shivering in the cold wind, having been dragged out of their hiding places, and assembled per his orders. It would take weeks to find them all, and drive, bribe or coerce them out of hiding, but it would be done. Some watched his men, as if watching a predator, warily; some stared vacantly at the Draconian soldiers, or the ground, or the sky, apparently resigned to this new terror. Others, the lucky ones, were too busy gobbling the precious field rations his men were passing out to watch anything. It had been his first order upon landing. A fed population was a quiescent population. And later, after order was restored, they would remember who, when their own would kill for a crust of bread, had fed them.

Overhead the sky rumbled, as if in protest at this latest indignity, and clouds gathered in sulky black masses. One of his men stepped forward, combat helmet obscuring his features. He glanced around at the corpse-littered ground. "What about them? Vaporize?"

Kor considered, lips pursed. "Not yet. Pile them somewhere. I want to talk to a native before I dispose of their dead." He, alone, did not wear a protective helmet. Behind the plasscreen, he could see respect in the men's eyes for that bit of arrogance.

His golden slit-pupiled eyes swept the ruined city and the starving natives. "Besides, they made this chaos, they can clean it up."

Illustrated by James Matt Frantz

He climbed the broken steps of the wide-pillared entrance to the once sumptuous Imperial Governor's Palace. It was small in comparison to those he had seen on larger, more important worlds, but it still had the characteristic winding stairs and wide-flung arched windows that marked Draconian architecture galaxy-wide. Of course, the palace currently lacked a roof, and the gaping, jagged holes in the walls detracted somewhat from its decor, but that could be fixed, and would be.

Fire had gutted most of it, and while his men searched the rooms for any sign of life, he stood in what had been the library, and fingered the charred and black-ened remains of a book. "Ah, Khovrecin, how could you let this get so out of control?" he murmured to himself. Books were a rare and expensive pastime, one for which the last governor had been noted. Even in this era of space travel, cargo space was at a premium, and books were a heavy and unnecessary load when the same information could be kept indefinitely on datacube for a hundredth of the mass. Kor tossed the burnt lump away. No one would be reading it now.

Toran, his second, jogged up, saluting smartly. "Lord, we have found a native who says he was on some sort of city council before the insurrection."

Kor pulled out a chair, touching it reluctantly even with his gloves, and set it in the center of the room, waving a negligent hand. "Then, by all means, show him in."

Toran gestured, and two armored officers brought in a bedraggled Iridelli, his once fine clothes rags, now. He was thin, though a jowly face showed that he had not always been so. His head barely came up to Kor's shoulder, and his long, thin prehensile tail hung limply.

On average, the Draconians were no taller than the Iridelli, but they were leaner, harder. The fine fur that covered Iridelli skin was not visible from any distance, but Kor knew it was there, and it was yet another difference between him and the Iridelli. The ruler and the ruled. One who had power and one who did not. The man, bare feet cringing from the cold marble floor, glared at his guards, and looked, with resentful awe, around the ruined palace.

"Your name?" Kor spoke the Lower Tongue, the language of commerce and conquest.

Startled, the Iridelli jumped. Apparently he had not seen Kor in the deepening twilight.

"Duan, Lord."

"Well, Duan. Come——sit." His voice was affable and pleasant, as if inviting the man for an afternoon social, not an interrogation. Duan sat, hesitantly, and Kor stepped out of the shadows so Duan could see him better. Kor did not suppose he would find any reassurance there, but then he wasn't supposed to.

"I am Rogan Kor, Commander of the Fourth Fleet, Second Division, and, now, Viceroy of Iridel."

He paused to allow the man some comment, if he had any to make. Apparently, he had none. Kor continued. "I have been sent by the Draconian Empire to make some sense out of this chaos, and to restore order. You would like to see order restored, wouldn't you, Duan?"

The man nodded hesitantly. "Good." With an offhand gesture, Kor dismissed his guards. Doubt showed on their normally impassive faces, but only his second, Toran, voiced it. "Sir?"

Kor tilted his head at the wide-eyed Iridelli. "Duan, here, wouldn't hurt me. Would you, Duan?"

Hastily the Iridelli shook his head, alarmed that anyone would even suggest such a thing. Kor waved a still-dubious Toran out.

He favored the man before him with a small smile. "Now, to business. Where is Governor Khovrecin?"

Duan looked startled, his dark eyes flashed warily. "Dead, Lord. Or so the rumors say."

Kor raised a brow and frowned. "I see. And your civic leaders?"

"They're dead too, Lord, or in hiding."

Kor clasped his hands behind his back and pondered. It was going to highly displease High Command if Khovrecin really had been killed while posted on a backwater world, a posting that had been considered a sinecure. Never in the history of the Empire had there been a successful revolt, and never the anarchy on the scale he had found here. Then again, with Khovrecin dead, there would be no doubt to whom blame would be assigned. That was going to make several ministers release held breaths.

Duan looked miserable as if he expected to be executed immediately for giving such news, and if Kor had been any of his colleagues, perhaps Duan would have been. But Kor had plans, and to carry them out he needed the natives to be, if not cooperative, at least only minimally hostile.

"Duan, I want you to feel free to talk to me. As a respected member of the community, before the . . . chaos broke out, you heard rumors, of course. You had some idea this was coming." That was assuming a lot, but Kor took a page from the Ministry of Intelligence. If you act like you know they know, your subject will usually decide he has been found out, and so tell you. "I need to know what happened here, if I am to make sense of this senseless"—he waved a hand out toward the darkening, tense city beyond the windows—"carnage."

He placed a long hand on his armored chest, his expression earnest. "I am here to restore order, not destroy it." He kept his voice low and soothing, reassuring. "High Command and the War Ministry want this world . . . cleansed of dissenters. I managed to talk them out of it . . . for the time being." There—just the right note of implied hope. "They will listen to me, as long as I can continue to report success. I am your best hope of survival, Duan, and not just yours alone, but that of your entire race."

Duan's dark eyes were huge, and the oncoming night stole age from his face, making him appear to be an overgrown Iridelli child, knowing he has misbehaved, and suddenly offered a reprieve from punishment. The sky rumbled again, in perfect counterpoint to the rhythms of Kor's voice. "I need a voice among your people, Duan. Someone they know, someone they trust. Someone who can mediate between the demands of the Empire and the needs of your struggling people. Someone to whom they can turn when my requests seem difficult to understand. . . ." He let his voice trail away, and read the response on the other's face. Fear, hope, longing, fear again, and mistrust.

Inwardly, he laughed. He did not lie, although his truth might be a little different than the Iridelli's. "Come, Duan. I am not asking you to betray your people. . . ."

Duan's eyes flashed to him, and Kor could read his thought plainly. *Now the devil lord can read minds. . . .* The Iridelli shifted bare feet.

Kor smiled. "Your people need leadership, especially during this trying time. They need guidance, if they are ever to rise from the ashes they have made." Duan kept his dark-pooled eyes on Kor, his lips firm, but his stance wavered. Kor paced slowly, his boots ringing on the floor.

"I am not a monster. I want only to help your people, Duan. I cannot do that alone. I believe this can be a cooperative effort, a true partnership between your people and mine." He kept his eyes leveled on the shaking Iridelli. "Give me the *choice*, Duan. Give me the option of working *with* your people. . . ."

One by one, drop by drop, puddles formed on the cracked marble floor, as the sky opened up and let forth its tears.

• • •

Duan entered the library, now the viceroy's office, with his usual trepidation. He had not realized what his status would be, once established as the viceroy's aide, and he would never feel comfortable passing the armed and armored guards with impunity. With such news as he had to report today, however, he was certain it would be only a temporary position. He did not expect to live much longer than it would take to give his report.

The viceroy sat behind his massive hand-carved desk. He called it his only luxury, which would have been laughable had it not been so sad. Over a hundred thousand people were still dependent on Draconian emergency rations, and every night Kor and his officers sat down to a meal made of fresh, real food. While his Iridelli subjects still boiled their water to cleanse it of impurities, he drank Draconian spiritwine from cut crystal goblets. Duan and his wife ate better than most, but every bite of fresh meat and fluffy bread was a searing pain in his gullet. He had not put on much weight at all.

Kor glanced up from under his brows, the same odd shade of dark bronze as his hair, and his golden eyes crinkled with a smile of sorts. "A few minutes, Duan. You might as well sit." Duan could not suppress the chill the first sight of those alien eyes always gave him. He would never get used to the gold iris swirling around the tapered slit pupil. He would never get used to the dark reflected light that shone there.

Commander Kor, Imperial Viceroy of Iridel, wore his armor, as always, a tight bodysuit made of tiny mesh rings. The cuirass, wrought to look like the hide of some scaly beast, gleamed in the late afternoon light. All Iridelli were familiar with that armor; all Draconians wore it. Duan had not yet noticed a distinguishing emblem or design. Only the faded tattoos just barely visible under the armor's collar set the viceroy apart from his troops. Tattoos similar to the late governor's, and that no other Draconian bore, that Duan had seen. No one, Duan included, ever mentioned them.

Kor finished his business, set the computer aside, steepling his long slate-gray hands in front of him, and politely gave Duan his attention.

"I assume you are here about today's council meeting?"

Duan swallowed hard and nodded. "Lord, they— they have refused to ratify the Farm Plan."

Kor raised a brow, and his eyes lidded. "On what grounds?"

"Lord, they believe the relocation of city residents to the country would be . . . disruptive."

Kor stood, and Duan shrank back. Kor did not appear to notice.

"I do not understand Iridelli, Duan, truly I don't. Do they not want to eat? Would they not prefer fresh food to ration bars? My emergency stores are not unlimited."

Kor waited for an answer but Duan could only shrug helplessly, eyes lowered. He could tell Kor of the pain of being separated from family. He could tell the Draconian of businesses lost, or homes abandoned, and Kor would listen courteously. Duan knew Kor wanted Iridelli cooperation. He gave fine speeches about the new era of peace between Iridelli and Draconian. He spoke of the coming day when Iridelli and Draconian would stand together before the Empire, both able to take pride in the restoration of their world to its former lush beauty.

In these orations, he never mentioned the lasguns every Draconian wore, weapons forbidden to Iridelli. He never mentioned the three battle cruisers in orbit above the planet.

He allowed them their illusions, to a point. When he spoke, his voice was very quiet. "Perhaps if you explain to them that relocation to the countryside would be far less disruptive than relocation to an offworld penal colony, they will be more amenable, hmm?"

Duan bowed his head.

• • •

Duan had not known that the collective farms were just the beginning. Two tendays after the council gave the order for the city to draw lots, deciding who would be sent to the country, a fourth imperial ship joined Kor's in orbit. The shuttle landed an entourage of Draconians garbed, not in the customary armor, but in soft rich robes. Kor feted them for three days, during which time Duan was called to the Governor's Palace only once.

"I don't care what you have to do, Duan, but keep them *quiet*. Throw a festival or declare a holiday, but keep your people on their best behavior."

Duan and the council did, indeed, declare a holiday. Work stopped and crews who had labored under guard, first during the rain and then the summer heat, took the time to play with their children and ease aching muscles. The city was quiet. It did not last. The day after the visitors flew off in their shiny little ship, Kor issued a general order for conscription of Iridelli workers to staff a repair facility for Draconian ships in this sector. It would be built, by Iridelli of course, in orbit around the nearest moon.

"But Lord," Duan had protested, "my people have no knowledge of the workings of your great ships."

Kor had given him a brilliant smile. "Ah, then you will learn something you didn't know before, won't you?"

"Lord, my people's religion forbids us to leave the planet. It is one of our oldest tenets. If we leave . . ." Duan's voice had gone soft in horror, his tail puffing.

Kor sighed and shot him a look of tried patience. "Bah. Superstitious nonsense. Duan, if you ever hope to stand on your own in this empire, you must have skills to handle technology. Khovrecin was remiss in this as in everything else. You people should have been trained long ago."

Duan did not tell him that Khovrecin had known and understood Iridelli beliefs and, superstition or not, had respected them. Khovrecin had been more concerned with his books and the old ruins outside the city than ruling the people he had been sent to govern. They had been almost free under Khovrecin. Duan stifled that thought. Khovrecin had brought the insurrection, and that had brought Kor, and there was no changing the past.

And so the training facility was built.

Immediately upon its completion, the order was issued for work crews to begin digging out the old ruins outside of the city. Draconians seemed to find the ruins fascinating, although Duan had never understood why.

"Why?" Kor had asked in disbelief, when Duan had mustered enough courage to ask. "Duan, ruins like those have been found all over the galaxy. Same materials, same workmanship. Same inscriptions. You know about the portals?"

Duan knew. For the Iridelli, the discovery of the existence of the portals that allowed travel through distant space had been brutal. How could any Iridelli forget that which had allowed their world to be conquered by outworlders?

"Every system that a portal leads to has ruins like these." Kor waved his arms expansively, his golden eyes alive with a burning light. "The materials are the same, the style the same. Who built them? Why? What happened to those people? It is the greatest mystery of all."

Duan nodded, swallowing his own opinion. He was thankful the rich robes Kor gave him covered his tail. The Draconian had been on Iridel long enough to learn the language of tails. "It would be wondrous to discover who could have left such ruins."

Kor sent him a smile that Duan was certain wasn't supposed to be perceived as condescending. "My dear Duan, it is hardly a matter for philosophers and historians only. If we could figure out how they made the portals . . . If we could learn to make them ourselves . . ." Gauntleted fists clenched, his eyes were far away, scanning vistas Duan could not even imagine. "Think of the possibilities."

Kor's smooth tones dropped to a whisper. "Think of the power. . . ."

• • •

At first glance, a visitor would see that the central market was busy, and perhaps comment approvingly that the city was starting to look like a city again. Work crews, Iridelli and Draconian, labored industriously, rebuilding the shattered civic center. Merchants filled the market, colorful wares bright under the canvas awnings. Iridelli residents mingled with offworld Draconians casually on the street, and the Draconians chatted at the various stalls. A more observant visitor might note the laser rifles toted by the Draconians. A truly astute observer would see the subtle contempt in Draconian eyes, and the wary fear in Iridelli.

Kor seemed to be in fine spirits, stopping frequently to chat with passersby or merchants in their stalls, or to beam at the work crews. He acted as if the city was his personal creation, pointing out this building and that statue, making notes to his second to remind him to check on the progress of various plans. Duan never wished to accompany him on these little excursions, but was also never consulted. Surrounded by Draconian guards, in the Imperial Viceroy's very shadow, few of his own would view him with anything but bitter loathing.

Kor stopped at a clothseller's stall. Although his wares were a far cry in quality and variety from what Duan had seen before the insurrection, the fact the man had any wares to sell at all was a good sign. The merchant eyed the group warily, swallowing convulsively.

"Duan," Kor turned to the Iridelli, "why don't you buy something for your wife? I am sure it has been some time since she has had anything new."

Duan's round black eyes widened. Lien would most likely hurl such a gift back in his face, and say something in her soft voice about it being bought with Iridelli blood. But he could hardly tell this to the viceroy.

"Lord, with things the way they are, I don't think she would care for new clothes."

Kor laughed. "Nonsense. Women always love clothes. Here, merchant." He pointed to the frightened man, apparently either unaware of his fright or choosing to ignore it. "This one is a vivid, happy color." He held up a bundle of cloth, a soft, rich red.

"Wrap it up." He directed the merchant to have it sent to the Governor's Palace. He winked at Duan, who was struggling to keep any expression off his face, and his voice became conspiratorial. "Perhaps it will soften her up toward me."

He walked off before Duan could respond, shock having frozen his tongue to the roof of his mouth. He could only stare after the man, sun shining off armor, silver bronze head ducking to speak to an old woman.

The viceroy seemed to forget about Duan, then, and he was glad of the reprieve. He leaned against a pillar and let the crowd mill around him, watching the viceroy, silver gray skin looking oddly dull in the bright light. Kor was in fine form this afternoon and his speech was replete with hand wavings and heartfelt displays. Duan let himself be lulled by the murmur of the crowd, the buzz of insects, and the somnolent heat.

A commotion started him awake, and barely had his eyes opened when a small figure barreled out of the crowd and straight into him. He managed to catch the figure before it could dart off, although it squirmed and kicked to be free. The crowd parted a second time, and with alacrity, when two Draconian soldiers pushed through. They spotted Duan and his hissing charge, and strode toward him, faces purposeful.

"Let me go!" wailed the small figure. He expected it to be a young urchin boy, but to his surprise, it wasn't a boy at all. It was an urchin girl, and she wasn't all that young. Deep brown eyes glared from a dirty face. Her tiny size gave the impression of youth, but, under the dirt, he could see the darkening of the fine down on her face that indicated she was at least past her majority. The Draconians stomped to a halt before him, obviously unsure how to proceed. They recognized him.

The girl darted behind him, and he could feel the eyes of the crowd on him. This, then, was to be his test. If he failed to protect the girl from the soldiers, his reputation as a Draconian pet would be sealed in the crowd's eyes. And in his own.

He drew himself up to his full height, still a span short of the Draconians, and his tail, covered by his councilor's robe, stiffened.

One soldier gestured peremptorily. "The girl. Give her to us."

"What was her crime?" Duan was proud of his voice. It did not shake, unlike his hands.

"She's a thief. I caught her poking around in my pack."

His companion nudged him urgently with his elbow. "We don't explain ourselves to the likes of *him*. You there, hand her over now. We are taking her into custody."

"I will not," Duan said quietly.

The soldier unslung his rifle, and the crowd that had gathered gasped and backed away. The girl squeaked.

"Will you fire on an unarmed man in front of all these witnesses, when your commander has explicitly stated that this . . . occupation . . . is a cooperative venture?"

"Cooperative venture, *hah!* You Iridelli couldn't take care of yourselves, so we're here to take care for you." He leveled the rifle and nodded to his companion.

"And we'll start by taking the girl." The other soldier started forward.

"Hold, soldier."

The new voice was deadly quiet, soft, and yet carried easily across the square. The two men's eyes widened and they hastily lowered their weapons, gray faces draining of what little color they usually had.

The viceroy stepped in between them, nostrils flared and eyes narrowed in cold anger. The crowd was absolutely silent. "*What* is going on here?"

The taller of the soldiers stepped forward hesitantly. "We were trying to apprehend a criminal, sir, when this . . . Iridelli interfered."

Kor turned his golden gaze on Duan. "Is this true, Duan?"

Duan was amazed at himself. He held the Draconian's eyes steadily. "Lord, I don't know what she may or may not have done, but she's little more than a child. She couldn't have done anything serious enough to warrant"—he shot a glare at the two men—"whatever they had in mind for her, sir."

Kor was angry, Duan knew. His anger burned cold, cold as the distant mountains, cold as the space from which he came. Golden eyes promised Duan he would not soon forget being put in this position.

"I will have the truth of this matter. Girl, come out here."

Behind him he felt the girl tremble, but when he let go of her, she did not run. She came forward, head held high. She was short, barely coming up to Kor's chest, and her hair was a tangled mane about her shoulders. Her clothes were little more than rags, and her dirty furry feet were bare.

Kor leveled his disturbing gaze on her and she flinched, but squared her shoulders. "Your name, girl."

The girl raised her chin, and her dark-pooled eyes were fathomless. "Ruenn a'Loer."

He took note of the lack of title with a raised brow, and Duan cringed. "You stand accused of theft, Ruenn a'Loer. Did you steal from these soldiers?"

She lifted her chin further. "No."

He raised both brows, and held her eyes until she fidgeted. "They say you did."

"They're wrong. I was hanging around the fruit-seller's stall, hoping to find work, when one of them made a . . ." she flushed and dropped her eyes, "a suggestion. I said no, and they said they could make me, and I—I ran."

The first soldier exploded. "She lies! She was stealing out of my pack." His hands came up, reaching, and to Duan's surprise, the girl darted behind Kor.

"You are out of line, soldier," Kor warned in a deadly tone. "And this is not the time or the place to settle this. You two are confined to quarters until further notice." Duan knew the man was not unaware of the avidly watching crowd. The two soldiers stiffened, and turned, as one, stalking through the crowd that parted hastily before them.

Kor turned to Duan and it was a look to chill even the warmest day.

"Since you seem to be the girl's champion, I remand her to your care," he said in an undertone. "Take her back to the palace." Duan ducked his head.

Kor turned to the eager faces surrounding the scene. "You may all carry on with your business now," he said with more than a hint of irony. "The drama is at an end." He smiled his most disarming smile, white teeth flashing. "The truth will be known, I assure you, and the matter settled fairly. The council will inform you of my decision." Scanning the crowd and apparently satisfied, he turned an arch look on Duan and the girl before striding off. His men followed, faces showing nothing of their feelings.

• • •

The matter was indeed settled, but Duan doubted anyone was satisfied, save Kor. That the soldiers were only given a stiff reprimand and put on half rations for a week outraged the Iridelli. That Duan was merely treated to a lecture on abusing Kor's favor offended the Draconians. That the girl was cleared of all charges and installed in the palace as Kor's new mistress horrified everyone in one way or another.

The last, Duan did not report to the council, although what the council reported to him was far more disturbing. The militant groups that had sprung up in the months since the Empire's return were becoming more vocal in their opposition of the new regime. The Empire had restored order, they said, had fed the people, but the price was too high. Kor had dismissed them as malcontents who would eventually settle down. The council was grimly pleased to announce that he was quite wrong. Several of them had been approached with thinly veiled threats if they ratified any more of the viceroy's plans or in any way aided the "imperial oppressor" in his occupation.

"They are arming," the council told Duan. "They have raided Draconian outposts in the country and are planning . . . something."

"What can they do?" he asked the gathering of Iridelli notables, scornfully. "They may as well be stinging insects for all they can hurt the Empire. Kor will take care of them, be certain. And if you go against him, he will take care of *you*. Ignore them, and do as you were doing. It's safest that way." He knew Kor wanted Iridelli cooperation, but would resort to drastic measures if he felt coerced. If the council suddenly balked at his proposals . . . Duan felt a dim sadness. Once, not so very long ago, his people had been peaceful, content. Violence had been almost unknown. The Iridelli were, indeed, learning much from their Draconian overlords.

●●●

"Now? It's after third watch. Does the man never sleep?" Lien a'Duan's wide eyes embarrassed her husband.

"He's a very busy man, Lien." Duan shrugged into his robes.

"Busy enough that he must call you out of bed in the middle of the night? What's he going to have you do this time, husband, read to him while he bathes? Sit and listen to another lecture on the Third Regime? Hand him sweetmeats while he—"

"Enough!" Duan instantly regretted his harsh tone when he saw the silent reproach in his wife's wide brown eyes. His tail lashed.

"What can I do, Lien, tell him, 'No, so sorry, I can't make it'? He wouldn't call me out if it wasn't important," he assured her. He did not tell her that Kor had stopped requiring Duan for trivial reasons since the incident in the square, not wishing to remind her of the role he had played in that affair. Like most Iridelli, Lien had been outraged, although Duan had been rather pleased with the outcome, himself. The girl's presence had ended the steady stream of Iridelli women in and out of Kor's bed, which gave the malcontents one thing less about which to complain. And she seemed to have a calming effect on the viceroy, which resulted in fewer lectures and fewer arbitrary commands.

The streets were empty, silent except for the chittering of a night animal and, in the distance, the raucous laughter of Draconian officers off duty for the night. Iridelli businesses that catered to the whims of garrison soldiers were allowed to operate after curfew and profited heartily from the privilege. Duan shivered. Under Khovrecin there had been no brothels, and no gambling houses. But Khovrecin had not been military, and had not brought three legions of soldiers with him.

He hurried through the streets, drawing his mantle about him, wishing he had kept a few of the ripped, ragged clothes from before the restoration. They would have been less conspicuous. It was a mark of the viceroy's favor that he wore such fine garments, but it branded him as one who served a function in the Covenant Government. Iridelli who worked ostensibly for the Iridelli people, but in reality served the viceroy in whatever capacity required, were often targeted by those who called them less flattering names than Covenanter.

"Well, look what we have here," purred a voice out of the darkness. Duan's hopes to make it to the palace unmarked and unremarked crashed at his feet, even as he bade them move faster. The guardpost was just ahead. He could see the moons' light gleaming off

Draconian laser rifles like a beacon. The irony of considering a Draconian guardpost as safety burned in his throat like bitter gall.

"Look at that nice mantle." Another voice joined the first, and then another, out of shadows so thick not even his Iridelli night vision could penetrate. They stepped forward. They were young, not yet to their majority, covered in ragged, tattered clothes, and bearing a darkness in their eyes deeper than any ingrained dirt. He knew who, or rather what, they were immediately, and wondered what someone brave would do now. The image that flashed through his mind was that of Kor, alone, facing unknown adversaries. The image laughed a laugh of rich contempt, shot them down and stepped jauntily over their bodies. Duan backed up, stepping frantically until he hit a wall and could go no further.

"A Covenanter, looks to me."

"Yeah. Well fed, too. No crusty ration bars for this one. Wonder which one he is?"

"Does it matter? They're all traitors as far as I'm concerned." The speaker was taller than the other two, and older. His eyes, perfectly round, pupils immense in the dark street, narrowed on Duan. He licked his lips and pulled a slim knife from his boot.

"He sits on their councils, he eats their food. He signs the orders to send *us* to labor camps." He fingered the knife, held it up so Duan could get a good look at it, and see the starlight gleam off its nicked and wicked length.

"I think we should leave a little gift for our good, kind, *generous* viceroy, one of his fine fat pets, all wrapped up in soft wool, on the steps of the Governor's Palace." The leader stepped up so close to Duan that he could smell his breath, redolent of alcohol. "With a message carved into his hide about what happens to those who betray their people."

The other two seemed less eager, shooting looks over their shoulders at the guardpost. "I don't know, Coret. Maybe we should take him somewhere first."

"You afraid of this pet's masters? They won't come in here alone, this time of night. He can scream to wake the dead, and they will sit right there and listen." He raised the blade to Duan's cheek, and Duan felt his tail stiffen in fear, his ears lying low on his head. "What's one more Iridelli scream?"

"Please—I—" He never knew what he would have said, for at that precise moment the Draconian soldiers did just what Coret had been so certain they wouldn't do. They left their post, and, girded in helmeted armor, loped into the streets, almost straight to where the four stood, transfixed. After one startled moment, Coret's friends ran, the movement showing them more clearly than a spotlight, and lasers flashed painfully, cutting the blackness, and Iridelli flesh, like lightning. Coret turned, snarling. The knife flashed, and Duan ducked instinctively, and felt burning pain in his shoulder. He sagged to the ground, aware of only his pain, the warm wetness seeping from him, running footsteps, and laser fire. He waited for the killing stroke.

After several hazy pain-ridden moments, he realized he hadn't died yet, and his vision cleared in time to see the booted foot coming toward him. He flinched, and a Draconian throat grunted.

"He's alive. Think he's the one the viceroy wants?"

"He'd better be. How are we supposed to tell them apart?"

They hauled him ungently to his feet, outraging his shoulder, but he managed not to black out, and fumbled in his pocket for his pass. Once he had it out, and they realized he wasn't struggling to be free of them, they relaxed their grip enough to allow him to hand them the pass.

"He's the one. The viceroy's going to be mighty unhappy his pet's been damaged."

Through his haze and pain, Duan could only laugh bitterly to himself, and wish Coret's aim had been just a little bit better.

•••

"Duan, whatever am I to do with you? I can't let you alone for a moment." Kor's voice was soft and indulgent, as Duan sat under a bright light in the library, trying to ignore the Draconian physician, Kor's own, who was bandaging his shoulder. It was wrong somehow to have one of them ministering to his wound.

He supposed Kor would insist on guards now. He had offered once before, concerned, he said, about ongoing violence in the streets. Duan had bitten back the response that had risen to his lips: "And who would protect me from *them?*" The viceroy had not pursued the matter, for which Duan had been deeply grateful.

Kor said nothing about guards, merely pacing thoughtfully, hands clasped behind his back, his customary posture when thinking. Even at this late hour, he wore his armor. Duan tried not to flinch under the physician's green gray hands. He disliked the feel of those hairless hands on his flesh and spared a moment's sympathy for Kor's mistress. That the physician was not any more pleased to be ministering to him helped not at all. He kept shooting black looks at the viceroy, who did not appear to notice.

Kor glanced up from under his brows, and his golden eyes smiled. "A few moments more, Duan. Be patient." If Kor had been anyone else, Duan would have sworn he saw worry in those odd, alien eyes, but he dismissed the thought as fanciful.

"I sent a message to your wife, to let her know you arrived safely."

Duan started, and the physician transferred his scowl from Kor to him, where it was marginally more successful.

Kor raised a sardonic brow. "It was the least I could do. You would hardly have been out on the streets at this hour had I not called for you."

Duan stared at the floor. "Thank you, sir. Lien does worry."

"Women do." Kor smiled at him. "It's part of their charm." He narrowed his eyes. "The ones who did this—did they take anything?"

"No, sir."

"You had nothing to take? Wise, that."

"Yes, sir." *Only my name, only my pride,* Duan thought. *Only my honor.*

He did not realize he had spoken the words aloud.

"What do you mean, Duan?"

He risked a look, and winced as the physician tightened a knot on the bandage. The Draconians had brought modern medical technology with them, but Draconian medicine was less than efficacious at treating Iridelli wounds, and there had been little motivation to try.

As soon as he saw Kor's face he wished he hadn't. The golden eyes were alight with cold fire, and it was a look chill enough to put out the sun. Duan was reminded forcefully of a jirabird he'd had when he had been a youngster. He had loved that bird, even when it bit him, even when it scratched his mother's best table. When he caught a clan-cousin teasing it cruelly, he had felt the purest protective rage.

"Sir, I . . ." He could not finish. If only the man were not so perceptive, so observant.

Kor dismissed the physician with a wave of a long hand. "Theft was not the motive, then. What was it?"

Duan mumbled something, and Kor frowned. "What *was* it, Duan?"

"That I work for you. Sir." Duan whispered.

"I see." Kor straightened. "Well, in any case, they will be caught and punished. That I promise you."

Duan steeled his courage, and hoped his tail was well hidden beneath his robes.

"Sir, I would prefer it if you didn't." Through great effort of will he met the disturbing golden eyes. They were surprised.

"Why ever not?"

"They were just boys, sir. Angry as many of my people are. They did not know what they were doing."

"Did not know?" Kor demanded incredulously. "That blade was at least a span long, Duan. And possession of such a blade is, of itself, a crime."

"I know."

Kor regarded him long enough to make Duan squirm. "Very well. At least now, I hope you will reconsider my offer of guards."

Duan swallowed, and decided, having risked Kor's wrath, he might as well continue. "Sir, I would really rather not."

Kor frowned. "I have grown rather fond of you, Duan. Aside from that, I would prefer not to have to train a replacement for you. If you will not accept guards, then I shall have you and your wife moved into the palace. There are more than enough rooms restored for you to have a suite." This solution seemed to please him mightily, and Duan's heart plummeted. Whatever small voice he might have left among his people would disappear completely if he were to move into the palace.

Kor, completely caught up in his plan, continued. "Yes, that is the perfect idea. That way, not only will you be protected, but you will be readily available to me. Ruenn would appreciate the company, and it would put an end to this ridiculous and dangerous traipsing all over town. . . ."

Duan stood, wincing as it jogged his shoulder. "Lord, I beg of you. Don't . . ."

Kor stopped and peered at him. "Well. That distresses you rather more, doesn't it?" He sighed, and clasped his hands behind his back again. "Duan, I do not wish to upset you more than absolutely necessary, but I will not have my ablest councilor, and my best voice among the Iridelli people, being hounded by riffraff. I must do *something*." He pursed his lips. "I could move you in here, will you or not."

Later, Duan would acknowledge the strangeness of this conversation, but for now, having found his courage, he realized he couldn't lose it again so easily. He held the Draconian's eyes.

"Yes, sir, you could."

Kor stared at him a long moment and Duan knew his tail had gone rigid enough to cut through the tension in the room like a blade. But he also knew the Draconian admired courage, often capriciously pardoning convicted Iridelli he thought had acted in some obscurely admirable fashion.

It seemed this principle was at work again. "As you wish. I will do nothing for now. If there is a repeat of this occurrence, however, I will be forced to act. I cannot have rabble attacking my most valuable councilors with impunity. You do understand, don't you, Duan?"

Duan, relief overwhelming him, dropped his eyes. "Yes, sir." He glanced up and his eyes locked with golden ones that regarded him with a mixture of irritation and surprised admiration.

Uncomfortable with both, he changed the subject. "Sir, why did you call me?"

Kor threw his head back and laughed. "I completely forgot. Great news, Duan. We have deciphered the inscriptions on the ruins. The secret—we have discovered the secret of the portals!"

• • •

Kor's exultation was short lived. What had seemed to be the key to the mystery of the portals turned out to be nothing more than a map leading to further ruins. In growling frustration, Kor redoubled his efforts, setting Iridelli crews to work night and day, digging the hitherto unknown temple out of the side of a mountain. This had the twofold effect of increasing his irritability and aggravating the city's unrest. Duan was certain it also led to the first assassination attempt.

During one of Kor's promenades through the square, "to take the city's moods," as he said, a bomb exploded not ten paces from where he stood. It wounded three of his guards, and killed an Iridelli merchant and two of her customers. Kor, enraged, had ordered a roundup of everyone suspected to be a member of any of the underground bands, and, after a summary tribunal, presided over their executions personally.

•••

"One of our primary functions on Iridel, citizens, is to restore and maintain order." His speech was being broadcast throughout the city on hastily erected viewscreens. He would have every Iridelli witness the manifest consequences of defiance. "Order we were well on our way to achieving."

His silver gray face, blown up to many times life size, was grave, his voice reproachful. "Are your children not being fed? Are your homes not being rebuilt? Is not the city being restored to its former beauty?" He spoke Iridelli, to ensure complete understanding, and his rich, cultured voice enunciated the liquid words as if born to them.

"I will forgive this barbaric mistake. For a mistake it was, I believe. A mistake born of fear, of impatience, of cowardice. This world will be great again, a world to be proud of, but I cannot do it alone, Iridel." His voice rang. "We must work together, for the good of all. Do not let a few malcontents blind you to the glorious future just on our horizon."

The screen resolved into the rows of men, hands bound before them, standing in the palace courtyard. Behind them, on a dais, stood the viceroy, flanked by helmeted guards and the Covenant Council. Kor's voice floated across the scene, and the Draconian soldiers raised their laser rifles to their shoulders.

"Harsh is our justice, yes. But swift. Imperial law calls for those convicted of murder to die over three days, by fire. I am not a monster." He paused for effect. "I hereby commute the sentence to death by laser."

He narrowed his eyes, and the watching crowd murmured. "No one may disrupt the order without paying the price. For the murder of your fellow citizens, by my command, and the command of the Covenant Council, the price these men will pay is their lives. No one escapes justice."

He raised one gauntleted fist over his head, holding it there until the very stones underfoot seemed to quiver with foreboding, and let it fall. The soldiers fired, the lasers flashed, searing Iridelli eyes, piercing Iridelli bodies. The bound men fell, twitching. "No one."

Duan turned away. The third man in the row had been Coret, round accusing eyes searing into Duan's soul. Duan would take those eyes to his grave.

• • •

The city moved into fall, the burning heat pushing down on the gleaming new buildings like a brutal hand, trying to grind them all into the earth. Tempers were short, but stifled, all warily guarding their words, and even their thoughts, for fear of reprisal. Iridelli scurried about their business, eyes flicking back and forth, always aware of impending danger. Draconians held tightly to their laser rifles, and watched every Iridelli man, woman, and child with suspicion. It was a lull pregnant with dangerous expectation, everyone waiting to see who would cause the next uproar.

Duan watched over his shoulder as much as everyone else, perhaps more so. Obsequious merchants

eyed him, and he read accusation in their eyes.
Draconian guards observed his approach and he saw
suspicion on their faces. His wife's eyes seemed to
reproach him. Coret's eyes followed him everywhere,
even into sleep. He performed his duties indifferently,
his body present in council chambers but his mind
rehearsing arguments he could have used to stop the
execution. He played out the scene a thousand times,
standing before the viceroy, his eloquence moving the
Draconian to mercy. He rehashed the unsaid words until
they were written in every line on his face, in every tense
slash of his tail. He went through the day listlessly, his
mind and heart aching with remorse for a tragedy he
might have been able to avert. In the end, he knew there
was nothing he could have done, but he throbbed with
the knowledge he should have *tried*.

When the underground finally approached him, he
felt a relief so profound it was spiritual. The representa-
tive met him in one of the small taverns that catered to
the harried Covenant Government near the Governor's
Palace and the viceroyalty. Duan sat alone at a small
table, and he recognized the man for what he was as
soon as he set eyes on him.

Garbed as richly as Duan if not better, the man seated
himself with a flourish and eyed him through obsidian
orbs.

"You aren't surprised."

Duan shrugged. "I knew it was only a matter of time.
Of anyone alive, I am in the best position to help you,
after all."

The man smiled, as coldly as any Draconian. "Not
quite *anyone*."

Duan cleared his throat. "She never leaves the palace
grounds."

The man hushed him, looking about. Duan smiled back, exactly, if he had but known it, like Kor.

"If anyone in here was going to run to the viceroy, don't you think it would be me?"

The other shrugged. "We took a risk. One never knows, these days, just how a person feels about the current state of affairs."

Duan stopped smiling. "How one feels is irrelevant to what must be done." He met the other's eyes squarely.

They regarded each other in perfect understanding. Duan, being one of the viceroy's personal staff, had unlimited credit at this tavern, so they drank bittersweet winter wine at Kor's expense to seal the pact.

• • •

Having made the decision to act, the accusing eyes ceased to haunt him, and he went about his duties with a surprising lightness of spirit. It would not end the occupation, he knew, but he was not thinking of freeing his people. He was thinking of freeing his soul . . . and his much sullied honor. He could look himself in the eye again, and stand straight, knowing that hundreds of deaths, and one in particular, would be avenged. He would be able to lay them to rest, and if he died for it, so much the better. He would be given a day's warning, time enough to send Lien out of the city. He would kiss her goodbye and smile into her warm brown eyes and know he had, at the last, been worthy of her love.

There was one person whose eyes he'd thought he would be unable to meet, but when it came down to it, Kor admired courage. Duan had no doubt, if their positions had been reversed, he would have struck long ago, and part of the contempt with which Kor and his fellow Draconians regarded their Iridelli subjects came from the Iridelli's very passivity. Certainly, had the Empire been met with open resistance, they would have slaughtered the untrained and unarmed Iridelli, but they would have respected them more for it. He met Kor's golden eyes steadily, never flinching.

This was fortunate for him, indeed, as the viceroy seemed to require Duan's presence more and more as the days turned and the slow-moving moons passed beyond view. Duan knew winter would soon slow the excavation of the caves, Kor's burning obsession. Duan realized now that Kor must have sought the secret to the ruins even before he landed, must have hoped for this all along. He was too ambitious to be satisfied with living on a remote planet, uninvolved in the great doings of the Empire. Duan might not fully understand the intricate maneuverings for power that accompanied ambition in the scheme-ridden imperial court, but he knew Rogan Kor, Commander of the Fourth Draconian Fleet, Imperial Viceroy of Iridel, had gambled his career on this one hope—that he could unravel the mystery of the portals. Duan rather hoped he would succeed before he died.

It seemed his wish was to be fulfilled when Kor called him to the palace on the first blustery day of winter. Meeting him excitedly in the library, Kor dragged Duan out to his armored flitter, barely giving Duan time to strap himself in before roaring off. Duan could not imagine what was so important that Kor would leave without guards, and wondered if the underground had decided to act on its own. Luring Kor out with some pretext, they could easily shoot the flitter out of the sky, or blow it up. Duan's worries were groundless and when Duan saw how many Draconian soldiers directed the Iridelli laborers at the site, he knew Kor was in no danger today.

But the administrator of the excavation met his commander with apprehension. "Sir, I am not certain this is a good idea. We don't know how stable that cave is or if there are any booby traps. We found several laid in the outer caves."

Kor was in a fire of impatience. "Nonsense. I am just as capable of disarming traps as any of my men, and there hasn't been any seismic activity in this region in years, if your reports are accurate."

"They are, they are, but, sir, the traps. Let me send in a few—" he stopped and eyed Duan. Obviously, he had been about to recommend sending in expendable Iridelli workers, to disarm—or trip—any traps. The officer was aware that *this* Iridelli had the viceroy's favor, however, possibly more than he did. Duan refused to think about how many of his people had died to bring them to this point. He returned the officer's gaze coolly.

Kor scoffed. "I said I would be the first to view this treasure, and first I shall be." He started toward the slender ladder that gave access to the narrow cave mouth. Climbing the first rungs, he shot a challenging look over his armored shoulder. "Coming, Duan?"

Duan twitched at his hindering robes, wishing Kor had warned him they would be climbing ladders and traipsing around rocky caves. Kor's form-fitting armor allowed much more ease of movement, but Duan finally removed his outer mantle and threw it over his shoulders. He shivered in his thin tights and under-tunic, but exertion soon warmed him.

The entrance to the cave was heavily carved with elaborate inscriptions and Duan found himself catching

Kor's excitement. He shivered from more than the wind which teasingly whisked and whistled around them.

"No'riendalya. Arnihm al'porya," Kor read. He had studied the ancient writings as diligently as the historians. "Those who enter, beware. The universe unfolds."

Taking deep breaths, they entered. Illumination from the hand-held beam lantern Kor brought only fell a few paces in front of them, and Kor had to advise him of low rock formations and jagged upthrusts. Duan decided the ancients must have been damnably short, if the whole cave system was this low. It never occurred to him to wonder that Kor took the lead, seeming quite content to warn Duan of the hazards of the journey, few that they were.

By the time the passage opened up, and Duan could stand straight, his back ached from the hunched posture and he was certain Kor's had to be worse, being the taller of the two. Straightening, he nearly ran into the Draconian's broad shoulders. He had stopped in awe.

Before them, catching and refracting the light from the beam lantern, was a wonder of nature. Crystalline formations shone on every surface. Extrusions hung from a ceiling high above, and grew, it seemed, from the very walls. The crystal begged to be touched. Duan drew a deep breath, and, without thinking, stepped forward, hand outstretched. A viselike hand gripped his arm.

"Wait," growled Kor, crouching to pick up a fallen piece of crystal. Motioning a chastened Duan back to the passage, he tossed the chip at the crystal formation before them.

There was no warning. With a roar loud enough to stir the very mountain itself, the wondrous crystal ceiling crashed down. The fall of crystal and rock seemed to go on forever, echoing in the chamber. It was some time before the dust settled and the reverberations in Duan's ears faded enough to risk a look. Coughing and spluttering, they cautiously stepped forward. The massive cave was completely filled with debris, the crystal losing its luminosity in the dust.

"The ancients guard their secrets well," Duan murmured.

Kor's face was filled with bitter disappointment. "Indeed. Too well." With a sigh, he gazed on the rock pile. "It will take them weeks to clear this, if there is even any point in it. This is the last cave. The rest of the mountain is solid. Whatever lay beyond that may well be out of reach forever." His eyes dulled, and he turned back to the narrow passageway.

Duan gazed around the eerily silent chamber, and turned to follow Kor before the light from the hand lantern faded. In that second, as his sharp Iridelli eyes adjusted to the natural darkness, he noticed a darkness that didn't belong.

"Wait," he called, stepping heedlessly over stones and rubble. Kor came up behind him, curious. He shone the light where Duan pointed. "There! There's some sort of . . . opening."

Pressing forward, Iridelli and Draconian stepped together into another, previously hidden, chamber.

Kor turned to Duan and clasped his shoulders in a painful grip. His gray face glowed with triumph as he shone the beam light on an intricately carved portal. "You've found it, Duan! You've found it!"

"What is it?" Duan asked, his voice hushed, wondrous.

Kor's voice rang. "It's a portal—a portal for people instead of ships. It's a portal!"

•••

Instead of being an answer, the portal became an ongoing question. This did not in any way diminish Kor's triumph in the discovery, however, and he delegated more and more duties to Duan and his officers and councilors, spending his days in the hastily erected prefab office at the base of the cliff. He devoted all of his time to deciphering this new puzzle, to the point that Duan was assigned his own flitter, in order to deliver reports to Kor on site.

The furor was not limited to the viceroy and the Draconians. Indeed, among certain Iridelli circles, the discovery of the portal fueled nationalistic sentiments. Iridelli took the portal's existence to mean they were descended from the ancient race that had built the portals. How could such an ancient culture, capable of so much, allow themselves to be ruled by an offworld, upstart race? Never mind that there was no proof that the Iridelli were actually related to the Builders, or the well-known fact that the Draconian race was the oldest on record. The Draconians might well be the heirs to the galactic legacy of the Builders, if they weren't already by default. The Iridelli ignored this possibility, however, in favor of more inspiring ones.

Duan began spending his days in the newly abandoned library in the Governor's Palace, pouring over statements and reports and all the myriad details it took to manage a planetary state, even a small one. He had all but forgotten his pact with the underground in the excitement. They, however, had not.

He was not expecting the summons, but when he received it, he did not hesitate to make his way through the city to the assigned meeting place. In the abandoned warehouse, Duan shivered, and wondered if it was some sort of trap. Had Kor's security people, so intent on rooting out the underground, decoded the elaborate set of signs and signals used by the resistance? Even now, were Draconian security officers making their way through the crowded streets to apprehend him, and drag him before the viceroy in chains? Many of Kor's senior staff would be only too pleased to show Iridelli faithlessness, blaming several recent terrorist acts on Kor's perceived laxness.

The face that appeared in the shadows, however, was reassuringly furred. The agent from the tavern, so many months ago—a lifetime ago—greeted him with the new arm clasp favored by nationalists.

"Are you ready?"

"I have been for months," Duan responded shortly.

The man raised his almost invisible brows. "Certain things had to be in place before we could act. We will rid ourselves of not just our good viceroy, but the entire pernicious Draconian presence."

Duan shook his head. "You are dreaming, man. You are a fool. We can kill them all, and it will change nothing. They will just send more. They are unlimited, friend, while we are not."

The underground man looked smug, his black eyes gleaming darkly. "We have friends off-world as well as enemies, Duan. Don't be so quick to dismiss our efforts." He cocked his head. "If you don't believe your action will make any difference, why are you doing it?"

Duan stared into the shadows. "Let's just say it is a debt I owe."

The other shrugged. "As you wish." He pulled a small metallic bundle out of his tunic. "This is a timed discharge device. We know you take reports to the

viceroy at his camp just after high noon every day. This
will detonate one hour after noon tomorrow. Be gone
from there before then, friend. Take your flitter and your
wife and flee far and fast. The city will not be safe for
you after that."

Duan held the palm-sized wrought metal ball in his
hand. It was cold to the touch. "It will do the job?"

The man snorted. "It will destroy everything within
two hundred spans."

Duan stared. "So small to be so powerful," he
murmured.

The underground agent smiled grimly, folding
Duan's fingers over the bomb. "A fitting metaphor for
the Iridelli, don't you think?"

• • •

The bomb fit easily into an inner pocket of his
mantle, and he struggled to forget its presence as he
returned to the palace. His hands shook as he seated
himself at Kor's desk. He had been using it steadily for
weeks now, and what would once have seemed brazen
foolhardiness no longer seemed even remarkable.

Today it felt too big for him, too cold.

Duan had always been the gentlest of men, never
striking his wife, or an animal, or anything else. He, who
found it difficult even to raise his voice in anger, would
kill a man tomorrow. *Not a man*, he told himself. *An
oppressor, a butcher. A murderer.* He felt a sharp pain in his
hands—*hands about to be covered in blood*—and realized
he was gripping a datacube so hard it dug into his
palms. He threw it from him.

He heard a gasp from the doorway and jumped, his
hand going to the pocket where the bomb lay. He

quelled the urge to run when he saw it was an Iridelli face staring at him, not a Draconian. A female face, to his surprise—the very pretty, very worried female face of Kor's mistress.

"Councilor," she said hesitantly.

"Lady Ruenn." It was a title of respect for one generally considered deserving of none. The market gossips branded her a worse traitor than Duan, a harlot, willing to sell herself for Draconian riches.

Duan knew differently, however, as she would not be standing in the doorway to the viceroy's office, her delicate brow raised questioningly, if not for him. He tried out a smile and found it not impossible.

She stepped inside, padding quietly on her clean, but still bare, feet. Servants' gossip said she never wore shoes, and certainly, if the viceroy denied her nothing, as rumor also whispered, then who was he to question?

"I . . . I—Are you all right?"

Duan wondered if she feared he might throw a datacube at *her*. "I think my lunch did not agree with me," he managed to grit out.

She nodded hesitantly, and came forward. He had only seen her a few times over the last months, as she kept to Kor's private chambers, one place he had little reason to go. Occasionally he had seen her about, however, arranging fresh flowers in different rooms, or speaking quietly to the servants. The first such time had been a shock; she was quite the most beautiful girl he had ever seen, her rich golden brown hair still a mane, only tamed with beads and braids in the latest fashion. Her markings were exquisite, highlighting her enormous brown eyes and delicate features. Kor robed her in only the finest silks and softest linens, of course, but she had been pretty in rags. He had flushed with embarrassment for staring then, and was afraid he fared no better now.

She was regarding him steadily, obviously giving him time to recover his composure, and when it appeared he had, she tried again. "I was wondering if you would do something for me."

"For you, Lady, of course."

She smiled dazzlingly, and held out a small datacube. "I know you are going out to the site tomorrow, and I was wondering if you would take this to Ro—— the viceroy for me. There is to be a general staff meeting, and he hates them so. I thought I might send him some words of encouragement."

Now, a small voice whispered in his head, *now you know why they chose tomorrow.* "I would be honored."

She smiled again, and sat in the chair opposite the desk, curling her legs up under her. Duan supposed he should not be surprised at her familiarity. After all, this was *her* home.

She looked about and her face fell. "It seems like it's been years since you found the portal." She sighed, fingering the 'cube. "I never thought I would say it, but I miss him when he's gone."

That startled an honest response out of Duan. "You do?"

She cocked her head. "Don't you?"

"I see him more often than you do," Duan covered, wary. He couldn't deny her eyes, though, and dropped his. "I—I have always felt responsible for my part in your . . . current position. I have always wanted to apologize for that."

She nodded, her face solemn. "You saved my honor and possibly my life that day. What those two had in mind for me . . ." She shuddered, but her chin lifted, still defiant. "I know there are those who say I should have slit my own throat before I let a Draconian touch me."

Duan was surprised by her candor, but he owed her at least his time to listen. "Many have suffered much worse than I and for much less. He is kind to me, and quite gentle. Patient with my"—her lips curved in a fond smile—"dreadfully unsophisticated ways."

Duan swallowed his response and she continued. "He is not the monster most think he is. He is harsh because his people are harsh. He is alone here, exiled among aliens, estranged from his own kind who are either jealous of his power, or distrusting of his policies." Her lilting voice turned fierce. "His is a dark and lonely place, and he has so few points of light. Your friendship is one, and I flatter myself that I am another."

Duan could not keep back the short bark of bitter laughter. "Friendship? I am a convenient tool, nothing more. I value my saw when I need to fell a tree and I treat it with care, lest it break and no longer be useful to me. But do I think of it as a friend? Hardly."

Her eyes were dark and grave. "You are wrong, Councilor. He speaks often of how you steady him. Would you want your saw there, on the most important day of your life? He was so excited to call you that day, the day they found the cave. You know what that means to him."

Duan looked down at the desk, unable to bear the reproach in her eyes. Like Lien's, they were all too expressive of that particular sentiment. Lien, *his* steadying force.

His words came from the heart, his bitter, bitter heart. "He may be fond of me—of *us*, Lady—but when he is recalled, when the Empire decides his particular talents are needed elsewhere, he will soon forget us, whereas we will never be the same. He destroys our lives so casually, and his is unchanged."

She shook her head ruefully and sighed, her eyes distant. "We are such hypocrites. When we were starving, we ate his food. When we were cold, we begged him to warm our homes. And then when we learned the price of salvation, we cried 'foul' and tried to drive him away. And now we castigate him for defending himself."

She stood and cocked her head, her rich brown eyes as deep as the night sky.

"He asks my opinion, you know, and sometimes I even think he listens. I comfort myself with that thought when I catch the market gossip." Her eyes were sad, but he saw the strength there that made a shaking young girl face and tame the conqueror of her world.

She stood and pressed the datacube into his hand, folding his fingers over it. He stared at his hand, thinking of another small metal object pressed so in his palm.

"Lady," Duan said, and he meant it, "I have to ask . . . were you really innocent of stealing from that soldier's pack that day?"

She smiled at him brilliantly, a laugh bubbling out of her. "Of course not. He had half a loaf of bread, Councilor, and I was hungry." She gave him a wink and a wave before slipping out.

Duan sat in Kor's chair, behind his massive carved desk, and watched the setting sun wash the walls in shades of blood.

• • •

"Duan." Kor clapped his shoulder in greeting, giving him a tight, exultant grin.

"You are just in time." The Draconian's eyes were alive with anticipation. "We will move the portal today."

He led Duan away from the landing site, guiding him through the maze of workers and tents and prefab buildings which gave the once barren plain the look of a thriving village. Kor's long legs carried him faster than Duan's could, and he paused impatiently for Duan to catch up, then peered at him. "Duan, you look like death. I am overworking you, aren't I, with all this uproar."

He couldn't look any worse than the Draconian. Kor's normally silver gray skin was a pale wraith of its usual shade. Duan had never known or wanted to know the Draconian's age, but he had known the Draconian was young for his position. The golden eyes, feverishly bright with excitement, were shadowed now, and the deep lines radiating from them aged him.

Duan ducked his head, afraid of what those keen eyes would see, and brought out the datacube. Kor took it, his brows questioning.

"It's a message from, ah, Lady Ruenn."

Kor smiled a very private smile and closed his fist around the 'cube, secreting it in his belt. They had reached Kor's temporary office, and he gestured with a long arm, describing the busy scene.

"We have been unable to defuse whatever substance in the rock inhibits our scanners, so we had to move the portal away from the energy field. It proved challenging." He pulled out a tall bottle with two small goblets, pouring high.

He handed one to Duan, whose startlement must have shown, because Kor chuckled. "It's Draconian spiritwine, my last bottle until we get a supply ship out here." He regarded Duan thoughtfully. "It's stronger than you're used to, so go easy."

Duan stared down at the rich amber liquid and decided the entire bottle would not be enough for him to "go easy" this day.

Kor was oblivious to the tumult in his councilor's soul, however, and continued. "It has taken ten days to find a way to move the portal without damaging it, but we are almost ready to begin."

His eyes lit up, and he held the glass high. "To success."

Duan drained his glass, not even flinching as the fiery liquid burned a trail to his stomach.

Kor regarded him with approval, and Duan felt hot shame rise in his throat like bile. *What am I doing? I sit here, smiling and drinking, when I am planning to kill him in less than an hour.* He set the glass hastily on the field table, before Kor could notice his shaking hands.

Kor, when he killed, did so openly, honestly, looking his enemy in the eye. It was an essential difference between them, and a clear indicator of the gulf between him and the Draconian. Duan would never have Kor's easy ability to end another's life if it suited him to do so. For Duan, killing might be necessary, but it would never be easy.

Kor was eyeing him oddly. "I have a lot of work today, Duan. Do you have anything for me?"

Duan swallowed a bark of laughter, and began to recite the council's decisions for the last few days. As his mouth shaped the words on the paper in front of him, other words, unbidden, echoed in Duan's head. *"If we could figure out how they made the portals . . . think of the power."* That was what he was doing. He was stopping this man before he had so much power he became unstoppable. He was laying to rest the outraged spirits of his people's dead.

He placed a small bundle of datacubes on Kor's desk, to be perused at leisure. The viceroy would never know it contained one other item.

Kor had spoken the words himself:

"Harsh is our justice, yes. . . . No one escapes justice."

•••

When he was finished with his reports, Duan rose. He was suddenly awkward, for he knew, if the Draconian didn't, that he would never seen this man again.

He paused in the doorway, looking back. Kor was already bent over the reports of food shipments, building necessities, and labor unrest. For the first time Duan saw what Ruenn must have seen. Not the alien silvered skin, or the hairless hands, or the golden slit-pupiled eyes. Not the armor, or the lasgun strapped to the strong thigh. He saw a ruler, by military decree, of a world not his own and the toll the position had taken on him. He saw a man with a heavy load of responsibility and very little resources with which to work. He saw a man who, from the moment his ships had appeared in the sky above the city, overtaking the sun, had been the focus of Duan's very existence.

"Sir, I—" The words caught in his throat.

Kor raised an inquiring brow. "Yes?"

"I—I never thanked you for that cloth you sent my wife that day," he finished lamely, his eyes saying so much more.

Kor seemed to understand. He nodded his dusky head gravely. "It was my pleasure, Duan."

Duan fled as if pursued by a demon.

•••

"I have grown rather fond of you, Duan." Kor's voice,
now indulgent, now exasperated, rose in Duan's ears,
followed him back to his flitter. *"Duan, whatever am I to
do with you? I can't let you alone for a moment."*

And from that first fateful night, *"Duan, here, wouldn't
hurt me. Would you, Duan?"*

As he climbed in the cold metal craft, he heard Lady
Ruenn: *"You are wrong, Councilor. He speaks often of how
you steady him. . . . He was so excited to call you that day, the
day they found the cave. You know what that means to him."*

Duan put his hands to his ears, as if that would shut
out the voices.

"I do not understand Iridelli, Duan, truly I don't."

I don't understand us, either, Lord, he cried back, soundlessly. *I don't understand how I can hate you so much and feel
this pain for your death. How?*

He knew the time, knew there was a quarter of an
hour until the bomb detonated. He saw, without seeing,
other flitters landing around him, and disembarking
Draconian officers making their way toward the prefab
office where Kor held court, unawares. He saw the
Iridelli workers backing off, unobtrusively moving out
of range. *They were warned,* he thought dully.

Duan knew he should fire up the flitter, flee to the
city, collect Lien and fly far, far away. There were small
villages along the coast where they could lose themselves, and start over. He would send the flitter to the
bottom of the sea, and they could pretend this last year
had never been. They could pretend it had never left its
mark on their souls.

Visions rose in his mind, visions of hunger and cold and misery. Visions from before Kor came. Once again, Iridelli would starve, trying to be something they had not been for over a hundred years. They knew too much now to be satisfied with the complacent, rustic, stagnant lives they had lived before the Empire came. Intentionally or not, Kor had broadened Iridelli vision, had awakened them to the universe around them. There was nothing to go back to.

"I will forgive this barbaric mistake. For a mistake it was, I believe. A mistake born of fear, of impatience, of cowardice." Kor's pronouncement at the execution, his voice smooth, refined, compassionate, resonated in Duan's head.

"You can forgive, Lord, but I can't," he whispered. "I can't."

He put his head in his hands and wept.

• • •

Duan crouched over the still, armored form, afraid even to touch it. He had never done so when Kor lived, and it seemed wrong to do so now. Around him, armored Draconian and unarmored Iridelli bodies alike lay like so many discarded toys. He stared with numb regret at the corpses, the knowledge that he had caused their deaths a dull pain in his chest. He didn't stir, even when he heard the shouts approaching. The Iridelli laborers, those who had not fled, returned to view the aftermath.

He hoped it satisfied them. He hoped they would never forget the sight of so many dead. He never would.

He rose, feeling old, old as the mountain before him, the silent stones bearing silent witness to his crime. Behind him, he heard a groan. The thought came to him that if any of the Draconians lived, he should stay with them, to make sure the Iridelli workers didn't slaughter them in their weakened state. He saw several armored bodies stir, and picked his way over those who didn't. As an afterthought, he knelt by one Draconian body, limbs missing, and pulled his lasgun out of its holster. The soldier wouldn't need it anymore, and Duan might, to fight off his own people.

"Planning to use that on me?" He heard the voice behind him with disbelief. Turning, he saw a Draconian struggle to rise. He held a hand to his bent head, obscuring his face, but Duan would know that voice anywhere. His heart, the heart he had thought died with the blast, began to pound fiercely.

"Sir? Lord—"

Kor sat up, shook his head to clear it, and wiped a hand across his face, rubbing his jaw.

Duan had never seen a sight so beautiful as that silver gray face. Dark Draconian blood ran from a wound on his head, and dirt and dust ran with it, but he was alive, gloriously alive. Duan dropped the laser and fell to his knees. He held out his hands, as if Kor were made of flame, and he would warm himself.

• • •

"They have it under control, now," Kor said to him, as they stood surveying the ruins of the excavation site. He watched the stretchers, guided by Iridelli drafted as medics, line up near the remains of his office. The blast had destroyed even the communication terminal, so Kor had sent one of his men, suffering only from cuts and scrapes, to the nearest Draconian outpost for help. Even injured, he held command easily, ordering all who could walk to tend to the wounded first, impartially, and then repair the comlink with the city and his orbiting ships. He stood staring at the rubble that was all that was left of the portal, dreams smashed to dust.

"Over thirty of my men killed, and almost a hundred of yours," he said, his eyes on the broken stone. He looked strange, to Duan, with the white bandage around his head, strange and vulnerable. Duan could not meet his eyes.

"If I hadn't answered your call, received your warning, I would be among them," he mused. He turned wondering golden eyes on his companion. "How did you know?"

Duan's mouth worked, the excuses rose to his lips. He could say something about signs and hints and timing. He could lie, and Kor would believe him. They could go on as before, with only Duan's heart to know his guilt.

He stood, shoulders bowed, head bent, and said nothing.

Kor's eyes, like lasers, seared his mind, his heart, pulled out his secrets and held them up to the light of day. After a long moment, he straightened, and his hand twitched over his holstered laser.

"I see."

Duan knew his reckoning was upon him. He would die now. He was not afraid. It would be a relief. It would be a rest from the image of those bodies, broken and bleeding by his hand, that spread out before him.

To his great disappointment, Kor did not kill him. He said, very quietly, "You have destroyed far more than you know. But you warned me, and so saved my life, along with most of my men. For *that* you will live."

Duan slowly raised his head, expecting to see hatred and contempt in the alien eyes. He could have dealt with those. He did not know how to deal with sympathy.

Kor smiled grimly. "I suspect you will punish yourself far better than I ever could for what you have done this day."

• • •

The city was on fire. The wounded soldier shouted his news before his damaged flitter even landed. At the precise time the bomb exploded in Kor's camp, several other bombs, preset, detonated all over the city. The granary, the merchants' square, and, most notably, the Governor's Palace were blown to bits, killing over two thousand farmers, merchants, patrons, and government employees. In the ensuing panic, accompanied by screams of terror, the citizens stampeded, trampling to death hundreds more. The remaining Draconian soldiers entrenched themselves in their barracks, and fired wildly on any who dared approach. Iridelli were rioting. It was the insurrection all over again.

Duan stood rooted to the ground, shock and horror freezing his face into a grotesque mask. His eyes flew to Kor, who gaped at his man, unable to believe what the wounded soldier kept repeating. *I did not know,* he cried voicelessly. *I did not know* . . . but he had. He had known they planned something, even if he hadn't known what.

Kor grabbed his arm and hauled him viciously aboard his armored skimmer, as his remaining unwounded men piled into the rest. "You will come with me. You will see what you have wrought," he vowed, over the roaring engines. Duan could only shake his head, not in refusal to come, but in refusal to admit this reality. Kor did not speak to him on the ride back, conferring with his officers about possible plans, for which Duan was grateful. His mouth was too dry to speak, his mind too numb to form words.

As they sped over the rolling terrain, once barren and burnt, now green and thriving, Duan could not admit the horror he had been party to. He saw peaceful farms, and collective or not, they were a good he could grasp. He held tight to that vision of agrarian serenity, and blocked his mind to anything else.

It was worse than they had been told, a vision out of his nightmares, a vision out of the insurrection. Fires raged, and people ran and screamed and burned. With grand disregard for the flitter's vulnerability, Kor sent it raging over the street outside the palace, he and his men firing wildly to drive back the howling mindless mob. By the time they beat them back enough to liberate the barracks, protected by covering laser fire from within, Duan had managed to make his escape.

•••

It took three days to regain control of the city; the Draconians had to fight not only panicked civilians but bands of armed and organized resistance. Even the most hardened Draconian soldiers recoiled from the ensuing blood bath, but once roused, the Draconians displayed a splendid wrath. Once they had pinned down the location of the resistance leaders, an enormous flaring beam of light shot from the sky, from the orbiting cruisers, like the wrath of the gods, searing a path of destruction from one end of the city to the other. It drove the mob into shelter, and the resistance back into hiding, but it cleared the streets.

In armored hovercraft, bristling with weapons, Kor's troops imposed order with an iron fist. Martial law locked down the entire city, mewing Iridelli in their homes, shops, and whatever other shelter they could find. They did not even venture forth for food. They were more terrified of the patrols than they were of hunger. The imperial troops had orders to shoot on sight anyone they deemed suspicious, and with the current temper of the city any Iridelli was deemed suspicious.

Duan was aware of none of it.

It had taken him several hours, after he had leapt from the flitter, to reach the house. He had avoided the areas with the most violence, keeping to back streets and alleys, jumping the fire lines. At one point he ran into a band of blood-crazed Iridelli, shouting and chanting slogans and waving stolen lasguns. They brandished scorched imperial armor like grotesque trophies. He fell in, yelling his throat raw, until he could slip away. He finally crawled into the city's drainage water system, and he realized, distantly, how they had planted the bombs.

Amazingly, his house still stood, an oasis of peace in a sea of chaos, and he wept to see it, nearly crawling the last few paces to his door. He had flung it open, expecting Lien to rush into his arms in relief. When she did not answer his calls, he ran from room to room, weeping, searching. "Lien, Lien, *Lien* . . ."

He found her body on a pole a few paces from the house, her throat slit, "Traitor" scrawled in her own blood across her chest.

• • •

He did not think of the danger when he crawled back into the gutters, hours or days later. He dimly hoped the resistance would not find him and kill him yet, though. If his life ended now, he would never find rest. But if he lived, if he could make it to his destination, he could exact his revenge. He could kill the one responsible, and end the pain, once and for all. Then he could join Lien in the land of the dead. His heart was there already.

●●●

When he emerged from the sewer, he poked his head carefully above the street and found it silent and deserted, as he'd hoped. The fires were gone, dowsed by Draconian chemicals, but a lingering acrid odor gave silent witness to their presence. He slithered away, ducking into shadows left by piles of burnt rubble, moving from one pool of darkness to another, making his way stealthily to his destination.

When it stood before him, the enormity of the disaster washed over him, as he gazed on the blackened walls of the Governor's Palace. It was silhouetted against the night sky like a skeleton, clawing fingers reaching toward the stars. That's where it belongs, he thought. It never belonged here.

He crept through the deserted halls, stepping carefully over exposed beams showing through gaping holes, until he reached the doors to the library, hanging crookedly from their hinges. That they hung at all surprised him; they crumbled at his touch. He paused, letting his eyes adjust to the darkness.

"So. You came. I knew you would."

The voice, the voice Duan knew so well, came out of the darkness like the whisper of a blade. A candle flared. Kor leaned against a wall at the far end of the room, casually, long arms resting on his knees.

Duan stepped in. He wondered that, even now, the Draconian could make him feel like an errant child.

"How could you know?" he snarled.

"Because *I* came. Because you could do nothing else. Because you and I are bound, Duan, beyond race, beyond blood. Because we are alike."

From under his sooty robes, Duan pulled a laser rifle, abandoned in the sewer during the chaos. It felt familiar in his hands. The first time he had held one had been to protect this man. He leveled the rifle, holding it so the light reflected off its lethal black barrel.

Kor chuckled, a grating rasping laugh, and raised one hand so Duan could clearly see the lasgun he held aimed straight at him.

"You see?" He rose stiffly, and gestured. "There is no need for these, I think," he said, laying his laser on the floor. Holding Duan's eyes, he kicked it away.

"I am nothing like you," Duan hissed, and kept tight grip on his rifle.

Kor chuckled again, and crossed his arms over his chest, leaning easily against the wall.

"Oh, we are more alike than you will ever admit, my friend. We both wanted what we thought was best for this world. We both killed to achieve it."

"I killed because I had no *choice*." The cry was wrenched from Duan's soul. He began to weep. "You killed because you could. You had the choice. . . ." He couldn't go on, his throat was too raw, and his tail lashed.

A fine, arched brow rose. "Did I? My choices were not free, Duan. No choices are ever free. I thought you understood that."

"You held power of life and death over an entire world! Who could force *you* to do anything?"

The flickering candlelight sent shadows over the hollows in Kor's face, distorting his features.

"Oh, my friend. After months of my company, how could you possibly remain so naive?" He threw his head back and laughed, the sound echoing in the empty chamber.

"I am just a minor part of a vast empire, Duan. Here, my power might have been absolute, but there," he waved an arm vaguely skyward, "I am answerable to superiors as far above me as I was above you."

He stepped away from the wall and Duan tensed, his finger twitching on the trigger. Kor noted it, but merely clasped his hands behind his back and looked up at the ceiling.

"And just as you tried to allay the injury I did your people, I mitigated the harm they would have done this world."

Duan shivered. The first time he had met this man, he had stood in this room and listened to those smooth tones tell him *he* was Iridel's best hope. He remembered orders for labor camps, orders for executions.

"It doesn't matter." Duan's tears had stopped. Strangely, he was not ashamed of showing that weakness before his enemy. He felt cleansed. "None of it matters, now. My world died, because of you. I will take your life in payment."

Kor regarded him solemnly. "I felt the same. I sent men to drag you back here in chains. I would have my revenge, I thought. To my surprise, they brought back—not my faithless councilor, but his wife, her body bloody and mutilated." His voice was very soft. "I saw what they wrote."

Duan began to shake, the laser rifle wobbling in his hands.

"That's when I knew you would come to me."

He bowed his head and sighed, then straightened, his armor creaking.

"Tomorrow a ship will come. I will leave this world—"

Duan was startled. "Leave?"

Kor's voice rasped across Duan's sensitive nerves. "Oh, yes. The message came by subspace this morning. Apparently, mass bombings and ruined portals are not what the High Command meant by 'results.' I am being . . . replaced."

Duan was stunned. He had wanted this, so long ago.

Kor smiled, a sardonic twitch of his lips. "Do not worry about me, Duan. I will regain all I have lost. I have fallen farther than this and yet risen."

Duan straightened, drawing himself up to his full height. The weight of the rifle made up for the stature he lost to the taller Draconian. "You will n-never leave this world." The tears had started again and rolled down his face, making tracks in the downy fur.

Kor held out his arms, his eyes old and sad, like a penitent asking grace. "She was my wife, you know."

"What?"

Kor cocked his bronze and silver head. "Ruenn. I married her months ago. Oh, it would not have been recognized under the Empire, of course, but it made her so happy. I had been building her a house on a distant world, a world far enough from the imperial center that they would never see or care." His arms fell to his sides, and he turned toward the broken, glassless window where the first pale shades of dawn lightened the sky.

"She was killed in the first wave of explosions, fortunately. She did not see the aftermath, what her people and mine did to each other."

His disturbing golden eyes, with their swirling irises and slit pupils, gleaming in the dark, grew before Duan's vision until he could see nothing else.

"Do you see, my friend? You will kill me, avenging your wife, and you will be killed by my men, or will die slowly from starvation, avenging mine. Although you no more caused that bomb to explode than I held the knife. We will be bound still, even in death."

Duan stared at him, at this alien man, ruler no longer, who stood before him unbowed and unflinching, the sorrow of worlds in his eyes, lines of pride and pain engraved on his face . . . and saw himself.

• • •

They came out of the sky like gods. Monstrous birds, the sun gleaming off lethal tapered hulls, wings outstretched. They blocked the sun, at once terrifying and familiar. No one yet living remembered the first time they had come, when they had, indeed, been thought gods. No one remembered a time when Iridel had not been ruled by outworlders. In wonder and terror, those who had said the gods were dead watched the birds disgorge their passengers for this, the last time.

The Empire set about restoring order with ruthless efficiency. The market square was demolished and work started immediately on a fortified citadel, bristling with the latest in weaponry. The collective farms were fenced and gated, and soldiers patrolled the perimeters, lasers always ready. Under heavily armed guard, shackled Iridelli crated up the ruins and sent them off to be studied by the finest minds the Empire could gather.

The Governor's Palace, bloodied and burnt, was razed to the ground and a statue of the Draconian Emperor erected in its place, a testament to power and pride. When the rains came, it seemed the statue wept with the city over which it stood.

No one paid any attention to the smaller bird climbing high as the new ones descended. Aboard the soaring ship, they stood at the viewport, and watched the planet fall away from them with mingled sorrow and regret. No longer ruler and ruled, neither were free. Both had been liberated. As the ancient portal opened, calling with its eternal mystery, one forbidden to stay turned his golden eyes to the vastness of space with impatience, plans for the future swirling in his head. One forbidden to leave turned his dark gaze towards the wonder of space with the first stirring hopes of peace.

OUT OF THE BLUE

Written by
Ron Collins

Illustrated by
Lukasz Laskowski

About the Author

Ron Collins is a husband and father, a basketball fan and an engineer, and is currently trying to learn as much as he can about how the Internet really works. But he also sold a story to Dragon Magazine and another to Mike Resnick's Return of the Dinosaurs anthology. And his published story was "The Disappearance of Josie Andrew," a finalist in L. Ron Hubbard Presents Writers of the Future, Volume XIV. Since then, he has sold several other fantasy and science fiction stories to a number of markets, including Analog. "Out of the Blue" results from an exercise he did for last year's WOTF workshop, and he would like to thank fellow workshopper Lisa Silverthorne for her assistance.

About the Illustrator

Born in Warsaw, Poland, in 1973, Lukasz Laskowski has for the last three years been studying the graphic applications of Macintosh computers, in Riverside, California. In Europe, he studied sculpture, photography, cinematography and major painting and graphics techniques. His goal is to bring the taste of the old school of art into the flavor of modern life.

For a moment, Sara McClintock found it easy to forget they were over fifty kilometers from the Ant Farm's relative safety. The crew worked along the southern edge of Belus Linea, a ragged network of silicate deposits that sluiced through Europa's icy surface with the apparent randomness of an errant river. Jupiter's massive presence dominated the eastern sky and cast a purple orange sheen across the floe. The horizon's razor edge cut through the pitch-black of deep space.

Across the ice, Lin Wi knelt to place a small package. August McGrath, another geologist, stood beside her, his white envirosuit now tinted Jupiter orange.

"Placing the charge," Lin said over the radio, her Oriental accent clipping the words.

"Copy," a voice from Mission Command came from across the ice floe. "Receiver is active."

The package housed a thin dart that, once driven into the ice, would activate a strain gauge, sonar system, and temperature sensor. A transmitter in the dart's tail would pass the data across Europa to scientists waiting at the Ant Farm. Sara carried another of the instruments and walked with Kris Callahan. Fifty meters to their left, Vernon Carey and Mustav Gapato were preparing another package. Combined, the three sensors would analyze the crust's thickness and let scientists develop mining techniques for future missions.

"Go ahead," Lin said as she stepped away from the device.

August hit the plunger.

The charge fired, and the ground shook. The vibration rumbled through Sara's boots, and a silvery plume of ice rose through thin atmosphere with a shape like exhalation from a humpback whale's blowhole.

Then all hell broke loose.

Europa's surface erupted. Silver orange arms of frost rose up like cresting waves, and the surface swirled with scintillating shades of blue. Lin's scream was cut ominously short. Other sounds were too jumbled for Sara to decipher.

The ground crumbled under Sara's feet. She fell, dropping the instrumentation package and hitting the ice ruggedly before sliding out of control on all fours along a downward slope. A vivid blue streak undulated through the ice with a motion that distinctly reminded Sara of a sea snake, circling her and pulsing wildly as she slid.

When the shaking stopped, Sara found herself in dark shadow at the bottom of a depression formed like a giant cereal bowl. Its rounded sides of silicate-impregnated ice loomed overhead, bringing a sudden spike of claustrophobic fear. She checked her suit for damage. No rips or cracks marred the exterior and the electronics seemed functional.

"Hello?" she said, clicking the radio.

The hollow sound of Sara's breathing echoed damply through her suit.

"Hello?" she said again.

● ● ●

That Sara made it to Europa at all was, perhaps, a miracle in itself.

She grew up in Crawford, Nebraska, a town of some five hundred farmers and few million acres of corn—a community that still sang "Amazing Grace" at church and went to neighbors' houses for lunch afterward, a place where her scholarship to Stanford made the front page and her Ph.D. in microbiology gave her instant celebrity.

Sara married Dan before they graduated, then spent three years with the Naval Microbiology Commission before being offered a position studying protoplankton at Sanibel Island. It was a great job. She loved waking up knowing she was going to spend the day on the ocean, fighting currents, tasting salt in the air and feeling the roll of a boat under her feet.

But slowly she realized something was wrong.

While at Stanford, Dan was everything she dreamed of, intelligent with a quirky sense of humor and a seemingly permanent Southern California tan. Once in Florida, he took an engineering job with a small contractor working on the International Space Station. The position turned out to be less than he imagined, and he found himself a continent away from home with a job that didn't interest him and a wife who worked twelve hours a day. He became moody, and Sara suddenly found herself unable to approach him.

The marriage ended badly. Dan used her professional life as a scapegoat throughout the proceedings, belittling her accomplishments and insinuating she had abandoned him.

Her parents wanted her to move back home then, and she almost did. But the idea of retreating to Crawford made her stomach queasy. No one would say

Illustrated by Lukasz Laskowski

anything directly, of course. But news traveled. Comments would be made. Sara hadn't been able to keep her marriage together, and she didn't think she could face the silent accusation and pity she knew would come from people in her hometown.

Instead, she slid further into her work. It was a good job to be alone in, a world where she could disappear under the water and fill her mind with problems that kept the rest of the world at a distance. She dove, and she took samples, and she ran studies. She stayed in Florida most of the time, keeping her life within the comfortable confines of walls she built around herself —only making it home for Christmas and a few special occasions. Slowly, she healed. Three years later Sara came up for air and took an associate professorship at the University of Florida.

That's where she was when the government came looking for scientists to go to Europa. Sara campaigned hard to get Dean Williams to back her nomination. They needed biologists, she argued, and she had kept herself in good physical shape. That she was an unattached female never came up, but was an obvious advantage.

That's how Sara came to be on a lonely sphere of ice orbiting Jupiter with the rest of a crew of twenty-five scientists, living in a connected series of insulated red tents they had immediately dubbed the Ant Farm.

They would be here another thirty standard days. Then they would pile back into the launcher and head for home.

•••

The radio crackled in Sara's ear.

"Uuugh." The voice was male, but she couldn't tell whose.

"Rover One, are you there?" Frederica Jackson at Mission Command said.

"I'm here, but we've run into problems," Vernon replied. As mission commander, Vernon Carey was responsible for the crew. "I still need to assess the situation. Will respond as soon as I have anything useful," he finished.

"Okay, Vernon. Will put Rover Two on standby."

"Roger," Vernon said.

Sara crawled cautiously out of the icy depression. Standing, she looked for Kris. Her partner lay on the ice, her suit shredded, a coppery pool of frozen blood underneath.

Sara's heart clutched and she nearly vomited.

"Oh, God," she whispered. "Oh, God."

"Sara?" Vernon asked from across the floe.

"Yes?" she managed, looking to her left.

Vernon knelt beside Mustav's prone body, glancing over his shoulder toward her. "How is Kris?"

"She's dead."

Vernon's voice dropped to a military pilot's monotone. "Okay, I'm working on Mustav. You check on August and Lin."

"Okay," she said, glad to move away from Kris's body.

The surface ahead looked like the fist of God had punched through it. Boulder-sized chunks of serrated ice jutted upward at awkward angles. Glass-clear shards gleamed from the floe like razor blades. A rainbow of blue and orange and purple floated inside a fog of microscopic ice crystals, a display of physics that would have been beautiful in almost any other circumstance.

"Lin?" she called. "August?"

She found Lin first.

A slab of ice the size of a pickup truck had crushed the lower half of her body. Exposure had taken care of the rest. Sara found nothing of August but a single blood-crusted boot sticking out of the ice like an obscene golf flag.

Internal pressure seemed to crush her chest. She put her hands on her knees and clenched her eyes shut. Her breath rasped inside her helmet.

"Sara?" Vernon's voice boomed in her ears.

"They're dead, Vernon. They're dead."

"Then get back here, now. I need your help."

Sara briefly considered trying to take the remains of her crewmates with her. But Vernon's order had been correct. They would retrieve the bodies later.

"Coming," she replied.

She raced toward Vernon, her steps crunching through her boots. She recalled the blue streak she had seen during the quake. Had she imagined it? It had seemed serpentine, so alive. Could it have been responsible for this destruction? Was it still here? She shook her head, clearing her thoughts. Whatever it was, there was no blue in Europa's ice now.

"Grab his other arm," Vernon said as Sara approached.

Mustav was unconscious. His envirosuit appeared intact, but his legs had been crushed and were twisted at grotesque angles that made Sara's stomach churn once again.

"Should we move him?" Sara asked.

"He's a dead man if we don't," Vernon snapped.

They lifted him gently, and made for the rover. Vernon limped heavily.

"Are you okay?" she asked.

"Yeah, I just bruised my thigh in the quake."

Sara nodded from within the bubble of her helmet.

Mustav was bulky, and they took pains to avoid causing him further damage. Even in Europa's light gravity, the inertia of his body was normal. The strain of moving him took its toll. Sara was out of breath after twenty meters, and her face was drenched with sweat after forty.

The rover appeared intact and undamaged. It was a small craft, a vehicle that resembled a bathysphere in many ways. It was heated to comfortable levels by energy reflected from Jupiter's surface and augmented with a battery backup. Floodlights illuminated their path, tiny wisps of steam rising from their artificial heat in the Europan cold. An array of sensors hung from a rack around the vehicle's rim, recording ice quality and the integrity of the surrounding surface.

Moving quickly, they hefted Mustav onto the airlock ramp. Sara pulled him into the cabin as soon as the doors processed their entry, Vernon right behind. The chamber was warm, and a luxurious sensation of heat soaked into her as she removed her helmet.

"You work on Mustav while I get us headed home," Vernon said. His eyes were wide. Sweat dripped from his brow and soaked his short-cropped sandy hair to a dark shade of walnut. Vernon was a leader, Sara knew, a man somehow bigger than his six-foot frame. He seemed to always have a hundred processes running inside his mind yet could focus on what was important at any particular moment. Sara, who assessed her leadership qualities as about as prevalent as elephants in the Everglades, had always marveled at his self-confidence and had found his calm demeanor intensely attractive.

The fact he was so obviously married made him somehow that much more intimidating.

She nodded and went to Mustav's side.

The vehicle lurched forward. Vernon's voice filled
the cabin. "Mission Command, this is Rover One. Mark
our current position at 11.77 degrees north latitude, and
227.98 west longitude."

Frederica's voice came from Mission Command.
"Do you have an update on the status of your crew?"

Vernon hesitated. Anguish flooded his brown eyes.
He was a strait-laced man who led by the book, and he
had just lost three crewmembers. A heavy mantle of
responsibility draped itself over him, and Sara watched
his shoulders sag with its weight.

Reactively, Sara thought of her dead compatriots.
Lin had just received word she was an aunt for the first
time, and delighted in passing images around to
everyone in the compound. Kris had been quiet like
Sara. She was artistic, and had been awarded degrees in
graphic arts and geology from Columbia. A handful of
brown freckles were scattered randomly across her nose
and cheeks, making her seem perpetually happy
despite her solitary nature. August had been a person
much like Sara's father, a man of humor and strength
whose presence put people immediately at ease. He
played practical jokes on various crewmembers with
the glee of a ten-year-old, and when he grinned, his
white teeth blazed against his black skin.

"We have three dead," Vernon said simply. "And
we're lifting Mustav Gapato back. Will require medical
assistance."

"Roger that, Vernon. Rover Two is suffering
mechanical difficulties and is unable to leave. Are you
okay to operate on your own?"

"Yeah," he replied. "We should be fine."

"What the hell happened, Vernon?" Frederica replied.

Vernon's gaze grew hard. He shook his head gently to himself, and his eyebrows raised. "The charge apparently caused structural problems on the floe," he said.

Sara considered commenting on the blue ice, but something in Vernon's demeanor made her stop. She wondered if he had even seen the streaks. Maybe she had hallucinated them. Maybe they hadn't been there at all. More likely the color was just the stress of the explosive discharge flowing through the ice. Like a schoolkid not wanting to sound silly, Sara stayed silent. But deep in her core, like that same child who continues to dream of princesses and faeries and white knights even as she grows through her teenaged years, Sara held on to the blue streaks as something important, something somehow alive.

The rover skimmed the ice with a slushy sound.

Mustav's face was ashen, his body shriveled. As gingerly as possible, Sara removed his envirosuit. The warm, coppery smell of blood filled the cabin. Mustav's legs were a tangled mess of flesh, blood and exposed bone. It was a miracle his suit hadn't been breached. She pulled a long strip of cloth from the emergency kit and tied a field tourniquet around his thigh, twisting it tight, and praying against all hope that Mustav could still be saved.

Grabbing antiseptic and fresh rags, Sara cleaned the wounds.

Mustav moaned. His eyes were wet and unfocused. They flickered and came to rest on Sara. He smiled weakly and whispered, "Did you see them?"

"Who?" she said.

"Blue snakes," he replied. Mustav was a scientist at heart, and the glint of discovery sizzled in his gaze. "Did you see the blue snakes?"

"Yes, Mustav," she said. "It was probably just stress flow in cold ice."

He shook his head, and his breath gurgled wetly. "You know better, do you not?"

She looked out the window. The ice was white and clean. It was a silly dream, really, finding life on Europa. The crew openly joked about it. But, inside, it was a dream that each of them secretly harbored. And now Mustav had seen the same snakes Sara had, the blue sheen that slithered through the ice, then slid silently away.

Wordlessly, she covered Mustav's wounds with plastic skin from a large tube provided in the first aid kit. She wrapped an electric blanket around him and pasted its sensors onto his body.

They drove in silence for several minutes. The vehicle vibrated with their progress. Sara leaned back and gazed at Mustav, thinking about the blue streak's movement, the rapid waving that so strongly matched that of sea snakes she had seen off Sanibel. Yes, it was too big of a leap to consider the blue streaks creatures, to label them as life. But Sara gave herself the luxury of thinking of them as such for a moment.

Her memory flashed to the day she told her parents she was going to Europa. "I'll be the most famous microbiologist in the world, Mom," she had said.

"Is that what you want?" her mother asked, with an anxious expression.

She remembered the question vividly. It *was* what she wanted. Ten years doing grunt research and teaching sophomore-level biochemistry to a bunch of kids who couldn't grasp the difference between a protein and an enzyme had changed her. She was in her late thirties. She had no husband, no real prospects, and wasn't even sure she wanted one anymore. She had no kids, and yes, her biological clock had been setting off alarms for the past five years.

Science was the one thing she did well. It had carried her through her toughest times. Now Sara dreamed of grants and articles and interviews, of other people's children smiling up at her as she addressed them. And, Sara admitted in those quiet moments when she looked deeply into her soul, she dreamed of Dan calling her and apologizing for his behavior during their divorce.

Yes, she understood the psychobabble—that Dan's anger was brought on by his own feelings of inadequacy. But his accusations had left scars that, perhaps, could never really heal. The thought of making him eat a little crow appealed to her in ways chocolate never could, and being a member of the party that discovered life on Europa would certainly fill that bill.

A jarring drop shook Sara out of her daydream.

"Ah, shit," Vernon grumbled.

"What happened?" Sara said, wheeling to face him. Tiny particles of ice scrubbed against the sides of the rover—blue ice, Sara realized—swirling blue and silver like a school of amber jack turning in perfect synchronicity. An ominous tingle rode her spine. Something wasn't right. Europa's atmosphere wasn't dense enough to support a storm like this.

Vernon ignored her question and peered out the rover's front window. He rubbed his eyes with quavering hands.

"What's wrong, Vernon?" Sara repeated.

His eyes were bloodshot and his gaze burned with fear and fatigue. The expression, so unlike Vernon's usual demeanor, was enough to scare her. He swallowed, struggling to speak. "We just threw a rail. I've got to take care of it or we'll never make it back." He stood up and grimaced, clutching his leg.

"Hold on a minute," Sara said, scrambling forward to examine his suit. Several needle-sized puncture marks appeared in the material along Vernon's leg, small enough that the suit had been able to compensate by injecting sealant between layers of insulation.

"You've been hit by something," Sara said.

"I'll live," he replied.

"I don't think you should go out there."

"Go out where?" he said, looking at her quizzically.

A spike of anger shot through her for an instant before Sara realized Vernon had truly forgotten what he had been doing. She looked at him closely, then. His eyes were glassy, and he appeared to be fighting to control his thoughts. He was sick. Whatever had pierced his suit had likely cut into his leg, exposing Vernon's system to its chemical content. "Outside to check the rover," she finally replied. "Why don't we just wait for Rover Two?"

"Rover Two is down, Sara. It could be hours before they get going again."

Something in the way Vernon's gaze wouldn't meet Sara's raised a warning within her. "What else, Vernon?"

Vernon sighed and shrugged his shoulders. "The storm is interfering with the compass, and I think I've gone off course somehow. Even if they do get everything fixed, Rover Two may not be able to find us."

"Let's call them and see when they might be ready," she said, almost pleading, her thoughts beginning to jumble.

Vernon nodded and went to the radio.

"Mission Command, this is Vernon. We've broken down, and we're trying to determine our next course of action. Can you give me an update of Rover Two's ETA?"

"Copy, Rover One," Frederica replied. "I have your location. Rover Two remains inoperable. They're working to correct the problem, but I have no estimate on readiness."

Vernon nodded and sighed resignedly. He clicked the radio off and turned to Sara. "No choice but to press on."

Sara didn't know what to do. Outside, a blue storm that shouldn't be there scrubbed against the rover. Vernon was obviously laboring. If they *were* lost, she thought, it was an even bet they had drifted off course as much a result of his lack of concentration as any problems with the compass.

But Mustav needed every minute they could give him.

"Go ahead," she finally whispered.

Vernon crawled deliberately to the air lock. He sealed the cabin and reached for the control mechanism.

"No!" Sara shouted, her heart racing. She lunged forward and pushed the autolock mechanism before it was too late. Vernon had forgotten to put his helmet on. If he had pulled that lever, Europa's savage climate would have killed him instantly. Sara's heart pounded, and she opened the cabin seal to pull him away from the controls.

He was worsening fast. His flesh was clammy and cold. His eyes were dilated, and his hair was wringing with his own sweat.

A shiver went up Sara's spine, a sensation of clarity and purpose that was oddly intoxicating. "You're sick, Vernon. Whatever hit you out there is doing you no good. You can't go." She pulled him back into the cabin and reached for her helmet. If anyone were going to fix the rover, it would have to be her.

"Stay here, okay, Vernon?" she said, speaking in the same voice she had used when she talked to fourth graders at Luther Elementary School.

"Uh-huh," Vernon mumbled as he sat down.

Sara sealed the cabin and clamped her helmet over her collar, breathing dry air that smelled of plastic. The electronic readouts glowed with neon red and blue at the edge of the helmet's display. The storm swirled outside, but had turned a gentle azure. Maybe the color was life, and maybe it wasn't. But now Mustav lay bleeding to death. Kris Callahan, Lin Wi and August McGrath had already died, and Vernon was growing worse by the minute. Whatever the blue was, five of the six people who had contacted it had come away worse for the experience.

A moment later, she was back on Europa's surface. The storm scrubbed her helmet with a sound like frying bacon, coalescing in curlicue waves of blue static before her. The surface was scintillating, its texture the rugged pebble of an uncut gem, its color a meshing kaleidoscope of intertwined blues. Was this a living creature? Could something actually have spawned under the ice shelves of Europa? A form of life that lived in water, or maybe one that used water as a human might use flesh and blood, each blue streak representing something more akin to a soul than a physical structure?

She imagined serpentine figures probing her envirosuit, searching for a crack or an edge, any separation that would give them access to her. Her heartbeat pounded audibly. A metallic flavor rode on her tongue.

Outside, Sara knew the temperature was 150 below zero Celsius. The ice was crusty and brittle, and all the oxygen in Europa's entire atmosphere would fit into a couple sports coliseums at Earth pressure. Her pulse rose. Her throat felt cotton-dry, and her hand shook with paralyzed fear as she placed it along the rover's body.

"Damn it, Sara, get a grip!" she yelled at herself, just as her mother had when she was a teenager. The sound of her own voice filled the tiny space inside her helmet and drowned out the scouring rasp of the blue ice. The thought of her mother brought Sara comfort. She lectured herself, using her mother's voice. She told herself she had swum with sharks in a hundred feet of water, and she had faced emergency situations before. She could do this.

Mission Command could hear her, she knew. But despite her self-consciousness, speaking aloud made her feel better. Without thinking, she started to hum a familiar tune, a song her mother had sung so often back in Nebraska, letting the melody carry her focus. There, on the surface of Europa, Sara hummed the melody of "Amazing Grace."

The storm paused, seeming to sync to her rhythm. The "wind" slowed to a stop, leaving a curtain of silver blue crystals floating downward. The surface ice swirled in patterns that folded themselves into large elements, then broke apart in cadence with the tune.

Sara hummed, feeling an odd sense of connection. The blue had powered the storm itself, she realized. And now it was pausing to reassess this visitor in its midst, curious like a pod of whales or a family of apes encountering a new beast.

She continued to hum, adding vigor to the song.

The blue stain slowed its motion and circled around her. The ice saturated, the color of deep ocean under her boots where the vibration was strongest, lightening to Caribbean green at its outer edges. She hummed, and the hue varied with her pitch. She sang a line and an aquamarine slash streaked through the surface.

Sara felt it then.

A feeling of power overwhelmed her, a feeling of millennia-old rightness, the emotion that came with watching porpoises play in the shallows or seeing a shark's silhouetted form slip stealthily into an area she had been diving. She had no explanation for what was happening, but she knew in her heart now that the blue coloration *was* life. And Sara knew that she was connected now in some inexplicable fashion. She was speaking with the blue, was telling them something of human life, perhaps even representing her species with a message embedded in the pitch and melody of the song.

A tear formed in the corner of her eye, and she spread her arms, bringing the song to its end.

Slowly, moving as if it didn't want to leave but felt it ought to, the blue color moved away. It dimmed to turquoise, then flared sapphire. Finally, it disappeared completely, leaving a silvery mist of ice crystals wafting noiselessly in the air as the only clue anything had ever been there.

Sara's heart pounded in her chest. She swallowed and glanced around the ice, feeling a loss at the sudden disappearance of the blue. Despite her suit's heating system, her fingers and toes were cold now. The pain brought her back to her situation. With almost physical effort, Sara turned her attention to the rover.

She quickly found the damaged blade. A section had broken off and jammed in the vehicle's rear axle. She hammered at it with the palm of her hand, and it dislodged. Sara picked up the broken blade and returned to the air-lock doors. Vernon was probably useless for the rest of the trip, but with any luck she could get the machine headed toward camp.

Sara pressed the device to open the air lock.

Nothing happened.

She tried again.

Again, nothing. Inside, Vernon sat slumped over like a drunk on a barstool. The red safety catch stuck out at an awkward angle to his left. For some unknown reason he had climbed into the air lock and flipped the latch to internal control.

He stared distantly into the horizon.

Sara pursed her lips. She wasn't going to get this far just to freeze out in the middle of an ice floe some 480 million miles from Earth.

"Come on, Vernon," she yelled, pounding desperately on the door and motioning him to release the air locks. "Vernon." She spoke into her radio in a voice suddenly calm. "Vernon?"

Vernon looked at her through wandering eyes.

"Get out of the air lock and release the safety."

Vernon nodded and turned to the latching mechanism.

"No!" Sara shouted. But it was too late this time. The doors swung open, exposing the entire cabin.

Sara stood slack jawed for a moment. This wasn't supposed to happen. She was supposed to fix the rover and make it home. She was supposed to save the whole crew. But the doors hung open like gates to an ancient crypt and Sara could almost picture a sign— *Abandon Hope All Ye Who Enter Here*—posted across the entrance, the bodies of her friends flash-frozen inside, preserved like modern mummies. The rover, as good as its environmental controls were, would certainly not attain a suitable temperature before her oxygen ran out, which—she glanced at her gauge—would be in about twenty minutes.

Her breathing rasped. Oxygen in, carbon dioxide out.

She looked at Mustav and Vernon. Their oxygen packs were still filled. A guilty chill made her shiver, but Sara ignored the feeling. They would want her to use the packs. The oxygen systems were stowed in the locker area, as well as an emergency pack—three more hours of life, maybe four.

Sara crawled into the forward compartment. The control panel was a flat display of numbers and tables. Afraid the plastic touch sheet might be too brittle in the Europan cold, she cautiously pressed buttons to close the air lock. The dash split silently across one panel, and the air lock doors remained open. The system was dead.

She sat down gingerly into the captain's chair and glanced around her. Every piece of electronic equipment in the cabin had just been subjected to a sudden temperature drop of over 200 degrees Celsius. What hadn't broken outright would be suspect in its operation. She couldn't trust any reading from here on out.

She clicked on her suit's radio connection. "Hello," she said, her voice faltering.

There was no answer.

"Mission Command?"

Still no answer.

The radios were fed through the rover's system, and that system was dead. There would be no more communications.

A familiar tingle spread through her then as if it had been injected directly into her heart, a sensation so thick she nearly smothered. It was the oddly hollow feeling of her house in Florida, the smell of a frozen dinner cooking in the microwave, the sound of a door closing after another first date. It was the empty, yet somehow comforting, echo of enforced solitude that only a person who has chosen to live her life alone could ever truly recognize.

Now though, it seemed to haunt her, to prod her like an invisible chef checking her readiness for the cooking pot.

She gritted her teeth and scanned the console, trying to ignore her emotions. Sara had not piloted the rover before, but like the rest of the crew, had taken emergency training on the system. The controls were like a car's— gas on the right, brake on the left. She engaged the drive and was almost surprised when the rover jerked forward.

She peered through the window.

Aerial imaging made it appear Europa's surface was as flat as a Kansas wheat field, but at ground level the terrain was amazingly rugged, gouged and cracked, a vast no man's land of trenches and ice formations. The compass indicated north was to the rear of the rover, but the readout floated between 150 and 220 degrees, a fluctuation on the compass point that could translate to kilometers of difference after an hour's trip.

"Which way?" she said aloud. "Goddamn it, which way?"

She set her jaw and turned right. Doubling back, she noticed the rover's tracks. An idea struck her. She could backtrack until she found where Vernon had strayed from the last path, then take the one leading back to the Ant Farm. She turned the wheel further. Muffled slushing filtered through her suit. The cabin view panned the landscape. Cold fingers crawled up Sara's neck as the rover drew nearer the trail. She drew a breath. She was going to live. She had the rover going, and was headed home. For whatever reason the fates had chosen, Sara was going to survive.

The weight of the entire solar system seemed to dislodge from her chest. A surge of adrenaline burned her veins. For a moment it was too much. She blinked away tears and breathed deeply several times before collecting herself. She was still a long way from home, and Sara knew it was too early to declare victory.

Without warning, the vehicle gave a sharp jolt and fell out from under her. Sara's helmet banged the back of her seat, and everything came to a silent stillness. With sick surety, she knew what had happened. The sensing array that ringed the vehicle had failed; the rover had rolled over brittle ice, and the floe had given way.

The cabin window looked up into a black curtain.

She lay back, crestfallen. Hope that had flared so strongly within her just a moment ago left her. She was not going to make it home. The enormity of this hit her. She had, perhaps, been part of the biggest discovery in the history of the human universe—life—the blue pool of color that floated through ice and water in some indescribable fashion. But she would not live to bring this find back. There would be no great notoriety. No grants. No interviews.

But in the end, she was surprised to realize that none of that really mattered to her.

It was the connection she thought of first, the odd sense of community she had felt when she first sang to the blue creatures, and the longing to know the other being that had dominated the moment. The feeling was water to desert sand.

That's what she would miss, she realized.

She would miss *knowing*.

Sara reviewed her existence then. She remembered things. The smell of s'mores in her freshman dorm room. Nights with Dan before things went sour. The delightfully triumphant sensation of being valedictorian of her high-school class. She thought of school friends and people she had spoken with in the weeks before the flight—college kids, hospital patients, and children in the Johnson County school system. But mostly, she thought of her parents and the firmness of their hugs the night before she launched.

Her heart swelled, and a sense of purpose crept over her that was so firm it nearly took her breath away. She was tied to these people, connected to them in a tangled way that she was at a loss to explain. To let them down would crush her. To let them down would be to let herself down.

She might die this day on Europa, but when her compatriots from the Ant Hill found Sara McClintock, she could not be sitting docilely in the cockpit of a disabled rover.

Sara could not give up. She would go it on foot, one step in front of the other, as long as it took. Her oxygen supply, she knew, would not get her back to the Ant Farm. But she would not quit. Who knew, maybe they would get the second rover working, and maybe, by some stroke of luck, they would manage to find her.

The oxygen system warning light flickered in the lower left of her helmet display, breaking her thought process. She clipped the emergency pack onto her second intake, then removed her old system. Pulling her dead companions' tanks along with her, Sara slipped out of the derelict rover.

From the outside, the vehicle sat silently at an awkward angle. Its front end jutted into dark space in

FREE

Send in this card and you'll receive a FREE POSTER while supplies last. No order required for this Special Offer! Mail your card today!

❑ Please send me a FREE poster.

❑ Please send me information about other books by L. Ron Hubbard.

ORDERS SHIPPED WITHIN 24 HRS OF RECEIPT

NEW RELEASE!

___ A Very Strange Trip

    __ Hardcover $25.00   _____

    __ Audio $25.00   _____

SCIENCE FICTION/FANTASY:

___ Ai! Pedritol When Intelligence Goes Wrong

    __ Hardcover $25.00   _____

    __ Audio $25.00   _____

___ Battlefield Earth paperback $7.99   _____

___ Battlefield Earth audio $29.95   _____

    MISSION EARTH® series (10 volumes)

___ paperbacks (specify volumes:_____)(each) $5.99   _____

___ audio (specify volumes:_____)(each) $15.95   _____

___ Final Blackout paperback $6.99   _____

___ Final Blackout audio   **SPECIAL** $11.95   _____

___ Fear paperback $6.99   _____

___ Fear audio   **SPECIAL** $9.95   _____

___ Slaves of Sleep & The Masters of Sleep hardcover $19.95   _____

___ Slaves of Sleep & The Masters of Sleep audio $19.95   _____

___ Typewriter in the Sky hardcover (Fantasy) $16.95   _____

___ Typewriter in the Sky audio $16.95   _____

___ Ole Doc Methuselah hardcover $18.95   _____

___ Ole Doc Methuselah audio $24.95   _____

___ *L. RON HUBBARD PRESENTS WRITERS OF THE FUTURE* Volumes: (paperback)

    ❑ Vol X $6.99   ❑ Vol XI $6.99

    ❑ Vol XIII $6.99 ❑ Vol XIV $6.99

CHECK AS APPLICABLE: **TAX*:**   _____

❑ Check/Money Order enclosed.   **TOTAL:**   _____

    (Use an envelope please)

❑ American Express ❑ Visa ❑ MasterCard ❑ Discover

* California residents add 8.25% sales tax.

Card#:_____

Exp. Date:_____Signature:_____

Credit Card Billing Address Zip Code :_____

NAME:_____

ADDRESS:_____

CITY:_____ STATE:_____ ZIP:_____

PHONE#:_____

Call us now with your Order 1-800-722-1733
http://www.bridgepub.com

© 1999 BPI. All Rights Reserved. MISSION EARTH and WRITERS OF THE FUTURE are trademarks owned by L. Ron Hubbard Library.

Name: _____

Address: _____

City: _____ State: _____ Zip: _____

the lonely way of a shipwreck under miles of ocean. The sun glinted in the distance, a cold ball of yellow light only slightly larger than a pinhead. Ganymede and Callisto were hidden behind Jupiter now. Io was a tiny disk of red silver to the giant planet's right. A handful of other moons glittered in the sky.

Metis. Amalthea. Thebe.

A sudden thrill crossed her spine. Sara McClintock had made it to Europa—a place no one else had ever been before. She smiled then, the dignified expression of an adventurer, of a gladiator entering the ring for his last bout. With a sigh, Sara retrieved a small sled and placed her remaining oxygen packs on it. Then she turned and walked toward the trail.

A pair of deep ruts cut black shadows in ice colored Jupiter orange. Sara walked, thinking. Jupiter, she knew, bombarded Europa with energy, and that energy initiated a chemical process that released traces of molecular oxygen into the atmosphere. Oxygen that slowly drifted away, eventually escaping the pull of Europa's gravity well, slipping into space like an elemental ghost, as if it had never existed.

Maybe she was like that, too. Maybe she would drift away and no one would ever find her. Maybe it would be as if she had never been to Europa at all.

The muffled crunching of her boots *whump-whumped* through her suit. Chill crept through her legs. Her breathing grew ragged. The oxygen packs slowly grew heavy. Sara walked between the rover's ruts like Dorothy following the yellow brick road, pulling Toto behind in her sled. But in her world there was no Scarecrow, no Tin Man, and no Cowardly Lion to help her cope. And in her world, clicking her heels together would not send her back home.

Minutes turned to hours. Somewhere she attached Vernon's oxygen supply, leaving her empty tank behind. She grew cold, and her suit stuck to her skin in unpleasant ways. Her feet became numb. Battery power had been running for a long time, and her heating system was failing. Her teeth chattered. Her muscles clenched as if they would tear themselves from her bones, but still she moved on.

She slipped and stumbled to the ice. Her body felt like rubber, but Sara picked herself up and moved on. Still nothing appeared on the horizon. No second rover. No Ant Farm. The melody of "Amazing Grace" came to her then, wrapped in the sound of her mother's voice. She was hallucinating, she knew, but Sara didn't care. She tried to sing along with her mother, her voice cracking in halted steps against her dehydrated throat.

A minute later—or was it an hour—Sara fell again. Her cheeks were cold and rigid, and a sensation of phantom heat tingled at her toes. She was freezing to death, she knew with her last lucid thought.

"Help me," she whispered, her voice rasping inside her helmet. "God, help me."

Another sound came to her then, a foreign voice, a low vibration that was sweet and sorrowful, filled with harmonics and overtones, deeper than anything Sara had ever heard before. She recognized a rhythm, and then she could pick out the melody.

The clear tune of "Amazing Grace," joining both her and her mother.

The ice grew blue around her.

She smiled, and hummed along with the song.

At that moment, Sara felt more at peace than at any other in her life.

BY OTHER WINDINGS

Written by
Franklin Thatcher

Illustrated by
Tomislav Tomic

About the Author

Franklin Thatcher has been writing for four decades, but it wasn't until he joined a Utah writing group called Pilgrimage—which included several people who were or would be winners in L. Ron Hubbard's Writers of the Future Contest—*that he began to progress as a fiction writer. Since winning First Prize in a quarter of the Contest, he has sold a story to the second* Star Trek: Strange New Worlds *anthology. He has written multimedia planetarium scripts, including an authorized adaptation of Isaac Asimov's perennial favorite "The Last Question," as well as a history and exploration of the planet Mars.*

About the Illustrator

Tomislav Tomic was born at the end of 1977 and lives with his parents and sister in Zapresic, a small town near Zagreb in Croatia. A graduate of the School of Fine Arts in Zagreb, he is now a student in the Academy of Fine Arts. He spends his days printing and painting in the Academy, and then drawing comics or illustrations when he returns home, or sharing time with his girlfriend. His placing in the Illustrators' Contest is his biggest success to date.

Night water stirs above me. Ebb and flow of sightless albino fish. Catch one if I could, but why? Couldn't starve again if I wanted to. And fish are never afraid.

Thud of pole against wood, rotted hull of Charon's boat. New slaves for Master. No grudge if I can steal one, though. I rise through abyssal depths.

Bow waves. Rippling silhouettes above, eyes blind as Master's uncatchable koi. Blind with fear and darkness and shame. Charon watches. Punishment for him if he loses one, but not for me. Catch one, and I feed.

Wait. Wait. Match the stroke of Charon's pole. Dance beneath India ink water. His pole, at last, swings across, sinks on the other side into sucking mud below. With a powerful kick of my fin-legs I rush through cold and stinking water. I hear Charon's pole pull free of the mud but he is not quick enough. I burst from water into a blast of burned and desiccating air and crash, roaring, against the rail. There is mayhem on the boat, and wherever the air burns my tongue I taste their fear. The boat heels as prisoners flee in mindless terror. Charon's pole flies from the water, but I have heard the scream and splash on the other side. I crash back into the water, clawing beneath the boat's encrusted keel. In the water I smell the screaming thing, find it by its panic.

Sometimes I rake their legs, grab their puny genitals, drag them down slowly, drinking their fear. But no time to dally with this one. I clutch a naked ankle, pull the thing down, and its screaming vanishes into bubbles. A splash above as Charon drives pole into water. I feel the squirming thing above clutch the slippery wood and fight against me, but its hand slips free of the pole. Back toward shore I pull it, into wake of the boat, knowing Charon won't turn around.

The squirming thing weakens and I take it up. Let it have hope, hope that even Master would be better than this. It struggles anew, its screams muted by the black water. I hear Charon's pole splash again, pushing on toward the opposite shore, and know the wriggling thing is mine.

I release it for a moment, swim around it. It is female, I can tell by the water-borne scent between its legs. How cruel it is, taunting me. My penis hangs erect and painful in the water, large as the rest of me, large as this woman-thing. Too large to be of any use against her.

I lunge forward, sinking fangs into a rounded breast, and again it screams, thrashing. Die, foul woman. Die again if you can. I back away. From below I watch curves and smoothness, limned in red. What part of herself did she love best? What part of her will become as big as my bloated and useless penis? Will she still have use of her little box? Will Master pleasure her with it, while taking from her all else that she will not give? Or was her box her undoing, as so many others were mine?

She kicks toward shore, and I lash upward, rake my claws between her legs. Evil box! She screams and doubles with pain. My webbed claws bite her flesh and drag her down again. Oh, my Little Box. If only you could see the part of me that I loved, the part that would have taken you there on Sevilla Road, amid the horse dung and the mud and the carts of pottery and chickens. Would you be horrified, my Little Box, if you could see it?

I am still toying with my Little Box when Charon returns, his boat empty. I free her, let her swim closer to the boat. Her nails claw and break against the sodden planks. Charon ignores her screams, her curses, her choking pleas. Master has already punished him. Why should he save her now?

She tries to keep up with the boat, but I pull her down again. Her fight has returned, born of hope in the stinking wood of the boat.

At last, she wearies. The pattern of my game grows old to her. Or perhaps she knows, at last, that she is mine. She does not struggle as I finally pull her down.

Perhaps I will hollow her out, use her for myself before Master comes to collect what is left, the river parting with steam and thunder before his heat as he walks past the poached and white-eyed fish. I stroke her perfect, ethereal flesh—unmarkable, unimpregnable, but still pawn to torment.

Perhaps I will discover her secret love, tear it from her and feast it down before her undying eyes. Maybe start with a hand, or a foot, or maybe just a finger. Always save the eyes for last. Make Little Box watch every horror I commit on her, the water around her sweet with hopelessness and fear. No escape for you, my Little Box.

But there is.

Light bursts in on me. Blinded, I am torn away, so fast that the water closes, thunderous applause, beneath me. Up through smoke and sulfur and stone, through burning water and then ice. I scream and claw at world-aged stone but it is gone, and I am powerless to halt or go back.

Illustrated by Tomislav Tomic

In a burst of flame, shower of dust, and clap of thunder, I stand, cold air rushing over me. My pebbled skin hisses and steams. I choke and vomit on the icy stone. The black and bloody detritus sets flame to mortar between the stones. Vaulted stone hangs above my head. At my feet, five points of light, each atop a peg of wax, burn my eyes, each peg atop the chalked point of a five-sided star.

My penis, flaccid now, lies against the frost-biting stone. I gather it up to escape the cold.

"Perfect."

At first, I do not recognize the sound as a word. My captor—tormentor—stands naked and painted and leering, emerald eyes blazing in candlelight. Breasts, round and thick but past their prime, jiggle as she laughs.

I roar and lash out, but my claws rend only the air, sparking and scraping at the boundaries of the circle. For an instant she recoils, startled, but then only laughs the more. I stare at my dulled and broken claws. "Mortal," I say, surprised at the forgotten sound of my own voice.

"Demon," she answers.

"You have taken me from important work. I will tear your breasts off and eat your little box from your living flesh."

She says nothing, only walks a circle around me, staying just beyond the chalked line, her naked feet padding silent on icy stone. "I have called you to a task," she says, "and will not release you until it is finished."

"I will see you to Master first."

"My *brother*"—she says it as she might address a pile of feces—"has married. As if I was not enough to keep him satisfied." She steps to the edge of the circle, her aureoles almost within my clawed reach. "She is heir to his wealth, the wealth to which I have driven him. My wealth! I need him alive. But I want her tormented. And then I want her dead."

I look coyly away, summon honey to my tongue. "I cannot kill, unless you release me from the circle."

She laughs again. "You think me a fool?" She whirls lithely away, sitting again on the freezing stone, her legs crossed, feet on thighs. In silence she sits, for how long I cannot tell. Within, I rage, promising that I will tear this woman's flesh from her bones one clawful at a time.

At last a candle gutters and dies and I throw myself at the gap in the circle. But the barrier repulses me, and I scream in anger and frustration, the sound reverberating from the dark and invisible walls beyond my pond of light. I pound my fists against the barrier, screaming again. The woman presses her hands over her ears, but does not move from her lotus position.

I stand again, facing her. She returns her hands to her knees, a smile teasing her lips. I imagine the feel of her blood dripping from my claws.

But I can only wait.

Another candle flickers out. I test the barrier with a claw and it rings, unyielding crystal beneath my touch. At the edge of light, her emerald eyes never leave me. She does not blink, but rolls her eyes until only the white remains, emerald green flashing back into place.

A third candle sputters and fades, and my eyes droop with sudden fatigue.

"Do you know what's happening to you?" she whispers.

Alert again, I test the unforgiving circle.

"You are dying," she says. "Not physically, but eternally. When the last candle dies you will vanish like the flame, irrevocably dispersed to oblivion. No longer even a tremor in the fabric of consciousness."

I say nothing. She would tell any lie to achieve her ends, as would I.

She fondles herself, my eyes fastened to her fingers as if by needles. I feel a sudden weakness, and without looking I know that the fourth candle has died.

•••

"Look at you," she says. My eyes snap open. She stands just beyond the circle. I did not hear her approach. "Your greatest attribute and you can't even get it up, no matter that I entertain you." She kneels before the last candle, a puddle of contorted wax and waning flame. Her breasts hang, framing yellow light. Her fingers stroke the flame and my eyelids flutter with its light.

"Obey me," she says, "and I will save you."

Soundlessly, my lips form the word "Never."

She stalks away, her limbs animated with rage. She returns, a new candle in hand. The air around her swims with shadows and ghostly forms.

"Why do you waste my time?" she demands. "Only you will pay the price of your defiance." But she is too eager. It will cost her, too. I know not how. But it is enough—to make her pay.

The swirling shadows close around me, all that I am diluting into the expanse of the universe. I cannot hold my eyes open any longer. I hear her screaming obscenities at me, demanding my obedience. Yes, she too will pay a price, whatever it be.

But if I am to die, why not have revenge first? I have butchered better than her. Of the dream state on the brink of death, my lying lips form the words "I will obey." When I open my eyes, she has placed the newly lighted candle in the circle, just as the last one flickers out. She brings more candles, transferring the living flame from one candle to the next and placing them where star-points meet circle, until all five burn again.

She turns to face me. "Again. Swear your oath to obey me."

To expect the truth of a demon. How much will she believe? How much time can I buy to find my own way back to the river? "First," I say, "I must have a token of our contract."

She hesitates, untrusting.

I raise a black stiletto claw before her eyes. "A drop of your blood, as troth."

Her eyes dart back and forth. "If you kill me, you will have nothing. You will die—for good and ever—when the candles fail."

I smile. "Of course."

She steps cautiously forward, offering her upturned wrist. She reaches unhindered through the circle.

I extend one claw toward her exposed skin, but my hand strikes out, clutching her wrist and pulling her into the circle. With my other hand I reach between her legs, and with a quick stroke, a whiff of seared flesh, she cries out. I release her and she stumbles back, clutching her wrist where my grip has charred her flesh. I raise my claw, the coating of red blood turning dark, bubbling, and then smoking.

She presses her hand between her legs and her fingers come away stained with blood.

"It will heal," I say, looking only at the dark coating on my black claw. "Now our contract is sealed." I examine her furtive emerald eyes. "I am your—humble servant."

•••

Floating in air, I follow the emerald-eyed woman through the cobble streets. The ethereal thread tugs insistently, pulling me back, binding to the physical manifestation of my body in the candle-bound circle.

She is cloaked now in purple silk, gold and ruby, clothed against the cold of the snow piled on pitched roofs, decorated sills and carved lintels. The smoke of a hundred chimneys mingles with the clouds which hang near enough to touch, suspended by mountain faces of snow and stone and evergreen.

We emerge from the narrow road into a square, and everywhere there are women: old women, young women, beautiful women, ugly women, little girls not yet in their time, old hags. My penis is huge and hard— I could not even move were it not as ethereal as the rest of me—and I ache for them all. I pass through a girl, first rag over the bud of her womanhood. I feel her new and unfamiliar desire, and I am caught as surely as in a web. I whisper to her, focus her craving. She looks around the marketplace, not understanding her sudden need. I heap desire deeper beneath her heart and she hunts blindly for some avenue of release, a means to spend the incomprehensible potency I feed her. For an instant, through her I can smell the other women in the square, hear their voices, the rustle of their dresses; I reel under ancient memories of power, of lust. I drive her forward, push against her want, and she becomes the huntress, seeking the means to fill the emptiness we both feel.

Obey! The woman's thought blows through me like cold wind off the mountain face. Her emerald eyes hold me, draw me out of the girl, who reels away frightened

and confused. Tears burst from the girl's eyes and she
flees, leaving me only the tapering air of her new and
vibrant womanhood. I stare at the emerald-eyed witch,
hiding my hate, my lust for her sex, for her death. I
remember the blackened blood on my claw, my oath to
her—to myself.

Follow. She turns away, and I trail after her.

From the windows of the stone dome before us
steam rises to the icy heavens. Within, the woman sheds
her cloak and sandals into the hands of one servant
while another pins up her hair. Through a curtain, she
vanishes into the vast and cloudy room beneath the
dome. Stone steps lead to an enormous pool of steaming
water, disappear beneath its rippling waves. Light from
above draws windows in the air, casting strange
shadows in the mist. The woman winces as the water
reaches where my claw cut her, but she continues,
holding the seared flesh of her wrist out of its reach.
Within the shadows of the mist are other women, naked
and lounging together in the steaming water, conversing
in words I cannot hear. The woman stops in the midst of
several others.

I move unfeeling through the water, pass into a
woman with large breasts and blonde hair pinned up on
her head. Like waking from sleep, I feel the sudden heat
of the water, smell its sulfurous tinge. The ripplings ring
in my ears, amid a symphony of soprano and alto
voices. Crystal laughter echoes from the vaulted ceiling
hidden in the mist above. My eyes pierce the fog to see
the water around me filled with women of every shape
and age.

". . . miserable day outside," the emerald-eyed
woman is saying.

"At least here we can escape our husbands," says
another, gray haired but with breasts so small as to look

like an adolescent. "All except you, Lo'Elenora." This she directs to the emerald-eyed woman.

I look at my tormentor, at last knowing her name, and she meets my eyes. Is it my eyes she sees, or the eyes of the woman I inhabit? No matter; she knows it is me.

A small woman sidles up to Lo'Elenora, her throat barely out of the water. "You mustn't listen to them, Elenora. Look at you. You're no old maid. Lo', indeed!"

There is laughter around the circle, some ingenuous, some afraid, some insinuating.

"No," says another woman, her voluminous red hair tressed by golden baubles—her best feature. "Not all of us enjoy the luxury of a wealthy brother."

Some of the women whisper at this, suspecting what I already know. My blonde and buxom woman feels the thrill of scandal. The small brunette woman brushes closer to Elenora, a touch at once familiar and servile. In utter silence I cross over to her.

The red-haired woman's voice drops to a whisper, conspiring with the others. "And what of his new bride? Will her brother's widow rule the house now?"

My small woman splashes water in the redhead's face, soaking her hair. Anger flares in the redhead's eyes, but she recovers her grace. She throws back her shoulders proudly, but the hair decorations are still her best feature. Elenora's face remains cool, no betrayal of secrets. Her calming hand touches my small woman's shoulder. At the touch, I feel in the small woman the thrill of hope, a tingling at her breasts, between her legs.

"Speaking of my dear sister-in-law," Elenora says, "where may I find her?"

"Where else?" says my small woman. "At the hottest end of the pool—trying to clear her complexion, no doubt." She laughs, but stops short when Elenora simply turns away, moving deeper into the mist.

I push the small woman after her, but she hesitates. Few go there where the mountain water is so new from the rocks beneath, the heat so deep and terrible. I push harder, but still she resists. *Elenora will love you if you follow,* I tell her. *She wants you with her.* I feel the stirrings within her and she presses forward, into the scalding current. The mist closes around us and the other women's voices fall behind. The water scalds my small woman's skin. Her sexual energy ebbs and she struggles to turn back, to retreat to cooler water. I direct her eyes to the muscles moving gracefully beneath Elenora's shoulders, the peaks of her shoulder blades beneath her skin. I direct her eyes down, to Elenora's hips hidden beneath the rippling water—and she follows. The water grows hotter with each step, and sweat trickles down my small woman's face, her hair sagging against her itching scalp. Elenora's back remains pristine, touched only by a sheen of condensation. The small woman's feet falter on the stones of the bottom, her eyes flutter in the heat. But I drive her lust forward, after Elenora.

At last in the mist ahead a shadow emerges. A figure no larger than my small woman. Her hair is long and sleek, brown as her eyes. Unlike the other women's, it hangs down, soaked against her skin and spreading on the water like a lily. Her skin is red from the braising water, her breasts adamantine beneath its rippling surface.

Elenora moves to her. "Miara," she says, takes the young woman by the shoulders and kisses her cheek.

Against the compounding heat, I stare at this creature through my small woman's eyes, at this gift from my mistress. How easy to destroy such an innocent. How disappointingly easy.

As Miara draws back from Elenora, her eyes are moist and red, as red as her flesh.

My small woman sways beneath the heat, moved by the current of the natural spring, and I find it easier to cull her thoughts, to drive her body to action. I consider pushing her forward, encircling her hands about Miara's throat, dragging her beneath the water until she grows quiet, and then retreating into the mist to tell the others of how Lo'Elenora strangled her sister while I stood terrified a distance off, unseen in the mist. Consumed by the scalding heat, my small woman would even believe it after the first telling. But she is too weak, too fevered. Her limbs quake beneath the water, and sweat burns in her eyes.

I dredge the shamble of melted thoughts in the small woman's mind. *Elenora's enemy,* I remind her, *and so yours as well.*

"Ya'Miara," the small woman says, her voice nearly crumbling. "A thief who steals what belongs to her better."

When Miara speaks, her voice is strained from the heat, but rich and deep, its quaking from her heart rather than her flesh. "No more than is offered, as my sister well knows. I am wife to my dead husband's brother. And because he wanted no wife, I am lower than the servants of the house."

"Really?" my small woman says. "And what sort of service do you provide?"

"Enough," Elenora says. "Dear sister, forgive Dirina's ill humor. I fear the heat has gotten the better of her." She takes Miara's arm on one side, my small woman's on the other, and pushes back toward cooler water.

The whispers of the other women emerge from the mist no sooner than their shadows, and whispered conversations stop as we approach.

"Ah," says the redhead upon seeing Miara, "the parboiled return." She comes forward, taking Miara away from Elenora. "Come, my dear. You've purified heart and soul enough for one day."

My small woman's heart pounds against her ribs now, ready to melt under the heat. Still, I cull her mind for some useful bit of innuendo. "Perhaps she seeks to cleanse more than heart and soul," I say, and my small woman's voice rasps it out. But the redhead, her curls drooping and wet against her face, does not wait to hear more.

"Among the other men," I say, "her husband brags of a secret wedding bed hidden in the cellar. And the Waiting Year not even half gone."

The other women gasp, and this time Miara pulls free of the redhead's grasp and turns back. When she speaks, her voice is subdued, but there are strong currents beneath. "Garvin is a good man. He has observed the law."

My small woman does not meet her challenge, only turns to the other women. "He says it is in the cellar so no one will hear her cries of ecstasy."

Elenora steps forward, a restraining hand on my small woman's shoulder. But her gesture is calculated for appearance rather than effect. The others have smelled the hunt, and the gray-haired one joins. "Well, as old as he is, he can't afford to wait." She laughs and there is nervous tittering around the circle.

"But we all waited," I cry. "Didn't we, ladies?" All are quick to agree.

My small woman is now shaking so badly that she can barely speak. I pass quickly to the gray-haired woman, and instantly Dirina staggers forward, struggling to escape the water. The others flutter after her, perceiving her distress. She claws up the steps and doubles, vomiting on the stone floor.

Miara is first to her side, holding her hair back from the foul smelling puddle, pressing a steadying hand against her back. Whispers pass among the women.

The redhead stands forth. "Dirina is spouting all manner of filth today, it would seem."

Miara says nothing, only strokes the small woman's face, and whispers soothingly.

My gray-haired woman's head is as empty as her breasts, her life composed of trifles—all she has left. I press her forward. "And yet, one can only wonder at Miara's first husband's death, before the Waiting Year was up. Two successive Waiting Years. Who could expect her to hold up?"

I pass quickly to the redhead. Here is a stronger mind, disciplined and thoughtful. But still, in deep recesses, there are doubts. How simple to twine them about one another, to whisper to them, to build them into words she does not expect.

"Perhaps it is true," I say, and the redhead dutifully repeats. Miara looks up, startled at this accusation from an unexpected quarter. "When the youth between her legs cries to be filled, one could hardly expect her to honor the memory of her dear, dead husband."

Tears burst from Miara's eyes. In an instant she is up and fleeing. I leave the redhead so quickly that she stumbles back.

Miara hardly takes time to wrap herself, fleeing without her sandals into the icy streets. Her skin and hair steam in the mountain air. She runs to a deserted side street, pressing herself into a corner where her shoulders shake with tears, her insufficient wrap pulled tight about her and crumpled in her fist. I circle around her. In the baths I saw every part of her flesh, and yet only now, as she stands weeping, do the stirrings rise in me, and I decide that I must have her before I kill her. Never in my mortality was the desire stronger. Never in my damnation was the hunger deeper. My hands follow the outline of her thighs, her hips, her back. I move through her—and in a startled instant her weeping stops. I leap away.

She looks about, as though expecting to see someone. Finally, she realizes that her feet are naked, and she scurries up the street alone.

I congratulate you, says the freezing wind. I turn and find Elenora behind me, watching Miara's flight. *It took me the better part of a month to evoke such a reaction.*

I say nothing, only look up the mountain-climbing cobble road and watch as the blue and gold of Miara's silk turns to a side path. I am compelled to follow her, but in that instant I sense that a part of me is gone—a weakness amounting to one-fifth. Through the eyes of my body, I see one flame replaced by a brief thread of smoke.

The candles are burning out, I say, and Elenora nods.

She turns back to the street. *There is time. Come. My brother.*

•••

Garvin is a man of forty years, but far older. In the house he wears a heavy coat and cap. He is a large man, soft from the touch of wealth. His buckles are gold, and his spectacles trimmed in silver. Within the house above where my body is imprisoned, he writes in his ledgers, adds his rows of numbers, and always they grow larger.

In the minds of passersby on the cobble street below I hear contempt and envy, fear and mockery. *Mi'Garvin,* they think, the selfish man who would never have married but for his younger brother's untimely death.

Da'Garvin, the man who married but who is still an old bachelor. *Ni'Garvin*, the landlord and moneylender. *Ha'Garvin*, the fool who cannot even see the beautiful young wife in his house. A hundred epithets on the mind and tongue of everyone in the city, but never spoken in his presence. Money buys silence and respect, however insincere.

Within, he is as cold and filthy as the cobbles in the street. Yet it is little of his own doing. His business affairs are the wall of stone and rubble where he hides from his acquaintances, his business associates, his sister. Beneath his dealings lies only half a man, willingly blinded by his money and his petty dealings, hiding behind an imperfect fortress of paper and coin. I cannot destroy him. He has already destroyed himself.

But I can use him.

Miara, I whisper in his mind, and his pen scrawls to a stop. I fill him with images of her, of what I saw in the baths. He shakes himself and moves his pen with renewed vigor. Strange morality from a man who has lain with his sister every month for the bulk of his life. The Waiting Year.

No one observes the Waiting Year, I whisper. *They laugh because you do.* Again the pen stops. Again I show him her body—never touched by another man—awaiting him.

He swallows so loudly I can hear it through his ears. He gets up and stands at the window. Beyond, the city suffuses into the mountainside as evening comes. A hundred chimneys greet the night with sooty columns. A hundred snowy rooftops huddle beneath the lowering clouds.

He is not yet ready. I leave him with an image of Miara prone and waiting, her arms outstretched and welcoming. I will visit him again tonight.

• • •

From my own eyes, I look across Elenora's hidden
cellar. The five candles burn brightly, two tall and new,
the wax just beginning to run. Elenora labors over a low
table strewn with jars of dark liquid and bundles of
dried herbs, the scraping of mortar and pestle following
the movement of her shoulders.

"Do not go to him," I say. "No matter how he begs."

She neither starts nor looks up from her work. "He
has not begged since before he was a Tradesman. He has
not asked since before he was a Guild Master. And he
has kept his door locked since she came here."

"As if you wouldn't have a key to every room in this
house."

A smile touches her lips but she does not look up.
"My intention is to let him think he keeps me—not the
other way around."

"Subtlety being your only virtue."

"It is worth a thousand of you."

"Hmmph."

I slip out of myself and move around the room.
Through the haze of my ethereal vision I peruse the
vaulted stone ceiling, the dusty shelves and cupboards.
Her eyes follow me as I move.

I look at myself within the candled circle, huddled
and still, head bowed as if in prayer. Never before have
I seen the whole of myself, great and hunchbacked, my
spine crenelated like some vast mountain ridge, the enormous phallus and scrotum filling—and overflowing
—the space between my legs. The scales of my skin pass
through grays, greens, and blues to black, patterns at
once striking and hideous. From webbed fingers and
toes, razor claws emerge, downward curving, sharpened
above and below.

I look to Elenora as her hands drive the pestle in the muted silence of my ethereal ears. She stops and looks at me. I hold her gaze, unwavering, and she returns to her work.

•••

Elenora sleeps, naked on her bed. The coals of the fire illuminating her spartan room, the stone walls bare and unadorned. The one window, high on the wall, peers out onto the cobble road as if from a prison cell. But her domain is devised to keep others out, rather than her in.

I perch on the wardrobe at the head of the bed, look down on her sleeping form, my claws twitching for her blood. *What do you dream of, witch? What are your unfulfilled desires?*

I dare not enter her sleep. I would do as well to tromp about the house in my physical form, leaving burned imprints of my splayed feet in the carpets and wooden floors.

But I hover over her, my claws at her eyes, her throat, her breasts, and her little box, dreaming of where I will first tear her flesh. I leave her, move upward into the stilled house.

The house is empty of servants, and the kitchen is dark and forbidding, only the reflections of copper pots and utensils shining to my eyes. Even at noonday my sight is dim. Now, the night conceals all but the largest and brightest objects.

Beyond the windows of the house, oil lamps burn in the streets, and the overwhelming whiteness of the snow reveals every detail to my dimmed eyes. A Candleman moves among the street lamps, snuffing them now that the streets are empty. I drift down to him.

The crisp and biting cold stings his fingers and nose. The new-fallen snow crunches as we trudge to the next lamp, and I hear a donkey's nasal braying, carried crisply from afar. He raises the snuffer, and the circle of light ebbs to darkness. Even so, through his mortal eyes the darkness has a brilliance and clarity denied to my ethereal eyes.

I turn him to look back at Garvin's house. It is dark-wood atop brown granite. Other houses—though none so grand—crowd around it, separated by cobbled walks, wrought-iron fences, and tiny patches of snow.

I feel the weight of the kerosene flask at the Candleman's belt, and I know there are sulfur matches in his powder box. I make him remove one glove, take a match, strike it, and hold it, watching the flame burn toward his fingers, ever closer, closer, holding it until at last the pain breaks my grip and he flings it away, cursing. He stoops, pressing his burned fingers to the snow, wondering whatever possessed him to waste a perfectly good match. I leave him huddled over the snow and drift back to the house.

Most of the upstairs rooms are empty: a sewing room with a loom before the window, a sitting room. At last I find a room with a figure in the bed. Garvin.

He wears ornate silk sleeping clothes, a silk cap tied down around his ears. His mouth is open. I circle his bed. *What gold fills the pockets of your dreams, Old Man?* I stoop close to his face. Like a cat, his eyes are slits, watching even in his sleep. *Is it death you watch for, Old Man?* I reach into his chest, feel the echoed beats of his burdened heart.

His inner eye is filled with a dark too perfect for dreamlessness. *Where are you, Old Man? I have come to rob your gold of you; to steal you from your silver.* There is only silence. No smell of fear to expose his hiding place. But I know he is watching. *Keep your precious metals, Old Man, your jewels, your silks and spices on your ships and caravans of llama. But you will never have the one thing you want, unless you come and get it.* For an instant the light is blinding, but still the darkness remains around it, untouched, undiscovered. When I open my eyes, Miara stands before me, white as an angel, terrible as an army with banners. I circle her, perusing her perfection in Garvin's mind. Her light presses against the darkness, pushing it back, slowly, unflinchingly, mercilessly. I feel the weight of Garvin's sleeping eyes, and I move closer to her. *Why do you suppose she's here, Old Man?* My claws snick through the straps of her white gown and it flutters down about her feet. I hear him hiss from the darkness. *For you, Old Man.* My hands stroke the curves of her breasts, her buttocks. My claws comb her soft fur. And at last I smell Garvin's fear.

I look squarely into the darkness. *She is yours, if you're man enough to come and take her. Are you afraid she'll see you?*

I snatch her gown from the floor, wrap it deftly around her head, covering her face, her eyes, her ears. And when I look again, Garvin stands at the edge of the darkness, dressed in his sleeping clothes.

I lean to her ear. *It is your husband, Miara,* and she takes a faltering step toward him.

He moves closer in halting steps. Suddenly behind him, I whisper, *Is that any way to meet your bride?* My claws cut through silk, pluck away his cap, leaving him naked before her. His hands struggle vainly to cover himself. In his dream, her arms raise up to welcome him. *See, Old Man. She wants you.* And I push him into her embrace.

I draw my hand from around Garvin's heart. At his hips, the tenting of the linens reveals my success. Enough for tonight. Always leave him wanting more.

In the next room is a great bed, covered with fine lace and blankets of the purest wool. The Bridal Bed, made the day of the wedding, untouched until the Waiting Year is over. I look back at the door to Garvin's room: we shall see.

Through the next door I find Miara, her hands clutching the sheet to her breasts, the pillow stained with her tears. Beyond her bed, the windowpanes are etched with intricate patterns, her breath made flesh against the panes. Beyond and below, the snow-covered roof of the adjacent house, the windows dark.

Miara's is a simple white and sleeveless gown, her arms protected from cold only by the vigor of youth. I watch for a time as each breath presses her sides against the blanket, takes her deeper into sleep. My eyes follow the hills and cups of the blanket over her body, and once again I know I must have her.

Behind her child's face, her mind is clouded with the shadows of sleep. Images come and pass in the beat of a hummingbird's wing. *Slower,* I whisper. *Show me.*

Miara sits at the loom at the center of her life, weaving images of her mother and father, of her first love, of her favorite aunt taken these later years by madness, of her dead husband. In the fabric is the stream of her years, dreams and tears. Yet beneath warp and weft, a hollowness in the fabric, a flaw: the quest for something she cannot quite name nor weave into the cloth.

Her throat moves as she weaves, a soundless tune. Her hands travel so fast as to elude the eye. Patterns emerge in the cloth: destiny for Garvin, for Elenora. And still her own future escapes her. I step closer and suddenly her hands still. *Who's there?* She turns and looks directly at me.

Suddenly she is gone, upright in bed. Her lips move as they did in the dream. "Who's there?" And then she looks at me. Not past me. Not through me. I know beyond doubt that she knows I am there.

I flee downward, through floors and ceilings, past soot-darkened candelabras, and darkwood tables, dirty carpets awaiting spring beating, the ancient and iron-hard beams of the floors, through stone, back to the secret chamber, back to myself.

• • •

Before dawn comes, I scratch the mortar from around one stone of the floor, lift the stone out, and hollow out a space beneath, tossing the dirt to far corners of the room where Elenora's naked feet will not find it. Using the stone, I tip the tallest candle, snuff the flame. My claw melts cleanly through the wax, leaving me with two candles. One I tip into the hole I have hollowed beneath the stone, the other I relight from another candle, and then push it back into place. By the time I hear the lock and chain slide on the outside of the door, I have four candle-halves in the hole. I slip the stone back into place and crouch on it as the door swings open.

Elenora takes fresh candles from a cupboard, begins replacing the shortest ones. "How are you going to kill her?"

I look at her, remembering my claws over her heart in the light of last night's coals. "The substance of our contract is that I torment her, and then kill her. My plans are my own."

She removes the candle she has just placed in the circle, blows out its flame. "I could leave you to die."

"Then you would have to bloody your own hands. And then they would find you—and kill you."

She considers this, relights the candle and replaces it in the circle. "Soon then."

• • •

Garvin sits at the table, the morning meal growing cold before him. He surreptitiously watches Miara, his eyes darting away when she looks in his direction. I give him the image from his dream: Miara, naked, her arms extended to receive him. He stares at her as she eats, his mind rendering her gown to nothing.

Tonight, I whisper.

And he believes.

• • •

Through the day, I follow Garvin, decanting the image of Miara into his mind at every turn. His travels about the city, his business dealings, his meals, all are colored with his rising passion, and trembling at what he imagines for this night. To the images of his lust I add the flavor of power, flashes of Miara's rebellion, imagined laughter of the crowds at his blind obedience to the Waiting Year.

After years of Elenora's manipulation, Garvin's mind is supple, the paths of submission and willful blindness deeply etched. As the sun wanes in the west, a strange calm comes over Garvin, a calm I know from my own mortality: certainty born of delusion, of power, of lust over all.

•••

Miara sits at her loom, her hands flying over the threads. The finished silk, red as blood, frames her hair, her neck, her shoulders. With how many others in my mortality did it begin this way? A phrase of music, the smell of flowers in a field, the taste of fine wine, a flash of brilliant color.

Garvin stands in the doorway, watching her, his heart pounding the tattoo of confidence wavering. Quietly, I speak to him of the dream images, of her willingness, her readiness. And his blood stirs, filling with the power of lust. Images of Miara on the Bridal Bed overflow Garvin's mind, emptying it of all else.

Garvin steps forward, his hands coming to rest on the warm skin of her neck. She starts, dropping the shuttle, but realizes it is him and her hands rise to cover his for but a moment. She tries to stoop, to collect the shuttle, but I tighten his hands, hold her motionless. With Garvin's hands I untie her gown and feel her tense beneath me. I push the fabric of her gown from her shoulders and she collects it against her arms, stopping its downward flight. She tries to speak, but so light is she that even Garvin's flabby arms control her every movement, and I lift her from the stool. As in the dream, Garvin does not wish to see her eyes, for her eyes to see him. Keeping her back to him, I move her into the hallway. Seeing the door to the bridal room already open she tenses against me, but I push her through and to the bed. She turns to face him, her eyes pleading, but I do not let Garvin see them. Hands shaking, he tears the gown from her, the sound of ripping fabric only heightening his frenzy of power and lust. She tries to pull away, to escape to the hallway, but I throw her onto the bed. Garvin sheds his dressing gown.

"Husband, no," is all she whispers, but Garvin's heart pounds in his ears. She tries to pull away, but I grab her ankle, dragging her back. I clutch her arm and she winces as Garvin's fingers bruise her flesh. Then he is on her, his mouth pressed to her, his hands groping her tender flesh. Each time she tries to pull away I close my fingers over her skin, leaving red palm-marks. Garvin's knees bruise her thighs. He thrusts and she cries out, struggling to escape, but I am in control of her—of him. The lust drives all that Garvin now is. All he feels, hears, sees, smells, and tastes is him within her, him controlling her, him taking what is rightfully his, silencing the laughing townspeople.

But I still see. In her face are the uncounted women I took in my mortality, the marks of my hands on their arms, their breasts. But her neck is still white and pure. I force Garvin's unfeeling hands to her throat, so fine that his hands wrap completely around. And I squeeze. Instantly her eyes fly wide with fear and her struggles increase. My fist comes away from her neck, striking her cheek, her hair flying with the force of the blow, and my fingers close again around her neck. Her nails bite into Garvin's sides but he feels nothing, so entrapped is he within her. Her fists beat against him, she claws at his face, at his eyes, but her strength is failing.

How many faces have I watched as life ebbed? How many women's eyes have fluttered to emptiness as I have reached ecstasy within them?

But Garvin's body is not my own and his excitement finishes too soon. Suddenly his eyes see her blue-tinged face, his ears hear the struggling of her mouth trying to speak. And suddenly he is fighting me. The muscles of his arms wrench and twist. He draws himself from her, uses his legs to pull away. My hands stay locked around her throat as her eyes flutter and close. But as he drags

her from the bed, we fall and her body twists away.
With a shrieking gasp she breathes again, panting as she
tumbles and crawls away from me. I struggle to rise, to
go after her, but Garvin is in control of his legs, and
slowly he takes the rest of him, until I only see and feel
and hear. He struggles to speak, to beg her forgiveness,
but I do not let him find the words. He struggles to
crawl forward, to fall in supplication at her ankles, but
Miara stumbles to her feet and bolts naked out the
doorway, the sound of her weeping vanishing behind
the door of her room.

Garvin lies on the floor, shaking, gasping for breath.
His stomach convulses and he vomits on the brocade
carpet. He grabs the bedpost, pulls himself up, his shoes
dragging through the detritus. There is blood on the
rumpled silk and lace of the Bridal Bed. Garvin reaches
with a shaking hand, but cannot make himself touch it.
He pulls his housecoat over his nakedness and struggles to Miara's door. Within she is weeping, but Garvin
cannot bring his hand to touch her door any more than
he could her virgin blood.

Within, he tears at himself, anguish flooding every
chamber of his mind. With it comes my own memory of
a young girl, my hands coming away from her throat
stilled to silence, the rush of her final breath escaping
her withering breast, hissing between her blue lips. The
image overwhelms me, washes into Garvin's mind, and
he flees to his room.

I fall to my knees, screaming my anguish to the stone-
arched ceiling of Elenora's secret chamber until my
lungs collapse on themselves and my head falls
forward, my eyes clenched against the indelible image
of death.

Elenora stands at her table, her eyes wide, the stool
overturned, herbs scattered on the floor. I turn to face

her, no longer hiding the murderous rage I feel for her, and she falls back against the wall. "Leave!"

Composing herself, she feels her way along the wall until she reaches the door, then turns and flees. The chain rattles against the wood as she fumbles to close the padlock, and her footsteps fade up the stone stairway.

In the enclosing silence, I summon this rediscovered echo of mortality.

A man more nearly a boy, alone in the camps outside the city, confusion under the cloud of marching armies.

She was alone, scavenging food, staying ahead of the packs of boys always looking for mischief. Her dress was tattered, but in the camps no one noticed. Her near nakedness was common enough and she took no pains to cover more of herself than essential. She hadn't counted on me.

Newfound lust raving within, I followed at an unremarkable distance, waiting, watching for a glimpse beneath her tattered dress; hunting, though I did not know it at the time. The more I followed her, the more I saw of her provocative flesh, the more I was compelled to draw closer, my thoughts entertaining ever greater liberties. Outside the city, alone as darkness fell, I overtook her, fought her to the ground, tearing the rags from her. Twice, three times, four times, I forced myself to her, but each time she squirmed away. I struck her again and again, until she fell silent, her eyes clamped shut, her shoulders shaking with soundless tears. But it was not enough for me simply to have her. Almost of their own mind, my hands crept about her throat, crushing the air from her. Horrified and fascinated I watched as she at last grew still. I fell back from her, frightened but entranced by her naked and still form in the dirt, her knees parted as if inviting my return. Lightning and thunder. Rain fell in torrents, turning the ground to mud, but washing her body until her skin fairly shone, washing the blood from her nose and lips, filling the hollows of her eyes, her mouth hanging open as the dead are wont to do. I fled, repeating to myself that it had not been me, that something else had happened to her while I was taking her. I prayed to my pounding feet to carry me away from the image of her empty eyes, her slack-jawed and still-throated drinking of the rain. But my own betraying mind played before me again and again the moment that her eyes grew silent, that moment the light left them. Through the rain I listened for the echo of an intruder's voice, some deceiver who had driven me to this madness that still made my heart race with excitement. But I found no voice, only the pounding of my own desire, the thrill of knowing such pleasure and power in the same ecstatic moment. And I knew then that I had wanted it.

But now, as I listen to that long-ago, I hear the voice that had led me, bred me, prepared me, for that moment of taking beauty that no one thereafter could have. In the five-candle light of Elenora's secret room, I at last hear the voice I had for so long thought to be my own—and recognize it.

Master.

How old had I been when he claimed me for his own? How long before I starved to death in that rat-infested prison had he marked a place for me in his filthy river? When had he made me his son? And when had I learned his lessons so well?

• • •

Garvin sits on the edge of his bed, eyes dried of tears. I do not circle him as prey, but face him as an equal, an equal I have made in my own image, just as Master made me.

But I will not add another hundred deaths to my ledger.

I lean close to Garvin's ear. *How long before you would let me kill with your hands? How long before you would do it on your own? You are the child of your sister, of me, nothing more. Will you go on from this moment? Will you live from horror to horror, until nothing stills your hunger but the axe or the noose? Are you ready to sell yourself for the pottage of woman's flesh?*

Garvin digs the heels of his hands into his eyes, as if to crush the images from his sight. I need not peer into his mind to know he sees his own hands around Miara's throat, feels himself thrusting between her unwilling legs.

Try if you wish, Old Man, but you will never forget what we have done tonight. And someday soon, you will only want it again for yourself.

Garvin stands unsteadily and drags himself to the window. Through the rippled panes the city is quiet, unaware. He stares at the cobble street three stories below. And opens the window. The icy wind snuffs the candle, leaving the room in darkness. But with the vanishing light, a serenity comes over him. A certainty of escape. A hope of salvation. Garvin closes his eyes, and lets himself tumble through the window.

At the snowy ledge, I look down at the broken form in the thin snow of the street, waiting for the Candleman to find it. *Sorry, Old Man. But perhaps I have saved you from Charon's boat, after all.*

● ● ●

The mourners are few in the candlelit sitting room. None of them are here for DaNiHaMi'Garvin, and all but one are Elenora's sycophants and tagalongs. The one for Miara—the redhead—is cloaked in black, penitent for her unexplainable cruelty two days ago at the baths.

Elenora lingers in the room like a jackal, angered that Miara has lived to be heir, unwilling to do anything about it so soon after Garvin's untimely death—afraid that I will choose this inopportune moment to exercise our contract.

She glances at me from time to time, disapproving of my hovering over the bier like a funerary gargoyle. She suspects me in Garvin's death, but she is not sure. And, for the moment, I am still valuable to her.

Miara—SaSa'Miara, they call her—twice widowed—sits at the head of the wooden coffin, candle wax dripping onto the sleeve of her black gown, taking no notice of it. The veil of black feathers and lace conveniently hides the bruises on her face.

Upon hearing of her second husband's death, Miara's weeping over her rape gave way to a desolate silence that has robbed her of all sound but the weeping of her heart, the whispering of her breath as it moves the concealing widow's veil.

All that was Garvin's is now hers, and yet her sole possession at this moment is the despondence of the scorned, the homeless and estranged. Why does she not sing and dance over the wealth she has acquired? Why is she not vindicated in the death of he who took the only possession she had left? How different she is from anything in my experience. In this moment, I find my only hunger is to know what she knows, to know the powers that drive her incomprehensible actions. Elenora watches my every gesture, but I ignore her, passing quietly into Miara—not to terrorize or humiliate, but to understand.

Within, I find only cathedral emptiness, and the weeping she has banished from her eyes, the echoes of legion tears. In the alcoves of this space lie memories dredged to new life, memories kept and honored.

Garvin, the elder brother.

At her wedding to Danrill, Garvin's brother, Garvin genteelly kisses her cheek, secretly presses something into her hand, whispers to tell no one. A hundred-crown gold piece—the dowry her family had not been able to afford.

In another alcove, a chance meeting with Garvin in the marketplace. She confides the amorous advances of her husband's landlord. Within a month, the landlord's investments fail. Within two, Garvin owns the residence.

At Danrill's funeral, Garvin does not wait for her to come pleading. At a moment of Elenora's absence, he tells her all—of himself, of Elenora, of their incestuous relationship. He tells her, not to frighten her away, but to save her the humiliation of his refusal to wed her, to save her from life within his house. Back in the sitting room, standing at her husband's coffin, she kneels before Garvin, before the assembled mourners, and petitions his mercy: Ad'Garvin, she addresses him—wise Garvin —her sign of forgiveness. He knows it for what it is, and accepts her before the assembled mourners.

And at last I know. Had Garvin come to her, even before the Waiting Year was through, she would not have refused him, but taken him into herself with welcoming arms. It is why she did not fight until I forced his hands around her throat. Miara's silent weeping is not for herself, but for him. Never, though she heard them, did the epithets—Da', Ni', Ha', Mi'—portend him in her mind. She was the only one—even counted against Elenora—who knew his true soul. As I now know hers—and know the danger she is in.

Elenora, I whisper. I need say nothing more.

Miara looks up. Through the whispered irreverences of Dirina and the others, Elenora looks back, and their eyes meet. In that moment, I know I have revealed my intent. In that moment, I know that Elenora has become my enemy—and I hers—and that I am now Miara's guardian. What Garvin could not finish, I must now complete.

•••

Tired by the funeral procession, and by the grief she hides, Miara excuses herself upon returning to the house.

Into the night, Elenora tolerates the loud and drunken presence of Dirina and the others, her patience growing thinner with each adoration of Miara's new wealth and status. When she is at last alone, Elenora prowls the house with the tolerance of a beleaguered panther.

I crouch on the stairs leading up to where Miara sleeps. Elenora does not speak to me, does not even acknowledge me beyond the occasional glance, as if taking stock of a hindrance to be circumvented. But her occasional glances beyond where I sit, to the gallery at the top of the stairs, reveal her mind.

Whether my presence, so solid to her conjuror's eyes, has deterred her assault on the stairs, or whether she has hesitated, waiting to resolve some indecision, she at last turns, taking the stairs two at a time. Instantly I am with her, and she turns within to repel me. Unlike the others, who are unaware of my presence, she recognizes every toehold I get, breaking it before I can secure myself within her. Even so, her body staggers, swaying, and finally tumbles down the stairs.

She looks up to find me once again positioned on the steps.

She turns away, toward her rooms below, and my body within the circle and the five-pointed star.

•••

I return to myself as the chain rattles against the door. I have added more candles to my tiny hoard beneath the stone, and those that remain in the circle burn low. Quickly I sink my claws into the candle farthest from the door, and pull it a short distance into the circle.

The door swings open. Elenora enters, stopping at the cupboards to collect the knife she uses for cutting her herbs. She approaches, stopping just beyond the circle, studying the five wavering candles.

She stoops before the first candle, holding the knife at ready, staying beyond the circle's limit. Quickly she tips the candle and snuffs the flame. I roar my anger, and strike out at her, the circle ringing as it deflects my assault. She extinguishes the next candle, and then the next. With each candle, my attack is more subdued—both from weakness and design—striking at her only with my clawed hand. Let her become confident. And careless.

As she reaches for the fourth candle, I lunge and she springs back, untouched. Coming forward again, her eyes remain on me as she reaches for the candle, not seeing that it is within the circle. As her fingers touch the candle, she glances down, but not soon enough. My hand flashes out, driving my claws through her palm and dragging her into the circle, knocking over the

fourth candle and extinguishing it. Reeling under
sudden dizziness, I sink my teeth into her breast, tearing
flesh, and her scream fills the stone-walled room. Her
hand flashes up, burying the blade in my throat, and I
recoil, roaring in pain. I strike for the death blow to her
throat, but she twists away and my claws plunge through
her shoulder, the searing blades emerging through the
shattered bone of her shoulder.

The knife still burning in my throat, I drive my claws
into the soft flesh between her legs, feeling them scrape
against the heavy bone of her pelvis. I fling her away,
her body making a dull smack against the wall and
leaving marks of blood on the stone. She tumbles down
beside the door, and lies still. But her emerald eyes
are open.

Tatters of cloth and flesh hang from my dagger teeth,
and the taste of her blood is sweet opium, nearly
blinding me to anything but the lust for more. But the
searing pain in my throat brings me back. I draw out the
blade, and it is coated with black blood that hisses and
bubbles. Amid the smell of her scorched flesh, I use the
knife to draw the fallen candles back into the circle, all
but the third which is too far to reach. I relight one of
them, setting it on one empty point of the star, feeling
vigor flow back into my limbs. I fling the knife away
and touch the wound at my throat. Already the
bleeding has stopped.

Through the tatters of Elenora's bloody gown, the
rents in her flesh are deep and dark. Where the cloth is
torn away over her breast, I see the white of her ribs.

Three claws are gone from my hand, broken against
her pelvis. I strike the broken stubs against the stone,
sending sympathetic vibrations through the lost shards,
and she cries out, doubling with the pain.

"Not dead yet, I see." I hunker down to wait. "But soon enough."

Bleeding from nose and mouth, she drags herself up against the wall. "I'll outlive you," she says. She pulls herself to her unwilling feet. "And her." Her back steadied against the wall, she finds the latch chain on the door. I project myself into her, but reel back at the explosion of pain from her wounds, and she easily repulses me. She pulls the door open and falls through onto the steps.

And I realize I have been a fool. A fool for not killing her when I had her. A fool for casting aside the knife when I could have plunged it into her heart even from the circle. Back to myself, I quickly dig at the rock that hides my cache of candles, but with three claws missing I am clumsy retrieving it. The door clumps shut as I raise the rock above me. Still I hurl it at the closed door, and the wooden beams shatter under the blow. But the rock's momentum is spent.

Elenora has left a trail of blood through the doorway. How long before she succumbs to her wounds? I cannot wait to see.

I project myself to Miara, into her dreams. I call to her again and again, but her sleep is deep, drugged with grief and tears, and she does not hear. I leave her.

Elenora lies at the bottom of the stairs on the main floor, her breast heaving against pain and loss of blood. She drags herself up a step, rests, then drags herself up another.

I return to Miara, but still I cannot reach her.

In the street, I search for someone else to use. A short distance away, I see a street lamp vanish, the Candleman invisible in the darkness beneath. In an instant, I am with him. Together, we make our way to the door of the house. I reach his hands forward and try the latch, but it is fast. I throw his shoulder against the door, but it remains secure. I drive his bundled elbow through the ornate glass and reach through, releasing the lock, and push my way in.

Elenora lies at the middle of the stairs. I fight to control the Candleman as he recoils from the sight of her savaged flesh. I push him forward, to stop her, to drag her back down the stairs until she is too weak to climb, too weak to threaten Miara.

She watches me as I climb to her, the steps slippery with her blood. As I stoop to drag her back, her hand flashes forward and for an instant I see a trail of silver in the air before the impact of pain drives me from the Candleman. From above I watch as his body tumbles back, the haft of the cook's knife echoing the last vibrations of his heart. As he falls, the heavy flask at his belt shatters, and yellow liquid courses down the steps.

Elenora tumbles after him and lies at the bottom of the stairs, her body shaking with pain and weakness. She reaches for the powder box at the Candleman's belt. Again I plunge into her, and again her pain and her power repulse me. I repeat it a second time and a third, as she opens the tin, removes a match, and strikes it. Instantly, the stairs erupt into flame, and the orange tongues easily climb the wooden walls and tapestries.

Elenora drags herself back as the flames creep over the Candleman's body. Finally, she stops, leaning against the brocade fabric of the divan. Smiling, she watches the flames creep upward toward Miara's room, watches until, at last, her emerald eyes fall still.

Within Miara's mind I call to her again, but still she sleeps. Desperately, I plunge my claws into the side of my head, pain lancing through my ethereal body. Cutting deep, I tear my ear away, screaming at the agony, struggling to stay at Miara's side. I press my severed ear to Miara's, waiting as the threads of her own ethereal matter twine around it, taking it in.

Miara!

She stirs under the covers. I call again, and her eyes flutter open. Instantly she smells the smoke. She climbs from the bed and flings the door open, only to have smoke pour in around her, choking her.

The window! I cry.

She starts at my voice, looks around the room, but the smoke obscures her vision. She pushes the door shut and turns back. Beyond the window, the snow-covered rooftop is a long way away, the wrought-iron fence jagged beneath it. She hesitates, looks back at the smoke coming around the closed door. She climbs to the windowsill, stoops there for a moment, shivering with fear and cold. I stand close at her side.

You can do it, I whisper, praying I am right.

Uncertain, she turns, as if to look back for the source of my voice. Flames burst through the smoke coming around the door.

Go! I cry.

And she is gone.

•••

I huddle in the faint light of the one candle I permit myself to burn. The cellar is cold now. The heat of the fire above, which melted two of my candles as they burned, is gone. The doorway and steps are filled with ash and blackened debris.

I move up through the ceiling, passing among the blackened beams. The house lies ruined, burned to its foundation, the snow settling on the charred timbers as if to erase what happened here. Two of the town's constables root among the rubble, tossing aside soot-stained kitchen implements and shattered crystal left by the flames. I watch as they find the bones of Elenora and the Candleman, blackened by the flames. I look to the roof of the adjacent house for the mark left by Miara's fall, but the snow was melted by the fire, and the roof recovered anew by the night's storm. I fear that she, too, is dead.

I descend back into the secret cellar.

Again, I try the circle, and it rings under the touch of my claw, the magic surviving its maker. It curves to a close above me, just below the vaulted stone of the ceiling, just as it closes in the earth beneath.

I have considered simply snuffing the candle, wondering if Elenora was lying, wondering if that is the key to breaking the circle. But that is an act best reserved for the final candle's desperation.

•••

It is night outside as I light the last candle and place it where a point meets the circle. I will not pray to Master, and I dare not pray to God, so I raise my voice to Miara, if perchance she can hear me.

•••

The candle is nearly gone when I hear movement above. I pass upward through the stone and cinders.

Wrapped in white fur and velvet, Miara stands among the ashes. I would sing if I could.

She looks around her as if for something forgotten, something not quite familiar. Her lips move, and I know she calls to me.

I am here, I say, and she steps suddenly forward, her hand rising to her breast. *I am trapped beneath you, in a room where Elenora kept me prisoner. I will die soon.*

She looks around, finally seeing the stairway filled with burnt timbers.

Below, I listen as she clears the stairway, and finally I see her feet, her legs, then her body profiled against the faint light from above. She peers into the darkness of the room. And suddenly I am afraid of her.

"Where are you?" she calls.

I turn my back to her. "Please. I don't want you to see me."

"You are the one who saved me from the fire," she says. "And who came to me three nights ago—in my dreams."

I keep my face turned from her. "And I am the one who drove Garvin to . . ."

"I know."

I hear her steps draw closer and I huddle lower, wishing I could vanish. I turn, ready to dash out the light of the candle, to send myself where Elenora had meant, but Miara's hand is over the flame. Her eyes meet mine and I turn away. "How can you look into my face and not flee?"

"You think my sight is limited to ugliness and misery?"

"I have nothing else to offer."

"You have a bold heart and a soul remade."

"Not much use, when you live under Charon's boat. Or when you're stuck in a dead woman's circle."

"More use than you know."

Miara looks down, studying the bounds of Elenora's circle. She puts her hands up as if following it in the air.

She steps into the circle, her legs straddling my enormous penis. She holds her hands out to me. "Take my hands."

"I'll burn you."

"No," she says. "You will never hurt me again."

I reach up, gently take her hands, and let her lead me from the circle.

And suddenly I am falling.

• • •

The woman is gone from where I bound her with the foul river-bottom weeds. In my absence, Master has come and collected her.

With my one remaining ear I hear Charon's boat above. I float quietly to the surface, looking up into the eyes of each prisoner on the deck. I shake my head and sink again, waiting.

Uncounted passages later, as I look up, I find emerald green eyes. And I smile.

I dive deep beneath the boat. Coming up, I build such speed that my impact splinters the planks of the hull, nearly tearing the ship in half. Charon comes forward, his pole at ready, but the boat lists suddenly with the inrushing water, and the pole only strikes a glancing blow off my back. I tear it from his hands, fling it into the water, and then dive after it. I tear through the prisoners, casting them aside as they flounder, until I see her again. In the same moment, she recognizes me, her eyes flying wide, her mouth open in an inarticulate cry of despair. I dive below, waiting, waiting until I taste her terror in the water, then come up, driving my claws between her legs and dragging her down, pulling her away from the wreck. Her struggles last longer than my others. She knows what she has to fear.

The other swimmers are long gone to shore when at last I drag her down, still screaming. She struggles as I bind her to the riverbed. I draw my claws over the breast whose mortal form I destroyed. Her perfect ethereal flesh gives beneath my touch, waiting for all I will do to her.

Thunder.

The water stirs and grows warm, and I know that Master is already coming to claim her.

But I remember the girl outside the city, when Master first spoke to me, when he watched and pleasured as I took my first innocent's life, and set me on the path to this place.

What was it Miara said?

A bold heart, and a soul remade.

I stretch my claws and turn to meet him.

HOW I'VE BEEN PASSING THE TIME UNTIL WAITING IS FILLED

Written by
K. D. Wentworth

About the Author

K. D. Wentworth lives in Tulsa with her husband, numerous finches and a 126-pound Akita, and teaches elementary school. She got her start in the L. Ron Hubbard Writers of the Future Contest in 1988 and has since sold short fiction to such markets as Aboriginal SF, F&SF, Hitchcock's Mystery Magazine, Return to the Twilight Zone, Did You Say Chicks?!, Tomorrow, and Realms of Fantasy.

She has also published four novels, Black on Black from Baen Books being the most recent. Her stories "Burning Bright" (Aboriginal SF) and "Tall One" (F&SF) were Nebula nominees for 1997 and 1998 respectively.

Ten years ago, I stood on a carpeted dais with twelve other writers at the United Nations and accepted my framed plaque for winning Third Place in the last quarter of the 1988 L. Ron Hubbard *Writers of the Future* Contest. The award was for "Daddy's Girls," my first published story. I felt I was on the brink of my career—I had gotten my foot in the door at last. What I had dreamed of for so many years was all about to happen. As it turned out, I was both right and wrong.

I went back to Tulsa and resumed teaching, kept in touch with some of my workshop friends, and wrote. Bridge Publications scheduled radio interviews for me all across the country, as well as a local newspaper interview. My name and picture were in *Locus*. I was invited to the local science fiction convention as a program participant. I was getting a lot of attention as well as good experience, but it was for just one story. And I was still getting rejections, lots of them, both on my short stories and the two novels I had completed up to that date.

Still, it was a heady sort of "honeymoon" period. I remember the first time a radio interviewer asked my opinion about something. My opinion? Someone, anyone, actually cared what I thought? The notion was dizzying. I wasn't in Oz yet, but the landscape did indeed seem to be changing.

As the months passed, though, I became much more discouraged than I had ever been before winning. Previously, I had expected selling my work to take a while, that I would have to pay my proverbial dues just like everybody else. Now my expectations had been raised, and the success I longed for just wasn't happening. One of the how-to-write books I had read said that succeeding as a writer was "fifty percent talent and fifty percent not giving up." Well, I told myself, no one has any control over the former, but you can darn well not give up.

Then, in December, a year after winning in the Contest, the initial waiting, as Heinlein's Michael Valentine Smith would say, was "filled." I sold a story to *Starshore*, a debuting pro-level magazine. It just so happened that particular story was the first one I wrote after attending the *Writers of the Future* Workshop (thanks, Algis!). A month later, *Pulphouse* accepted another story. A few small press sales followed in the summer. Then that October, I had one dizzying week in which I sold three stories, including one to *Aboriginal SF*, which made my third professional sale and qualified me for Active Membership in the Science Fiction Writers of America, the professionals' not-quite trade union.

By that time, I was beginning to be able to glimpse the difference between work that sold and work that didn't. I wrote a third novel, sneaking in a few stories here and there for short-term gratification. I received a good rejection from DAW Books on my second novel, saying they had liked it. The occasional short fiction sale made waiting less painful, but my desire to sell a novel was growing so intense that it's a good thing no one came along right about then to bargain for my soul.

Late in 1990, I wrote a story that garnered my first personal rejection from *The Magazine of Fantasy & Science Fiction*, then sold to *Hitchcock's*.

Through the following year, the stories I had been selling began to see print and I churned out a fourth novel, a sequel to the unsold second. I wasn't altogether sure it was wise to write a sequel at that point, but it did provide a chance to learn how to do it when no deadlines loomed to make me crazy.

My first rewrite request came from *Pulphouse* in 1991, just after I won a scholarship to the Wesleyan Writers Conference in a "Fields Publications Teachers as Writers" contest. I headed up to Connecticut to Wesleyan and spent ten days there working on the rewrite, as well as attending classes and seeing a new side of the writing game. Rewriting proved a definite challenge, but Dean Smith's suggestions were spot on and I learned from the experience. Up to that point, no one had liked any of my rejected stories enough to ask me for a rewrite. The new version was accepted by *Pulphouse*, and I felt another inch closer to becoming a professional.

Then I had a rewrite request from *F&SF*. Gee, this was great! Again, I learned a great deal in the process. I gave the story a new ending and it became my first sale to *F&SF*. I had moved up one more tiny step on the ladder to success.

From time to time during these years, I tormented myself by querying agents and asking them to consider representing me. They either didn't answer me at all, or had me send them a manuscript, only to take months before reading it, or to never get around to it at all. Time would melt away and then I would be right back where I started.

I wrote a fifth novel in 1992, *The Imperium Game*, but when I finished the first draft, I couldn't bring myself to revise it. You're an idiot! I told myself. You spend all your time writing novels, but you can't even give one away! You're selling short fiction to good markets, so you should just stick to that for a while.

It was a decision born of tooth-grinding frustration, but it turned out to be exactly the right thing to do, in more than one way. I put aside the manuscript for five months, wrote more short stories, sold some of them, and when I finally did get back to the novel, saw much more clearly what needed to be done. I had gained enough emotional distance from the writing to be objective. I spent four months rewriting and then sent it off to Del Rey Books, because I'd read about their Discovery program for new writers.

Later that year, a former editor in the field decided to become an agent and signed with a top firm. She called around to the magazines for the names of new writers who were considered "up and coming," as she put it, and didn't yet have representation. She got my name from *F&SF* and gave me a call.

"Have you written any novels?" she asked.

"Only five," I said, not sure whether to be pleased or ashamed that I had five unsold novels to my credit.

She told me to pick one and send it her way. Three weeks later, she agreed to represent me. Three weeks after that, Del Rey bought *The Imperium Game*.

Here follows another heady period in which I sold three novels to Del Rey in eighteen months, the second two being *Moonspeaker* and its sequel, *House of Moons*. The opportunity to work with a good editor at Del Rey was invaluable. Mine took the time to help me see the kinds of mistakes new writers make in general and the ones in particular I was prone to making myself. I did pages of corrections and changes on all three books, and in the end, knew a whole lot more about the novel-writing process and how not to mess up in the first place.

I was on my way, I remember thinking after selling the third book. This is it. I'll write novels, kiss the day job of grading papers goodbye and live my dream life. It's all finally happening (sound familiar?).

Only, in today's market with game-tie-in and media-tie-in novels, shelf space for new writers is shrinking fast. Selling a novel turns out to be just the tip of the marketing iceberg. After that, you have to get the book into the stores, and, in this brave new world of computer ordering, that's a lot harder than it sounds. Almost four years would pass before I sold another book.

At any rate, after three novels, there I was, washed up on the shoals. When the going gets tough, when life gives you lemons—I'm sure you know all the litanies. What else is there to do when things aren't going your way, but work harder and harder and harder? I'll "dance with what brung me," I told myself in the dialect of my region. I'll write more short fiction while I work on a new novel.

It helped somewhat that I was beginning to receive the occasional invitation to write for anthologies, but the subconscious is a sly beast. Mine worried endlessly that I wasn't good enough, that I would never really succeed. It kept whispering that I had hit the wall and gone as far as I would ever get in the writing game.

This cost me a year of endlessly writing and rewriting the first ten chapters of a novel-in-progress before I finally realized what I was experiencing was a failure of nerve. *Self*, I said sternly, once I figured out that all this rewriting was producing only the illusion of forward progress, *finish the blamed thing!* What did it matter if it did turn out to be terrible? No one wanted to buy it anyway! So I did, at last, manage to complete it.

In the middle of all this, last year, my short story "Burning Bright," published in *Aboriginal SF*, became a finalist for the SFWA's Nebula Award.

Shortly thereafter, I sold another novel, *Black on Black*, providing me with the chance to get back on the horse that had thrown me, so to speak, and once again hold on for dear life as I head for the elusive finish line.

The last year has in many ways been very good to me. A publisher asked me to contribute a cover quote for a writer's first novel. The author of a how-to-write book on "openings that sell" recently requested a story beginning and comment from me. I was asked to judge the Oklahoma Writers Federation SF Novel Excerpt Contest. I had a story published in the second volume of the *Chicks in Chainmail* series, *Did You Say Chicks?!*, and sold another to the third; and I sold fiction to *F&SF*, *Marion Zimmer Bradley's Fantasy Magazine*, *Cemetery Sonata*, *The Science Fiction Law Journal*, *Quantum*, and *Realms of Fantasy*, among others. My fourth novel, *Black on Black*, was published and I recently learned my latest *F&SF* story, "Tall One," is another Nebula finalist.

So, how does it feel to stand here, ten years later, with a second Nebula nomination for short fiction, over forty stories either in print or about to be, and my fourth book careening down that crowded bookstore race-track? It feels . . . like I finally understand what I'm doing, that I'm on the brink, about to make the grade, and it's all really going to happen this time.

But, mostly, it feels like I need to work harder.

MY SON, MY SELF

Written by
Amy Sterling Casil

Illustrated by
Lee Seed

About the Author

Amy Sterling Casil has led quite a life of letters since graduating from the Clarion Writers' Workshop in 1984. She contributes regularly to Speculations, *the publication for writers, is the moderator of the America Online Fiction Writers Workshop, is a staff member for The Writers' Club on the Web, and teaches in a number of other places. Last year, she published "Jenny with the Stars in Her Hair," a finalist story in L. Ron Hubbard Presents* Writers of the Future, *Volume XIV. This year, she is a prize winner.*

She received her MFA in creative writing from Chapman University in Orange, California.

About the Illustrator

Lee Seed began professional art lessons at the age of ten. With a background of costume illustration and design for the stage, Lee turned to science fiction and fantasy illustration upon attending her first convention and discovering the work of Michael Whelan.

Since placing in the L. Ron Hubbard's Illustrators of the Future Contest, she has gone to work for ICE Games, DNA Publications, Pirate Writings Magazine, and has formed her own charity organization, Art Against AIDS, which raises money to benefit pediatric AIDS hospices.

Lee currently resides in Houston, Texas.

The doctors could have given me the news over a cup of Jamaican Blue Mountain coffee or whispered it in my ear with a kiss on the cheek, a Judas kiss: Oh, by the way, Gerald Knight, you have advanced cancer of the pancreas. Instead, they mailed me a typed green half-sheet of paper addressed to Mr. Gerald Knight, with "Your Cancer Support Group is Tuesday Night at 7:30 p.m. in the Fontana Health Center Lounge" scrawled across the bottom by some clerk with a capitalization fetish.

I had to call Lou.

"Good morning, Knight AIA, this is Lou."

"Get Rennie home on a plane right now." Click.

Sweet Lula Lou, better than a wife. Get my sixteen-year-old Rennie on a plane from two thousand miles away. She would do it. Was Rennie still chunky? I was "husky" until sixteen or so, then I shot up. High-water Jerry. Ma Dearest could only afford the fake Sears Levis and she got my T-shirts six to a pack. The collars fell off after three washings. High-water Jerry with his navy blue PF Flyers, the closest I could come to cool shoes— Hush Puppies or Doc Martens. One shining moment junior year, the five-buck K-Mart black polyester loafers had been in style and I had a pair.

They told me that I had an aptitude for using a template and a CAD program. No one could see my high-water pants or the holes in my socks on a UC application form. I ate Top Ramen for eight years.

Back then, there was Kendra. I always figured that Kendra left because she was sick of rotting while I studied half the night. Maybe she was sick of paying for every dinner and every movie and buying my Hush Puppies and Pierre Cardin socks and a half-price double-breasted Armani suit for my big interviews.

Kendra straddling my thighs, wearing one of my white T-shirts with a frayed neck, the scent of some tropical fruit on her breath and the scent of musky vanilla in her hair as it brushed my lips like feathers.

Now, I am an important man, Gerald Knight the architect, so important and desirable that cancer cells want to hang out at my place for a while. Hang out *in* my place. I get phone calls, Kendra, from beautiful women. Kendra is probably fat now, with four kids, a minivan, a golden retriever and an equally fat husband smashing down her pretty tits every night.

I am not alone. I have Rennie. Flesh of my flesh.

When I designed the Rancourt Center for the Performing Arts seventeen years ago, they gave me a check big enough to start my own practice. I opened the office, I hired Lou, and what was left over was enough to clone Rennie.

I worried for a long time that the woman who carried Rennie for nine months might want him, might sue, some of that stupid crap I saw on realvid. But it never happened. Rennie came home from the hospital and I fed him and cradled him and he grew up just fine. Him and me and sometimes Lou, who was good with babies and little kids.

I didn't want him going to school here, not in Redlands. No high-water Rennie, not with me to look after him, but there are more subtle and painful forms of persecution than razzing a guy's short pants or his worn-out sneakers. Stuff I don't like to talk about. Rennie was safe in Connecticut at the Braxton School.

I hadn't seen him for four years.

•••

Rennie said his room was "fine, Dad, fine." This morning the sun was as sharp as light glinting off a stainless steel steak knife. Rennie's hair was smooth like a beaver's back, damp from the shower. Smooth, clear light brown. Rennie, when you are forty-five, you will have silver hairs threading the brown, at your temples and on the crown of your head. They will be wiry and thicker than the rest of your hair. You'll pluck them one at a time when you first notice them. You'll consider a tube of metal-based "natural" color which feels like Brylcreem. Then you will realize that the green turd-colored hair of your golf buddies comes from this crap.

At sixteen, were my cheekbones as sharp as Rennie's? Did I have that fuzzy down on my jaw and my upper lip when my pants turned into clam diggers in the space of two weeks?

"I'm going for a bike ride." Rennie picked up his Italian ceramic bowl and slurped the milk which remained, licking a cornflake from the rim.

The stitch in my side had turned into a pair of needle-nosed pliers. The air was crisp, the sun bright as steel. The gardener had just ridden over the lawn and the odor of the fresh-cut grass filtered into the kitchen, mixed with the milk and the coffee and the cornflakes.

"Glad I got the bike. Can I come?"

"Gonna go now," Rennie said, flashing his white, slightly crooked teeth.

Illustrated by Lee Seed

I was still in my robe and bare feet. "Go out and make sure Jose got the clippings off the sidewalk," I said. I could throw on jogging shorts and a sweatshirt. The Marlboro Grand Prix shirt was clean.

Rennie shrugged.

I trotted back to the bedroom, the pliers twisting every step. "No," I said to the cancer, "you're taking a holiday today." At eleven, I had my second appointment with The Specialist. Chin-Yeh or Yeh-Chin. I rehearsed what I would say to him. "I'm fine, Doctor Chin-Yeh (or Yeh-Chin), I went bike riding with my boy this morning. I bet you'll find those bad-boy cells have made a major retreat into my bladder, and I have peed them all out."

Somewhere in the Cancer Support Group pap, there was a line about "Attitude Can Win!" I would think those cells into retreat. I was the general, marshaling my immune system into formation, attacking and killing the perverted cells infiltrating my pancreas.

I found if I held my thigh a certain way, I didn't limp when I went into the garage to get the bikes. If I leaned over the bike seat, the needle-nosed pliers released. Rennie would suspect nothing.

If you ride east from the house, it's flat for a quarter of a mile, then all downhill, turn after twisting turn, a gleeful joyride of wind in your face. A Bronco or a Beemer might suddenly loom around one of those curves, chrome bumper and personalized license plate right in front of your front wheel. I'd taken Rennie down this hill when he still had training wheels, me jogging after him, yelling encouragement.

But there were no Beemers. It was after nine, everyone was off, to work or the country club. We reached the foot of the hill. I was sucking air, curled over in a racing posture. "Speed racer," I said to Rennie, trying to grin, though my mouth had dried out and it wasn't a racing posture, it was a plier-avoidance posture.

Rennie braked beside the patch of weeds and wildflowers the city fathers called a "nature zone," and put one long, pale leg out to prop the bike. He turned, frowning.

"Dad, is this about Jack?"

I didn't know who he meant. I shrugged and curled my arm inward to press down the pain in my side.

"I mean, did you bring me home like this because of me and Jack?" Beads of sweat dotted Rennie's downy upper lip. It was hotter than I'd thought it would be. The Marlboro Grand Prix shirt flapped wetly against my back. Rennie's monthly e-mails. He'd talked about a friend, maybe his name had been Jack.

"No," I said. "Why would I have a problem with your friend?" What was up? Him and Jack, smuggling six-packs into the dorm? Smoking joints? Groping town girls after curfew?

I remembered something Rennie had written about this Jack being on the rugby team. Big kid, most likely. "Is this the guy who played rugby?"

Rennie nodded. "I thought you might have been upset," he said.

One of the long muscles twitched in Rennie's slender thigh. "No," I said. "I thought maybe you could take some time off. I wanted . . ." I wanted to bring home my boy, because I'm dying.

"I'm kind of pissed," Rennie said, looking down at the split tarmac which bordered the "nature zone" as if he might find a twenty-dollar bill. "Jack and I, well, I'm gonna miss him. He was pretty pissed, too. I mean, I've only got a couple of semesters left. We were talking about colleges and stuff. Maybe Dartmouth or Yale. Jack's into law."

Jack=friend=pissed=miss him. Your boy has grown from a gangly-kneed laser-tag fan into a young man.

"You can see your friend again. Maybe over the summer."

"You don't understand," Rennie said, then flipped up the kickstand and started back up the hill.

He was already a block away by the time I got my bike turned around and started after him. "It's okay," I called. His brown hair was flying, his sleeveless shirt flapping around his waist. I thought he probably heard, but he didn't turn. His legs were pumping furiously.

I stood on my pedals and tried to catch up. The needle-nosed pliers twisted. My face felt freeze-dried. The sweatshirt was soaked. Then came the other pain in my gut, the snakes, twisting around. Rennie pedaled faster. He rounded a curve. The sun was like a blind penny in the sky, heated white-hot. Somebody took the penny and threw it into my gut, where it burned and seared.

I've known pain. Sometimes I've even enjoyed pain. Like tonguing a sore tooth. You can't help yourself. But this wasn't an aching tooth. This was a puking, twisting bayonet.

I would not get off the bike. Rennie would not see his father sweating like a five-hundred-pound woman, walking the bike up the driveway. I pedaled, each downward stroke of my legs a fresh agony. I couldn't see anything, just chunks of asphalt torn up which I had to avoid so I wouldn't do a header and kill myself, and I found myself making the way back up to the house, two and a half miles, by counting the chunks of pavement. Ten . . . twenty . . . thirty. If I counted, I could breathe. Hee-hee-haw. Breathing out, just breathing out, that was it.

As I crept up the driveway, I saw Rennie's bike, leaning against the garage door.

I stopped halfway up the driveway, got off the bike as the snakes did an undulating tango in my abdomen.

Sometimes things happen you can't do anything about. Like when a bunch of reptiles wrap themselves around your stomach and you toss everything you've eaten for the last twenty-four hours over the freshly mown lawn, and you curse the day you ever put in the used-brick lawn border because it hurts like hell when your nose slams into it.

"Rennie." I vomited again. The grass was cool. It didn't stink. I was all wet. I thought I'd dried off after my shower.

"Dad," I heard Rennie saying from somewhere very far away. Someone grabbed my shoulders and turned me over, so I could see the white-hot-penny sun. Why was I so cold? Who had shot me? Someone shot me in the side, and I couldn't move.

"Dad, what's the matter?"

"I'm fine," I said, very clearly and distinctly. "There is absolutely nothing the matter."

Rennie was crying.

•••

"The unfortunate thing about this type of cancer," Dr. Yeh-Chin was saying, "is that we seldom see it until it is advanced." Asymptomatic, he called it. Until it was too late. He had prefaced this information with five minutes of lecture featuring the words "fool" and "idiot," in relation to my bike ride with Rennie.

There were the usual doctor's office furnishings, diplomas, certificates, medical books for show, and some things I hadn't expected. Yeh-Chin had a holographic model of the L-5 station on his bookcase. Astronaut models. A space nut. His desk was made of bird's-eye maple and probably cost as much as he paid his receptionist in a year. Yeh-Chin's face was broad, his eyes tiny and unreadable, set close to his broad, freckled nose. I hadn't realized that Chinese people got freckles. Well, why not? They looked like little flecks of dirt.

He had been silent for a long while. I asked him how long I'd had the cancer.

"Probably about ten years."

So, I hadn't had it when they did Rennie. Imagine a kid growing up with cancer. And Rennie was exactly like—

"Interesting," Yeh-Chin said, flicking a button on his datapad and squinting at the glowing display. "You have a viable clone."

"Will he get it? What can be done?" I scooted forward in the slippery leather chair, holding my side.

Yeh-Chin scratched his chin and cocked his head. "What I meant, Mr. Knight, is that you are most fortunate in having the clone. Our best alternative is harvesting and transplantation."

It took a few moments. The pain in my side was excruciating. When I tried to think, the pliers seemed to twist in my head at the same time they were twisting in my side. He meant Rennie. I shook my head.

Yeh-Chin nodded in misunderstanding. "Yes, this would be the best method," he said.

My god, I was tired. And yellow. I'd been avoiding the mirror, because every time I looked, I'd see the whites of my eyes the same dull color as creamed corn, shot with tiny red veins. "I've heard," I said, and I had to pause to catch my breath, "I've heard you can grow a new pancreas for me. From Rennie."

Yeh-Chin shook his head. "There isn't sufficient time. Your entire pancreas is cancerous and there is invasion of surrounding tissue. Soon there will be involvement of the spine and the liver. By the time the patient feels pain or discomfort, it is far past our ability to treat with less . . . bold . . . procedures."

"Why don't you just put my head on his body, then?"

Yeh-Chin took me seriously. "Possibly," he said. "Though a simple transplant and directed laser therapy is what is indicated."

I knew the answer, but still I had to ask. Yeh-Chin was putting the datapad away. "If you transplant Rennie's pancreas into me, what happens to him?"

Yeh-Chin raised one sparse, black eyebrow and smiled without showing his teeth. "As you are discovering, Mr. Knight, one cannot live without a functioning pancreas. I assure you, in these cases, it is quite painless for the donor. We will euthanize immediately after the surgery."

He was clearing his desk. His hands were small and neat, the nails clipped blunt. Then he took a chrome letter opener and began to scrape under his thumbnail. He thought I was like one of those rich people cloning for transplants: eyes, hearts, livers. They could turn their liver into a gray, twisted hunk of scar tissue and have a perfect one waiting.

My side was on fire again and my hands had begun to tremble. I wrapped my arm around my stomach and stood, bent over, feeling like "old age" in that painting of the three ages of man. Would my teeth drop out of my mouth into my hand? "I don't want any of that," I said. "Just send me home. Give me something for the pain."

The letter opener clattered to his smoothly polished bird's-eye maple desk. Yeh-Chin stood, and there was something different in his face. His small black eyes met mine, then his hand was on my arm, the other hand went around my side.

"Please," he said. "Sit down, Mr. Knight."

I let him guide me to the chair. He knelt beside the chair. Big round bald spot on the top of his head. Little tufts of hair. Freckles there, too. Maybe he golfed.

I put my head in my hands.

"There are conventional treatments. The odds are not good. As it is, you have perhaps three months. Or not more than a week. There is no way to tell in these cases, without invasive tests which I would not advise."

I turned so he would not see me cry. "Rennie is my son," I said. "He's only sixteen."

"There are treatments for the pain. I will prescribe something."

A junkie in my dying days. "Morphine," I said.

"Oh, no," Yeh-Chin said, and his voice was gentle. "We no longer use opiates to any extent. But for the nausea, I will prescribe cannabis. That should not cause too many ill effects."

"I don't want Rennie to see me smoking pot," I said.

"You can take it orally," he replied. "And you must let me know in a week what it is you've decided. Beyond that, I can assure nothing, even with the transplant."

•••

Rennie was not home when I got back. Note on the kitchen counter. He'd gone to the mall, be back before dinner. I fixed a double Glenlivet and water and sat on the patio, staring at the freshly mown backyard. It was 3:30. The shadows were cast deep across the mountains. The snow was hanging on. Skiing. Maybe Rennie would want to go skiing. He'd enjoyed that, cross-country, mostly, in Connecticut. So I remembered from his letters. I rehearsed what I would say to him. Big rehearsal. Rennie, your father is dying. I'm dying, Rennie. I'm kicking the bucket, I've got the Big C, and it's having a party in my guts.

I hadn't taken one of the pink horse pills Yeh-Chin had prescribed yet. There was no way they were going to convince me that they wouldn't make me dopey. Painless painkillers. The bottle said that one of the side effects was nausea, as if I needed more of that. The cannabis pills looked like pellets of horse crap. The pharmacist, a bald guy with a ring through his nose like a Pamplona bull, had told me that smoking the dope was always more effective than the pills.

"In a lot of pain, huh?" he'd asked in a smartass voice.

I'd wanted to yank the ring right out of his nose. Hey, Jerry, got the brass ring! Instead, I got out.

"Sheesh, some people," I'd heard him say as I left.

It was getting hot on the patio. Sweaty again. I'd lost another five pounds. It wasn't fat sweat. Sick sweat. Railroad-tie-rib sweat. Time to go inside.

The door to Rennie's room was ajar. He'd left it a mess, hadn't made the bed. I went in to straighten the covers and picked up his duffel bag where he'd left it. Papers spilled out, mostly yellow ruled sheets.

"I'm gonna miss you, can't wait to kiss you," one of them said, in loopy red letters. Big love letter. I started to stuff it back in the bag, but the red letters drew me like a magnet. One of Rennie's conquests. Well, he was a good-looking kid.

It was really sappy love stuff. Flowers and hearts and "I'll always love you, baby, Your my love thang." It was signed "you know who."

I didn't know. I put it back in the bag. Rennie would tell me if he wanted to. She couldn't have been very important, or he would have already said something, or at least I wanted to think that.

There was a little zippered leather pouch in the duffel bag. Maybe it was the Glenlivet. The ice was melting down into what little booze remained, the glass sitting making a water circle on Rennie's kid desk. Had to get him a new one, I decided. I'd order it tomorrow. One of my subs did custom desks. He could have one that took up the whole side of the room. I'd call about private schools, too. Valley Prep, that was the name of one of them. Didn't kids from there go to Harvard and Yale? It wouldn't be so much of an adjustment for him, not going to a school like that.

I unzipped the pouch. Drugs? No way, not Rennie. There were more letters inside, the same yellow paper. Maybe this girl did mean something. I opened the first letter.

"I just want to suck you're big dick," it said.

This was not a nice girl.

More of the same. That loopy handwriting, the lousy spelling.

"Luv, Jack," it said.

I folded the paper, stuffed it back in the pouch, pulled the zipper very tight, and kicked the duffel back into the half-open closet. Then I swallowed the last of the

Glenlivet and stared at the *R* on the side of the mountain, and chewed the ice.

Boys had crushes. Sure. Like I'd ever had a crush like that, or sucked another guy's dick. Maybe I'd thought about it a couple of times, for about five seconds. Psych 101. Every person has an attraction to the same sex, in greater or lesser degree. Yeah, sure.

More Glenlivet. If I took about ten of the pink pills and washed them down with the scotch, maybe I would just go to sleep and not wake up. Maybe I wouldn't puke the mess up and Rennie wouldn't find me and call the paramedics and they wouldn't pump my stomach and "save" me. Dad's just sleeping it off, Nancy Boy. Dad's just going to take a long nap and never wake up.

My son was a fucking faggot. A prancing queen, a dick-sucking fairy. A butt-fuck buddy.

I cried like a woman. And then it occurred to me. Was I a fag, too? Why couldn't I ever get it together with a woman? Good old Jerry, was that why Kendra took off? Stupid, stupid, I'd always had this fantasy that Rennie would grow up, find a decent woman, a beautiful girl, get married, have kids the right way, the normal way. God, I pictured it, Rennie and this faggot jock Jack, or some other big macho guy, Rennie wearing an apron and pushing their little boy baby down the street in a baby carriage, keeping it all in the gender. Just one big happy faggot family.

I knew what guys did together. What I hadn't known, I learned from that letter. The nausea again. Another slug of scotch, this time straight from the bottle. It went down, hot and shuddering. I gagged over the kitchen sink.

Rennie came in. He was humming.

"Dad, you're sick again." He put his hand on my shoulder. Faggot hand.

Then his nose wrinkled. He smelled the booze.

"You got something to tell me?" My God, now I was slurring like one of my "uncles." Probably had a blue shadow on my chin. Probably smelled like sweat and puke and evil just the way all of Ma Dearest's revolving-door "uncles" did. I wanted to smash Rennie's pretty, soft, downy face. My face. My son, my self. He was white and his chin trembled.

"Dad, what's the matter?" He touched me again with slim pale fingers.

"Get your hand off me, you little fairy," I said. The old bull is sick, the old bull is dying, but he can still charge.

Rennie backed into the other corner of the kitchen. He put the butcher's block island where I chopped vegetables between us.

"You got into my stuff."

I nodded, then drained the last of the Glenlivet. "Not deliberately," I said.

"Well, maybe I wanted you to find it." He crossed his arms, bunched his shoulders. His hair fell into his face. He looked like he was about five, then, and I wanted to put my arms around him.

We stood there a long time. He brushed his hair back, then took a deep breath. "I've known for a long time," he said. "I just didn't know how to tell you. You were always so—"

"How can you be a fag? How? You're me." I wasn't. I knew that. I wasn't.

Rennie shook his head. A tear slid down his cheek. "You keep telling me that. But I don't know. I'm not you. I'm not like you. I've never been like you." He pounded the counter with his fist, his voice choked, cheeks reddening. "Why did you do this to me?"

"Oh, shit, Rennie," I said. "Come here." I held out my arms. He came forward slowly, step by step, then I grabbed him and drew him to me. His head rested against my shoulder.

"I'm scared," he said.

I stroked his hair, so soft, so beautifully clear brown, so fine. "I'm scared too," I said after a while. He thought I meant about him. Maybe that was what I meant.

• • •

Rennie was helpful around the house. I told him that I had a virus I'd picked up somewhere. That was why I was so sick. He didn't know about the pink horse pills and the cannabis pellets. I hid those. The pink pills helped. But my head wasn't clear. Colors looked different. The pliers went away, though. Almost completely away, except at the end of the day.

Rennie used the net all the time. I was watching him click back and forth between all this stuff, the music sites he liked, surfing, skiing stuff. It occurred to me that I might find Kendra. I'd been thinking about her every night. Reaching under the T-shirt, stroking her full breasts in my dreams, wet dreams; even in my yellow state, I still had those.

It took about thirty seconds and I found a listing for a Kendra R. Collins, Ph.D., in Alta Loma. The same last name. A phone number. I called, and it was an office of some sort. A secretary took the message.

Kendra called back two days later. "Jerry?" she said.

"Hi." There was a long moment of silence.

"Are you okay?" The same voice, a little huskier. Her voice had always been husky.

Are you fat with four kids, Kendra? Married? Divorced? Remarried? "Can I see you?" I asked.

Another long pause. "Are you still in Redlands?"

"Yeah. How did you know?"

"I knew you'd go home, Jerry. The place had infected you."

"You've got a Ph.D. What are you doing?"

"I'm a psychologist. I've been in practice here a long time. Kids."

Gee, let me tell you something, Doc. There's this guy, and he was so screwed up after you left him that he didn't touch another woman for five years. He wanted a kid, but he couldn't bear the thought of screwing up his genes with some woman who wasn't you and so he went and cloned himself. Just like one of those crazy rich people with no moral fiber. And now he's forty-five and he's got a cancerous tumor the shape of an eggplant sucking the life out of him. And the clone kid? It's a nice joke, Doc; the identical clone of this guy you fucked about eight million times is—this is a really good one, Doc—gay. I'm straight and my clone is gay. Maybe I should sell it to realvid. What do you think?

"That sounds like a good thing to do," I said.

I heard her breathing, lightly. "I'm not comfortable with talking to you," she said. "I don't know why I returned your call."

"Please," I said. "I have a son. Rennie. He's sixteen. And I'm not—"

"I hope you're happy, Jerry. I really do. I wish the best for you."

"Kendra—"

"I always have." Then she hung up.

"I'm dying," I said to the dial tone.

•••

It hadn't occurred to me before that Dr. Yeh-Chin resembled a Buddha. He did. His face was round, his belly was round. He was calm, and he never smiled with his teeth. When he talked, his front teeth gapped. It produced a slight speech impediment.

There was a kit which he ordered and presented to me. It came in a blue plastic box. "Not intended for home use," it said.

"Theoretically, this must be administered under medical supervision," he said. "Legally, however, you have every right to do this. Since you have told me that the subject is sixteen and has been raised as your own son, I think that it would be best if you administered it yourself, preferably while he is asleep."

I nodded. Dr. Yeh-Chin explained the procedure. I was to pierce the vial with the needle and draw five cc's of something called a "soporific" from it. Then I should inject it in a muscular area. The butt or the thigh or the upper arm. Then, I should call him, and he would call the medical transport van.

He had me practice with another needle and a vial of water.

He produced an orange. I pierced the thick skin of the orange with the needle.

"That should give you a good idea," he said. "How is the medication working?"

"Fine. No more pliers."

His brow raised. "Ah," he said. "How unpleasant."

"I don't know," I said.

"I must be honest with you," he said. "I cannot understand your choice regarding—"

"I don't understand," I said, interrupting him.

He crossed his arms and regarded me, rubbing his thumb and forefinger together in an unusual gesture. I'd seen him do it before. Maybe it relaxed him. "We have thoughts on this," he said. "Chinese thoughts. That perhaps this person you feel is your son is really a ghost. A ghost of yourself."

I hadn't spoken of Rennie's sexuality. I shook my head.

"What I wanted to say is that you mustn't feel badly. The fate has led a certain way. It is unfortunate, but unavoidable."

"I don't know if I can do it or not," I said. And I did not know.

"You will know," Dr. Yeh-Chin said. "I am not sure I am expressing it properly, but I believe that such things are all preordained. There will be no pain."

The blue plastic case was very cold, and heavier than I'd thought it would be. I suppose they had kept it in the refrigerator.

"Rennie likes to ski," I told him. "He likes to ride his bike. He's a whiz on the net. His grades are tops."

"Yes," he said. "Of course."

•••

"Dad," Rennie said. "Jack's flying out for a long weekend. Maybe we could go skiing together, since you're feeling so much better."

"Beating this virus back," I said, flexing my arm. Rennie's face was shining.

"Next week, do you want to go visit that school you were telling me about?"

"Sure," I said.

"Lou said maybe you'd be starting back to work next week. She's glad you're feeling better, too."

I nodded. "Yeah."

He'd just returned from a bike ride. His shoulders glistened with sweat. Then he ran up and hugged me. I pressed my face into his hair. It smelled sweet and fruity—no, more like musky vanilla.

I wanted to say something else, but I couldn't. I just patted his shoulder, then released him.

We had tri-tip on the grill. I had a couple of beers. Rennie had a cherry Coke. He told me about school, the tough teachers, the easy ones. He preferred the tough ones, because at least he was learning. Jack had a harder time, he said. Jack was smart, but not about school. Smart in other ways, Rennie said.

I had another beer while the food digested. Rennie didn't seem to notice when I forked most of my tri-tip into the trash. On the side of the mountain, there was the *R*, and I told him about it, how it was mostly chunks of concrete and white granite rocks, and every year a group from the high school would take a bus up there and sweat all day long clearing away the brush so it would look white and perfect from a distance, the way it did now.

"You didn't like school, did you?" Rennie said.

"Sure," I said. "I liked it fine."

"I'm glad Jack is coming," he said.

I took a long pull from my beer. "Rennie, I guess I can handle how you feel."

"Dad, I'm so glad," he said, and he smiled.

"I wonder if you'll have a family. Do you want a family? I mean a real one—"

"I can make a family. Jack wants a family."

Jack is your high-school crush, even if he does have hair on his chest. You think this is forever, but it's never forever. "Not like that," I said.

"There's no reason either of us can't do the same as you did," he said. "After all, when you didn't want to get married, you figured it out."

There was the *R* on the mountain. White and clean-edged and perfect. An acre on each side. It took all day to clean the brush away. We were proud of it, coming home sweaty, legs ripped up from the thorny saw grass and stinking creosote, hands all ripped from heaving the concrete around. All those rich kids hadn't looked much better than you, Jerry, by the time that was all done. Your short pants hadn't mattered much, by the end of that day. Rennie sat beside me in his immaculate shirt and chinos, which broke nicely over his deck shoes.

"Jack's plane gets in Friday at 3:00. Lou said she'd take me to the airport to pick him up."

"Good for Jack," I said. Then I reached over and squeezed Rennie's hand.

That night, I tucked Rennie in, and sat in the living room. The blue case had been in the refrigerator the whole time. Rennie hadn't noticed it, or if he'd noticed, he hadn't said.

I dialed Kendra's number. It rang six times, then I heard a click.

"I'm in session," Kendra said.

"I guess you work late."

All I could hear was her breathing. "You're taking me away from the patient," she said.

I cleared my throat. There was a huge lump there, like I'd swallowed an egg. "I need—"

"You need? That was always it, wasn't it?" Her hand covered the receiver, and I heard her saying something, just the sound of her voice, not the words. Then she was back. "I had hoped you would have grown up, Jerry, but it was always you. Whatever Jerry wants. Jerry's the only person in the world. Someday you'll learn there's more to life than that."

"Kendra, I'm dying," I said.

She took a deep breath. "I'm not a medical doctor," she said. "I can recommend some counselors in Redlands. My secretary will call with their names tomorrow." She hung up. The dial tone echoed. I put the receiver down, gently.

I went to the patio again and stared at the mountain, which was now like a torn sheet of black paper against the night. Then I went inside.

Rennie was sleeping. His shoulder was uncovered. The sheet had slipped. His hair feathered over his cheek. His breathing was soft, regular, untroubled.

The bottle was cold, the needle colder. I broke the plastic covering and thrust the needle into the liquid. Five cc's. It took five seconds.

Rennie's shoulder did not feel like an orange.

He stirred once, moaned, then was quiet.

THE PRICE
OF TEA IN CHINA

Written by
DAVID W. HILL

Illustrated by
Robert G. Kmiec

About the Author

David W. Hill lives in New York City, where he works for a management consulting firm. His work has appeared in many small-press magazines, and he has received honorable mentions three times in The Year's Best Fantasy and Horror. *In 1998 a story of his garnered several recommendations for an SFWA Nebula Award.*

About the Illustrator

Robert G. Kmiec was born in 1973 in Boston, and still lives, draws and paints there. After an up-and-down career in school, livened only by consistent good reviews for his art, he graduated from the Massachusetts College of Art with a degree in illustration. His principal inspiration came from discovering a calendar full of art by Frank Frazetta. It was at that moment he knew he had seen the pinnacle of science fiction–fantasy art.

He now teaches at Catholic Memorial School, where he instructs in art history, studio art, drafting and digital art to students in grades eleven and twelve.

They took him from his family because of the thing he did in kindergarten.

It wasn't simply because Jimmy died, although that was what the court officer told his parents. If it had only been a matter of murder, the black van would have carried him across town to the Bellevue pediatric psychiatry ward instead of upstate, past Poughkeepsie, to the vast walled grounds of the Haldane Federal School. No, the important fact wasn't that he had actually *killed* Jimmy; it was *why* he had chosen to defenestrate Jimmy instead of, say, Kareem or Abner or Darwin, bullies all, and all, at first glance, much more deserving of such unkind attention.

"Not right," he told Dr. Powers around a mouthful of cereal, his favorite snack. He'd been eating it all his life. He'd just turned five.

"What wasn't right, William? You can tell me. I want to know."

"He wasn't right. Jimmy. You understand. Not right."

"How wasn't Jimmy right? I'm a little confused."

Will spread his hands, trying to encompass what he wanted to say, but the words slipped from him like minnows through his fingers, like the green slimy glop that he'd gotten for Christmas, the ideas too large to handle. He wanted to tell the doctor about how things had changed at school ever since Jimmy enrolled, all because of Jimmy; not that you'd ever guess it was Jimmy instigating the rule of terror in the hallways and in the schoolyard, since he was slick, and never made a move outright but only through other boys. But Will had *known*, known who orchestrated it all with the perfect word here and the precise whisper there . . . getting Abner to beat up on the little kids for no reason, just because, with only a sidelong glance, not a single sentence passing between them . . . or provoking Kareem to do what he did to Sara so obscurely that even Kareem didn't realize why he'd pulled her skirt up over her head and her panties down around her ankles, sending her stumbling and screaming away *to tell on him* . . . or egging Darwin on with the slightest nudge, so that, hours later, Fred and Winona ended up red eyed and gagging in the sandbox.

Jimmy was bad. He wasn't right. And no one else saw it—not the other kids nor the teachers nor his parents nor any other adult. They all thought that Jimmy was merely a small, rather quiet child, perhaps a little shy, but that was because he was from a *dysfunctional* family and new to the neighborhood. Only Will saw the truth—that was his *gift*; that was what he did well: he understood processes; he could cut straight to the heart of the matter, although he couldn't quite put what he knew into words. It wasn't even that Will had identified Jimmy as being a "malignant sociopath"—the words he overheard the doctors using to describe Jimmy after posthumous examination of his psychological records. Will couldn't have cared less what Jimmy *was*. All he knew was that before Jimmy enrolled, school had worked, it had been fun, kids had, more or less, gotten along. Jimmy's arrival had *broken* something, interfered somewhere, perverted the normal pattern of the school day into something that didn't work, that wasn't fun, that needed *fixing*.

Talking wouldn't correct the situation, either. Nor would telling. Not fighting, not passive resistance, not evasion. There was only one way to deal with Jimmy. And Will understood instinctively what it was. That was his other *gift*.

"Jimmy was a bad boy," he tried to explain, mumbling a little because of the volume of cereal he'd crammed into his mouth. "He wouldn't listen. He didn't care. He had *fish eyes*."

That was as close as Will could approach to expressing how Jimmy stared right through you, as if you weren't there, which you weren't, not to him, not really, since Jimmy wasn't truly a human being, not inside, not where it counted. He was something *inhuman* right smack in the middle of a *human* system; that was what was wrong. "You know," Will continued, struggling to pass on the sense of what he had grasped intuitively, "Jimmy didn't *fit*. Like . . . like *this*." With sudden inspiration he went to the bottom shelves where all the toys were kept and brought the doctor a board with differently shaped holes cut into it and an assortment of plastic blocks fitting those holes. He took a block shaped like a triangle and forced it into the square hole, where it jammed fast. "See!" Will exclaimed. "That's Jimmy."

"The triangle?" Dr. Powers asked.

"Uh-huh! And he got stuck. He got us all stuck."

Will ran back to the toy shelves, returning with a plastic hammer. He took careful aim and hit the triangle with all his might, propelling the block right out of the square hole and across the room.

"See," he said, smiling at the memory, remembering the window. "I *fixed* it."

2

The Haldane Federal School wasn't like other schools. There weren't any teachers, any adults, just A-one caretakers. There weren't any schedules, either—no rules, no regulations, no required courses, no electives, no grades, no report cards. And instead of science and mathematics and social studies and the like, the entire curriculum consisted of puzzles and games and brain teasers—games played indoors and games played outside, games played alone and games played in teams, physical games and mental games, word games and board games and computer games and jigsaws with a million pieces, games of skill and games of chance and games of pure intellect, games ten thousand years old and games invented only yesterday . . . Monopoly and poker and Doom 18 and chess and football and checkers and tag and mahjong and Othello and tic-tac-toe and Seventieth Guest and bridge and Parcheesi and hopscotch and hockey and hangman and Risk—games without number, games without end.

Will loved the school from the very first day, from the very first *hour*, when he was escorted by an automatic chaperon from the black van through the massive gates and along marble corridors to his new room, where a note on his bed welcomed him to Haldane and asked:

Using only four straight lines, without lifting your pencil from the paper, and without going back over any lines, can you connect these nine dots?

Illustrated by Robert G. Kmiec

Of course he could, and within seconds, too, which proved nothing to the ubiquitous overhead surveillance cameras except that the correct decision had been made about recruiting him, and to Will himself that he was going to have fun, which he *did*, almost enough fun to make up for the fact that neither he nor the other kids were ever allowed to leave the school grounds or to see or speak with their parents and families and friends again.

In short he had been brought straight to heaven, or at least to a place that would be heaven to just about any kid and particularly so to Will and the others, who all loved games, not even for the sake of winning, but simply for the pure pleasure of figuring out what was going on, what the rules were, and *playing.* And play they did, from dawn to dusk and late into the night, on weekdays and on weekends, before meals and after meals and during meals, in ones and twos and threes and in great impromptu gatherings of hundreds, in teams and alone, face to face and on-line, against each other or against A ones, using boards and pieces and cards and balls and joysticks and markers or nothing at all.

With so much going on, it was terribly easy to live in the moment. It was easy to let the years pass by and to forget how remarkable the school was, easy to accept Haldane at face value, easy not to question why, easy to forget that there were no adults, just the robots, nor any kids older than twelve.

At least until you started growing up yourself.

When Will turned ten, being twelve was pure abstraction. Even when he turned eleven, his next birthday seemed a lifetime away. But six months later the eighth of September seemed just around the corner.

Everyone knew what they were doing at the school. *What* was the simple question; their job was to play, that was the *process*. But *why* they were at Haldane was another question altogether. The prevailing schoolwide myth, subscribed to by just about the entire student body, embraced with nothing less than religious fervor, was that they were the *chosen few*, admitted into the promised land at an early age. But that didn't explain what they were chosen for. Or the empty rooms where twelve-year-olds had gone to sleep the night before.

And as he grew older, Will had to know—

How many had *graduated*?

And how many had *failed*?

3

He awoke and everything was different. For one thing he was in a strange room in a strange bed wearing clothes that weren't his. And when he inspected his face in the battered metal mirror on the dirty gray wall, a stranger regarded him in return, a stranger with blond hair and blue eyes and a thin nose and cruelly pale lips. He was *white*.

There was a note in his hand:

> Your name is Erik Smith. You have been enrolled in the Kings County Juvenile Educational Facility for torching your foster parents. Something's *broken* here. *Fix* it.

The paper crumbled into ash.

Then the door slammed open and in marched four boys wearing identical outfits of coarse brown polyester. Two of them grabbed his arms and held him while the others punched him repeatedly in the stomach, groin, and face, leaving him on the cement floor in a puddle of blood and vomit and teeth.

An eternity later the door opened again to admit a fat man in the olive uniform of the Department of Social Services. He lifted Will's head from the concrete by the hair and thumbed up an eyelid.

"Welcome to Kings County, Will, my boy. Your home away from home. Be that as it may, I'm Warren Clap; Proctor Clap to you, or just plain *sir.* I wanted to let you know that I've read your file. I know all about what you did to those folks who tried to do good by you. You remember them, yes? Well, in any case, and so there's no misunderstanding, I asked some of the other lads to make you comfortable. Looks like they did a fine job of it, too. Any questions, son? No, I didn't think so."

Proctor Clap let Will's face slap back against the floor. He put his lips close to Will's ear and said softly, "Get cleaned up. First period begins in half an hour. I personally wouldn't want to be late."

Kings County Juvenile Educational Facility consisted of four dreary buildings constructed around a barren quadrangle. It housed fifteen hundred children between the ages of ten and eighteen; boys in the north and west wings, girls in the south and east. It wasn't a school, of course, not for decades, no matter what it was called. It was more a *prison,* despite the fact that each child—each *inmate*—was required to attend a daily schedule of classes.

Will kept his head down and his mouth shut. He survived.

What kept him alive those first horrific weeks was the memory of the note he had held in his hand. It wasn't a *dream.* He *hadn't* been forgotten. He hadn't been sent to hell. He hadn't failed. He'd been given a task. It was up to him to discover what the assignment was, what was *broken* here, and *fix* it.

Will let the rhythm of the place enter him. He blacked out any deliberate effort of analysis or speculation, allowing his innate *talent* to absorb the rules of the game that was being played throughout the grim place and to sort them out far back in his mind, in that strange space beyond intelligence and reason and conscious thought.

Then he went to see Principal Merchant.

She was straight and tall and severe. She wore her hair pulled tight back from her forehead, parted down the center with geometric precision. The creases of her olive-drab uniform were equally meticulous. But there was something tired at the back of her eyes, something weary, something that hinted at the presence of a real individual lost deep inside, perhaps the spirit of the teacher she once had been, ten or twenty or thirty years before, before experience and the Department of Social Services and Kings County itself had corrupted her, before accommodations, before compromises. She regarded Will expressionlessly, her face as blank as the steel desk between them.

"You have two minutes to explain why you requested this appointment."

"Please, ma'am—" Will allowed his face to crumple, tears to well, a catch to come to his voice. He had to get through to her. He had to set free the person she once had been.

"Please, ma'am—I want to *learn*. And I *can't*. Will you *help* me? Please?"

It was maudlin, it was plaintive, it was sentimental, it was pathetic, it was pitiable; it was precisely the *right* thing to say, as nothing else could have been—a bullet straight through the years armoring Principal Merchant's soul, piercing through the accretion of cynicism and distrust, directly into her heart. Will could see it, see the effect the words had on her, no matter how she tried to dissemble.

"I'm not alone, ma'am," he went on earnestly. "There are others. Others like me. Kids who want to learn. Kids who want to be somebody. But we can't. Not here. They won't let us."

"They? What do you mean—they?"

"You know, ma'am. The system. The way things are. This is a prison, but it could be a school again. The way it used to be. Someday. With *your* help."

Were those tears in her eyes? Will didn't dare look closely.

"It's too late."

"It's not, ma'am. Truly it isn't. It's never too late to change."

"But I—I wouldn't know where to begin."

"Maybe not, ma'am. But *I* do."

4

It took a year to transform Kings County Juvenile Educational Facility from the penal institution it had become into a better school than it had ever been, with six Daiwa scholarships, reading levels two grades above state average, and the highest math scores in the city. They did it by the rules that Will had roughed out during his time of doubt and fear and pain, by the rules of *cultural change.*

They moved fast, they went flat out, because change isn't something that can happen slowly. Principal

Merchant *championed the process,* because organizational transformation requires a mandate from the top. She *built a power base,* bringing in a new breed of eccentrics and freethinkers, making *casualties* of those who, no matter how loyal, refused to change. She was a woman possessed, *living the vision* of what Kings County could be, focusing on the future, deliberately *destabilizing* the administrative and bureaucratic infrastructure, creating self-directed educational teams of students and teachers, rewarding inspiration rather than obedience, *communicating* rather than commanding, *involving everyone.* The Board of Education began an inquiry into her methods. But by then they had already begun to achieve hard results and had some *quick wins* to show the investigative committee, and were allowed to continue without interference.

Will remained in the background, his relationship with Principal Merchant carefully obscured, meeting with her only under cover of disciplinary conferences, counseling discussions, and remedial tutoring sessions. No one suspected the role he played—no one, that is, at King's County.

But when he awoke on the morning of his second anniversary at the school, Will once more found himself in another place, arising from good linen instead of the threadbare bedding to which he'd become accustomed, surrounded by soft lighting instead of the harsh glare of bare fluorescent tubing. There was a mirror on one wall and Will went to it and stared a very long time at the dark reflection there. He had his own face back.

"Good job, son."

He hadn't heard the door open. His visitor was middle aged, gray haired, wearing an old cardigan sweater and loose corduroy trousers, an unlit pipe in one hand. The other was outstretched. Will accepted it gingerly.

"So I passed?"

"With honors."

"I was wondering."

His guest chuckled. "I'm Dr. Frost, by the way. Aaron Frost. Your guidance counselor, so to speak, for the next couple semesters."

"Semesters?"

"It's time to hit the books, Will. Let me explain."

Haldane Beneath encompassed kilometers of corridors, dormitories, classrooms, and lecture halls, all buried far below the aboveground campus. The student body consisted of those who, like Will, had survived their trials by fire—their *work/study programs*—after graduating from Haldane On Top. Here there was a human staff in addition to automatic instructors and A ones, and the curriculum, while not the usual academic subjects with which Will had become familiar while at King's County, was far more explicit than before: chaos and order theory; organizational structure; applied leadership; the principles of dynamic systems; advanced weather analysis; fractals and the calculus of strange attractors; the dialectics of both Hegel and Marx; the anatomy of natural and artificial constructions on the micro and macro levels; comparative sociology and anthropology; the philosophy of recurring patterns; post-Darwinian evolutionary hypotheses; quantum mechanics and subatomic physics. They still *played*, of course—that was, after all, the whole point, to master *processes*—but they also *studied*. There were courses; there were classes; there were lectures; there were seminars; there were papers and dissertations; there were discussion groups. Entirely missing, however, were tests and grades.

"What would be the point?" Dr. Frost asked. "You either get it or you don't. You either pass or you fail. It's as simple as that, Will. All this"—he waved his pipe to take in the entirety of Haldane Beneath—"is, essentially, superfluous. What counts in the end is what you have in here."

He tapped the stem of his pipe against his forehead.

"I'm not sure I follow you, Doctor."

Dr. Frost didn't answer Will directly. "The twenty-first century is a terrifying place for humanity," he said with the professorial hyperbole that Will had come to expect from him. "Our world is far too complex for any ordinary understanding. It's been like that for hundreds of years, perhaps thousands, perhaps since Aristotle. But not until this century has our ignorance been so utterly dangerous to our species as a whole. Not until this century have we come up against the real possibility of destroying our planet and extinguishing ourselves as a race. Not maliciously, mind you. But through simple ignorance. Logic, reason, deduction, cause and effect, all the old tools of thought that allowed us to achieve what we have achieved, are utterly inadequate in the face of the global challenges now before us. We need a new way of thinking, a way of understanding the *whole* without necessarily understanding the *part*, a way to be *right* because we can't afford to be *wrong*."

Dr. Frost looked at Will expectantly.

"Which brings the discussion to—*me*."

"And the others here like you. Of course. We don't know what you are, Will. Not for certain. But what we *hope* is that evolution is throwing up a mutation capable of adapting to the changing circumstances of our environment. *Homo nova*, if you will. One able to make correct decisions intuitively, through instinct rather than through trial and error. A new kind of man, an *organization* man, more at home with processes than with components, able to think four-dimensionally rather than linearly or even in three dimensions. That's what this is all about. We're giving you your chance, *sport.*" Dr. Frost smiled at his own pun. "Your chance to seize the future, unfettered by the past. So what do you say, Will? Are you with us?"

5

He awoke and everything was different—*again.* It was the day after he turned eighteen. The lanky body he wore was his own but once more his face belonged to someone else. The room around him was an anonymous utilitarian cubicle. Well-used denim work clothes were folded on a chair beside the bed, a pair of scuffed boots lined up on the floor.

There was a note in his hand:

> Your name is Jim Ditmar. You are employed as a machine operator by International Extraction, Inc. You're a member in good standing of Local 1122 of the Amalgamated Miners Union. There is currently a state of undeclared industrial action. Something's *broken* here. *Fix* it.

The paper crumbled into ash.

Will dressed slowly and left the vast dreary beehive of a building, the only housing for miles, rising from the badlands like some appalling stele—the company town, of course—and found his way to the mine gates. Armed guards examined his ID and thumbed him inside, where he joined the queue of miners entering the main adit and descending in high-speed elevators thousands of meters to the reef of shale they were working. It was a food mine. A measurable percentage of the populations of Colorado, Arizona, New Mexico, and Oklahoma were dependent on the calories being extracted from the rock here. For the past seven months production had been at less than 50 percent of capacity. People were *starving*.

"Screw 'em," Todd Fawcette remarked as he and Will wrestled their huge hammer into position and ducked behind its blast shield as the machine began screaming and flooding the tunnel with shrapnel. "Thirty dollars an hour hardly keeps my kid in diapers, for Christ's sake. Let 'em come down to hell with us and dig up their own meals if they're so goddamned hungry."

There was a lot of truth in this. By the end of each shift Will felt as if he had died and been condemned to suffer, deafened in spite of ear protectors, every muscle afire, lacerated by rock splinters, coated from head to toe with dust and grime, coughing black wads of it from his lungs regardless of his respirator. Yet the terrible physical effort required of the miners wasn't at the heart of the matter—most, as miners had for millennia, took a certain perverse professional pride in enduring. There was something else going on, and once again Will blanked out any conscious effort at understanding, allowing facts and events to sink without interpretation into his brain, there to be absorbed, evaluated, and processed by *intuition* alone, without the limitations of preconception, of logic, of theory, not even what he'd learned in Haldane Beneath—that, too, as Dr. Frost had predicted, was essentially immaterial in the face of his innate *talent*.

Daylight was a glimpse of heaven. Will showered with the rest of his shift and joined the line of tired miners approaching the main exit. Off to the left was the executive parking lot, filled mostly with Mercedes and Porsches and BMWs and a Lexus or two. One beautiful gleaming gray Rolls Royce gunned its engine and rose slowly into the air. With startling speed a SAM missile shrieked out of the west and impacted the car. The men alongside Will cheered as fire flowered and wreckage fell to earth and the breeze brought to them the stink of burning human flesh and human fat and human skin.

"Serves the bastards right," Todd Fawcette observed to Will as sirens throbbed in the distance and as they passed together through the gates under the grim inspection of the security guards. "Thirty damned dollars per, while those sons of bitches drive Jaguars. What's minimum wage these days anyway? Why, Jim, for just five bucks less, we could be bagging groceries, for God's sake."

But money wasn't the real crux, either, although money was the single topic at union meetings, despite the fact that the sole agenda items of ongoing labor/management discussions concerned overtime and dirty pay and hazard bonuses. No, it came to Will that driving the entire situation, the paradigm below the surface, invisible and unremarked upon but nonetheless manipulating the whole confrontation, the rhinoceros head on the table in the middle of the room that everyone was pretending wasn't there, was a vast well of *alienation.* Cut off from any control over their own lives, denied the least authority over their own destinies by an entrenched administrative establishment that regarded them as, at worst, hostile, and, at best, incompetent, the miners had become *disassociated,* unconnected, unable to identify any relationship whatsoever between themselves as human beings and those they worked for or the urban populations they fed.

What was needed was a radical *transformation* in the prevailing social contract. In July Will was elected union delegate by his crew. Six weeks later he had a seat on the negotiating committee.

Bulletproof glass separated the parties. On one side of the table were the *suits* and their lawyers; on the other, the *reps* and their attorneys. The meeting droned on interminably, neither faction giving or taking, yielding an inch, compromising at all. Will swallowed nervously, tense in spite of the groundwork he'd laid during months of politicking and diplomacy. Then he stood up, and stared deliberately from one group to the other, and hesitation left him. He tore the agenda he held in half and let the papers fall to the floor.

"Gentlemen," he said, first addressing management, "this whole discussion is meaningless. *Wages* aren't the issue here. Not that you're in a position to do anything constructive, anyway. IE shares are at an eighteen-month low. Your operating capital is approaching zero. And your line of credit is overextended. You couldn't afford a one-cent across-the-board increase even if you were inclined to provide one. On the other hand"—now Will faced his fellow delegates—"on the other hand, our pension fund is flush. What I'm proposing is that Amalgamated Miners tender an offer for 27 percent of IE stock at thirty-six and an eighth, which is a fair deal, five dollars and change above current price per share."

Shouting drowned his next words. Will waited patiently. One senior vice-president shook a soft pale index finger at him. "And then we're out, is that it, Ditmar? Well, believe me, we'll take this company down before we let you through the gates."

And on his own side of the thick glass the union members were nodding slowly. "Just try it, Cornwall," one replied to the SVP. "You'll be the first through the window without a goddamned golden parachute."

Will lifted his hand. "I said this wasn't about *wages*. It's not about *revenge*, either. What we don't need is a Pyrrhic victory. What we do need is to *all* win. A partnership. A chance for everyone to have a *stake* in the success of this company, to be part of a shared future, of a common vision; a say on the Board is just the beginning. You won't be *out*, gentlemen, but to succeed we'll *all* have to work differently. We'll have to think outside of the box. We'll have to improvise. Take *risks*. I don't have all the answers, maybe not even many of them. Not hardly. But a starting point might be the creation of cross-functional supervisory teams. The flattening of the corporate hierarchy. Tying compensation to performance, from the CEO on down. Allowing line employees to set their own goals and respecting their judgment as to what *is* possible and what *isn't*. Insisting that management, too, spend time at the front in order to appreciate the sweat and tears that pour into every single pound of rock we take from the ground. Maybe I'm idealistic. Maybe I'm naive. But I don't think so. I think that if we talk straight and walk the talk, we can do it. So what do you say, gentlemen?"

Will allowed his gaze to pan slowly from one group to the other.

"Are you with me?"

6

"Production at 109 percent of estimated capacity within eight months? Operating expenses down 22 percent? ROI at thirty cents on the dollar? Not to mention the virtual elimination of industrial accidents and guerrilla activity. *And* the ending of food riots in both Denver and Oklahoma City." Dr. Frost beamed. "Well done, my boy. *Very* well done."

Will shrugged, embarrassed by his mentor's accolades. Not because of modesty but because his achievements were a result of what he *was*, of his genetic heritage, of what was innate in him, not because of any personal conscious effort for which he could honestly take credit.

"So what's next, Aaron? More study? Or another assignment?"

He had woken this time in Deeper Haldane, a complex below both Haldane On Top and Haldane Beneath and much smaller than either, since the student body here numbered less than a dozen.

"You've graduated, Will. From this point on you chart your own course."

"What if I wanted simply to quit?"

"We'd be disappointed. But we wouldn't stand in your way. If you're not with us of your own accord by now, you'd be valueless to the project, anyway."

"That's what I want to do, then. I'm twenty-one, Aaron. I've been at Haldane since I was five. I am what you've made me. What my genes have made me into. But who am I really? I don't know. I need to find out."

"Do it, then." Dr. Frost stabbed the air with his pipe stem. "We'll keep the door open for you, Will." He winked. "And a light in the window."

For the first time that he remembered, Will stood outside wearing his real face. A chill acrid wind knifed through the canyons of Queens, the sun all but invisible overhead, a pale nimbus obscured by smog. He gagged and quickly latched his respirator and joined the throngs similarly anonymous in micropore protective clothing and filters. He hailed a rickshaw and let the taxi take him into Manhattan via the LIE. Amazingly, the driver had enough breath left over to talk during the miles of running without his pace once faltering.

"What do you say about them Democrats? Think they have a chance?"

"I don't know."

"*Of course* they do. Damned Independents let the country go straight to hell. It's time for a change."

"I don't see as there's any real difference between either party."

"Difference? Sure as shit there's a difference. Pardon my tip, sir, but what planet do you hail from?"

Will had to smile. "This one, I hope."

But he wondered. He rented a room at the Chelsea Hotel and for the first couple of weeks mainly stayed indoors, surfing the seven hundred plus channels available on television, slowly becoming acclimated to the world he had left so long before. But nothing made sense—no, that wasn't it. The problem was that everyone, all the thousands of commentators and panelists and pundits and experts and analysts who flooded the airwaves and the optical cables day in and day out, were talking about the *wrong* things, about surface facts and trends, without ever once approaching the truth, without ever grasping what was actually going on.

Yes, the current round of disarmament talks between Brazil and Denmark was interesting, but no one recognized that the cause of the conflict lay in the unequal balance of trade between Copenhagen and Istanbul. Yes, concern about the prime rate—now at 26 percent— was valid, but not one person acknowledged the link between the escalating inflation and the extinction of

Australia's Great Barrier Reef and the hole in the ozone layer over Europe. Connections that were brilliantly obvious to Will just weren't discussed. It was as if he spoke a separate language with a private lexicon that no one besides himself could decipher.

Not even Maria. She was a doctoral candidate at The Newer School and had an intelligence as sharp and lovely as her features, a cap of curls as dark and lustrous as night. They met on Grove Street on an afternoon when Will was drifting from one café to another in an effort to submerge himself in the everyday life of other people. Coming up against her in the crowd, it was as if an electric arc shot between them. Within a month he'd moved into her studio on West Fourth. But within another month they were bickering.

"I can't figure out what it is with you, Will," Maria said, lifting herself on an elbow to face him across the narrow bed. "I try to talk seriously, and you go off on *tangents*."

"I don't mean to. It's just that things aren't as—as *straightforward* as you imagine they are."

"Straightforward? Well, you tell me what correlation there could possibly be between the price of tofu in Mexico City and the Miami insurrection. Seriously, Will, I'd like to know."

But he couldn't explain, not out loud, not in words, because he didn't know himself, not in any rational way, not with any certainty born of logic and reason, of induction and deduction, of intellect or common sense.

So he remained silent. The whisper of her fingertips on his cheek only emphasized the gulf separating them. "Oh, Will," she whispered. "What's to become of us?"

He had *that* answer, too, although, again, he didn't reply—he understood *processes*, after all. And *solutions*, even when there wasn't one. That was his other gift. In the morning Will packed his clothes and caught a bus heading upstate, past Poughkeepsie. By noon he was home. He had work to do.

A couple days afterward he was someone else.

7

First there was a stint as Harry Wallace, human resources generalist for a Fortune 100 conglomerate involved in ethically ambiguous transactions with the Irish and Florida juntas, deals that were, unfortunately, encouraging factories in Baltimore and Caracas to generate unacceptable amounts of environmental toxins while protected by local ordinances propped up by that same Fortune 100 company. Then he was Phil Stringer, and then Davis Appleby, and then Fred Touhy and Bill Smith and Jack Springer. Eventually Will lost track of the men he had become, of the roles he'd played, of the problems he'd encountered, of the solutions he'd put in place. Some assignments were handed to him; others he chose himself; what linked them all was that more and more of them, no matter how seemingly provincial, were essentially *global*, and yielded only to global resolutions. Old Dr. Frost, now a decade retired, had been frighteningly correct—the twenty-first century *was* a terrifying place for mankind, and the flutter of a butterfly's wings in Sydney truly did cause tornadoes in Montreal; the outcome of a school board election in Laredo, Texas, *inevitably* instigated genocide in Mozambique. As the years passed, Will began to fear that all his efforts, and those of the few like him who had passed from Haldane On Top to Haldane Beneath and finally to Deeper Haldane— those few examples of *Homo nova* that the project had managed to identify—simply wouldn't be enough to save humanity from itself, not in the face of a system as utterly complicated as international technological civilization.

But then he learned that Dr. Frost had misled him long ago. He hadn't graduated at all. He'd merely been allowed some *independent study*.

•••

Will awoke sitting in a comfortable chair behind a polished desk in a formal office with walls almost entirely covered by the framed portraits of statesmen. His hands, emerging from crisp French cuffs beneath sleeves that heralded from Brooks Brothers, were manicured and plump. Will felt no need to find a mirror to discover what face he wore, or even to scan the note in his fingers before it crumbled into ash—he knew exactly who he was. But he glanced at the slip of paper anyway.

Something's *broken* here, Mr. President. *Fix* it.

THE GREAT
WIZARD JOEY

Written by
W. G. Rowland

Illustrated by
Ludmila Ryabets

About the Author

W. G. (pronounced Bill) Rowland was born in Glendale, California, in 1971. When he was eleven, he and his mother moved to Modesto. There, some years later, he met his wife, Alisan, and they promptly moved to San Diego, where they've been living ever since.

Over the years, he wrote hundreds of story beginnings, but never finished most of them. However, his wife, a graduate student of English and a long-time reader, encouraged him to keep trying. "Joey" started out as a writing exercise, but lo and behold, he finished it. Since successfully submitting the story here, he's finished four more. There's no telling where this will end.

About the Illustrator

Ludmila Ryabets grew up in southern Ukraine, and now lives in Kiev. She has enjoyed drawing since childhood. She has completed Art Studio, where she specialized in graphic design and drawing.

She graduated from Ukrainian Building University and is now working as an assistant architect.

Oh stars, what a night! The Kats were already drunk; the Drugar so deep into their cups of Millamberwine one could dance on their beards and not catch their wrath. The players' music swirled almost visibly through the hall—a whirlwind that reached beyond the dancers and into the hearts of everyone not too drunk to listen. The dancers themselves twirled around in the light haze of drugged incense that filled the wood-paneled hall like dervishes created from the smoke and possessed by the music. In several corners I could see couples, not initiated to the effects of smoked Seana weed, making love on, near, and, in one case, under, their tables.

I too felt the intoxication of the night. Not the Seana weed; to me that was no more than a light buzzing behind my eyes, and although I had downed my share of wine and then some, I had not yet lost track of my senses.

My exhilaration was of an entirely different nature.

Mine had to do with escape.

Mine was the joy of newfound freedom.

Not hard-earned freedom, perhaps, but freedom nonetheless.

And, for the first time since the beginning of my long flight, there was the chance that I might stay free.

At least I hoped so, for, short of the frozen wilds of the north or getting myself lost at sea to the east, there was no further place I could run to avoid detection by my master, Jerroth-Kine. Best not to think of that, though. With any luck at all, the decoy I left behind had convinced Jerroth that I was dead. I had, after all, worked quite hard at convincing my trackers that I had fallen from the cliffs back in Denelor, and even though illusion is not my strongest craft, I still thought it was a convincing performance.

I really did jump from the precipice, and in my terror I don't think I could have made a sound loud enough to be heard over the waves crashing below me as I clung to the hanging vines in the dark and rain, waiting for the guards either to spot me or be convinced of the phantom double I sent screaming into the freezing waters below.

If their report carried any weight with Jerroth, then, hidden and disguised on the other side of the world, I might be able to scrape together some sort of life—assuming I could convince the world that I knew nothing of magic. If not, well, an apprentice Storm-Warder who's abandoned his master has, by guild law, given up all his rights—including the right to live. Jerroth would stop at nothing to track me down, and no one would lift a finger to help me.

Even if Jerroth-Kine was a coldblooded murderer.

Still, with the music playing and the incense enchanting the room, I allowed myself hope. Everyone catches a bit of luck at some point. I certainly felt overdue for some. Perhaps not deserving—I could have attempted to expose Jerroth instead of running like a coward—but due.

My mug came up dry, and a rather pretty serving girl came and refilled it. I noticed her eye on me as she worked, more than one smile crossing her lips. That warmed the heart. Perhaps I could settle here? Farming might be beneath my station, but certainly no more so than the executioner's block. I let my mind wander to visions of a farmhouse and a plow, a fat wife and a brood of children, sowing and reaping. The music here was fine, the women pretty, the wine, no worse than elsewhere. Yes, I thought, given the alternatives, I could live in this.

And so, mind wandering towards the future, cup tipped back, and spirits rising, I had no warning as Jerroth-Kine entered the room behind me.

"I must admit, child, your thinking grows beyond my ken," came the sonorous, almost fatherly, voice like ice water down my spine. "Under my tutelage you would have been nearly as rich as any city's lord and twice as powerful . . . and yet you chose instead to throw your life away like this? I thought I knew you better."

If not for the alcohol in my system, I surely would have fallen from my chair. Instead, I whirled around and, through more luck than grace, ended on my feet, face to face with my master, as the chair clattered to the floor behind me. Jerroth was alone, looking regal in black robes carrying the guild's blue-and-red insignia. Even drunk, I could feel the power of the spell he was holding; his hands glowed bright blue with its power, plain as day for anyone trained to see it.

I took two steps back, into an aisle between the tables so that at least something was separating us, as he continued. "You couldn't have thought you'd escape me. You're not stupid. Headstrong, perhaps; foolish, without question; but not stupid. So whatever gave you the idea that you could run from me, Dornan? Call it a curiosity, but I must know this. It's almost as important to me as retrieving you was to my reputation."

Illustrated by Ludmila Ryabets

I had no idea what to say. The man had never addressed me with anything other than my family name, Lor. Jerroth never called his students by their first names, except in rage—even me, his star pupil. Terror was working hard at sobering me up.

At first I thought no one had noticed my plight, but out of the corners of my eyes I observed a subtle shift in the room: the players still played, and the dancers danced, but all its charm had departed. People were actively ignoring the scene in the center of the room, which made sense. No one intruded on a StormWarder's business without a good reason and a lot of backing. I wondered what made them stay, until—as I backed up a step further, coming out on the far side of the aisle between the tables—I noticed two of his henchmen, armed with long knives, near the main entrance. A fair-sized window was behind me, and, foolish as it was, I was thinking of using it.

Summoning all the bravado I possessed, I answered, "Call me hopeful, I guess."

"Hopeful?" He sounded intrigued, but I could see the strain in his eyes. They were puffy, the bags underneath dark, almost a bruised color. The calm figure before me was a mask, and a thin one. "You must mean the little charade back in Denelor? Yes, Dornan, my child"—there it was again, fatherly, comforting, yet the last boy he'd called by his given name had been whipped near to death—"that was impressive, I must admit. I've given you no schooling in illusion, yet you had my guards convinced of your demise. You've been studying in my private library, haven't you?"

I flushed, even now feeling the guilt of a schoolboy caught in the act.

A wry grin cracked Jerroth's face. "Such an enterprising student," he mused. "Why, oh, why did you choose to leave?"

"You know exactly why I left," I spat.

"What, Kerek? Come now, Dornan, you and I both know Kerek would never have made initiate. So I made use of his other qualifications. What of it? I may be old, but even I have needs. He should have been grateful to serve any use at all!"

That kindled my anger, at least as much as fear would allow. Kerek had been my friend. He had no great talent for the learning, but what Jerroth had done to the boy was unconscionable, and Kerek had been only half my age—not even the start of a beard on his chin. The thought of Kerek at Jerroth's mercy, along with the rest of the old lecher's coterie of boys, set my rage free. My fear boiled away in an instant.

"You killed him, you bastard!" I shouted, and at that, everything in the hall stopped. No one openly insulted a StormWarder.

"I owned him! He was mine to use as I pleased." A sadistic smile curled his lip. "As are you."

"Never!" I screamed, flinging the wine tin in my hand at Jerroth's face. The cup flew end over end in a timeless spiral and connected squarely with the sorcerer's nose. He drew his arm up, sneezing blood onto his sleeve. When he lowered it, all pretense at civility was gone. The dark fury that replaced it pummeled at my resolve.

Jerroth spread his arms wide and released the spell he had been holding. Twin beasts—gray, leathery-skinned things that somehow looked like giant hairless hounds—rose up from the thin air under Jerroth's hands. Huge muscles rippled underneath their skins.

Their hind legs were long, almost froglike, except for the thick black claws at their ends. Their teeth were equally thick and black. Not good for cutting, but more than adequate for ripping and crushing. Their lidless red eyes were large—set forward for hunting. As they sat, surveying the room and focusing mostly on Jerroth, I caught a whiff of them. I'd never smelled charred flesh before, but that was what the smell made me think of.

So much for hope. I was about to die.

If the room had been still before, it was all motion and sound as soon as Jerroth released his summoning. The K'tarins hissed, almost as if they recognized the beasts—which may well have been true; who knows what world Jerroth had called them from, perhaps the Kats' home world? The K'tarins' fur bristled as they rushed the entrance to escape, along with everyone else. Even the Drugar, last to leave a fight and usually the last ones standing, backed cautiously away. The two guards stepped aside, avoiding the stampede. The sound of frenzied feet blended with the patter of heavy rain outside.

Jerroth ignored all of this. His focus, and that of the "dogs," was on me. The pretense at serenity had returned. Now that he was back in control, only his eyes hinted at his true feelings.

"You know, Dornan, I had truly hoped to bring you back with me." With Jerroth's penchant for torture, I had no doubt he would have liked to get me alone, where no one could watch. "You were the most promising student I'd seen in decades. You truly would have been a Master StormWarder. It is such a shame."

He turned to the dog on his left, who gazed up at him like an obedient puppy. He did the same with the dog on his right. Then turning to me with a satisfied smile on his face, he issued a single command.

"Kill."

Both dogs leapt at once.

Praise the Makers that Jerroth was a blowhard. If not for his little speech I would have had no time to prepare. Not that it helped much. The alcohol in my system was stronger than I had thought. Not only had it allowed Jerroth to sneak up on me, it was also sapping my ability to use magic. I needed concentration to draw power for a spell, and time to direct it. As it was I could barely draw any power at all, and had no time to properly channel it. So when the beasts leapt on me, there was only one thing I could do.

I drew the power on myself.

Even the youngest guild initiate will tell you that this is a fast way to get killed. The mortal body is not built to hold raw magic of any kind, and the incredible strength it affords the wielder is as likely to strip the muscles off his bones as it is to be useful.

But I had no choice.

With a grunt I heaved the tables before me at the dogs, straining the muscles in my arms and back. The tables went flying, the thick wood colliding with the beasts. The one on my left went sprawling, but the one on my right crashed through, unharmed. Splintered wood flew everywhere.

The dog was stunned, but far from out. I had no time to wait. I turned and leapt with all my might—which, magically augmented, was substantial—at the window behind me. The glass exploded around me, jagged shards raining down on my head and back, as I landed in the mud outside.

Without thinking I got up and ran, ignoring the cuts and hoping my body would hold out against the power that surged through it.

I could already hear the dogs making their way through the window behind me. Without thinking, I ran blindly into the storm. My heart was hammering. My blood, saturated with magic, burned. I could feel muscles straining and tearing as I moved, but I was too afraid to stop.

Now, call it a moment of madness if you will, but I really didn't notice until it was too late. That it was raining, I knew. That the tavern I'd stopped into was at the edge of town, I also knew. That I was an initiate of the StormWarders' guild, and that it is our business above all others to know better, I also knew. But with two beast-hounds and my master clamoring for my blood behind me, the fact that I was running, unprotected, into a raging Chaos Storm did not strike me until the first bolt of red lightning flashed down, and a tree the size of a house and all the ground for two-dozen steps around it vanished before me.

Now I was truly, truly dead.

Chaos Storms are the StormWarder's stock in trade. They are the reason for the guild's existence, and the reason the guild is as powerful as it is. From the beginning of history—known history, anyway; everything before the One War is all myth and debate—the whole of the world outside the protected cities was subject to Chaos Storms. It is said that the Makers themselves are responsible for the storms, but that, as any StormWarder will tell you, is unprovable myth. The science of the storms is much more readily apparent.

The storms themselves carry two dangers. The red lightning, as I had just witnessed, eliminates a bubble of space of anywhere from twenty to a hundred steps from the center of its impact. It, as the missing tree ahead of me would attest to, is the much more common of the two threats.

Blue lightning, on the other hand, is much rarer.

Which is why I was shocked to see an arc of it streak by overhead to land somewhere behind me.

I couldn't help but stop. I'd spent twelve years studying the storms, their effects, and the magics meant to divert their path, but I'd never actually been in one. Neither, apparently, had the hounds behind me.

Or hound, I should say.

It stood there, sniffing at the remains of its mate and making an odd keening noise. Of course, the thing twitching its last on the ground next to it bore little resemblance to the hound's mate. Not surprising. Blue lightning, unlike the red that destroys, changes whatever it touches.

At least, that's the popular version.

The truth, which I discovered while stealing through Jerroth's private library, is that blue lightning replaces whatever it touches with something summoned from somewhere else—just as the Old Ones supposedly summoned the Kats and the Vagra during the One War. Just as Jerroth had summoned those beasts.

The remaining one of which was now running towards me.

Praying to the Makers one last time to save a young fool, I turned to flee.

As I did, I realized that I was the biggest fool of all. Like metal to a magnet, Chaos Lightning is drawn to certain types of magic and repelled by others. The guild's power and influence derived from its ability to use magic to divert the storms, and yet, like a fool, I was running blindly through such a storm, filled with raw magic. I was a walking lightning rod.

I realized this just in time to see the truth of it. For, just then, two arcs of lightning streaked down—one red, one blue.

Both with me as their target.

•••

Jerroth-Kine stood in the aftermath of the blast, arms tensed at his sides, mouth twisted into a snarl. His eyes burned with the afterimage of the twin strikes, the final moments etched into his retinas. The hound, shocked and confused at the departure of both brother and prey, whined into the night. The sound raised gooseflesh along Jerroth's back. As his eyes slowly regained focus, Jerroth sought out the beast.

Sighting the gray monstrosity keening pathetically over the remains of what had originally been its mate, he focused his attention on the ugly beast, drawing energy into the area around it until, finally, a flash of red lapped down from the sky like a hungry tongue, and the remaining beast was no more.

Jerroth smiled in the newfound quiet.

All around him the storm raged. Lightning, misdirected by his own personal ward, lashed down everywhere he wasn't, sucking up part and parcel of the land around and leaving a pocked and cratered waste in its wake. Wherever lightning flashed, Jerroth's heightened senses could make out the fine cord that stretched from the strike point away into the heavens. Like a funnel, Jerroth could see the essence of the land being sucked up the red cords and taken Creators knew where. Then the cord would wink out, vanishing like its prey. Likewise, blue cords appeared—though like the lightning that called them, much less often—carrying foreign energy to deposit here, before vanishing into the night like an uncaring mother.

All of these wonders were Jerroth's alone. Not another StormWarder living could see what he saw. Not one even knew to look. The full truth of the storms was Jerroth's to hoard and control. At least until that damnable boy started sneaking around his private estate—his libraries, his own private quarters.

But none of that mattered now. What drew Jerroth's focus and held him frozen until his rage at Dornan's loss drained away sat in the center of the storm. Right at the spot where Dornan Lor had made his final escape. There, rising out of the crater, a single cord—neither red nor blue, but purple—snaked away into the night.

"Extraordinary," he breathed, to no one in particular.

For a moment he wondered if the boy had somehow known—running into the storm by design instead of blind, bumbling panic. But that was folly. The boy's learning was no more than he could steal from Jerroth's own learning, hidden away in journals that were supposed to be private, and this was beyond even Jerroth's experience: that red and blue lightning might mix.

No one could have guessed that.

No, once again, blind luck had favored Lor, and, perhaps, this time Jerroth as well. For as he watched, the cord remained, holding true and strong, unlike either of its fitful parents. And that held possibility. For perhaps the first time Jerroth would actually be able to study the connection between worlds that these fleeting cords represented, and the possibilities created by that could be endless.

Not the least of which would be retrieving Dornan.

It wasn't until the salty tang of blood from his freshly broken nose reached his lips that Jerroth broke from his contemplation.

Ignoring the cold, he wrapped his arms around himself and shut his eyes. In the darkness behind his lids he replayed the events of the last few seconds over and over. Eyes closed, he strode forward in the rain, deftly avoiding both fresh lightning and the gaping craters it left in the ground.

At last he reached the edge of the pit that marked Dornan Lor's final, foolish stand against his master, and opened his eyes.

The crater resonated with energy. To Jerroth it appeared as a violet mist that wafted up from the newly opened earth. In the darkness it made the ground look alive—and wounded. He could feel the power of it pulsing at his feet. Resonating in a way unlike anything he'd ever felt before.

"Oh, thank you, Dornan," he said, smiling. "This may well be the discovery that marks my ascension to Grand Master of the Guild."

As he spoke he stooped, reaching down to touch the energy before him, to gather it for examination and study; but as he did, the mist moved, pulling away from the edge of the crater and receding into its depths. Jerroth started, jerking his hand back and watching the slithering mist recede into the center of the crater towards the base of the cord, snaking endlessly upwards. After a second he followed after it, watching it coil and wind, creating a small vortex at the base of the crater. For a second he paused, remembering the sight of Dornan, struck by both red and blue lightning at once, watching the lightning mix and coil around his helpless body, turning a deep angry violet. He remembered with relish the brief but intense look of agony on the apprentice's face as the energy saturated his body and, then, nothing. Apprentice, lightning, and land—all gone.

Only the cord remaining.

He remembered the look of Lor's essence, like a fiery golden liquid, rushing up the cord and away; then the energy of another—drawn in by the blue lightning stroke—rushing down. That light was blue and of a softer, gentler hue.

Pulling out of his thoughts, his gaze returned to the vortex, now no larger than a candle flame, and for the first time he noticed its source. At the bottom of the crater lay a small spherical stone of deepest amber. From one side sprung the now tiny vortex; from the other rose the cord. The stone was foreign, unfamiliar, and after a second, Jerroth realized why. With a wry grin, Jerroth reached down and scooped up the altered remains of his former student. How delightful it was that he should be left with a souvenir to remind him of his former prodigy.

When he touched it, however, all mirth vanished. A sensation, sharp and electrical, burst up his fingertips and along his arm, finally reaching his skull with a bone-shaking rattle. The whole world seemed to fall away, and Jerroth was washed in energy stronger and stranger than anything he'd ever felt.

In a moment the feeling ebbed and he looked down at the vortex emanating from the stone. Through it he could see, as if looking into a tunnel, a vision that brought back his former mirth. Wrapped in violet energy the image of a tiny newborn babe floated. It looked back at Jerroth with bright wondering blue eyes, and through those eyes Jerroth could see Dornan, lost and confused in a foreign place, but very much alive.

Looking down once again at the stone, Jerroth smiled and crooned to it. Oh yes, he thought, much work to do. Learning to channel this new energy might take ages, but it would come. My final revenge on you might have to wait a bit, but don't worry. Punishing your little school chums will keep my fires burning until the time is right. Yes, indeed, Dornan, my boy, killing you is going to be the education of a lifetime!

Part II

I wanted to scream, but the force of the blast ripped the sound from my throat. For a moment I could see Jerroth, grinning sadistically at me as I twisted in pain, and then the whole world fell apart and everything was replaced by warm purple light and the sensation of flying. I was sure I was dead, and, for the first time, wondered what came after.

A little late, that thought, but I had been so certain I was going to live forever.

I don't know how long it lasted. There was nothing to mark the time, nothing to mark change at all, except for one brief instant when I was struck with the sensation of not being myself. It happened quickly. One instant I was myself and terrified; then there was a flash of blue and I was someone else, devoid of thought and filled with a wondering innocence unlike anything I could describe. It only lasted a moment, and then I was myself again—less innocent and still terrified.

Then, abruptly, the journey ended. There was a blinding flash of light and color, and I felt myself surrounded by the warm wetness of blood. My equilibrium left me, and I felt as if I had literally been hoisted upside down. A cacophony of frantic voices surrounded me, but I couldn't understand any of what was said. And as I hung, helpless and confused, with shapes of color and light that seemed to want to make sense but couldn't, I realized with alarm that I was also unable to breathe.

My lungs burned, straining in desperation for air that would not come. All the blood rushed to my head, the fire in my chest grew, and as it did, the swirling shapes around me began to coalesce into a bewildering scene that denied the reality of my own death.

Everything was upside down and simultaneously foreign and familiar. I was in a room; despite the desperate swaying and swirling, I could make out definite walls. Someone, a woman by the sound of her, lay in a bed with her legs held aloft. Next to her stood another, this one male, but his features were lost in the constant swaying. Bright white light flooded up at me from the floor—which was actually the ceiling. There was no lamp that I could see. Square panels in the ceiling seemed to glow of their own accord. The light was white, but as I strained for air, it and everything else slowly turned crimson.

As I looked up at the lights I was finally able to see what held me aloft as the life slowly choked out of me.

A giant dressed in a pale robe and wearing a mask and cap that covered everything except his eyes held me by my ankles in a single, enormous hand. And just as I thought I would die from lack of air, I discovered his other hand, descending in a short, sharp arc behind me.

It landed squarely and with titanic force on my helpless posterior. My lungs surged to life, filling with sharp, sweet air.

And finally, released from my silence, I screamed like the damned.

I was mortified! I could marshal neither my reflexes to escape nor my voice to protest. I was utterly helpless as the titanic barbarian, whose handprint I feared would forever emblazon my backside, passed me off to another. This one, a harpy of a giantess, bundled me into her arms and carried me over to some sort of shiny metal cradle.

Once there, she plopped me down, backside first, into the cradle. The metal was frigid. Chills rolled through my body everywhere except my backside which, irritated by the slap, burned all the more fiercely. The harpy vanished for an all-too-brief moment, only to return carrying some sort of metallic wand.

This instrument emitted a deep crimson light that she shone first in my left eye, then my right, leaving me seeing stars. This was promptly followed by another instrument, this one shoved in each ear, and then a wooden stick shoved in my mouth. Then, before I'd even had a chance to clear my vision, and without so much as a by-your-leave, she picked me up and flopped me over on my belly—exposing the rest of my delicate anatomy to the iciness of the metal cradle—and walked off again.

The world was spinning, and I felt as if I might get sick at any moment. Promptly she returned. I caught a glimpse of something she carried, another wand, this one made of crystal. Then she was out of sight behind me. I stretched, trying to see what was going on, when suddenly I felt her hand push down on my back, and the tip of the crystal wand being inserted in my helpless posterior!

For a second there was peace—if frozen testicles and foreign instruments up your backside could be considered peaceful—and I wondered if I might not have been better off at the mercy of Jerroth. I had no idea where I was, what was happening, who these people were, or what their sadistic interest in my backside was about.

The only time in my life I can remember being poked and prodded so thoroughly was when as a child I'd been stricken with a deadly fever and my father had summoned the palace doctor.

Without preamble I was rudely pulled from my thoughts as the harpy yanked the crystal wand out of my behind, then, of all things, drew it up to her face and examined it.

Repulsed by what I was beginning to believe was some sort of medical examination, I tried to pull myself up and make an escape. No sooner had I grabbed the sides of my cradle for leverage when the harpy seized me by the waist and started hauling me away.

I struggled, trying my best to hold on to the crib as she lifted me up, until I noticed my reflection in its shiny metal surface. The sight of myself, and the final realization of what had happened to me, squelched all of my rebellious instincts. I let go of the cradle.

As she carried me away, I could not help but stare at my reflection in the crib. The ruddy face of a mewling babe, receding in the distance, watched back.

Fate is a fickle mistress, I decided, as I lay alone in a bed barely larger than I, surrounded by the wailing of infants.

At an early age, Fate had embraced me, whispering promises of a good life in my ear. Dornan Lor, born into a royal family, had the guarantee of wealth and easy living. Not the responsibilities of a true city lord—I was sixth in a line of many sons and daughters—but wealth and status.

Then Fate, that vile harlot, abandoned me, taking my promised future with her.

At seven, I, along with all but the first born of my siblings, was sent away to GuildHall in Caladan, mostly as punishment for mischievousness. Initiate training took two years, and most would get sent back, but that was not the point.

The point was that we would be gone for two years.

Except, as it turned out, I had a talent.

At the end of those two years all my siblings went back, and I stayed at GuildHall. I made initiate quickly and was rapidly advancing in rank and skill, until finally I was put under the tutelage of a Master.

Jerroth-Kine.

Fate, finding a young mage on his way up in place of the princeling she'd abandoned, returned, promising power and prestige if I was willing to work for it.

And I did work, sucking up all that Jerroth would teach, with rapidity that made the tedious learning of my guild mates torturous and slow.

So, in secret, I began my own learning.

In Jerroth-Kine's private library.

Stealing away in the dark of the night, I made a habit of sneaking into his private chambers and laboriously studying his many journals. Jerroth's curiosity, it turned out, matched my own. Over the years he'd bought, borrowed, or outright stolen magical rituals from over a dozen other guilds—fire magics from the Miners' guild, illusionary arts from the Travelers, arts of transportation and transmutation, ways of summoning power from the Dragon, and others. City law forbade many of the secrets I learned; others were forbidden by mandate of the High King himself. The practice of much of what Jerroth knew was punishable by death.

Like a beggar at a banquet, I swallowed everything I could lay hands on.

Finally, I discovered Jerroth's research journals. There I learned the true secrets of Chaos Storms: proof that these brief flashes of light and color are actually connections to other worlds and that Jerroth had somehow learned to see the connections, though how exactly this was done, he did not explain. These were things he was keeping secret even from his own guild!

One night, secreted in a corner of Jerroth's library and reading a tome on the lost races from before the One War, I heard noises coming from Jerroth's bedchambers. Bored with my reading and surprised to hear anything this late at night, I crept down the servants' passage to Jerroth's chambers. Light shone through the cracks around the edges of the servants' entrance, and I used them to peek in and see what was happening.

That's when I discovered Fate had abandoned me again.

Inside I saw Jerroth, naked as the day he was born, raging around the room. He was an odd combination of age and power. His skin sagged, but there was still muscle on the wiry frame underneath. It seemed as if I was looking at the remains of a larger man, eaten away from the inside. He was stomping around the room, waving his arms and cursing. At what, I couldn't discern, until I noticed the bed.

Kerek, my best friend, was lying there, face down, also naked. His backside was covered in blood. After a second, I realized he wasn't breathing.

The choice of whether to run or to slink away in the night and pretend I hadn't seen was never mine to make. Seeing Kerek on the bed, his chest neither rising nor falling, blood dripping from him, my body made its own choice. I cried out in anguish—and my career as a StormWarder ended.

After that I spent four months eluding Jerroth's henchmen. When I thought I was safe, Fate presented herself again. Mockingly, she gave me a new choice: a simple farmer's life in a nowhere town, pretending I was anyone other than myself, or death. I chose the former.

She chose the latter.

But even death wasn't enough for cruel Fate.

Death was supposed to be peaceful—a quiet respite from the ignominy of living—but, oh no, nothing so dignified for me. Struck down by Death in red, and again by Death in blue, I was now subjected to a fate worse than death.

Not only had I been transported to another world, but somehow I had managed to swap bodies with a newborn babe.

So, amidst a chorus of squalling infants, I found myself cursing Fate yet again, and fuming over the impending sentence of lifelong humiliation and embarrassment that renewed infanthood would bring.

Or so I thought.

In reality it turned out to be quite amusing, at least at first.

Within an hour or so of my deliverance to the baby ward, I was again collected, this time by a much less severe looking giantess—or adult, I should say—and returned to the room of my birth.

Right side up, the room wasn't nearly so terrifying. The walls were a serene blue. Sadly, the room—and the whole building for that matter—smelled dead. There was no sense of decay, the place seemed impeccably clean, but it smelled as if every organic thing had been utterly removed. I could only hope that the whole planet was not like this. Who would want to live in such a sterile place?

In the corner, on a bed, lay my new mother. Remove the blood and the disarray of childbirth and she was rather pretty. She had beautiful, slightly curling auburn hair that spread about her on the pillow, as I'd always imagined a woman's hair would look in bed—sadly, like priesthood, the life of an apprentice is very cloistered and completely celibate. Her face was equally lovely. Soft brown eyes set in an alabaster face that was only a shade too pale—and pale with good reason. The rest of her was hidden away by unflattering bed sheets, but the silhouette they formed was most enticing.

Sadly, a billion stabs of reality shattered the romantic tension as I was carried to where she lay.

The first of which was the man sitting next to her and holding her hand. Strange that I should be feeling pangs of jealousy towards a man whom, by all rights, I should be calling Daddy. Yet there it was, and in the light of male competition, I found a fault to offset every perfection I'd noticed in her. He was too thin, too gangly; his hair was too short, his beard too small; his eyes bulged ever so slightly and his teeth were crooked.

Rude, I know. Unfair, likewise, but lust and jealousy are potent things in the aging virgin.

But, of course, my virility was the next thing to crumble in the unflattering light of reality.

Distance is deceiving. And from the corner of the room, my new mother was attractive and my father annoying. But as I was carried closer, they grew, and grew, and grew, until, as I was passed into her waiting arms, she was simply enormous, and my father, ghastly.

There's no greater blow to one's manhood that being made to feel small. And right then, I felt infinitesimal.

So you can imagine my shock as the woman proceeded to lower her sheet, open her gown, and present to me perhaps the single largest breast the rudest minds all of mankind might ever conceive.

I was aghast!

In my lifetime I had admired small women, and I had greatly admired large women, but here I was presented with the object of my desire magnified to the point of absurdity, and without warning, the woman gently cupped me behind the head and pressed my face into the thing.

It shall forever shame me, but I must admit, at that point I completely lost my senses. Panic overtook me, and I proceeded to scream and flail until, finally, the monster breast was removed. That seemed to upset everyone in the room, but I simply couldn't help it, and, a few minutes later, when the whole process was tried anew, I panicked a second time.

Finally, the woman who'd brought me left and returned a few minutes later with a bottle capped by some sort of artificial teat. It looked strange and terrible as it was presented to me, but considering the alternative feeding method, I took the bottle immediately.

That was how I spent my first few days. In the daytime in the arms of these strange new parents, in the evening in the baby ward. Food was made available whenever I made noise—in this new body I was unable to form words. I had no control of my body either, which made for some new embarrassments. But even these shameful and uncontrollable bodily functions were quickly tended to. Crying seemed to be the incantation that summoned help whenever needed.

And like all magic, I learned the incantation thoroughly.

Unfortunately, real magic seemed all but absent from this world, at least as far as I was able to sense it. I didn't think I was completely helpless, for I could feel a faint whisper of my own personal magical aura—that field from which some create magic and others use to draw external magic—but I was unable to do any more than sense it.

I was going to have to learn my real skills all over again, and if I couldn't call on the abundant magic of my home world's chaotic atmosphere, I might have to learn some new skills as well.

So, all ability to do aught but eat and sleep taken from me, I spent a lot of those first few days sleeping. And I had the strangest dreams.

Normally when one shuts his eyes—at least when I shut my own—they are greeted by blackness at night, and by the crimson of their own eyelids when lit by day; and yet in this new world, whenever I closed my eyes I found myself surrounded by brown, the color of tanned hide. And stranger than that, whenever I closed my eyes I heard noises, not strange in themselves—except that they should be found residing in the confines of my own skull—yet quite definite. Every time I closed my eyes, the sight of leather and the sound of horses' hooves striking earth greeted me.

These things, fleeting with the blink of a wakeful eye, grew stranger when I went to sleep. For there, instead of dreaming, it was always the same. For a stretch of hours I would reside inside some sort of sack, nearly black at times, at others lit slightly from cracks. Everything was moving at a constant bounce as if the whole earth were shaking in time with the constant sound of the horse.

On occasion I could even hear voices amidst the cantering herd. They were faint, and most of it was lost amidst the more constant sound of the horses. But they were there, and stranger still, they spoke the common tongue of my own homeland.

But, of course, contemplation was fleeting and futile. I was still trapped in this uncoordinated body, and with more important matters to consider.

For on the third day my new parents took me home.

● ● ●

Jerroth-Kine snarled at the bastard sun that blazed down on his head, and cursed the confines of public appearance. If not for the contingent of men-at-arms riding with him, he might simply cast a tunnel between that worthless backwater on the edge of nowhere that Dornan had drawn him to and his beloved home. Instead, he was forced into this interminable mule ride across the High King's Road all the way through FreeHold, holing up each night at one of the myriad public inns that sprouted like sores around every High King's Watch.

Because the world could not know the depth of his knowledge, it would be at least two months before Jerroth saw home again.

His master-at-arms called the men to a halt in front of the large barn that passed as the inn's stables, and they quickly set to dismounting and leading the horses inside. Jerroth sat, staring off in the direction of home until a guardsman took up the horse's reins.

Jerroth dismounted, taking pains to retrieve the saddlebags from his horse before letting the man lead it away. Tossing the small burden over his shoulder, he finally turned and walked to the inn.

Inside, Jerroth was suitably pleased at the populace's reaction, which was mainly fear, lightly disguised as respect and servitude. Even the common field agents of the guild in their gray robes would seldom be seen passing this way. It never stormed over the High King's Road. So the sight of a Master StormWarder in his black robe was a unique experience to these common folk, and not a pleasant one.

The place was packed. Not a seat in the serving area was empty. It looked like a trade caravan returning from a successful venture. Money and wine were passing freely.

After a second, the proprietor—a small man with blond hair and a thick belt that was supposed to make him look strong, but only succeeded in making him look fat—approached, a plaintive look on his face that said they had no rooms available.

Before he was able to turn the look into words, Jerroth fixed him with an icy stare that made the man shrivel where he stood and said, "I need a room, and provisions for twenty men. The correct response is 'Yes, sir.' Do not test me by giving an incorrect one."

The innkeep stammered, looked away at the men about the room—and no doubt the size of each purse at their hips—and then back at Jerroth. For a brief second a flash of protest flitted across the man's features. Without moving, Jerroth cast the slightest of illusions, just a simple trick that brought a swirl of blue light flashing across his dark eyes. The sight of it made the man jump.

"A room will be made ready," he stammered, then nearly tumbled over himself in his rush to get away.

An hour later, Jerroth was in a private room. His saddlebags lay across the smelly straw mattress. Below the bags lay his trophy, the amber stone that was all that remained of Dornan Lor. He took careful pains to make sure it stayed out of contact with his skin, touching it only with gloves or linens. For whenever he did make contact, that strange sensation would burn through him, almost as if it were trying, briefly, to suck him into the violet vortex that still swirled over one side of its amber surface.

In the passing of idle time, Jerroth had begun experimenting with his newfound toy, reaching out with his will across the length of the purple cord that bound his world to this new one. Along the way, he found that he was able not only to see into the new world, but to cast some rudimentary spells and have their effects reach all the way into the alien lands.

His first spells, as befit his greedy nature, were summonings. But these early experiments had produced the worthless results one would expect from such a random test: a rock, some sort of bizarre shoe, some sort of animal flesh—no doubt sorely missed by its owner, but nothing useful.

Today he hoped for better luck.

The casting was a simple thing. He merely closed his eyes and detached his attention from his physical body, and, free of his physical body, let his mind ride along the purple cord that connected his world to Dornan's newfound one. The journey was quick, almost instantaneous. A rush of violet color and the sensation of flying and then he would find his mind floating freely in the new world. The only problem was maintaining the connection. It never led directly to Dornan; instead, for reasons yet unfathomed, his mind would jump off at some point before the violet tether's final destination.

This time he found himself floating in a room full of uniformed men.

He'd noted before a strange parallel between this world and his own, and was struck by it again in this new place. Though the surroundings were strange and almost completely alien to the comforts of this world, the inhabitants bore an uncanny resemblance to the stocky, ill-bred humanity that was common to FreeHold. If the legends of the One War were true, then many of the common races originated from other worlds. It made him wonder.

The room was full of many objects, and, after a moment, he spotted the one he would try for. Focusing his concentration on the object, he could feel his mind surrounding it—he was getting better at this—and finally, when his grip felt as secure as he could make it, he pulled. There was a soft thump before him, and when Jerroth opened his eyes, he discovered the object settling to a rest on the mattress before him.

He picked the object up. It was cold metal, although of what type he was uncertain. The dull gray surface reflected the room ever so slightly along its surface. The shape was simple and functional: a simple handle, and atop it a single metal pipe with an opening at one end and a small hinged hammer at the other. Set in the joint where the handle met the tube was a small metal lever.

He had just started toying with the lever when he was jolted by a knock at the door.

In that moment of surprise his aging fingers twitched over the small lever. The hinged hammer at the back of the thing pulled back, then kicked forward and the whole contraption exploded in his hands, sending an incredible recoil that shot up his arms and made him drop the device. His nostrils were seared by the sharp tang of burnt sulfur and his arms and back tingled from the shock. Several seconds passed before he noticed the gaping hole in the door across the room.

Jerroth leapt up and rushed to examine the door. The thick wood was shattered around a fist-sized hole about midway down the door. Through it he could see the innkeeper lying on the floor, a similar fist-sized hole about halfway down his frame.

Pulling the door open Jerroth shouted, "Oh, I *like* this!" at no one in particular.

Just then, two of his men-at-arms appeared, no doubt seeking the cause of the explosion. At the sight of their master, they stopped, then gasped at the sight of the bleeding corpse at his feet.

Jerroth snorted in derision. "Clean this up," he ordered, then receded into his room, slamming the door behind him.

Returning to his bed, he picked up the amber stone using a linen hand towel, and returned it to the saddlebag that would be its resting place for the two months it took to get back home. After that he returned to the examination of his new toy, this time handling it delicately. It was intact, in spite of the damage it had caused, and the tube was now warm to the touch. He turned it over in his hands, taking careful pains to avoid the "trigger." Along the side of the tube he discovered a set of strange runes carved into the handle. Excited by the discovery he quickly fumbled his notebook out of the other saddlebag, and, after inking a slender stylus, he set to copying the runes.

Though he had no clue what the strange characters meant, he found something in them strangely familiar. He'd studied many arcane languages in his long quest for knowledge, and perhaps with time he could decipher these as well.

After several minutes of studied labor, he set down the stylus. His work was exact, and as he sat listening to the sounds of his men grumbling over their cleanup duties, he stared at the alien characters he'd written:

SMITH AND WESSON TM.

•••

The life of an adult hidden in the body of an infant was a lot nicer than one would first expect. Taken to my new home, I came to enjoy a regular routine of feeding, washing, constant attention, and the genuine affection of two parents who, over the course of several weeks, I came to appreciate as possibly the first truly nice adults—alien or otherwise—I had ever met.

Alcohol, women, and only a slight increase in muscular coordination and bladder control would be all one would need to advance from this lifestyle to that of a petty nobleman!

Of course, like nobility, there were certain downsides as well—the first and foremost being a total lack of freedom, followed by an equally complete lack of privacy. The combination made it practically impossible to try to find a way home, while at the same time gave me ample opportunity to examine this new world.

I quickly discovered that, in spite of my initial observation, this world was rich with magic, though of a different kind than any I had ever encountered. Magic here seemed to be used to power devices of various shapes and ingenious uses never imagined in our world. As far as I was able to gather, it emanated from the very walls themselves, traveling to small "contact points" scattered about the walls near the floor. From these, all manner of devices were attached by wires plugged into these "contact points"—which I was determined one day to examine up close and in detail.

One of these objects, which I quickly grew quite attached to, was a large box with a pane of glass set in one side. One would think that a box with a window in its side would show the contents of the box, but instead, whenever Mother or Father would pick up a small, oddly shaped wand and point it at the box, it would light up and show fantastic moving images of other things and places. It was almost as if someone, somewhere, were holding up a mirror to the world, and its reflection appeared here, in the box.

There were numerous other contraptions, though most were more mundane in their function, if not their method. Cookeries that heated themselves at the turn of a dial. Basins and tubs that filled with water—cold and hot—at the turn of a spigot. There was a strange collection of boxes, one similar to the viewing box I watched with Mother, which Father frequently occupied himself with.

At first I had assumed my new parents to be relatively poor, judging by an apparent lack of servants and helpers, but, as I later came to think, they must be quite wealthy to afford such automated wonders.

Father, it seemed, was some sort of tradesman—at least I assumed such, as daily he left for a third of the day or more, only to return, tired, but lacking the soot and dirty fingernails of the common worker. Mother stayed at home with me, which I found a quite agreeable situation—especially after the notion of breast-feeding was completely abandoned. I quickly came to be embarrassed by my initial assessment of Father's appearance. Jealousy, it seems, can go quite a long way towards distorting perceptions, and I soon came to realize that Father's face bore more than a passing resemblance to my own—at least before the lightning had transformed me.

I saw almost nothing of the outside world, except rare trips to the domiciles of others. Most of what I learned came from the images I viewed through the magical box Mother and I often watched, and the world it portrayed filled me with wonder and shock.

Not at its strangeness, but at its frightful familiarity.

What struck me first as the days stretched into weeks, and then into months, was that the language of these people, who looked so similar to my own kind, was the common tongue of my own people.

It took me some time to realize this, as the language was guttural and so strange of dialect that the words were as foreign as familiar; but slowly I began to recognize word after word, so close to my own tongue that I could draw no other conclusion. Most of the words were unintelligible chatter, but in between those words I began to make connections.

"Something *was* something else."

"Someone *went* somewhere *to meet* someone else."

As I heard these things, the gibberish began to make sense. Nouns may have been meaningless—why should they be otherwise, when most of the objects they described were completely alien to me?—but as I came to recognize the placeholders between words, I started piecing together what the gibberish meant.

The viewing box we watched was a *television*.

Mother cooked *food* on the *stove*—and in the morning it was *breakfast*, at noon *lunch*, and in the evening *dinner*.

In time, I realized that my mother's name was *Diane*, my father was *Patrick,* and that I had a name as well:

Joey.

The impossibility of all this kept me up at nights seeking an explanation for how inhabitants of one world might speak the same tongue as those on another.

Unfortunately, I thought I knew the answer.

In GuildHall, I had never been one to shirk my studies, even the frivolous ones. I assumed all legends of the One War and before to be without value, but now I could not help but wonder at them.

The legends of our world's origin were steeped in myth. In the beginning the Creators walked the earth, teaching the eldest race of man the ways of life. The Creators quarreled over teaching the Old Ones the ways of magic, one of them opposing the other three, claiming that it would destroy the natural balance of the universe. They ignored him. That one—known by some as the

White One, by others as the GodKing—struck down the others, casting them from the world. In the conflict the land was split apart, and the few Old Ones that survived the rending of the land hid in the far corners of the world. In the absence of the other gods, the GodKing summoned a race of beings to his service. Their reason for existence was to seek out and destroy every living thing on the planet; to wipe the slate clean so that perfection might be restored.

Of course, this led to the One War. The great conflict that changed the world forever into what we know it to be today, and wasted nearly three months of my education on theology when I could have been studying magic.

But now, I couldn't help but remember the end of that history.

According to the High King, bearer of the Creators' warning to their creations, at the end of the One War a stranger had come to the land. The High King and his followers believe that the stranger was one of the Creators reborn, others that he was from another world, but this everyone agrees upon: The stranger, using magics unknown, shared the contents of his mind with that of every living being on the planet, and in that moment when his mind contacted theirs, every being on the planet knew the only possible outcome of war.

Of course, with most of the elder races having gone into seclusion at the end of the One War, there weren't many left, outside of the High King, who could confirm or deny this; but in my classes a strong case was made defending the concept that the stranger *did* exist, and came from another world. First and foremost of which was the common speech. This language, which from that day on was known to every inhabitant of the land, bears no relation to any other known language on the planet.

To me the story of the One War had always seemed the worst of religious drivel, not that I would ever admit it—the High King and his army of Watchmen based their lives on belief in the One War, and the prophecy that followed it—but I couldn't help but wonder about that stranger. It is said that he came from a world where war and all its horror were commonplace, a place whose language had needs for words like *annihilation* and *holocaust*. And as the weeks passed, I quickly came to discover that this was a world where war was common.

I'd seen images of buildings and vehicles destroyed, homes on fire, people crying. I'd even seen people chase and kill each other in the streets, all with Mother—so sweet and loving in every other aspect—watching with rapt attention.

Might this be the same world?

Of course, not every second of those early months was spent exploring the new world. At night, for instance, I was put to bed in a cradle which was at first in the same room with my parents, then later in the room next door. During these times, when the lights were off and I was alone, I had nothing to do but think and watch the strange journey that was unfolding behind my closed eyes.

Night after night I found myself jouncing along inside that same leather world, surrounded by the sounds of horses and the muted shouts of men. On several horrible occasions I heard another voice, too muffled to recognize, that nevertheless managed to send chills up my spine.

But the monotony of this strange experience made my mind wander, and I found myself thinking of old friends.

Especially of Kerek.

Kerek had been such a fine friend. At twelve, he strove to make initiate in spite of his poor ability, all because of the prestige it would afford his poor family. His talent was meager, and his education more so, but his honesty and sincerity were enough to win over even a royal-born snob like myself.

If only I hadn't been so selfish.

I could have tutored him instead of spending all my time stealing knowledge from Jerroth. If Kerek had shown any more talent, Jerroth might have left him alone. If only I'd been as good a friend to him as he was towards me, he might still be alive.

I shut my eyes against shame and depression, and found myself instead staring at the face of horror itself.

In the darkness behind my closed lids, I discovered that the slight comfort of my leather abode had been replaced by new surroundings. Ones a great deal more familiar. And a great deal more terrifying.

Behind closed eyes, I saw Jerroth-Kine's study, as plain as I ever remembered it, and in the center of the view, Jerroth-Kine himself stood over me, grinning.

In that instant the complete reality of my situation came crashing down on me with the full weight of doom behind it.

Red lightning transports.

Blue lightning transforms.

The combination of the two had done both: transporting my spirit to a new world, and somehow transforming my body into something small enough for Jerroth to carry with him in a saddlebag.

And if I was able to see my home world through that object, then it and I were somehow still connected.

Which meant Jerroth could probably see me.

I immediately tried to call upon my months of infant training, but with Jerroth staring, seemingly right at me, I couldn't muster enough voice to scream, which was a shame, since the fright was enough to scare away my bladder control.

So I lay, breathless and wet and angry, watching in silence.

Outside I could hear the television playing—louder than usual. Father had worked an exceptionally long day, and I'd thought to give him some peace, pretending to sleep so that Mother might attend him for a while instead of me.

Now, as I watched Jerroth move in and out of view, intently working on something I couldn't make out, I wished desperately that they would come. But the tiny fearful croaks that my throat kept producing were not enough to get their attention.

Then I felt it: a faint violet flash suffused my vision, and my skin prickled in a way I hadn't felt in months. Instantly my eyes popped open, and my fear doubled as I noticed a pale violet light drifting up from me to the ceiling. It was a faint magic, but in this world it set off klaxons in my head like thunderclaps. A spell had been cast.

Somewhere nearby.

My heart thudded in my tiny chest, my mind quickly throwing argument after argument in defense of the idea that I was wrong. Jerroth couldn't actually see me; he didn't really know where I was.

But the tiny voice of fear had a different argument. In the din of fierce rationalization, fear quietly asserted that Jerroth-Kine knew my secret and had only been biding his time.

He'd found me.

Now I screamed in earnest, crawling to the edge of my crib and trying my best to climb up the wooden bars. Above the noise of the sitting room, my parents heard nothing. No one came.

In my fear I was oblivious to the fact that I was standing upright for the first time in this body, but I could not escape the confines of the crib. My bed had become a prison.

Then I heard it.

From the wall separating the bedroom from the front yard came a hideous scratching noise. A sound like rats chewing on wood, but louder.

I screamed with all the force my tiny lungs could muster, until my voice grew hoarse. Turning to the door, I prayed to powers greater than mine for deliverance. Still nothing came.

And the noise outside was getting louder.

The sound of wood splintering joined it.

I grabbed the bars of my cage with both hands and threw my weight against it. My voice was gone, and now I coughed uncontrollably from the exertion. The crib jiggled with my tiny effort, but nothing more.

"Come," came a horrific voice through the scratching. It was my own language, parroted by something that sounded unaccustomed to speech.

"Come to bring you home," it hissed.

And, looking behind me, I saw the ends of long razorlike fingers making gashes in the wall.

"Come. Come to take you back to Master."

I watched in horror as the long fingertips wrapped around a chunk of wall and pulled it out, revealing a bright yellow eye surrounded by gnarled brown flesh.

"Jerroth-Kine, want you. Baby boy he like. Want you back, does he. Want to use you, like Kerek. Only worse." It snickered at that, and another chunk of the wall was pulled outside.

What was left in my bowels immediately departed.

Jerroth didn't want to kill me. He wanted . . . he wanted to . . .

Frantic, I turned back to the gate of the crib as the creature thrust one arm through the opening and started squeezing himself through. I rattled the gate with all my strength, feeling it move in my hands as if it wanted to swing open, but couldn't. Something was catching. I'd watched Mother open the thing a thousand times. How had she done it?

How?

That's when I saw it. A simple metal clasp at the top of the gate—out of my reach all this time because I had been flat on my back.

But I was standing now.

Leaning against the gate, I reached for the clasp. My motor skills were pathetic, but fear helped the learning process. I reached the clasp and pushed . . . And with the weight of my body against it, the gate swung open, spilling me head first, trailing my blanket and all the toys on it onto the floor behind.

I landed with a thud, and the metallic taste of blood filled my mouth. The impact stunned me. I couldn't focus my eyes, but I could hear the creature crawling through the hole it had made. Its clawlike fingers scratched the wall, and more wood splintered as it strained to force its malformed head through.

I belly-crawled away as fast as I could, bumping into my rattle as I moved, then realized that I had nowhere to go. The doorway to the hall was shut. There was no way I could reach the knob.

I was stuck.

And as I looked back, I realized it was also too late. The creature was through the hole.

The monster was simultaneously horrifying and fascinating. Its extremities were large, malformed. Its head was a twisted brown lump that looked, somehow, like a knot of rotted wood. Its feet were talons. Its hands held long thin fingers that ended in razor-sharp tips. All of them were terrifying, separately or together. Yet the body that held it together was a tiny thing—neck, arms, legs, torso, were all so thin as to look like sticks. It stood no taller than I—if I could stand, that is.

But most terrifying of all was the fact that, as I turned to look at it, it was already reaching for my leg.

Grasping hold in a grip like iron, and drawing blood in several places along my calf, it flipped me over on my back, easily. My hand flopped down on my toy rattle.

"Time to go home now," it hissed. "Master is waiting."

Terror strengthening me, I swung blindly, using the rattle as if it were a club. The creature was too slow, expecting no resistance from a baby. The rattle caught the beast squarely on the side of its head, and to my surprise the stick man went flying like so many twigs. Its claws raked along my bare calf, drawing more blood. I screamed and backed away.

The thing crashed into the far wall, near its hole, but was quick to regain its feet.

"Owwww," it complained. "I hurt you for that!" Then it started back towards me.

Frantic, I reached. Summoning the small trickle of magic I could command here, I raced trying to think of something I could do. Anything!

"Going to cut you. Going to gut you," it snarled as it neared.

Then the thought hit me.

Simple spell. One syllable command. Easy gesture. My only hope.

As it reached for me, claws outstretched, I pointed my finger at the beast, and said in my own language:

"Burn."

To my surprise, not only did the beast catch fire, it actually erupted into flame, flying backward and crashing into the hole, where it exploded. I collapsed, exhausted, into tears.

Finally, as if some barrier had been lifted with the creature's passing, I heard my parents rushing up the hall to my room. They burst in together. Their eyes went wide as they surveyed the room. Me on the floor, bleeding in several places. The crib, open and over-turned. And, finally, the hole in the wall where the fire was slowly beginning to spread.

Mother came to me instantly, scooping me up and cradling me in her arms. Father vanished around a corner, only to return carrying a giant red tube with a hose attached. He pointed the hose at the flames, and gray smoke shot out. Strangely enough, the smoke actu-ally extinguished the flames rather quickly.

After that, the evening was spent rushing around. Men in yellow uniforms arrived in a giant red vehicle, basically, it seemed, to mill around the house and look at the hole. Mother rushed me off to be seen by more doctors, bandaged, examined, prodded and poked. On the way home Mother bought me a furry stuffed doll she called *Teddy Bear*.

Neither Mother nor Father seemed angry with me, which was quite a shock. In fact, they were both incred-ibly loving in spite of the fact that I'd nearly burned them out of their home. The conclusion of the yellow-jacketed men, whose job it seemed was to rate the severity of a fire after it was over, was that this was an *electrical fire*, and that the *wiring* needed to be *checked* by an *electrician*. Which I assumed to mean that the mage who had ensorceled the house to run all of Mother and Father's conveniences was in trouble and had to come out and fix things.

I hoped his guild wasn't as severe as my own.

Within two days, everything was back to normal. I was back to sleeping in the same room with Mother and Father, but everything else remained unchanged.

Unfortunately, I was no longer able to avoid the urgency of my situation. Jerroth knew I was alive. He knew where I was. And he *did* have the ability to reach me.

Which meant I didn't have a lot of time.

Fortunately, my perilous position wasn't the only discovery of that evening. In Jerroth's eagerness to capture me he'd made several important mistakes. I'd felt the spell Jerroth had used to send that awful little creature to me. I'd been too frightened to realize it at the time, but I'd also *seen* the spell Jerroth had cast.

After the melee was over, and my nerves had calmed themselves, I'd noticed that the purple light I'd seen was still there. It was faint, like the afterimage from a lightning strike, but I was clearly able to make out a thin purple cord that stretched away from me, through the ceiling of the room and beyond.

I could see the tether that joined my world to this one.

And, though my own personal magical aura was weak, I could feel the power of my home world through that cord. I think the spell I had cast against the creature had drawn power through the connection. There was no other explanation I could conceive to explain why it had been so strong.

Which meant I had power.

Jerroth's second mistake was his choice of spells. Not an actual summoning—the creature he'd sent here had been no more alive than the lump of wood he'd fashioned it from. Jerroth had instead chosen to animate the creature using much darker arts.

Which, combined with the gift my parents had given me, gave me an idea of my own.

I apologize to the Makers for the practice of dark arts I used to enact my plan, but the creature that had died to make the gift Diane called *Teddy Bear* would feel no worse for having its old skin walk and talk one last time, even if only as a puppet walks and talks under the control of a puppeteer.

And I needed a vessel I could send back home.

Part III

It felt good to be on the move again, to be home again, if only in effigy. Jerroth's teachings—even his inadvertent ones—had proven sound. For the next week I worked while my parents slept. Though it had been a struggle, I had been able to successfully animate the *Teddy Bear.* It had been quite a sight watching the thing walk about the new crib. After that, it had been a fairly simple matter to give it my senses, so that when I closed my eyes I saw through its eyes, heard through its ears, felt through its skin.

For a moment, I was free of the visions of Jerroth's study, having replaced them with my own, but it was very brief. For my plan to succeed I needed to be able to act in my own world, and Jerroth had given me all the tools I'd need to be able to do just that.

I reenacted the spell I had watched him use to send the wood-beast here, and used it to send Teddy to Jerroth. As I was his best student, the spell worked, landing my puppet just outside Jerroth's study. Pulling out of the spell for a moment, I checked my surroundings at home. My parents still slept; my sending hadn't aroused them. Then I closed my eyes and returned to Jerroth's manor.

I thought I had felt small before, but landing here, in my master's lair, standing in the body of a foot-tall, walking, talking piece of fluff, I was terrified.

But I had to stop him, once and for all.

No one was around, so I scuttled my fluffy feet up to the door of Jerroth's study and peeked underneath. No sign of anyone—which would have been perfect except for one unforeseen problem.

After a few seconds of comical leaping and acrobatics, I came to the conclusion that being one foot tall, there was no way I was going to reach the doorknob to let myself in.

I had to find another way.

Just then I heard a noise. My heart skipped a beat, and I froze for an instant before mustering the will to dive under the nearest table to avoid detection. Peeking out from underneath, I watched as two servants pushed a large cart down the hall, holding a steaming tray of something I couldn't see. With the servants intent on their work, neither of them noticed me jump under the cart, which wheeled slowly around a corner and through a door into the servants' passageways.

Along the way the cart passed a full-length mirror, and I couldn't avoid looking at myself as I passed. The image of myself—floppy hat atop a furry round head, button eyes and nose scrunched up in a conspiratorial grimace, ridiculous blue button overcoat, with furry feet sticking out the bottom—was so comical that I had to stifle a laugh.

This was the champion who would finally end Jerroth's days?

I must be mad.

Although I'd never seen it from this vantage point, I recognized the doors as we passed—Jerroth's study, then his bedroom—and we finally stopped at a door I'd never been through, which the servants promptly opened.

I'd only smelled charred flesh once before. The smell had accompanied my pursuers as I ran for my life through a Chaos Storm, filling me with fear so strong that I would forget a lifetime's training and allow myself to be struck by the very lightning I was trained to avoid. The smell surrounded me as the cart I rode on wheeled into the room.

Seeing another low table to hide under, I dashed off the cart. From there I was able to see into the room. Jerroth was there, with several men-at-arms and servants surrounding him. Seeing him there filled me with so much fear that I wanted to run, but the servants' door had closed behind me.

I was trapped.

The room looked like some sort of enormous indoor arena. A round walkway surrounded a shallow pit at the center of the room.

Snarling and stench poured out of the hole like smoke, and though I couldn't see into it, I could imagine what was down there. Fortunately, my furry knees didn't make any noise as they quaked.

Something was going on, but I couldn't make it out from here. I couldn't get closer without being spotted, so I had to find a way to reach higher ground.

Luckily, like every corner of every room in Jerroth's manor, this room was lined with bookshelves, and while all backs were turned I rallied my courage long enough to climb up one and hide behind a tome on the top shelf.

From there I could see everything.

As I'd feared, two snarling beast-hounds, like the ones I had seen before, circled at the base of the pit. Jerroth threw meat—not just cuts of meat but whole cooked carcasses—from the cart down to them, which the beasts devoured instantly.

After the bloody feeding was done, another servant entered, carrying a small bundle. It took me a moment to realize that I recognized the woman. Saleigh had been much larger—with child—when last I'd seen her, and I assumed that the bundle she carried must have been the new child.

Oddly enough, in spite of my fear, I found myself wondering what she'd named it.

Jerroth ordered the woman to hand the child over to one of the guards, which she did. Then he ordered the guards into the pit.

With some trepidation the guards descended the spiral ramp that led to the base of the pit. There—working hard to circumvent the hounds, who still wore bits of dead animal carcass in their teeth—they made their way to a small dais in the far corner of the pit.

For a horrified moment I feared that Jerroth intended to feed the child to the beasts as well, but instead the guards set the baby—who had been squalling from the moment it was removed from its mother—down on the dais, and at Jerroth's order took up positions between it and the beasts.

"Now remember," Jerroth yelled at them, "guard that child as if it were your own. This woman depends on it." Both men saluted and began drawing their swords.

Then, Jerroth pointed at the baby, and commanded the hounds: "Fetch!"

I watched in horror as the bloody scene unfolded.

Both guards were dead before their swords had left their scabbards.

I bit down on a furry paw to keep from crying out. The servants backed away, leaving only the woman crying at the edge of the pit. Jerroth merely looked on, smiling.

I wanted to kill him.

After that, as gingerly as a noblewoman sipping at tea, one hound went to the child, lifted it up in its mouth—still dripping with the spilt gore of the fallen guardsman—and cantered up the pathway, with its mate following close behind.

My muscles tensed as I waited for the beasts to bite down, killing the helpless child. My heart ached to help Saleigh and the baby, but if I moved we'd all be dead.

Cowardice held me rigid.

At the top of the path, Jerroth met the beast, which gently dropped the child into Jerroth's waiting arms. Jerroth smiled, patting the nearest hound's head, and praising, "Good boy!" He then handed the blood-soaked bundle back to Saleigh, who bolted from the room, barely stifling a scream as she fled. The other servants followed quickly behind.

Alone with the beasts, he cooed to them while pulling something from his robe. I didn't recognize the item, until I noticed the faint violet cord snaking away from it towards the ceiling. In my fright I hadn't noticed it earlier. But at the sight of the purple cord, I knew instantly that Jerroth held my transformed mortal remains in the palm of his hand.

My body, my whole life, had been turned into a rock.

I had no time to contemplate the situation—or curse Fate, as she richly deserved—as Jerroth was already moving. Holding the amber stone above his head, he quickly started incanting a spell I recognized instantly, but before I could react, the spell was finished. The two hounds vanished, replaced by a fiery white light that rose through the cord and into the heavens.

The dogs were gone.

Jerroth was alone.

Now was my chance to move.

And then it dawned on me. The whole display: two guards protecting a small infant that the hounds retrieved for Jerroth. It was all a test. The dogs were trained to retrieve a child, and were speeding on their way to where my sleeping parents and I were alone, undefended.

I'd seen what the beasts had done to those guards. What would they do to my parents? I had to stop them!

Opening my eyes, I was temporarily lost in the darkness of the room. Everything was quiet, save the light snoring that came surprisingly, not from Father, but instead from Mother. I strained in the darkness, trying to make out any motion, any threat, but I could see nothing.

All the fear I had felt since my journey home had manifested itself in my diaper, but I had no time to worry about that now.

There was a noise outside.

I didn't recognize it at first. It was loud, but muffled by the wall. It sounded vaguely like someone working madly on a bellows, pumping deep bursts of air in and out, quickly. Then I realized it was the hounds. Sniffing.

Sniffing for me.

As soon as I realized what it was, it was already too late. There was a brief pause, like the silent moment between inhaling and exhaling, where nothing moved, and then the wall above my parents' bed exploded inwards, showering everything in debris.

Light and smoke and dust flooded the room, all working together to blind me. An enormous thud sounded in front of me, followed by Diane screaming. Something, a scrap from the splintered wall perhaps, struck me in the head, knocking me flat on my back. I winced.

And when I recovered, the hounds were there standing between my crib and my parents' bed. Two silhouettes of death in the moonlight.

As they started to move towards me, I was relieved to see that both Patrick and Diane were alive. Diane screamed at the beasts, trying to draw their attention away from me, but they ignored her. Patrick, quiet as a mouse, picked up a board from the devastated wall, and moved to attack one of the beasts.

Makers, they were brave!

As soon as he moved, one of the beasts turned and snarled at him. The sound shook the room, and Patrick recoiled as if struck. The beasts' vile reek was everywhere, so strong it shriveled my stomach and singed my nose. The beast was moving towards Patrick, and I had to stop that.

Summoning power from the violet cord, I cast a detonation—a spell the Miners' guild used to break rock and expose ore—at the ground between the crib and the bed. The room erupted a second time. My crib flew backwards; my parents' bed upended, knocking them through the hole and out of the house altogether; the hounds scattered.

I landed with a jolt that was padded by the many layers of blankets in the crib. Using the confusion, I scrambled out the bedroom door and into the hall, all the while praying that Mother and Father were all right.

I could hear the beasts stirring in the bedroom behind me. To gain time I summoned an illusion, doing my best to copy the sight, sound and smell of myself and creating an image of my screaming form crawling down the opposite end of the hall as I slipped into my old bedroom.

Fate smiled. The hole the wood-beast had created earlier had not yet been repaired. Only a thin translucent sheet of material separated me from the backyard. Through it I could see that it was raining.

I heard a crash from the hallway, followed by the sound of powerful feet running away down the hall.

Not wanting to waste the opportunity, I scrambled to the hole. The material was stronger than I'd guessed, but I summoned a small trickle of the same fire I'd used to burn the wood-beast, and the material melted away before me.

I crawled through the hole.

I don't know whose eyes went wider—mine on seeing my parents alive and scrambling for a way back in, or theirs on seeing me emerge, unscathed—but it was a wonderful reunion as Mother raced to me, scooping me up in her arms and running with Father towards the back gate.

My illusion must have failed quickly, for no sooner was Mother reaching for the latch on the gate, when the hounds emerged into the backyard—one bursting through the upturned bed in my parents' room, the other through the window in mine. My parents, being only human, had a natural reaction at the sight of the beasts.

They froze.

Lightning flashed above us. In spite of my perilous situation, I couldn't help but stare at it. The lightning crackled, striking down somewhere in the distance, neither red nor blue, but bright white. I'd never seen its like.

But it got me thinking.

I started summoning energy from the cord, not a trickle, but massive amounts. All I could muster. I wrapped the beasts in the energy until their auras glowed bright with it, as they sauntered forward, smug in their apparent victory.

But nothing happened.

I had hoped that I might be able to summon lightning down on them like I'd accidentally done to myself before, but they were halfway across the yard, and nothing was happening.

We were doomed.

I was shocked when, of all things, Mother recovered from her fright, and pushed the gate open. Grabbing Patrick by the shoulder she dove through the door.

White lightning flashed in the yard behind us.

The lightning touched down, striking the violet aura I'd summoned around the hounds, and turning bright red. After that, the hounds, the yard, and a four-foot bubble of fence vanished before my eyes.

The hounds were gone.

Patrick and Diane were safe.

Now it was Jerroth's turn.

I closed my eyes, and, returning to my furry host, I found the arena empty. I scrambled down the book-shelf, taking pains not to look at the gore congealing in the pit below. The door to the servants' hall had been left open, and after a quick peek to make sure no one was there, I dashed into the hall and made my way to the servants' entrance to Jerroth's study.

Pushing my furry face down so I could see under the door, I spied Jerroth hovering over his desk. His back was turned towards me.

Now was my chance.

The door to the servants' entrance had no latch, just a lock on the inside that Jerroth never used. Praying that he hadn't changed his habits, I pushed with all my might, and was rewarded. The door slid open silently.

Moving on padded feet, I stalked Jerroth, sum-moning the energy for the spell I would use to kill him. He was undefended, unprepared. One small spell of fire aimed right at his heart, and he would never hurt anyone ever again.

Four feet away from him I stopped. Looking at him, enormous and regal in his black robes, I focused the energy, aimed it at his heart, and . . .

He vanished.

I stood there a moment, stunned beyond words. My concentration obliterated, the spell I'd been preparing crumbled.

Vanished.

Then I realized. I'd been duped by illusion, from the same source I'd learned the craft: Jerroth-Kine.

"I was wondering when you'd get here," came the sonorous voice from behind me. "I knew you'd find a way, but I must admit," it chuckled, "your choice of vessels is . . . amusing to say the least."

Jerroth-Kine.

I turned slowly, not wanting to see what I knew was waiting. Jerroth stood in the servants' doorway, the door shut behind him. From my perspective he towered like a nightmare above me. Jerroth-Kine, torturer, murderer, Master. Jerroth in control.

"How?" I stammered.

Jerroth smiled broadly. "You departed rather abruptly after I sent my pets to fetch you," he explained, taking a step forward. I couldn't move. "When your puppet fell inanimate, it dropped the book you'd been hiding behind. Nearly scared me to death." He laughed briefly, then all mirth drained from his face.

"Nearly."

He bent down, scooping me up in one hand like the rag doll that I was. I struggled, beating his hands with my tiny fists.

I couldn't have been more pathetic.

He walked to his desk and thrust me down, pinning me on the desktop with one hand. With the other, he scooped up a small pile of thin spikes he'd apparently set aside just for the occasion, and used them, one at a time, to pin down my limbs.

Puppet body or no, those spikes hurt, and I wailed as he nailed me to the desk.

Satisfied that I wasn't going anywhere, Jerroth let go of me. "You really were a wonderful student, Dornan. I almost wish circumstances were different, so we might study this together." As he spoke, he pulled the amber stone from his robes and set it down next to my head.

The violet cord snaked down from the ceiling and entered one side of the stone. On the other side a tiny vortex emerged, swirling around an image I hadn't thought of until now.

Joey.

The real Joey. His spirit hung, trapped in the stone, as mine was in his body back on his world.

I couldn't run away, couldn't abandon the spell that animated the puppet. Not as long as Jerroth held Joey's spirit for ransom.

"Oh, well," Jerroth mused. "If you hadn't run, I wouldn't have this to play with," he said, indicating the stone. "So I guess it did all work out for the best."

"What are you going to do to me?" I asked.

Jerroth smiled, and gestured to a book laying open on the other side of the desk. Even with it open I recognized it. It was Jerroth's liturgy on Necromancy, and it was open to a ritual of Binding.

Jerroth was going to bind my spirit to Teddy, trapping me in this form.

I gaped up at him.

He laughed again. "Well, I certainly can't have you running around mucking things up. This world you've discovered is rich with wonders I wish to exploit." As if making an example, he pulled another object from his robes. This one I recognized from the *television* Mother and I watched. It was called a *gun*.

"No one is going to get in my way." He pointed the device at my chest.

"Least of all, you." And pulled the trigger.

Sound and pain exploded in my chest. The whole desk shook beneath me. I screamed and screamed, but the pain didn't cease, until finally I blacked out.

When I came to, Jerroth was gathering up the components of his spell. A brief glance showed a hole in my stomach, the fur around it singed and smoky. The stone was still next to my head, resonating with energy. Joey stared at me from inside, an unspoken plea in his bright blue eyes.

"How does it work? Why doesn't the connection wink out, like all the others?" I asked, my student's curiosity arising from my stupor before my cautious common sense.

Jerroth seemed pleased at the question. He turned to me, all the hostility of a few moments ago replaced by the teacher he harbored inside. "You know, I've been asking that question now for months, and I finally think I know the answer."

He picked up the stone, and for a second a look crossed his face. Whether it was agony or ecstasy, I couldn't tell.

"It's an odd thing. Whenever you touch the stone it pulls at you, almost as if it's trying to draw you into it, but something is stopping it. And I think, therein, lies the key.

"Chaos Lightning," he continued, turning his answer into a speech, "is like a siphon as far as I can determine, sucking things up and spitting them out. Red in one direction, blue in the other. When the twin strikes that took you mixed, it seemed to do both at once. Sucking you and the infant in the stone up at the same time, and trying to spit you out in each other's places.

"But it seems as if, somehow, you both got stuck.

"You both arrived in your successive destinations, and yet the cord remains, its ends attached to each of you, as if you are both stuck. It explains a lot. Why the cord remains stable, why objects sent along the path jump off before reaching their final destination. You and the infant are like corks. While you exist in the child's body he can move neither forward nor back, and while he exists in yours—or what's left of it—you are equally trapped." He smiled as if tickled by the thought.

I stared at him. "You mean we're holding the passage open."

Jerroth smiled, "Indeed."

"Then won't moving my spirit into this body close the connection?"

Jerroth frowned as if explaining things to a dullard.

"Of course it would, unless I put someone in to replace you. I thought Saleigh's new child would do nicely."

I cursed inwardly, thinking, *Please, not another child's death on my hands,* but something Jerroth had said had given me an idea. I fell silent and waited for Jerroth to finish his preparations.

While he moved, collecting objects, checking notes, conferring with guards—who eventually brought in Saleigh's baby—I used the privacy to try and free one of my hands. The spike tore at my paw as if it were my own flesh, but I stifled my screams. I had to be ready.

Finally the time came. Jerroth returned; having arranged a series of candles and stones around me and the stone on the desk, he lit the candles, one by one, chuckling to himself as he did.

"I'm sure you realize that when your mortal spirit enters this damaged vessel it's not going to survive for very long." As he spoke, he traced a finger along the inside of the hole he had produced. The pain was intense; the smile on his face while he did it, more so.

"Any last requests, Dornan?"

Trying not to cry out, I replied, in as even a tone as I could muster. "Yes, just one."

Jerroth raised an eyebrow.

"Think of Kerek."

That made him frown, but in a second he shrugged it off and began the incantation that would draw my essence from Joey's body so that he could place it in the body of Teddy.

The room swirled. As he spoke I could feel myself in two places at once. The sensation was like standing and falling simultaneously. As he continued, it grew worse, feeling more like falling than standing. This was it. It was now or never.

Using the last of my strength I shouted Jerroth's name.

Shocked from his chanting, he looked down, a vague, dreamy look in his eyes. Ignoring the pain, I ripped my paw free of the spike, grabbed the stone and threw it at him, yelling, "Catch!"

Reflexively he caught the stone in one hand.

As he did, I spoke the last line of the spell.

The world came unglued. I felt the purple cord pull loose from me with a snap, and my spirit hovered free above the now inanimate Teddy Bear. As soon as my end of the connection was freed, Joey slid out of the amber stone, his pale blue essence zooming up the cord and away. Joey was going home to his parents.

That left Jerroth, shocked and confused, with the now empty amber stone pulling at him, I gave him no time to rally his defenses. Summoning my essence into a single point I aimed myself at Jerroth and pushed.

As I'd hoped, my essence slipped into Jerroth's body.

And his essence slipped into the stone.

He was trapped.

Feeling the heavy weight of the weapon he'd used to blow a hole in Teddy's chest, I quickly pulled the object from Jerroth's—my—robes. Setting the stone down on the table, I looked at Jerroth's image in the stone.

"Think of Kerek, you bastard," I repeated, then raising the weapon, I shot the stone, blowing it and Jerroth into dust. The cord vanished.

I was free!

Joey was safe. His—our—parents were safe. Saleigh's baby was safe.

And I now inhabited the body of one of the most powerful members of the StormWarders' guild.

Things were going to change for the better, I thought.

Then Jerroth's aging bladder let loose.

I sighed, realizing that my new aged body, like my previous one, was incontinent.

Oh, well, maybe not everything.

Epilogue

Patrick bolted from his computer chair as he heard his wife's excited cry from the bedroom, banging his shoulder on the doorjamb as he rounded the corner. "Diane, what is it? Is Joey okay?" But before he even got the words out he knew the answer.

In the two years that had followed that insane day, when their first house was destroyed and they'd nearly lost their lives, things had changed. They'd bought a new home. Joey had grown, started walking. Things had, mostly, gone back to normal.

Diane had Joey in her arms, swinging back and forth in an arc almost as wide as the smile on her face. Her big brown eyes were shining and misty, a tear hung in the corner of one. She was beaming so brightly at the giggly bundle in her arms that Patrick thought he would explode if she didn't speak.

"What is it? What is it? What happened?"

Diane looked from Joey to Patrick beaming pure unadulterated joy through her eyes straight at Patrick. He fell in love with her all over again.

Almost sobbing she explained, "He spoke, honey. I was holding him after his feeding, and he just looked up at me and spoke."

Pat was staggered. Joey had been babbling forever. Chattering away all the time in what sounded almost like a foreign tongue, but he'd never spoken a single word of English until now. They'd both been thinking— even if they were afraid to air their fears out loud—that something might be wrong with him.

Pat walked over and put his arm around his wife, cradling the struggling bundle between them. He kissed his wife's brow, then Joey's.

"What did he say?"

Diane looked down at the toddler, tears rolling now, and asked, "Joey, talk to Daddy, okay? Tell him what you told me."

Without hesitation, Joey looked up at his father and said, in a voice clear as day, "Magic!" and then burst into giggles as if he'd just told the funniest joke in the world.

HOLDING
BOGART'S FORT

Written by
Tim Powers

About the Author

Tim Powers was born in Buffalo, New York, on Leap Year Day in 1952, but has lived in Southern California since 1959. He graduated from California State University at Fullerton with a B.A. in English in 1976; the same year saw the publication of his first two novels, The Skies Discrowned *and* Epitaph in Rust *(both from Laser Books).*

Powers's subsequent novels are The Drawing of the Dark *(Del Rey, 1979),* The Anubis Gates *(Ace, 1983, winner of the Philip K. Dick Memorial Award and the Prix Apollo),* Dinner at Deviant's Palace *(Ace, 1985, winner of the Philip K. Dick Memorial Award),* On Stranger Tides *(Ace, 1987),* The Stress of Her Regard *(Ace, 1989),* Last Call *(Morrow, 1992, winner of the World Fantasy Award), and* Expiration Date *(Tor, 1996). His newest novel is a contemporary fantasy set in San Francisco,* Earthquake Weather *(Tor, 1997).*

Powers has taught at the Clarion Science Fiction Writers' Workshop at Michigan State University five times, and has twice co-taught the Writers of the Future Workshop *with Algis Budrys in Long Island, New York.*

A week or so ago I got a call from the lady who's running L. Ron Hubbard's *Writers of the Future* Contest in Hollywood, and she asked me if I would agree to be a story judge for the Contest's upcoming quarter.

"Why don't you make a sign," I told her, "and hang it on the wall: POWERS WILL ALWAYS AGREE TO BE A JUDGE."

I think I've been a judge for most of the quarters in the last ten or twelve years. This means that several times a year I get a stack of manuscript photocopies via next-day mail, and take a day off from my own writing to read them all and evaluate them; this is no chore, since Dave Wolverton has already culled these from the total volume of submissions, and invariably there is at least one story that I'm grateful to have a chance to read. I send my verdicts in, and usually I hang on to a couple of the photocopies, just because I want to have the chance to read them again before the actual anthology is published.

The stories at this point have no provenance beyond their titles—I don't know the genders or ages or addresses of the writers; and not all of them turn out to live in North America, by any means. The only thing I can be fairly sure of is that I have not read anything by any of these writers before.

(Over the years, I have read a lot of subsequent books from many of them, with their names right there on the spines and their photos on the dustjacket flap—though since I'm not a very up-to-date reader, I generally don't get around to reading them until they've been nominated for Hugos or Nebulas or World Fantasy Awards.)

It's at the awards event weekend that I first get to put faces and names to the stories I've read. In previous years the event has been held in Manhattan, Houston, and Cape Canaveral; last year it was at the theater at Author Services, Inc., the agency which represents all the works of L. Ron Hubbard, and at the elegant Manor Hotel in Hollywood, which is the restored Chateau Elysée, built in 1929 for the wife of pioneer movie director Thomas Ince. In its day as the Chateau Elysée, it hosted such folk as Edgar Rice Burroughs, Humphrey Bogart and Ginger Rogers.

I generally get to give an hour's talk to the writers at the end of the four-day workshop at which Algis Budrys and Dave Wolverton have been instructors; twice I've been an instructor at it myself—once when Wolverton was one of the new writers! I know that the new writers all work like mad, learning, through action, truths about writing that would otherwise require many years of trial-and-costly-error work. I think my advice generally boils down to this: Take your writing seriously, because nothing but your aching best will do at all.

Here I finally get to meet and shake the hands of the people who wrote those anonymous stories, and on the terraces and lawns of the Manor the distinction between judges and judged—many-times-published and newly published—evaporates as the sun goes down behind the Columbia Records building across the freeway. In the company of writers like Jack Williamson or Frederik Pohl, I'm as awed as any of the Contest winners, at first. But in no time we're all clustered together at the tables, along with Niven and Pournelle and Budrys and Benford; and in the gossipy talk some hundreds of years of insightful writing experience is unlocked and genially passed around in the warm breeze under the California stars.

It was at one of these informal gatherings that Jerry Pournelle told me something about plot mechanics that has changed every book I've written since; Julius Schwartz has fascinated us with reminiscences about H. P. Lovecraft and the history of the field; and stories about good and bad editors and agents fly every which way. The new writers, and myself too, realize that we're part of a special company here, among whom the writing of science fiction and fantasy is recognized as something important enough to spend one's life at. Later we'll all have to go home, and preserve that conviction without a lot of evidence—but for these several days we're confirmed in our faith.

At these weekends I have over the years been thrilled to meet and chat with Robert Bloch, A. E. van Vogt and Isaac Asimov; I've shaken hands with Frank Frazetta; and in Cape Canaveral, sitting on a bleacher seat among Algis Budrys, Jack Williamson and Frederik Pohl, my wife and I got to watch the space shuttle *Atlantis* light up the night sky and torch its way right out of Earth's atmosphere and into orbit.

The awards ceremony itself happens on a Saturday, and culminates in the unveiling and passing around of the new *Writers of the Future* anthology. I always make a point of grabbing a copy and then getting all the writers to sign it; in this way I have got autographs on the first-appearances-in-print of writers like Stephen Baxter,

M. Shayne Bell, J. R. Dunn, Ray Aldridge, Jamil Nasir and Howard V. Hendrix. And there are several names from the most recent couple of anthologies that I'm confident I will be bragging about in years to come. It's fun, too, to approach one of the new writers with a copy of the book and a pen; I hold them out for an autograph, and say, "You'd better get used to this kind of thing."

Now there are the stories in this book. I won't be seeing the book for a few months yet, myself—for me right now the authors of these stories are still ciphers. But on a not-too-distant Saturday night, I will be holding a copy of the book you're holding now, and sidling through the crowd to get the writers to sign their stories. Sometimes the signatures are the first they have ever written below a printed byline—but chances are they won't be the last, by a long shot; and I think the ghosts of Bogart and Burroughs and Claude Rains must recognize that their old castle is likely to be remembered, too, for some newer names than theirs.

The odds are very good that some of those newer names are right here, on either side of me.

GREAT WHITE HUNTER

Written by
Don Solosan

Illustrated by
Scott Schomburg

About the Author

Raised in suburban Michigan, Don Solosan spent four years in the U.S. Navy, working with reconnaissance photography. He then received a bachelor's degree from the University of Michigan, where he won several awards for screenplays. He also has a master's degree from Ohio University.

After graduation he moved to the Los Angeles area. By day, he works for the RAND think tank, and by night he continues a mild flirtation with Hollywood.

About the Illustrator

Scott Schomburg—no relation to the late Alex Schomburg—lives with his parents in rural Prescott, Wisconsin. Scott has attended the University of Wisconsin and studied illustration at the Fashion Institute of Technology in New York City. Next fall he will be attending the Minneapolis College of Art and Design. He enjoys illustration, painting and sculpture, and he hopes to someday illustrate a children's book, and to eventually work in creative development for TV and film.

1945

Entering Berlin, a black-and-gray world. It's noon, but the streets are cast in shifting shadows. The sky is angry, roiling with dust and smoke. I'm in little danger from the German army; they're nowhere to be seen. The Russian artillery is another question. What they lack in accuracy, they're making up in volume. And even having studied the Allies' aerials of the pockmarked streets is no guarantee that I won't stumble into a shell.

But being something of an expert on making tough decisions, I get to the Chancellery unharmed. By now, the Russians have been hammering it pretty steadily for days. The garden wall has been breached and I enter, passing a pyramid of petrol cans. Still no alarm. I step over the stiffened body of a dog—the entrance I want is around here somewhere—turn a corner and come face to face with a tiny girl.

We both freeze in surprise.

She clenches and releases her little fists, unsure. I make a playful conspiratorial gesture and she understands: we're playing a game. She scampers away, jabbering in German.

In the Chancellery proper now. I'm amazed at how many people have stayed behind under this bombardment. And not all of them are soldiers; there are a lot of servants scurrying around. The Russians are less than a mile away and these people are frightened, but focused. They still have work to do.

By the third room, an officer I recognize as Goebbels gets in my way. "And where do you think you're going?" he asks, not waiting for an answer. He pulls a knife. I take it away from him and bury it in his chest, never breaking stride.

A few more soldiers try to stop me and I kill them quickly. They mean nothing to me.

Here are the stairs. Some fifty feet below the Chancellery is the *Führerbunker*. I pause at the door and draw my blaster. A deep breath—

Then I'm in.

There are two people in the bunker, a man and a woman. He has dazed black eyes set in a pale, greasy face with an exclamation point of a mustache. She has been crying, her eyes red rimmed. I don't think she's swallowed the poison yet.

Before he remembers he's holding a pistol, I slap the primitive weapon from his hand.

"I don't understand—" Hitler stammers.

"Punk!" I snarl, then shove the cannon in the little bastard's mouth and blow his brains all over Eva Braun's satin party dress.

2076

Back at the walled city, I don't have to consult ancient history; I know what it says: Facing capture by the Russian forces bearing down on him, Adolf Hitler shoots himself with a handgun; Eva Braun swallows poison. The bodies are hauled into the garden where they're doused with gasoline and burned over and over again. Goebbels and Bormann stand over the bonfire giving the Nazi salute. Then the remains are gathered up and sealed in a wall. An almost festive mood descends on the remaining faithful, and they joke and smoke cigarettes, something the *Führer* does not allow while breathing.

There is no mention anywhere of Hitler's skull being atomized, no word of *der Schattenungeheuer,* a dark maniac stalking the halls before slaughtering the *Führer.*

It never happens at all.

1906

Remy tries to kill me in an old hotel called the Eschaton, located along the Embarcadero. Even without his inept help, the Victorian building is destroyed in several hours when a great earthquake triggers a firestorm that razes most of San Francisco.

I spend the night fast asleep; the next three days promise to be very busy and I need my rest. I wake around 4:00 a.m., have a brisk shower and devour a large breakfast.

When descending the grand staircase, the bellhop on duty snaps to attention. "Good morning, sir! Say, Mr. M, you're up awful early!"

Then I see Remy step out from behind a pillar, his face gaunt, laced with fresh scars.

"Hello, Remy. You're looking unwell."

"Not again, for the love of Christ. Don't do this again."

I take a few leisured steps down. What's on my mind right this instant is *time.* According to the clock over the desk, now visible from my new position on the stairs, it's

Illustrated by Scott Schomburg

5:11. By all accounts, the quake starts at either 5:12 (seismologist's record), 5:14 (police chief's report), or 5:15 (as reported in the newspapers of the day). Remy shifts his position, blocking the foot of the stairs; I notice there's a bulge under his duster at the right armpit.

"It seems I can't change my stripes any more than you can," I explain calmly. "I've gone over it again and again, but it always comes out the same. I have to go out this morning, just as you have to try to stop me—for all the wrong reasons, I might add. Why can't you just accept that and go home?"

"Enough!" he cries. "Be reasonable, please."

"If we're being reasonable, why the heat?"

"The what?"

"What kind of historian are you?" I snap. "The *blaster*."

Remy seems to become aware of the weapon's weight at that moment, and it makes up his mind. He brushes the duster aside, yanks the blaster free from its holster and levels it.

I don't move.

But the earth *does*. Five-thirteen (figures—everyone's wrong) and the building is leaping up and down and roaring. The bellhop and desk clerk, up to this point staring in amazement at our exchange, race out the front door. Remy reels around bewildered, trying to aim. The blaster goes off and a great rip opens in the ceiling; a divan and a woman wearing a man's suspenders (God, I love this city!) rain down. I roll over the railing and escape out into the back alley, the plaster and wood of the walls exploding around my head.

The shaking only lasts a minute, but the disruption it causes brings out a wide assortment of ghouls. In the Mission District, to more quickly steal some gold rings, a man cuts off a woman's fingers and leaves her to die. And down in the Tenderloin, a group of men kidnap a little girl and take turns raping her behind a burning warehouse. After they finish, they throw the injured child into the flames to cover their deed. History may have misplaced their names, but I will find them.

They all belong to me.

1881

I first meet Remy in the cool darkness of the Maxwell House hotel/saloon in old Fort Sumner, New Mexico, his sleek Franco good looks edged in lamplight as he crosses the sawdust-covered floor. Instantly I know he's trouble. I've seen the look of desperate men before, but it's nothing a good blaster can't cure.

And I know he's a traveler. Don't ask me how, but it's true. You can always spot someone out of time. It's not that I've seen a lot of travelers, partly because there are so many times to disappear into and partly because there aren't a whole lot of us to begin with, but there's something that sets us apart. We wear our time the same way you can date a fashion photograph by the models.

He's fumbling about theatrically for matches, a Gitanes poised on his lips. A helpless gesture and a motion to the box on the table before me. I nod. After he lights the Gitanes and takes a deep drag, he motions again. This time to the chair opposite me. "Do you mind?"

I draw on my cigar and blow a smoke ring into the air over his head. "Be my guest."

He thrusts a soft hand toward me. "Remy Arnaud."

"Call me M."

We shake. He sits and toys a moment with the box of matches: Eschaton Hotel, San Francisco, reads the cover. "Thank you," he whispers and pushes the box across the table.

"Not at all. What brings you to New Mexico in this god-awful heat?"

"I'm looking for a man," he replies. "A special kind of man. Someone who gets around, if you catch my meaning."

"You mean temporally, sir?"

"Exactly! Exactly so!" He snubs out the cigarette on the floor and turns to me, eyes glinting. "You're the Shadow Man."

I merely shrug.

A hundred emotions cross his face. Awe edges out revulsion and fear. "It just occurred to me: you've actually met Adolf Hitler."

"I have that distinction."

"Is it true he had only one testicle?"

"Ask Eva—or better yet, ask Adolf."

"I can't," he protests.

"He's baptized in a Roman Catholic church in another eight years. You can substitute yourself for the parish priest, lift up his little tunic and end decades of academic squabbling."

He seems utterly appalled. "I can't—how you say?—interfere."

"Once you leave, everything is erased," I assure him. "Time is a river you can swim in without getting wet."

"But *you* change history. How do I account for that?"

"I'm not from your timeline."

"I suspected just such a thing!" he exclaims. "You can travel between timelines and are not bound by our temporal restrictions." He thinks a moment about the import of what he has just said. "But how can you assume such an awesome power?"

Another shrug.

"How do you find me, Remy?" I venture, dragging him away from his dark thoughts.

"I travel quite a bit; very low-key, you understand? It's all sanctioned and controlled by my government. They need to find out discreet facts, I gather those facts. I am their official historian. Then one day I returned to Paris and found that my world had changed.

"Suddenly Germany didn't exist anymore," he says, eyeing me as if he's looking upon a god and might be blinded.

1934

Killing Hitler is fun, so I do it again.

The Sixth Nazi Party Congress is held in Nuremberg, and it's a big do. One of Germany's finest filmmakers, Leni Reifenstal, has been tapped to document the event, which is tailored to the camera: massive, majestic, unfolding in geometric precision. The resulting film, *Triumph of the Will*, is meant to reveal to the world what the German people already know in their hearts—that the little bastard is one swell guy.

How can I resist?

1881

Seated across from me in the Maxwell House hotel/saloon, Remy is sweating, wild-eyed. "One day Hitler was assassinated in Berlin and the next, it was

Nuremberg. And no one knew but me! Reifenstal caught it all on film in *Failure of the Will,* just like Zapruder. Their heads exploded like they were filled with red dust. Horrible. *Horrible!* You have a signature, M, and it reveals the immense dimensions of your sick ego."

"I don't do Kennedy," I protest.

"That's not what the Warren Report says."

"No one ever believes the Warren Report."

"This is irrelevant!" Remy shouts and the bar settles into nervous quiet. When gunfire is not exchanged, the locals resume their recreational drinking. "Tortured over their failure to protect the *Führer,* the German people as a whole lost their will to exist and were crushed under a Russian assault. All because of you, a century and a half later, Germany is nothing but a distant memory for my people. But I"—here Remy taps his forehead—"I know differently. While traveling, I'm immune to your changes in the timeline."

Just then, a rawboned man with a handlebar mustache appears in the saloon door. Diamond-sharp eyes survey the dim interior. A subtle glance is exchanged with the bartender before committing. He enters.

As the rawboned man crosses the floor, the atmosphere feels charged with electricity, but I know it's only me. The locals, well lubricated with cheap booze, sense nothing. He pauses by the bar long enough for a whisper—at most a few words—but it's enough.

The man continues down the hall. After a moment's pause, there's a light tap at a door.

Almost imperceptibly comes the response: "Who is it?"

The door is forced open and a single shot fired. The locals don't seem to have noticed and it occurs to me that it's impossible for me to have heard anything but the gunshot over their raucous celebration. Then I notice that I'm gripping the table, white knuckled. Remy is gaping at me.

"Who was that?" he whispers.

"What's your area of expertise, historian?"

"Twentieth century, particularly the Second World War."

One in a trillion, I think.

How do I explain that almost nothing but myth survives about the men known as Pat Garrett and Billy the Kid? That it seems Garrett is not the true-blue lawman, nor Billy the heartless killer, that we've been led to believe? My jaunt has turned up nothing but ambiguity. One man shot in the heart by a friend; years later, the other shot in the back while taking a piss. There's a thrilling testament to the human race, boys. Now turn out the lights. . . .

"It's no one important," I say.

"This is how it is with you, I think. No one is important but yourself. But everything you do matters! You've been given a tremendous gift, and . . . and you squander it for selfish indulgence, like a child!"

I smile wanly, pour a shot and tip it back in salute. My blaster is aimed at his belly under the table. It would be ridiculously easy to gut this annoying Frenchman and leave him to die gasping like a fish out of water in the nineteenth century. Instead I stand suddenly, bringing the table up with me. It flips over, knocking him to the floor while I storm out, startled cowpokes scattering before me.

One in a trillion. Sweet baby Jesus.

2076

San Francisco, the Idyllwhile Hotel, Remy's timeline. It's not the Eschaton, but it'll do. In particular, the view from the balcony is inspiring. Even though San Francisco is destroyed in cataclysms of biblical proportions in 1906 and 2011, people rebuild. They raise new homes bigger and brighter than the last and pour their hearts into the place. Maybe that's why I love this city.

I port to the Nexus and do a little research.

Fact: The destruction of the German state sets back rocket science decades.

Fact: Bloated with stolen European wealth, Russian expansion radically speeds up the release of greenhouse gases.

Out of curiosity, I reference "Shadow Man" and find a doorway to the ramblings of the mainstream conspiracy culture.

Conjecture: The dark maniac in Nuremberg is also seen in tintypes of Billy the Kid's funeral and news footage circa 1970 of the brutal assassination of one "Pogo the Clown" while entertaining children in a Chicago suburb. Furthermore, his style has been linked to over two dozen other killings scattered throughout history. The Shadow Man, they believe, is of alien origin and acting to destroy civilization as they know it. Which actually is not that far off the mark. The problem with killing mad dogs like John Wayne Gacy *before* they start to foam is mainly one of PR, it seems. But what they'll never realize is that they've been spared the horror of digging out Gacy's crawl space, not to mention his clown paintings from prison.

Remy Arnaud, the "official historian," looks at these scattered events and sees something else: a threat to his position.

They say one in every trillion humans has the ability to time travel, though few realize their full potential. But it's not necessarily a sign of intellectual advancement or genetic superiority. They say that a startled Neanderthal suddenly appears at a circus in Madison Square Garden. Everyone thinks he's a part of the festivities and then—just as suddenly—he vanishes. When I think of the Frenchman, I'm reminded of that caveman, hopelessly lost and struggling to understand what he sees.

I bring up the University of Paris's dossier on their star professor. With a perverse sense of humor, I hardcopy Remy's photograph and tuck it into my wallet.

I spend most of the night on the balcony watching the slow ebb and flow of the city, then return to the walled city.

By now I've been awake for over forty-eight hours and I'm exhausted. I shower, have a quick sandwich, and then climb into bed. Sleep never comes easy and today is no different. There's a high-pitched tone which rings in my ears and sometimes I have a feeling of vertigo. The whirr of a fan or light music can help blot it out, but the thought of getting back up is as bad as these demons plaguing me. I should know better than to try to sleep during the day. During the day, the howling from outside seeps through the walls, penetrates every crack and crevice and will not be ignored.

If only that howling were just the wind.

Fact: In my world, Remy Arnaud is stillborn in 2049.

1907

Hitler is eighteen years old when he withdraws his life savings and hits the road. Today he finishes the two-day entrance exam to the Vienna Academy of Fine Arts. He strolls the city's tree-lined boulevards this fine October afternoon, an ivory cane in one hand, his portfolio in the other. Despite his humble beginnings and his despicable ends, he likes to pretend that he is a gentleman. There is no reason on Earth why Adolf Hitler won't take his place in the Academy. He is confident, content.

Then I step out of an alley.

"Mr. Hitler," I say, "I have news. The school has sent me to locate you."

Hitler anxiously clutches his portfolio to his thin chest.

"I'm afraid they want me to tell you that they simply cannot accept your admission."

"But . . . but . . ." he stammers. "Why?"

"Because you're a lousy artist," I reply and fire. The blaster punches clean through the leather case and the little bastard. He stands there a moment, startled, then crumples on his back. When the body hits the ground, a smoke ring rises from the giant hole in his chest.

1929, 1975, 1969

Exit the Metropol Hotel into the brisk Moscow night. It would be nice to skip away a few years and see how the unstoppable mad monk Rasputin stands up to a blaster. But this is not a time for games and as I push the friendly thought away like a playful puppy, a man steps into my path.

Remy Arnaud.

He glances over his shoulder at patrons filing into the Bolshoi. "Come for the ballet, did you?"

At once my buoyant mood is spoiled. "No."

"No, of course not. Not bloody enough for you, M."

"Now, Remy—so quarrelsome, and after I give you such a nice present."

He seems confused. "Germany," I explain. "I pick off Hitler in his prime. Eighteen years old and never been matriculated. Germany exists again."

"That doesn't make it right!"

"It doesn't make it *wrong*, either," I counter. "Think of the millions who don't have to die."

"We survived that!" Remy shouts. "We learned hard lessons!"

"Listen to you, Remy: Survived. Learned. You talk like the past is over and as dead as your boring history texts. If that's true, then what are you doing here in 1929? Let me give you a little clue, my friend.

"Everything. Happens. *Now*.

"Everything is up for grabs, every moment, for all time. It's high stakes and I play to win. You don't even understand the game. Now get out of my way."

"The future will curse you for this," Remy hisses as I brush past him.

"I've seen your future and it's a disgrace. You've never been there, have you?"

I see the truth in his face.

"You're a fool, Remy; here for your professional pride and nothing more."

Then he makes the mistake of pulling a knife on me. With no difficulty at all, I take the weapon from him and throw him against a wall. I snap the blade on stone and throw away the handle. The Frenchman crumples before me. I pull my blaster and backhand him with it, a good shot that draws blood from his mouth. His grunt of pain only spurs me on; I pistol-whip the man into unconsciousness before suddenly pulling back, my breath ragged in the frigid air.

Without a word I turn and hurry down the street. I come to the Kremlin and enter like a monsoon wind, scattering everything before me. They have nothing to stop me. Bodies, barely seen, fly apart. Past palaces, towers and cathedrals; their symbols mean nothing to me. In the inner sanctum, I locate Joseph Stalin and blow him away and enter the humid jungles of Cambodia, still moving inexorably, to the lair of Pol Pot, who flies across the compound like a leaf before the monsoon. The blaster throws him onto a heap of dead soldiers and I leave him to rot.

I've shaved the weapon's emitter cone with a penknife, which distorts the beam. Now it no longer cuts like a laser, clean and precise, but more like a chain saw, ragged and brutal. Which is more in keeping with my mood as I move fast across the parched California desert to a low ranch house. I reduce the front door to splinters as I enter and at once there are panicked cries of "Raid!" "It's the cops!" Tex Watson charges out of a bedroom, shirtless, and levels a shotgun. I clip him fast and he splashes across the wall, and these doped-up maniacs start to grasp that they are in the presence of some very serious shit.

Squeaky Fromme releases an attack dog. I cut the beast in two. Before she can haul out her hand cannon, I blow Squeaky's head off. Shrieks. Doors slamming. Gunshots boom as these desperados squeeze off shots without aiming. One, two, three, they drop, reduced to tattered meat and rags. In the middle of the carnage I see Charles Manson, that furry little ape, his head tucked down trying to sneak out. He's got one hand on Mary Brunner on his left and his eyes go wide as she erupts in gore beside him. He staggers to the right, where another of his merry band of reptiles blows up. Manson reels in the other direction to face one of the faithful, a zoned-out girl trying to speak, but she too explodes. Manson jerks back, slipping on a pool of blood. He falls and starts crawling away from me.

It's just the two of us now.

Manson hits the far wall and stops; but the message doesn't reach his legs somehow and they keep churning away, his mad eyes darting.

I step out of the smoke and shadows, a wraith drenched in blood and a fearsome righteousness, and cross the floor to tower over him.

Manson stares at me, his mouth working. "Christ Almighty!" he blurts before he dies.

"I'm just like you, man," I reply. "I'm *misunderstood.*"

I am the Shadow Man; I am the Right Hand of God and I am damned. Howling fills my head and I wonder how much longer I can go on.

1963

Noon in Dallas, Texas; late autumn, about the only bearable time in this state. A crowd has gathered on the sidewalks and grass lining Elm Street. I walk among the people, observing. There is Abraham Zapruder with his 8 mm Bell & Howell, checking the film load for the hundredth time. There is the Man With the Umbrella, standing under an unbroken blue sky. There is James Tague by the underpass, here by accident and about to catch a piece of shrapnel. People are excited, expectant. Word has reached them that the President of the United States has landed at Love Field; the motorcade is on the way to Dealey Plaza.

I'm strolling the grassy knoll, searching the bushes for co-conspirators, when the motorcade appears on

Houston Street. The energy level of the crowd increases tenfold and an invisible force seems to pull them to the curbs. As the first car turns onto Elm, I hear heavy footsteps behind me, then a truncheon crunches against my scalp. My feet go out from under me and in the distance I see the cars veering off; they're racing away on Houston, away from the crowd. A voice nearby says, "Yeah, we got him all right," as if speaking into a radio and then I black out.

I never even see Kennedy.

The next two days are spent in the congenial company of the Dallas police and United States Secret Service agents. The station is crowded with police, their staff, family and friends of the police, friends of the staff, and apparently, just about any passerby who wants to get a gander at the enigma. I am fingerprinted three times, moved in and out of cells, put through several lineups and questioned at length. Through it all I say nothing.

The officer in charge is Captain J. S. "Will" Fritz, a purposeful man facing an impossible conundrum. They don't know who I am and so far all the fingerprint experts in the country haven't been able to help. I carry no identification papers and offer nothing in the way of explanation. Even the blaster, recognizable as a weapon of sorts but inert in their clumsy hands, is a mystery to them.

Detective Rollings fingers it, sitting on a desk and leaning over me. "Maybe it's something special the Rooshians give 'im," he offers the other men with a leering grin before turning to me. "Is that right? Are you a Rooshian spy and that's why you won't talk?"

"Mebbe he don't speak English. Had you thought of that?" a cop offers.

Rollings turns his attention back to me. "Is that the problem here, amigo? Don't you habla no Englaise?"

My silence enrages him and he clips me across the forehead.

The other men pull Rollings away and Fritz leads me into his office. A trickle of blood courses down into my eye, but the manacles won't allow me to do anything about it.

"Clamming up isn't helping you at all," he says quietly, taking out his handkerchief and dabbing at the wound. "If you're a square citizen, just down in Dealey Plaza to see the president, well, you've got to say so. Keeping your mouth shut only makes you look guilty."

He folds the handkerchief, searching for a clean spot.

"Right now it don't look good for you, not at all. I'm being honest with you, son. We were watching you; you were acting mighty suspicious the way you were checking out the crowd. Made me think of a predator lining up its next meal. We got you with that funny little gun. And we got a witness says you were threatening to harm the president a few hours before the motorcade came through. That alone can buy you a mighty deep hole. So won't you help us both out now and tell me your name?"

Stare at the wall. Feel nothing. Show nothing.

A frustrated sigh. Then it's back into interrogation and several hours with the Secret Service.

Evening. A beat cop enters. "Boss, we've got a stiff at the Carousel Club."

"Don't tell me," Fritz replies, "somebody finally whacked that hood Ruby." Chuckles from the local badges.

"How'd you know?" the beat cop asks.

This piques the captain's interest. "What've you got?"

"Tippit's down there, says maybe the perp caught him opening up the club. It smells like robbery."

"His wallet missing?"

"No, but the strippers started showing up. One of 'em says Ruby always carried a little pistol; that's gone."

Suddenly, a roaring noise fills my head.

"This witness of yours, Captain—" I say slowly, drawing the attention of everyone in the room at my first words since the arrest. "Does he happen to have a French accent?"

●●●

Eleven a.m. on the morning of November 24, two days after my incarceration, the police prepare to move me from the city cells to the county jail. My manacles are put back into place before the cell is opened, then several officers gather around me. Captain Fritz and Patrol Officer J. D. Tippit grab my arms and lead me down the back stairs to the Dallas police station's basement where a car is waiting.

We hit the basement and my first thought is that a convention's being held in this cavern: hundreds of people are milling around, dozens have cameras slung about their necks, and there's even an old-style television camera. As soon as we're through the door, the crowd goes berserk. Men are yelling, I see cameras held at arm's length, flashbulbs popping. We keep moving, but as the detectives deal with the more unruly men, they end up forced off to either side so that Fritz and Tippit are escorting me straight into the crowd with no protection in front. And that's when a slight man separates from the melee, aiming his stolen pistol.

Remy's eyes are hollow, his clothes hang on his once full frame. *Some men are not born to carry this burden,* I reflect.

The Shadow Man smiles and it unnerves him.

"Remy Arnaud! Freeze!" Fritz bellows and the Frenchman flinches. He knows he's trapped. I've even provided the police with his photograph. Why else would I be here now? Manacles and jail cells are no obstacle to a man who gets around.

He starts firing.

Fire blossoms in my belly while flashbulbs isolate cross sections of the next few moments. Sparks from the gun barrel. Tippit folding beside me. The sudden panic of the crowd. A rush of bright blood down my legs. A dozen service revolvers knocking chunks out of the Frenchman. Remy spinning, collapsing to the concrete. Remy dying.

Darkness gathers over me. No longer supported by the police, I slip to the floor. Before unconsciousness can claim me, I throw myself.

2077

Home.

A home not far removed from the score of hotel rooms I've ghosted over the years. Plain, utilitarian, anonymous. It's true I have the luxury of being able to live anywhere I want, any time I want. But everyone wants a place to call home. That's what I think anyway. *This is my home,* I tell myself, turning to take in the tiny suite. With that small comfort, I program the medico to pull the slugs out of my belly, then go to bed and try not to listen to the howling.

Everything you do matters. Remy has that right at least. When I travel timelines like the Frenchman's, I'm struck by the countless people acting blindly. Billions upon billions of senseless acts of greed and stupidity slowly accumulating in a tidal wave of decay.

•••

I visit Remy's timeline once more, far into the twenty-second century. It's not the best of all possible worlds, but it'll do. They inhabit the Moon and Mars, and are ready to push out farther.

Soon I'll be ready to go out again, to sift the timelines for another Earth doomed to become a blackened cinder. And I'll start all over, making the hard decisions.

How I wish someone would do the same for us.

THE VAMPIRE SHORTSTOP

Written by
Scott Nicholson

Illustrated by
Igor Pogodin

About the Author

Scott Nicholson had a 1997 finalist story, "Metabolism," published in Volume XIV. Following that, he sold to semiprofessional magazines and anthologies, but to have "The Vampire Shortstop" be a First Prize winner in this year's Contest was the turning point. He is currently at work on a series of dark fantasy novels set in the Blue Ridge Mountains of North Carolina, where he lives and works as a newspaper writer. "The Vampire Shortstop" is dedicated to his mother-in-law, Mary, an inveterate Braves fan.

About the Illustrator

Igor Pogodin was born in Ukraine in 1965, by the sea. The presence of the sea and his formation as an artist have become an integral part of his imagination. He has trained in the College of Arts since 1981. Since 1995, he has been working in Lugansk, as a designer.

Jerry Shepherd showed up at the first practice. I mean, *showed*, as if he'd just popped into thin air at the edge of the woods that bordered Sawyer Field. Most kids, they come to first practice bookended by their parents, who glower like Mafia heavies willing to break your kneecaps if their kid rides the pine for so much as an inning. So, in a way, it was a relief to see Jerry materialize like that, with no threat implied.

But in another way, he made me nervous. Every year us Little League coaches get handed two or three players who either recently moved into the area or were given their release (yeah, we're that serious) by their former teams. And there's one thing that's just about universal, and that's the fact that these Johnny-come-latelys couldn't hit their way out of a paper bag. So I figured, here's this spooky kid standing there at the fence, just chewing on his glove, real scared-like, so at least there's one brat that's not going to be squealing for playing time.

I figured him for a vampire right away. He had that pale complexion, the color of a brand-new baseball before the outfield grass scuffs up the horsehide. But, hey, these are enlightened times; everybody's cool with everybody, especially since "Transylvania" Wayne Kasloski broke the major league undead barrier back in '29. And that old myth about vampires melting in the sun is just that, an old myth.

The league powers figured I wouldn't raise a fuss if they dumped an undesirable on me. I had eleven kids on the roster, only five of them holdovers from the year before, so I was starting from scratch anyway. I didn't mind a new face, even if I was pretty much guaranteed that the vampire kid had two left feet. Coming off a three and thirteen season, the Maynard Solar Red Sox didn't have great expectations to live up to.

All the other players had clustered around me as if I were giving out tickets to see a rock band, but Jerry just hung out around first base like a slow-thawing cryogenic.

"I'm Coach Ruttlemyer," I said, loudly enough to reach Jerry's pointy ears. "Some of you guys know each other and some of you don't. But on my team, it's not who you know that counts, it's how hard you play."

At this point in the first preseason speech, you will always catch some kid with a finger in his or her nose. That year it was a sweet-faced redheaded girl. She had, at that moment, banished herself to right field.

"Now, everybody's going to play in every game," I said. "We're here to have fun, not just to win."

The kids looked at me like they didn't buy that line of bull. I barely believed it myself. But I always said it extra loud so the parents could hear. It gave me something to fall back on at the end of a crappy season.

"We're going to be practicing hard because we only have two weeks before our first game," I said, pulling the bill of my cap down low over my eyes so they could see what a serious guy I was. "Now let's see who's who."

I went down the roster alphabetically, calling out each kid's name. When he or she answered "Here," I glanced first at the kid, then up into the bleachers to see which parents were grinning and straining their necks.

That's a good way to tell right off who's going to want their kid to pitch: the beefy, red-faced dad who's wearing sunglasses and too-tight polyester shorts, and the mom who's busy organizing which parent is bringing what snack for which game.

When I called out Jerry's name, he croaked out a weak syllable and grimaced, showing the tips of his fangs. I waved him over to join the rest of the team. He tucked his glove in his armpit and jogged to the end of the line. I was watching him out of the corner of my eye, waiting for him to trip over the baseline chalk. But he didn't stumble once, and that's when I got my first glimmer of hope that maybe he'd be able to swipe a couple of bases for me. He was gaunt, which means that if he's clumsy you call him "gangly," but if he's well coordinated you call him "sleek." So maybe we're not as enlightened as we claim to be, but, hey, we're making progress.

I like to start first practice by having them all get on the infield dirt and snag grounders. You can tell just about everything you need to know about a player that way. And I don't mean just gloving the ball and pegging it over to first. I mean footwork, hand-eye, hustle, aggressiveness, vision, all those little extras that separate the cellar-dwellers from the also-rans from the team that takes home a Sawyer Cup at the end of the season. And it's not just the way they act when it's their turn; you get a lot of clues by how they back each other up, whether they sit down between turns, whether they punch each other on the arm or hunt for four-leaf clovers.

By the first run through, ten ground balls had skittered through to the deep grass in center field. But one, *one*, made up for all those other errors. Jerry Shepherd's grounder. He skimmed the ball off the dirt and whizzed

Illustrated by Igor Pogodin

it over to first base as if the ball were a yo-yo and he held the string. My assistant coach and darling wife, Dana, grinned at me when the ball thwacked into her mitt. I winked at her, hoping the play wasn't a fluke.

But it was no fluke. Six turns through, and six perfect scoops and tosses by Jerry Shepherd. Some of the other kids were fifty-fifty risks, and one, you'd have guessed the poor little kid had the glove on the wrong hand. You know the kind, parents probably raised him on computer chess and wheat bran. Oops, there I go again, acting all unenlightened.

Another bright spot was Elise Stewart, who was my best returning player. She only made the one error on her first turn, and I could chalk that up to a long winter's layoff. She was not only sure handed, she was also the kind of girl you'd want your son to date in high school. She had a happy heart and you just knew she'd be good at algebra.

All in all, I was pleased with the personnel. In fifteen years of coaching Little League, this was probably the best crop of raw talent I'd ever had. Now, I wasn't quite having visions of being hauled out of the dugout on these guys' shoulders (me crushing their bones and hoisting the championship trophy above my head), but with a little work we had a chance at a winning season.

I made a boy named Biff put on the catcher's gear and get behind the plate. In the baseball films, the chunky kid always plays catcher, but if you've ever watched even one inning of a real Little League game, you know the catcher needs to be quick. He spends all his time against the backstop, stumbling over his mask and jerking his head around looking for the baseball. Besides, Biff had a great name for a catcher, and what more could you ask for?

I threw batting practice, and again each kid had a turn while the others fanned out across the diamond. I didn't worry as much about hitting as I did fielding, because I knew hitting was mostly a matter of practice and concentration. It was a skill that could be taught. So I kind of expected the team to be a little slow with the bat, and they didn't disappoint me.

Except when Jerry dug into the batter's box. He stared at me with his pupils glinting red under the brim of his batting helmet, just daring me to bring the heat. I chuckled to myself. I liked this kid's cockiness. But I used to be a decent scholarship prospect, and I still had a little of the old vanity myself. So instead of lobbing a cream puff over, I kicked up my leg and brought the Ruttlemyer Express.

His line drive would have parted my hair, except for two things: I was wearing a cap and my hairline barely reached above my ears. But I felt the heat off his scorcher all the same, and it had whistled like a bullet from a gun. I picked up the rosin bag and tossed it in the air a few times. Some of the parents had stopped talking among themselves and watched the confrontation.

Jerry dug in and Biff gave me a target painting the black on the inside corner. I snapped off a two-seamer curveball, hoping the poor batter didn't break his spine when he lunged at the ball as it dipped. But he kept his hips square, then twisted his wrists and roped the ball to right field for what would have been a stand-up double. I'd never seen a Little Leaguer who could go with a pitch like that. I tossed him a knuckle ball, and most grown-ups couldn't have hit it with a tennis racket, but Jerry drilled it over the fence in left center.

Okay. *Okay*.

He did miss one pitch, and hit a couple of fouls, during his turn. I guess even vampires are only human.

After practice, I passed out uniforms and schedules and talked to the parents. I was hoping to tell Jerry what a good job he'd done and how I'd be counting on him to be a team leader, but he snatched up his goods and left before I had the chance. He got to the edge of the woods, then turned into a bat (the flying kind, not the kind you hit with) and flitted into the trees, his red jersey dangling from one of his little claws. His glove weighed him down a little and he was blind, of course, so he bumped into a couple of tree limbs before he got out of sight.

And so went the two weeks. Jerry was a natural shortstop; even the other kids saw that. Usually, everybody wanted to pitch and play shortstop (both positions at the same time, you know), but nobody grumbled when I said Jerry would be our starting shortstop. Elise was starting pitcher, and Wheat Bran and the redhead were "designated pinch hitters." I told everybody to get a good night's sleep, because we would be taking on the Piedmont Electric Half-Watts, who were always one of the better teams.

I could hardly sleep that night, I was so excited. Dana rolled over at about one a.m. and stole back her pillow.

"What's wrong?" she grunted, when I rolled over.

"The game," I said. I was running through lineups in my mind, planning strategies for situations that might arise in the sixth inning.

"Go to sleep. Deadline's tomorrow."

"Yeah, yeah, yeah." I was editor of the *Sawyer Creek E-Weekly,* and Thursday noon was press time. I still had some unfinished articles. "That's just my job, but baseball is my lifeblood."

Thinking of lifeblood made me think of Jerry. The poor kid must not have any parents. Back a few centuries ago, there had been a lot of purging and staking and garlic-baiting. Yeah, like I said, we're making progress, but sometimes I wonder if you can ever really change the human animal. I hoped nothing would come up about his being a vampire.

I knew how cruel Little League could be. Not the kids. They could play and play and play, making up rules as they went along, working things out. No, it was the parents who sometimes made things ugly, who threw tantrums and called names and threatened coaches. I'd heard parents boo their own kids.

In one respect, I was glad Jerry didn't have parents. At least I didn't have to worry about them changing into wolves and leaping over the chain-link fence and ripping my throat out over a bad managerial decision. Not that vampires perpetrated that sort of violence. But still, all myths contain a kernel of truth, and even a myth can make you shiver.

I finally went to sleep, woke up and got the paper to press. I drove out to the ballfield and there were four dozen vehicles in the parking lot. There's not much entertainment in Sawyer Creek. Like I said, Little League's a big deal in these parts, plus it was a beautiful April day, with the clouds all puffy and soft in the blue sky. Dana was already there, passing out baseballs so the kids could warm up. I looked around and noticed Jerry hadn't arrived.

"He'll be here," Dana said, reading my nervousness.

We took infield and I was filling out my lineup card when Elise pointed to center field.

"Hey, looky there," she said.

Over the fence loped a big black dog, with red socks and shirt and white pinstriped pants. Propped between the two stiff ears was a cockeyed cap. A worn leather glove was hooked over the upraised tail that whipped back and forth in the breeze. The dog turned into Jerry when it got to second base.

I heard a murmur ripple through the crowd. I felt sorry for Jerry then. The world may be enlightened, but the light's a little slower in reaching Sawyer Creek than it is most places. There are always a few bigots around. Red, yellow, black and white, we had all got along and interbred and become one race. But when you get down to the equality of the living and the living dead, some people just don't take to that notion of unity as easily.

And there was something else that set the crowd on edge, and even bothered *me* for a second. Hanging by a strap around his neck was one of those sports bottles all the kids have these days. Most of them put in juice or Super-Ade or something advertised by their favorite big leaguers. But Jerry's drink was thick and blood-red. Perfectly blood-red.

"Sorry I'm late," he said, sitting down on the end of the bench. I winced as he squirted some of the contents of the sports bottle into his throat.

"Play ball," the umpire yelled, and Elise went up to the plate and led off with a clean single to right. The next kid bunted her over, then Jerry got up. The first pitch bounced halfway to home plate and Elise stole third. Dana, who was coaching third base, gave her the "hold" sign. I wanted to give Jerry a chance to drive her in.

The next pitch was a little high, but Jerry reached out easily with the bat. The ball dinged off the aluminum into center and we were up, one to nothing. And that was the final score, with Elise pitching a three-hitter and Jerry taking away a handful of hits from deep in the hole. Jerry walked once and hit another double, but Wheat Bran struck out to leave him stranded in the fifth.

Still, I was pleased with the team effort, and a "W" is a "W," no matter how you get it. The kids gathered around the snack cooler after the game, all happy and noisy and ready to play soccer or something. But not Jerry. He had slipped away before I could slap him on the back.

"Ain't no fair, you playing a slanty-eyed vampire," came a gruff voice behind me. "Next thing you know, they'll allow droids and other such trash to mix in. Baseball's supposed to be for normal folks."

I turned to find myself face to face with Roscoe Turnbull, Sawyer Creek's Mister Baseball. Coach of the reigning champs for the past seven years. He'd been watching from the stands, scouting the opposition the way he always did.

"Hey, he's got just as much right to play as anybody," I said. "I know you're not big on reading, but someday you ought to pick up the U.S. Constitution and check out the Forty-Third Amendment."

The Red Sox had never beaten one of Turnbull's teams, but at least I could be smug in my intellectual superiority.

"Big words don't mean nothing when they're giving out the Sawyer Cup," Turnbull hissed through his Yogi Berra teeth. He had a point. He'd had to build an addition onto his house just so he could store all the hardware his teams had won.

"We'll see," I said, something I would never have dared to say in previous years. Turnbull grunted and got in his panel truck. His son Ted was in the passenger seat, wearing the family scowl. I waved to him and went back to my team.

We won the next five games. Jerry was batting something like .900 and had made only one error, which occurred when a stray moth bobbed around his head in the infield. He'd snatched it out of the air with his mouth at the same moment the batter sent a three-hopper his way. I didn't say anything. I mean, instincts are instincts. Plus, we were winning, and that was all that mattered.

The seventh game was trouble. I'd been dreading that line on the schedule ever since I realized that my best player was a vampire. Maynard Solar Red Sox versus The Dead Reckoning Funeral Parlor Pallbearers. Now, no self-respecting funeral parlors were *selling* the blood that they drained. But there had been rumors of underground activity, a black market for blood supplies.

And Jerry had slowly been catching the heat, anyway. The grumbles from the stands had gotten louder, and whenever Jerry got up to bat or made a play in the field, some remark would come from the other team's bleachers. Oh, they were the usual unimaginative kind, like the old "Kill the vampire," the play on the resemblance between the words *vampire* and *umpire*. The other common one was "Vampires suck." And these were parents, mind you. They wonder where kids get it from.

The cruelest one, and the one that caught on the fastest, came from the unlikely mouth of Roscoe Turnbull, who'd made a habit of bringing his son Ted to our games just so they could ride Jerry's case. Jerry had launched a three-run homer to win in the last inning in one of our games. As he crossed the plate, Turnbull yelled out, "Hey, look, everybody, it's the Unnatural."

You know, a play on the old Robert Redford film. Even *I* had to grudgingly admit that was a good one.

Now we were playing a funeral parlor and I didn't know where Jerry got his blood. I usually didn't make it my business to keep up with how kids lived their lives off the diamond. But Jerry didn't have any parents, any guidance. Maybe he could be bribed to throw a game if the enticements were right.

So I was worried when Jerry came to bat in the sixth with two outs. We were down, 4–3. Biff was on second. It was a situation where there was really no coaching strategy. Jerry either got a hit or made an out.

He had made hits in his three previous trips, but they were all in meaningless situations. So I couldn't tell if he was setting us up to lose. Until that moment.

"Come on, Jerry," I said, clapping my hands. "I know you can do it."

If you *want* to, I silently added.

Jerry took two strikes over the heart of the plate. The bat never left his shoulder. All my secret little fantasies of an undefeated season were about to go up in smoke. I started mentally rehearsing my after-game speech, about how we gave it all we had, we'll get 'em next time, blah blah blah.

The beanpole on the mound kicked up his leg and brought the cheese. Jerry laced it off the fence in right-center. Dana waved Biff around to score, and Jerry was rounding second. I didn't know whether I hoped Dana would motion him to try for third, because Wheat Bran was coming up next, and he'd yet to hit even a foul tip all season. But the issue was decided when their short-stop, the undertaker's kid, rifled the relay throw over the third baseman's head as Jerry was pounding down the base path. We won, 5–4.

"I never doubted you guys for a second," I told the team afterward, but of course Jerry had already pulled his disappearing act.

Dana was blunt at dinner, as I served up some tasti-whiz and fauxburger. I'd popped a cork on some decent wine to celebrate.

"Steve, I think you're getting to like winning just a little too much," she said, ever the concerned wife.

I grinned around a mouthful of food. "It gets in your blood," I said. "Can't help it."

"What about all those seasons you told the kids to just give it their best, back when you were plenty satisfied if everyone only showed a little improvement over the course of the season?"

"Back when I was just trying to build their self-esteem? Well, nothing builds character like winning. I can just *feel* the little guys exploding with character."

"I wish you were doing more for Jerry," she said. "He still doesn't act like part of the team. And the way he looks at you, like he wants you for a father figure. I think he's down on himself."

"Down on himself? *Down* on himself?" I almost sprayed my mouthful of wine across the table, and that stuff was ten bucks a bottle. I gulped and continued. "I could trade him for an entire *team* if I wanted. He's the best player to come out of Sawyer Creek since—"

"—since Roscoe Turnbull, and you see how *he* ended up."

I didn't like the way this discussion was headed. "I'm sure Jerry's proud of his play. And the team likes him."

"Only because the team's winning. But I wonder how they would have reacted, how their *parents* would have reacted, if Jerry had struck out that last time today?

I mean, nobody's exactly inviting him for sleepovers as it is."

"He's just quiet. A lone wolf. Nothing wrong with that," I said, a little unsure of myself.

"Nothing wrong with vampires as long as they hit .921, is that what you mean?"

"Hey, we're winning, and that's what counts."

"I don't know," Dana said, shaking her pretty and sad head. "You're starting to sound like Roscoe Turnbull."

That killed *my* mood, all right. That killed my mood for a lot of things around the house for a while. Lying in bed that night with a frigid two feet between us, I stared out the window at the full moon. A shape fluttered across it, a small lonely speck lost in that great circle of white. It most likely wasn't Jerry, but I felt an ache in my heart for him all the same.

At practice, I sometimes noticed the other players whispering to each other while Jerry was at bat. I don't think for a minute that children are born evil. But they have parents who teach and guide them. Parents who were brought up on the same whispered myths.

I tried to be friendly toward Jerry, and kept turning my head so I could catch that look that Dana said he was giving me. But all I saw were a pair of bright eyes that could pierce the back of a person's skull if they wanted. Truth be told, he *did* give me the creeps, a little. And I could always pretend my philosophy was to show no favoritism, despite Dana's urging me to reach out to him.

She was a loyal assistant despite our difference of opinion. She helped co-pilot the Red Sox through the next eight victories. Jerry continued to tear up the league's pitching and play shortstop like a strip of flypaper, even though he was booed constantly. Elise was pitching well and the rest of the kids were coming along, improving every game. I was almost sad when we got to the last game. I didn't want the season to end.

Naturally, we had to play the Turnbull Construction Claw Hammers for the championship. They'd gone undefeated in their division again. Ted had a fastball that could shatter a brick. And Roscoe Turnbull started scouting his draft picks while they were still in kindergarten, so he had the market cornered on talent.

I was so nervous I couldn't eat the day of the game. I got to the field early, while the caretaker was still trimming the outfield. Turnbull was there, too. He was in the home team's dugout shaving down a wooden bat. Wooden bats weren't even used in the majors anymore. Turnbull could afford lithium compound bats. That's when I first started getting suspicious.

"I'm looking forward to the big game," Turnbull said, showing the gap between his front teeth.

"Me, too," I said, determined not to show that I cared. "And may the best team win."

"What do you mean? The best team always wins."

I didn't like the way he was running that wood-shaver down the bat handle.

"You getting all nostalgic?" I asked, tremblingly nonchalant. "Going back to wood?"

"Good enough for my daddy. And my great-grandpaw on my mother's side. Maybe you heard of him. Tyrus Cobb."

The Hall-of-Famer. The Georgia Peach. The greatest hitter in any league, ever. Or the dirtiest player ever to set foot on a diamond, depending on whom you asked.

"Yeah, I've heard of him," I said. "That's quite a bloodline."

"Well, *we've* always managed to win without no low-down, stinking vampires on our team."

"Jerry Shepherd deserves to play as much as any other boy or girl."

"It ain't right. Here this"—he made a spitting face—"*creature* has all these advantages like being able to change into an animal or to throw the hocus-pocus on other players."

"You know that's against the rules. We'd be disqualified if he tried something like that. There's no advantage."

Turnbull held the tip of the bat up in the air. It was whittled to a fine menacing point. "Sometimes, you got to *make* your advantages," he said.

"Even you wouldn't stoop that low," I said. "Not just to win a game."

A thin stream of saliva shot from the gap in his teeth and landed on the infield dirt. Then he smiled again, and it was the ugliest smile imaginable. "Gotta keep a little something on deck. Just in case."

I shuddered and walked back to my dugout. Turnbull wasn't that bloodthirsty. He was just trying to gain a psychological edge. Sure, that was all.

Psychological edges work if you let them, so I spent the next fifteen minutes picking rocks from the infield. The kids were starting to arrive by then, so I watched them warm up. Jerry was late, as usual, but he walked out of the woods just as I was writing his name into the lineup. We were batting first.

Ted was starting for the Claw Hammers, of course. He was the kind of pitcher who would throw a brush-back pitch at his own grandmother, if he thought she was digging in on him. He stood on the mound and practiced his glare, then whipped the ball into the catcher's mitt. I had to admit, the goon sure knew how to bring it to the plate.

Half the town had turned out. The championship game always drew better than town elections. Dana patted me on the back. She wasn't one to hold a grudge when times were tough.

"Play ball," the umpire yelled, and we did.

Elise strode confidently to the plate.

"Go after her, Tedder," Turnbull shouted through his cupped hands. "You can do it, big guy."

The first pitch missed her helmet by three inches. She dusted herself off and stood deeper in the batter's box. The next pitch made her hop. Ball two. But she was getting a little shaky. No one likes being used for target practice. The next pitch hit her bat as she was ducking away. Foul, strike one.

Elise was trembling now. I hated the strategy they were using, but unfortunately it was working. The umpire didn't say a word.

"Attaboy," Turnbull yelled from his dugout. "Now go in for the kill."

Ted whizzed two more strikes past her while she was still off balance. Biff grounded out weakly to second. Jerry went up to the plate and dug in. Ted's next offering hit Jerry flush in the face.

Jerry went down like a shot. I ran up to him and knelt in the dirt, expecting to see broken teeth and blood and worse. But Jerry's eyes snapped open. Another myth about vampires was that they didn't feel pain. There are other kinds of pain besides physical, and I saw them in Jerry's red irises. He could hear the crowd cheering as clearly as I could.

"Kill the vampire," one parent said.

"Stick a stake in him," another shouted.

"The Unnatural strikes again," a woman yelled.

I looked into the home team's dugout and saw Turnbull beaming as if he'd just won a trip to Alpha Centauri.

I helped Jerry up and he jogged to first base. I could see a flush of pink on the back of his usually pale neck. I wondered whether the color was due to rage or embarrassment. I was going to have Dana give him the "steal" sign, but the redhead popped up to the catcher on the next pitch.

We held them scoreless in their half, despite Ted's getting a triple. My heart was pounding like a kid's toy drum on Xmas Day, but I couldn't let the players know that I cared one way or the other. When we got that third out, I calmly gave the kids high-fives as they came off the field. Sure, this was just another game, like the Mona Lisa was just another painting.

So it went for another couple of innings, with no runners getting past second. Jerry got beaned on the helmet his next trip up. The crowd was cheering like mad as he fell. I looked out at the mob sitting in the bleachers, and the scariest thing was that it wasn't just our opponent's fans who were applauding.

There was the sheriff, pumping his fist in the air. The mayor looked around secretively, checked the majority opinion, then added his jeers to the din. Biff's mother almost wriggled out of her tanktop, she was screaming so enthusiastically. A little old lady in the front row was bellowing death threats into her megaphone.

I protested the beaning to the umpire. He was a plump guy and his face was weighed down by his jowls. He looked like he'd umpired back before the days of protective masks and had taken a few foul tips to the face.

"You've got to warn the pitcher against throwing at my players," I said.

"Can't hurt a vampire, so what's the point?" the umpire snarled, spitting brown juice towards my shoes. So that was how it was going to be.

"Then you should throw the pitcher out of the game because of poor sportsmanship."

"And I ought to throw *you* out for delay of game." He yanked the mask back over his face, which was a great improvement on his looks.

I patted Jerry on the shoulder and looked him fully in the eyes for the first time since I'd known him. Maybe I'd been afraid he would mesmerize me.

"Jerry, I'm going to put in a pinch runner for you," I said. "It's not fair for you to put up with this kind of treatment."

I'd said the words that practically guaranteed losing the game, but I wasn't thinking about that then. The decision was made on instinct, and instinct is always truer and more revealing than a rationalizing mind. Later on, that thought gave me my only comfort. I started signaling Dana to send in a replacement.

But Jerry's eyes blazed like a hot ember and his face contorted into various animal faces: wolf, bat, tiger, wolverine, then settled back into its usual wan constitution.

"No," he grunted, "I'm staying in."

He jogged to first before I could stop him.

"Batter up," the umpire yelled.

I went into the dugout. Dana gave me a hug. There were tears in her eyes. Mine, too, though I made sure no one noticed.

Jerry stole second and then third. Wheat Bran was at the plate, waving his bat back and forth. I knew his eyes were closed. Two strikes, two outs. I was preparing to send the troops back out into the field when Wheat Bran blooped a single down the line in right. Jerry scored standing up.

Elise shut down the Claw Hammers until the bottom of the sixth. This was ulcer time, and I'd quit pretending not to care about winning. Sweat pooled under my arms and the band of my hat was soaked. I kept clapping my hands, but my throat was too tight to yell much encouragement.

Their first batter struck out. The second batter sent a hard grounder to Jerry. I was mentally ringing up the second out when someone in the stands shouted, "Bite me, blood-breath!" The ball bounced off Jerry's glove and went into the outfield. The runner made it to second by sliding on his belly. Jerry was staring at the dirt.

"Shake it off, Jerry," I was saying, but my voice was lost in the chorus of spectators who were calling my shortstop every ugly name you could think of. The next batter grounded out to first, advancing the runner to third.

Two outs, and you know the way these things always work. Big Ted Turnbull was digging into the batter's box. He had the sharpened wooden bat. But I wasn't going to let him hurt us. I did what you always do to a dangerous hitter with first base open: I took the bat out of his hands. I told Elise to walk him intentionally.

Roscoe Turnbull was glaring at me with death in his eyes, but I had to protect my shortstop and give us the best chance to win. Ted reached first base and called time out, then jogged over to his team's bench. Roscoe gave me a smile. That smile made my stomach squirm as if I'd swallowed a dozen live snakes.

Ted sat down and was changing his shoes. I didn't understand until he walked back onto the infield. The bottom of his cleats were so thick that they looked like those shoes that the disco dancers wore after disco made its fourth comeback. The shoes made Ted about six inches taller. The worst part was what the spikes were made of. Wood.

I thought of Ted's ancestor, Ty Cobb, how Cobb was legendary for sliding into second with his spikes high. I rocketed off the bench.

"Time!" I screamed. "Time out!"

The umpire lifted his mask.

"What now?" he said.

I pointed to the cleats. "Those are illegal."

"The rule book only bans *metal* cleats," he said. "Now, batter up."

"Second baseman takes the throw on a steal," I shouted as instruction to my fielders.

"No," Jerry shouted back. He pointed to the plate. "Left-handed batter."

Shortstop takes the throw when a lefty's up. The tradition of playing the percentages was as old as baseball itself. Even with the danger, I couldn't buck the lords of the game. I sat on the bench with my heart against my tonsils.

The crowd was chanting, "Spike him, spike him, spike him!" over and over. Dana sat beside me and held my hand, a strange mixture of accusation and empathy in her eyes.

"Maybe the next batter will pop up," she said. "There probably won't even *be* a play at second."

"Probably not."

She didn't say anything about testosterone or my stubborn devotion to the percentages. I knew what she was thinking, though.

"I'd do it even if it was my own son out there," I muttered. I almost even believed it.

They tried a double steal on the next pitch. It was a delayed steal, where the runner on third waits for the catcher to throw down to second, then tries for home. Not a great strategy for the game situation, but I had a feeling Turnbull had a lower purpose in mind.

Biff gunned a perfect strike to Jerry at second. I saw the play as if it were unfolding in slow motion. Ted was already leaning back, ready to launch into his slide.

Please step away, Jerry, I was praying. The runner on third was halfway home. If Jerry didn't make the tag, we'd be tied. But I didn't care. I'd gladly trade safe for safe.

Jerry didn't step away. His instincts were probably screaming at him to change into a bat and flutter above the danger, or to paralyze Ted in his tracks with a long look. But maybe he knew that would have caused us to forfeit the game and the championship. Or maybe he was stubborn.

He gritted his teeth, his two sharp incisors hanging over his lips in concentration. Ted was sliding into the bag, wooden spikes high in the air. Jerry stooped into the cloud of dust. He applied the tag just before the spikes caught him flush in the chest.

The field umpire reflexively threw his thumb back over his shoulder to signal the third out. But all I could see through my blurry eyes was Jerry writhing in the dirt, his teammates hustling to gather around him. I ran out to my vampire shortstop, kneeling beside his body just as the smoke was starting to rise from his flesh.

He looked up at me, the pain dousing the fire in his eyes. The crowd was silent, hushed by the horror of seeing their wish come true. The Red Sox had solemnly removed their hats. I'd never heard such a joyless championship celebration. Jerry looked at me and smiled, even as his features dissolved around his lips.

"We won, Coach," he whispered, then he was dust, forever part of the infield.

Dana took the pitcher's mound, weeping without shame. She stared into the crowd, at the umpires, into Turnbull's dugout, and I knew she was meeting the eye of every single person at Sawyer Field that day.

"Look at yourselves," she said, her voice strong despite the knots I knew were in her chest. "Just take a good long look."

Everybody did. I could hear a hot-dog wrapper blowing against the backstop.

"All he wanted was to play," she said. "All he wanted was to be just like you."

Sure, her words were for everybody. But she had twenty-two years of experience as Mrs. Ruttlemyer. We both knew to whom she was really talking.

"Just like you," she whispered, her words barely squeezing out yet somehow filling the outfield, the sky, the little place in your heart where you like to hide bad things. She walked off the mound with her head down, like a pitcher that had just given up the game-losing hit.

So many tears were shed that the field would have been unplayable. People had tasted the wormwood of their prejudice. They had seen how vicious the human animal could be. Even vampires didn't kill their young, even when the young might be decades old.

There was no memorial service. I wrote a eulogy, but nobody ever got to read it, not even Dana. There was talk of filing criminal charges against the Turnbulls, but nobody had the stomach to carry through on the threat.

What happened that day was something that people spent a lot of time trying to forget.

But that victory rang out across the ensuing years, a Liberty Bell for the living dead in Sawyer Creek. Vampires were embraced by the community, welcomed into the Chamber of Commerce, one was even elected mayor. Roscoe Turnbull had three of them on his team last season.

That Sawyer Cup still sits on my mantel, even though I never set foot on a diamond after that day. Sometimes when I look at the trophy, I imagine that it is full of blood. They say that winning takes sacrifice. But that's just a myth.

Still, all myths contain a kernel of truth, and even a myth can make you shiver.

FIFTEEN YEARS OF L. RON HUBBARD'S WRITERS OF THE FUTURE

Written by
Algis Budrys

About the Author

Algis Budrys was the founding Coordinating Judge of L. Ron Hubbard's Writers of the Future *Contest, as well as an advisor to L. Ron Hubbard's* Illustrators of the Future *Contest. He was—and is—an instructor at the writing workshop series in which the winning writers participate. He was also the founding editor of this anthology series. After relinquishing the Coordinating Judge role and the editorship to pursue various career opportunities—the editorship of* Tomorrow SF, *now www.tomorrowsf.com, the novel* Hard Landing, *and the Unifont Company literary agency—he continued to judge many quarters of the Contest. And now he has returned to edit this anthology.*

iikfteen years ago, L. Ron Hubbard did the remarkable; he founded the Contest which bears his name. It is difficult to remember, now, how unlikely were its prospects for success, if you were to ask certain "experts" in the field. But LRH knew there was a vast reservoir of talent waiting to be found. He knew the old days, of editors nurturing talent, were over. He saw that most writing courses were intended to make new writers subservient to the secluded ideals of academe, instead of being storytellers to the public. He did something about that, and you see the result.

When this Contest began, there was not, at first, the thought that Bridge Publications, Inc., would anthologize the winners. But the chance was taken. And those of you who have access to the first in this series will note that it does not state it is Volume I. We did not know if there would ever be a Volume II . . . that is, most of us did not know.

We gathered together in the side room of Chasen's restaurant, in Beverly Hills, and marked the release of that first volume. We were judges Gregory Benford, myself, Stephen Goldin, C. L. Moore, Robert Silverberg, Theodore Sturgeon, Jack Williamson and Roger Zelazny, with guests Ray Bradbury and A. E. van Vogt, and the Contest winners. We did not dream that in the not too distant future, we would be conducting an experimental writing workshop in Taos, New Mexico, and then institutionalizing that workshop as an annual event; that we would begin awarding a special trophy and prize to the author of the best Contest story of the year and the best illustration, or that we would be gathering at the United Nations, among other prestigious places. That is, most of us did not dream. I am confident that LRH would have laughed at us for the timidity of our expectations. He knew that given a chance, the writers and illustrators of the Contests would burst forth, would swiftly acquire an enthusiastic public, and would continue to flourish.

And they did.

But let me explain how the writers' contest works:

The Contest year ends September 30. The preceding twelve months are divided into four quarters. Entrants must not have published more than three short stories or one novelette. They send their entries in to Contest headquarters, where the administrator removes all traces of the authors' identities and then turns over the now anonymous stories to the preliminary judge. That judge winnows down the stories to the ones he feels are publishable. And those surviving entries are given to a blue-ribbon panel, which decides which stories are the First, Second and Third Prize winners. Four times a year, then, these are the quarterly winners, and the prizes—$1,000, $750 and $500, and trophies—are awarded. Once each year, the four quarterly First Prize winners are rejudged and that blue-ribbon panel awards an additional $4,000, and a special trophy, to one individual. All this comes from Author Services, Inc., which is L. Ron Hubbard's literary agency and administers his estate.

Much the same process is undergone by entrants in the illustrators' contest, except that they are given the winning stories, illustrate them, and are judged on the basis of the illustrations they produce. Their judges are some of the top artists of the day. For more details on both Contests, see the rules pages elsewhere in this book.

The anthology, from Bridge Publications, Inc., complements the Contests. It pays $1,000 for the stories by winners in the Writing Contest, and big-ticket prices for the illustrations. It pays honoraria to the people who contribute essays to the book.

And, of course, there are the workshops, one for the writers and one for the illustrators, preceding the awards ceremony, to which the winners are brought and which, for the contestants and the judges, mark one of the high points of their lives. In other words, the Contests and the anthology are first-class events in every way—which is the way L. Ron Hubbard did things.

These were the judges for the 1998 year in the _Writers of the Future_ Contest.

Gregory Benford	Jerry Pournelle
Algis Budrys	Tim Powers
Eric Kotani	Robert Silverberg
Anne McCaffrey	Jack Williamson
Larry Niven	Dave Wolverton
Andre Norton	Kevin J. Anderson
Frederik Pohl	Doug Beason

Judges for the 1998 year in the _Illustrators of the Future_ Contest were

Edd Cartier	Frank Kelly Freas
Leo Dillon	Dr. Laura Brodian Freas

Diane Dillon
Bob Eggleton
Will Eisner
Vincent Di Fate
Frank Frazetta

Shun Kijima
Paul Lehr*
Ron Lindahn
Val Lakey Lindahn
H. R. van Dongen

Winners for the year in the *Writers of the Future* Contest were

First Quarter

1. Jim Hines
   Blade of the Bunny
2. Gregory Janks
   The One-Eyed Man
3. Amy Sterling Casil
   My Son, My Self

Second Quarter

1. Scott Nicholson
   The Vampire Shortstop
2. G. Scott Huggins
   Bearing the Pattern
3. Manfred Gabriel
   A Man More Ordinary

Third Quarter

1. Franklin Thatcher
   By Other Windings
2. Nicole Montgomery
   The Unbound
3. Ron Collins
   Out of the Blue

Fourth Quarter

1. W. G. Rowland
   The Great Wizard Joey
2. David W. Hill
   The Price of Tea in China
3. Don Solosan
   Great White Hunter

*Now deceased, and very much missed.

Winners for the year in the *Illustrators of the Future* Contest were

Paul Butler	Ludmila Ryabets
James Matt Frantz	Scott Schomburg
Robert G. Kmiec	Lee Seed
Lukasz Laskowski	Yuri Chari
Julia Armstrong Murphy	Tomislav Tomic
Igor Pogodin	Victory

Honor them. They worked hard, and hoped and dreamed of the future.

CONTEST RULES

1. No entry fee is required and all rights in the story remain the property of the author. All types of science fiction, fantasy and horror with fantastic elements are welcome; every entry is judged on its own merits only.

2. All entries must be original works in English. Plagiarism, which includes poetry, song lyrics, characters or another person's world will result in disqualification. Submitted works may not have been previously published in professional media.

3. Eligible entries must be works of prose under 17,000 words in length. We regret we cannot consider poetry or works intended for children. Excessive violence or sex will result in disqualification.

4. The Contest is open only to those who have not had published (more than 5,000 copies) a novel or short novel, or more than three short stories, or more than one novelette, in any medium.

5. Entries must be typewritten and double-spaced with numbered pages (computer-printer output okay). Each entry must have a cover page with the title of the work, the author's name, address and telephone number and an approximate word count. The manuscript itself should be titled and numbered on every page, but the AUTHOR'S NAME SHOULD BE DELETED to facilitate fair judging.

6. Manuscripts will be returned after judging. Entries MUST include a self-addressed return envelope. U.S. return envelopes MUST be stamped; others may enclose international postal reply coupons.

7. There shall be three cash prizes in each quarter: 1st Prize of $1,000, 2nd Prize of $750, and 3rd Prize of $500, in U.S. dollars or the recipient's local equivalent amount. In addition, there shall be a further cash prize of $4,000 to the Grand Prize winner, who will be selected from among the 1st Prize winners for the period of October 1, 1999, through September 30, 2000. All winners will also receive trophies or certificates.

8. The Contest will continue through September 30, 2000, on the following quarterly basis:

October 1–December 31, 1999   January 1–March 31, 2000

April 1–June 30, 2000   July 1–September 30, 2000

Information regarding subsequent contests may be obtained by sending a self-addressed, stamped business-size envelope to the address on the previous page.

To be eligible for the quarterly judging, an entry must be postmarked no later than midnight on the last day of the quarter.

9. Each entrant may submit only one manuscript per quarter. Contest winners are ineligible to make further entries.

10. All entries for each quarter are final. No revisions are accepted.

11. Entries will be judged by professional authors. The decisions of the judges are entirely their own, and are final.

12. Winners in each quarter will be individually notified of the results by mail.

This Contest is void where prohibited by law.

L. Ron Hubbard's

ILLUSTRATORS
OF THE
FUTURE
CONTEST

OPEN TO NEW SCIENCE FICTION
AND FANTASY ARTISTS
WORLDWIDE

All Judging by Professional Artists Only

$1,500 in Prizes Each Quarter
No entry fee.   Entrants retain all rights.

Quarterly winners compete for
$4,000 additional ANNUAL PRIZE

L. Ron Hubbard's
Illustrators of the Future Contest
P.O. Box 3190
Los Angeles, CA 90078

1. The Contest is open to entrants from all nations. (However, entrants should provide themselves with some means for written communication in English.) All themes of science fiction and fantasy illustration are welcome: every entry is judged on its own merits only. No entry fee is required, and all rights in the entries remain the property of the artists.

2. By submitting work to the Contest, the entrant agrees to abide by all Contest rules.

3. This Contest is open to those who have not previously published more than three black-and-white story illustrations, or more than one process-color painting, in media distributed nationally to the general public, such as magazines or books sold at newsstands, or books sold in stores merchandising to the general public. The submitted entry shall not have been previously published in professional media as exampled above.

If you are not sure of your eligibility, write to the Contest address with details, enclosing a business-size self-addressed envelope with return postage. The Contest Administration will reply with a determination.

Winners in previous quarters are not eligible to make further entries.

4. Only one entry per quarter is permitted. The entry must be original to the entrant. Plagiarism, infringement of the rights of others, or other violations of the Contest rules will result in disqualification.

5. An entry shall consist of three illustrations done by the entrant in a black-and-white medium. Each must represent a theme different from the other two.

6. ENTRIES SHOULD NOT BE THE ORIGINAL DRAWINGS, but should be large black-and-white photocopies of a quality satisfactory to the entrant. Entries must be submitted unfolded and flat, in an envelope no larger than 9 inches by 12 inches.

All entries must be accompanied by a self-addressed return envelope of the appropriate size, with correct U.S. postage affixed. (Non-U.S. entrants should enclose international postal reply coupons.) If the entrant does not want the photocopies returned, the entry should be clearly marked DISPOSABLE COPIES: DO NOT RETURN.

A business-size self-addressed envelope with correct postage should be included so that judging results can be returned to the entrant.

7. To facilitate anonymous judging, each of the three photocopies must be accompanied by a removable cover sheet bearing the artist's name, address and telephone number, and an identifying title for that work. The photocopy of the work should carry the same identifying title, and the artist's signature should be deleted from the photocopy.

The Contest Administration will remove and file the cover sheets, and forward only the anonymous entry to the judges.

8. To be eligible for a quarterly judging, an entry must be postmarked no later than the last day of the quarter.

Late entries will be included in the following quarter, and the Contest Administration will so notify the entrant.

9. There will be three co-winners in each quarter. Each winner will receive an outright cash grant of U.S. $500, and a certificate of merit. Such winners also receive eligibility to compete for the annual Grand Prize of an additional outright cash grant of $4,000 together with the annual Grand Prize trophy.

10. Competition for the Grand Prize is designed to acquaint the entrant with customary practices in the field of professional illustrating. It will be conducted in the following manner:

Each winner in each quarter will be furnished a Specification Sheet giving details on the size and kind of black-and-white illustration work required by Grand Prize competition. Requirements will be of the sort customarily stated by professional publishing companies.

These specifications will be furnished to the entrant by the Contest Administration, using Return Receipt Requested mail or its equivalent.

Also furnished will be a copy of a science fiction or fantasy story, to be illustrated by the entrant. This story will have been selected for that purpose by the Coordinating Judge of the Contest. Thereafter, the entrant will work toward completing the assigned illustration.

In order to retain eligibility for the Grand Prize, each entrant shall, within thirty (30) days of receipt of the said story assignment, send to the Contest address the entrant's black-and-white page illustration of the assigned story in accordance with the Specification Sheet.

The entrant's finished illustration shall be in the form of camera-ready art prepared in accordance with the Specification Sheet and securely packed, shipped at the entrant's own risk. The Contest will exercise due care in handling all submissions as received.

The said illustration will then be judged in competition for the Grand Prize on the following basis only:

Each Grand Prize judge's personal opinion on the extent to which it makes the judge want to read the story it illustrates.

The entrant shall retain copyright in the said illustration.

11. The Contest year will continue through September 30, 1999, with the following quarterly period (see Rule 8):

July 1–September 30, 1999

The next Contest will continue through September 30, 2000, on the following quarterly basis:

October 1–December 31, 1999   January 1–March 31, 2000

April 1–June 30, 2000   July 1–September 30, 2000

Entrants in each quarter will be individually notified of the quarter's judging results by mail. Winning entrants' participation in the Contest shall continue until the results of the Grand Prize judging have been announced.

Information regarding subsequent contests may be obtained by sending a self-addressed business-size envelope, with postage, to the Contest address.

12. The Grand Prize winner will be announced at the L. Ron Hubbard Awards events to be held in the calendar year of 2000.

13. Entries will be judged by professional artists only. Each quarterly judging and the Grand Prize judging may have a different panel of judges. The decisions of the judges are entirely their own, and are final.

14. This Contest is void where prohibited by law.

A VERY STRANGE TRIP

AN ORIGINAL STORY BY
L. RON HUBBARD

NOVEL BY
DAVE WOLVERTON

NEW YORK TIMES BESTSELLER

"A WILD, HIGH-TECH RIDE!"

— Brian Herbert, co-author,
Dune: House Atreides

While transporting a contraband Russian time machine and developmental weaponry, Private Everett Dumphee finds himself cast into new settings when the device suddenly activates. What follows are fantastic high-tech experiences that might be called the *ultimate off-road adventure*.

For the determined Dumphee—narrowly escaping with his life and three beautiful women—it is not necessarily a matter of will he make his destination, but when. These four vivid characters trek through this fun and fast moving journey like there's no tomorrow. Wherever that may be.

New York Times bestselling authors L. Ron Hubbard (*Battlefield Earth* and *Mission Earth*®) and Dave Wolverton (*Star Wars: The Courtship of Princess Leia*) deliver a highly absorbing and entertaining story with more than one interesting twist.

Buy Your Copy Wherever Books Are Sold!

$25.00 US, $33.50 Canada

Also available in Audio

$25.00 US, $33.50 Canada

The New York Times Bestseller

BATTLEFIELD
-EARTH-

Now in Production as a Major Motion Picture

by L. Ron Hubbard

IF YOU LIKED *STAR WARS*, *INDEPENDENCE DAY* AND THE CREATIVE STYLE OF *THE MATRIX*, YOU'LL BE FASCINATED BY *BATTLEFIELD EARTH*. THE BIGGEST SCIENCE FICTION BOOK OF ALL TIME!

THIS THOUGHT PROVOKING AND IMAGINATIVE STORY IS SET IN THE YEAR 3000, WHEN MOST HUMANS HAVE BEEN DESTROYED AND EARTH IS RULED BY THE PSYCHLOS, A CRUEL, TOUGH, ALIEN RACE OF INVADERS WHOSE ONLY INTEREST IN THE PLANET IS ITS MINERAL RESOURCES AND WEALTH, WHICH THEY CONTINUE TO PLUNDER. BUT WHEN ONE LONE MAN, JONNIE GOODBOY TYLER, DECIDES TO BREAK AWAY FROM A SMALL BAND OF SURVIVORS TO CHALLENGE THE POWER AND MIGHT OF THE PSYCHLOS, THE SCENE IS SET FOR A FAST-MOVING, COMPELLING ADVENTURE WHICH YOU WON'T BE ABLE TO PUT DOWN. THE FILM RELEASE OF THIS EPIC SCIENCE FICTION NOVEL IS SCHEDULED FOR THE YEAR 2000.

Buy Your Copy Today
Wherever Books Are Sold!
$7.99 US, $9.99 Canada

Also available in audio
$24.95 US, $29.95 Canada

"This has everything: suspense, pathos, politics, war, humor, diplomacy and intergalactic finance."

—PUBLISHERS WEEKLY

Ai! Pedrito!

— When Intelligence Goes Wrong

"Ai! Pedrito! is a fast paced adventure in the style of James Bond and Indiana Jones."

—ED GORMAN
MYSTERY SCENE

Pedrito, while admired by many, leaves behind a throng of foes out for his blood when he heads north to assume Smith's identity. Smith meanwhile, has been out-foxed, arriving in South America for a quiet vacation only to be attacked in a setup by a foreign intelligence agency.

As this intriguing page-turner builds and the plot unfolds, New York Times bestselling authors L. Ron Hubbard (*Battlefield Earth* and the *Mission Earth®* series) and Kevin J. Anderson (*X-files* and *Star Wars*) take Smith—and the reader—on a rollicking and unpredictable adventure through the world of spies and double agents, lovers and enemies (often one and the same).

ORIGINAL STORY BY
L. Ron Hubbard
NOVELIZED BY
Kevin J. Anderson

Mission Earth

BY

L. RON HUBBARD

"You will lose sleep, you will miss appointments, if you don't force yourself to put it down."

—Orson Scott Card

They look like us, they talk like us...

We are not alone. They are here now, living and walking amongst us. Some are here to help, some are here to harm. Only one of them is here to salvage our dying planet—Royal Fleet Combat Engineer, Jettero Heller.

In a race that is fiercely pitted against time, Heller is sent on a desperate mission to stop the self-destruction of Earth—wholly unaware that a secret branch of his own government (the Coordinated Information Apparatus) has dispatched its own agent—whose sole purpose is to sabotage Heller at all costs, as part of its own clandestine operation.

In a narrative told from the eyes of the alien invaders—the tale is crowded with sharply memorable characters, biting satire, imaginative plot twists and disasters and triumphs as the two protagonists struggle against incredible odds in this intergalactic game where the future of Earth hangs in the balance.

"A superbly imaginative, intricately plotted invasion of Earth." —Chicago Tribune

"All the entertainment anybody could ask for." —New York Newsday

All Volumes New York Times Best Sellers:

Available in paperback for $6.99 or audio for $15.95 each

Vol. 1. The Invaders Plan

Vol. 2. Black Genesis

Vol. 3. The Enemy Within

Vol. 4. An Alien Affair

Vol. 5. Fortune of Fear

Vol. 6. Death Quest

Vol. 7. Voyage of Vengeance

Vol. 8. Disaster

Vol. 9. Villainy Victorious

Vol. 10. The Doomed Planet

BUY YOUR COPIES TODAY!

Call: 1-800-722-1733/Internet: www.bridgepub.com
or mail the tear-off card with your order to:
Bridge Publications, Inc.
4751 Fountain Ave., Dept. MEPB99
Los Angeles, CA 90029